I0614473

Alfred the Great; Viking Invasion

By Bruce Corbett

Copyright © 2023, by Bruce Corbett

All rights reserved.

ISBN: 978-1-7380048-1-2

This story is a work of fiction. All fictional characters are the product of the author's imagination. Any resemblance to any person, living or dead, is coincidental.

Dedication:

To my wife - the light of my life,

Cynthia.

FOREWORD

This is the seventh book in the Ambrose historical adventure series, and this and the next novel cover a time when England came very close to becoming a Danish kingdom. I have followed the Anglo-Saxon Chronicles as closely as I can, but it is a rather bare-bones listing of long-ago events. I therefore took it upon myself to fill in the gaps with literary license. The title of the books have changed, since the main character from now on is Alfred the Great, though Ambrose, Polonius and Phillip will continue to play a major part in the war against the pagan Danes.

In 875 A.D., Alfred, eventually to be known as the Great, is the king of Wessex, a Saxon Kingdom that stretches from Dover to the western tip of Cornwall, and from the southern coast north to the Thames and (eventually) Watling Street. Ten years before, the three sons of Ragnar Lodbrok: Ubbi, Halfdan and Ivar, had arrived with the 'Great Army', the largest Viking invasion army ever seen in England until that time.

Instead of lightning raids or seasonal forays, as had been the pattern for the previous two generations, the Danes conquered, one by one, every single Angle and Saxon kingdom in England except Wessex. As this story opens, King Guthrum of Denmark is about to lead a strong Viking force south into Wessex. This is the story of that struggle.

Most of the events you are about to read about, although fictionalized, really did occur, more or less in the order in which I describe them. There seems to some question about if the treaty with King Guthrum that allowed Wessex to expand north of the Thames was signed right after his baptism (878) or was signed considerably later. My version of the Anglo-Saxon Chronicles reported that Alfred took London about 886, so that is the timeline I followed. The story (and the text) of Alfred's second treaty with Guthrum is to be found in my next adventure, **Alfred the Great; King's Revenge**.

The quotes are from the Anglo-Saxon Chronicles. Alfred really did put together a fleet and defeat seven enemy vessels, though he did this in 875 A.D., the year before Guthrum arrived with his army. *Words in italics generally have special meaning and the details may be found in Appendix III.*

The author,

Bruce Corbett

CAST OF CHARACTERS

Aldwin: (Fictitious) Was a thane of a small village in the woods of Selwood. He asked Ethelnoth to act as judge in a rape case.

Alfred: The younger brother of Ambrose, Ethelbert, and Ethelred. He was an intensely curious man who unexpectedly became king at the death of his brother, in 871 AD. A great general, he drove King Guthrum out of Wessex, but was almost taken captive in a surprise winter attack. Hiding first in the forests, and then at his island base of Athelney, he started to strike back at the hated enemy. When his men rallied to him in the spring, he was able to defeat Guthrum. Surprisingly, he treated Guthrum generously, and became his godfather.

Ambrose: (Fictitious) He was an Anglo-Saxon bastard prince of Wessex. Kidnapped by Viking slavers as a boy, he was taken to Denmark, and then fled to Norway and Sweden. Chased by the Danes, he joined Gunnar of the Rus, who sent him and his two companions, Phillip and Polonius, to trade on his behalf down the Russian rivers. Ambrose set up trading posts in Novgorod, and then Kiev. Finally, he traveled to Constantinople as an emissary for the Kiev leaders. From there, he eventually returned to England to help his brothers fight against the Viking raiders.
He and his friends became a legend when they first joined the Danish Great Army, and then stole a princess from a Norse ruler in Ireland.

Anwell: (Fictitious) He was the Ealdorman of Cornwall who had made an alliance with the Danes in return for nominal independence. Polonius and Ambrose captured his sons, and he was forced to support Alfred.

Asser: A bishop who later lived at King Alfred's court and was his biographer. He actually joined the court in 886 AD.

Axton: (Fictitious) A thane of Devon, he was chief lieutenant to Ealdorman Odda.

Boc: (Fictitious) A senior thane who delivered a message to Anwell of Cornwall.

Burgtun: (Fictitious) A thane of Alfred, who commanded the scouts at Wareham when Guthrum escaped.

Brok: (Fictitious) A messenger who breathlessly reported to Ethelnoth that the Vikings were attacking a village.

Byram: (Fictitious) A ship officer aboard Alfred's **Leaping Stag,** he was the thane who went out to collect all the boats beached at Chippenham.

Calldwr: (Fictitious) Thane at the siege of Chippenham who sent boats up and down-river to destroy any vessels they couldn't use.

Claeg: (Fictitious) Stewart of the royal estate where the queen stopped on her flight from Chippenham.

Cliftun: (Fictitious) A boy accused of raping Naomi, who was tried by Ethelnoth.

Cyne: (Fictitious) A cousin & acolyte of Bishop Asser.

Delwyn: (Fictitious) A thane of Ethelwold who was blamed for Guthrum's escape at Wareham. Ethelwold had him hanged to hide the truth.

Eadric: (Fictitious) A forester who lived in the forest of Selwood, and went to get Alfred's men when the king twisted his ankle.

Ealhswith: Wife of Alfred.

Egbert: He was an ancestor of Alfred's. He ruled Wessex from 802 to 839 AD.

Ethelnoth: Ealdorman of Somerset, he was a loyal friend to Alfred, and hid him in his forest territory of Selwood, and later at Athelney.

Ethelwold: Alfred's nephew and Ealdorman of Dorset. His father was Ethelred, older brother of Alfred, and king of Wessex from AD. 866 until his death in 871.

Glydan: (Fictitious) The shrewish wife of EADRIC, a forester who provided shelter to King Alfred. It was she who attacked the king with a broom.

Galar: (Fictitious) The commander of the thirty thanes who escorted the royal family from Winchester to Selwood Forest.

Gretchen: (Fictitious) Was the daughter of Osmond, Ealdorman of East Anglia, and distant cousin to the royal family of Wessex. She first met Ambrose at the Wessex court, and then nursed him back to health when he was wounded during his earlier escape from the Danes. They were betrothed, but Gretchen is first kidnapped by Welsh, and then Viking brigands. Ambrose traveled to Ireland to free her. After many adventures, they were married.

Godwin: (Fictitious) Was a thane and member of King Alfred's Personal Guard.

Guthrum: A king of Denmark who conquered East Anglia. He attacked Wessex, was bought off, and then attacked from Mercia at Christmas of 878.

Halfdan: He was an elder brother of Ubbi and Ivar the Boneless. He was one of the three leaders of the Great Army in England. His father was Ragnar Lodbrok.

Hamar: (Fictitious) Was the name Ambrose used when he pretended to be a Swedish trader in Guthrum's camp at Chippenham.

Halsig: (Fictitious) Was the thane who held Twineham against the Viking Fleet.

Hrycg: (Fictitious) A faithful thane of Alfred's, who agreed to pay Danegeld to Guthrum so Ambrose could sneak into the camp.

Ivar the Boneless: The brother of Halfdan and Ubbi and joint leader of the Great Army. His father was Ragnar Lodbrok. He died in 873.

Korni: (Fictitious) A commander of Ubbi's from when the army landed on the Dorset coast.

Kuralla: (Fictitious) She was a Slav chieftain's daughter whose village defied Bothi, a Rus warrior settled near Novgorod. Bothi ordered her father tortured and killed, and she was about to be given to his warriors when Ambrose purchased her to save her life. Polonius married her before they returned with Ambrose to England.

Matilda: (Fictitious) Was the flaxen-headed and sharp-tongued wife of Phillip.

Naomi: (Fictitious) A young maiden raped by a Saxon boy named Cliftun.

Odda: The Ealdorman of Devon, he raised an army to face Halfdan when the Viking arrived with his fleet on the northern Devon coast. Having retreated to the fort at Countisbury, he sallied forth and surprised and defeated the Danish army. Later, his force kept Ethelwold from joining Guthrum's army and betraying Alfred.

Oskar: (Fictitious) Danish commander of the fort just across the Avon River from Chippenham. He later commanded the Viking force chasing Alfred into the swamps near Athelney.

Owein: (Fictitious) A Cornishman, he was one of Anwell's two sons.

Phillip: (Fictitious) A giant of a man, he was the free-born guardian of Ambrose. Often called the weapons-master, he had trained several generations of athelings in the military arts. Wherever Ambrose went, there was Phillip. His great goal in life was to protect his prince.

Pitanig: (Fictitious) A loyal thane to Odda, the Ealdorman of Devon.

Polonius: (Fictitious) He was born to noble Byzantine parents, and given an excellent education. When his family had financial reverses, he and his sisters were sold into slavery. He was taken to Lombardy, France, and eventually Frisia. There, he chanced to meet Ambrose and Phillip. Together they embarked on a series of adventures that took them to Norway, Sweden, Novgorod, Kiev, and eventually Constantinople itself. An expert linguist and knife-thrower, he returned to England with Ambrose, helped him spy on the Danish Great Army, and steal Gretchen back from the Irish Vikings. He taught Alfred to read, and acted as his senior military advisor and spy master.

Pyt: (Fictitious) Thane of Alfred's Personal Guard, who arranged to hang the hostages at Chippenham.

Radnor: (Fictitious) Was a loyal thane to Odda, the Ealdorman of Devon.

Ragnar Lodbrok: A powerful Danish chieftain who invaded England and France. Legend had it that he was killed in Northumbria by being thrown in a pit of snakes. His three sons were Halfdan, Ivar the Boneless, and Ubbi.

Ryscford: (Fictitious) Thane of a little marsh village near Athelney, he arranged for transportation for Alfred's fighting thanes.

Saer: (Fictitious) A Cornishman, he was the second son of Anwell.

Seger: (Fictitious) A faithful thane of Ealdorman Ethelwold. He rode to Alfred in Selwood Forest in the hopes of capturing the king. If that was impossible, he was expected to invite him to visit Ethelwold.

Sitric Ivarsson: The son of Ivar the Boneless. He previously met Ambrose at the Wessex court, where he was a spy with the identity of a Frisian peddler by the name of Harold. Phillip rescued him later, and they shared adventures in Ireland together. He did not join his uncle on the attack on Wessex.

Thawian: (Fictitious) A messenger who brought proof to Alfred of the sinking of the Danish fleet at Swanwich.

Thormond: (Fictitious) The commander, after Seger was sent back, of the Dorsetmen sent to capture King Alfred for Ethelwold.

Ubbi: He was a younger brother of Halfdan and Ivar the Boneless. He inadvertently allowed Ambrose, Phillip and Polonius to join the Great Army. Furious when he found out they were spies, he sent out hundreds of warriors to track the fugitives down. In this story, he arrived from southern Wales. He landed in Dorset, besieged Odda, and was then killed in a surprise dawn attack. His father was Ragnar Lodbrok.

Uigbiorn: (Fictitious) Danish sub-commander of the Viking force chasing Alfred into the swamps near Athelney.

Ura: (Fictitious) A Jarl, he was one of Guthrum's commanders. He was sent to negotiate with King Alfred at the siege of Wareham and Exeter.

TABLE OF CONTENTS

CHAPTER 1

"This summer King Alfred went out to sea with an armed fleet, and fought with seven ship-rovers, one of whom he took and dispersed the others."

The clatter of galloping hooves could be heard over the rustle of wind in the trees and the rigging of the little fleet that lay tethered along the riverbank. The staccato sound indicated a message, and an urgent one. Alfred, king of Wessex and all its tributary domains, stood expectantly.

The rider followed the river trail along the shoreline. He was riding hard and when he saw his king, he galloped directly to him. The excitement was alive in his eyes and his voice.

"Majesty, there are seven craft coasting westward. They're long-ships, and they're Viking!"

Alfred's face wore a wolfish grin. He turned to his brother and his two companions.

"Ambrose, I told you some of the devil spawn would come. Phillip, pass the word to board, and quickly! Let us go and welcome our guests properly."

At Phillip's shouted instructions, ship commanders ran to fetch their crews. In only minutes, the crews of all eleven vessels were boarded and at their stations. The rowers eagerly pushed their oars into the water, while the extra crewmen untied the vessels and removed the boarding planks. The Angle and Saxon crews had been practicing for weeks, and the vessels, double crewed and stripped for action, were soon pulling strongly out to sea. King Alfred had prepared a special greeting for his uninvited visitors.

The eleven vessels cleared the headland. Seven enemy vessels suddenly hove into sight, strung along in a ragged line. Their masts were stepped, in anticipation of a favoring breeze, but the sails were furled. As the winds this close to land were contrary, the Vikings were forced to man their oars.

Alfred smiled. "Well, brother, it looks like we will get some serious exercise today. Increase the beat and let's catch the devil's hounds!"

Ambrose relayed the order to the ship's commander and the drummer beat a faster cadence. The men, fresh and well-trained, easily increased the speed of their stroke. Polonius and Ambrose, having spent considerable time on Byzantine *dromons*, had recommended to Alfred that they adopt some of the simpler code systems of the sophisticated Eastern Romans. The friends, traveling to the Golden City itself, had watched in awe as hundreds of Byzantine vessels had sailed as if they were but various parts of one single giant organism. The code flag that instructed the crew to increase the beat was hoisted, and the other ships followed suit. The Saxon fleet sped through the choppy water.

It had been centuries since the Saxons of *Angleland* had been feared as sea-rovers. The only war fleets that normally coasted these shores were Danish or *Norse*. The seven Viking vessels stopped in confusion when the intercepting fleet was spotted, but they soon went about. The Viking commanders were no fools, the Norse and the Danes were not always friends, and it was not unknown for Danes to attack Danes. The fleet that had just slipped out of the river mouth was flying no identifying pennants, but, faced with a strange fleet of superior size, the Vikings rowed for their lives.

Alfred smiled as his larger fleet gradually closed the gap. Most of the ships of his new fleet were Viking in construction, but the pagans were not naively trusting. He had helped design the lead ship, his flagship, himself, and the *Frisian* craftsmen had done their job well. Alfred had ordered them to strip out the normal storage areas and add more oars and room for his doubled crews. The pagan Danes had to travel long distances by sea and they were forced to carry the supplies necessary for weeks afloat.

Alfred had ordered that his vessels be designed or modified for use as short-range fighting vessels. They were supplied from shore. Several south-coast sea ports had been assigned to repair and re-supply them. The vessels were filled with fighting men who never needed to be at sea for more than a few hours.

Alfred turned to his bastard brother. "At last, Ambrose! Our people have endured onslaught after onslaught by these savage northern barbarians. I thank merciful God we are finally able to strike back at the curse that had fallen on Angleland's shores. Control of the sea has for too long given these devils the ability to land and pillage where they please, and then provides them an escape route once our *fyrdmen* finally catch up with them. Today we will show these Viking dogs that Saxons have sharp teeth, too!"

The ship-commander saw the headlong pace faltering. "Sire, the men are tiring. I would suggest a change of rowers."

Alfred looked down at his men pulling hard on the oars. Some smiled back, even as they struggled to keep up the brutal pace.

"Aye. We will lose a little headway, but the crews are practiced and can switch quickly."

Polonius ran up the appropriate signal-flag, and Alfred knew that each of his other ship-commanders would follow suit. The gap widened briefly, but then began to close again as the fresh rowers began to synchronize their strokes.

Alfred's command vessel, the *Leaping Stag*, led the formation. Alfred had ordered his Frisian builders to build it with a deep keel and high sides. It tracked beautifully, and, with its extra oars and crew, could easily match the pace of the smaller Viking vessels.

As the last enemy vessel came into bowshot, Alfred ordered his Hampshire archers to empty their quivers. A hail of arrows soon arced down on the long-ship, and several of the Viking crewmen fell wounded over their oars. The enemy tried to reciprocate, but most of their men were needed to row, and the higher sides of Alfred's ship protected both the archers and the rowers.

As more Vikings fell wounded or killed, their oars tangled with their neighbors', and the stroke faltered. Alfred's flagship closed rapidly, and the king turned to his ship officers.

"Phillip! Have the nearside crew watch for my signal. I want the oars drawn in when I drop my right arm! Byram! Run to the stern and tell the steersmen to turn hard into the enemy ship at the same signal. I want to sheer into their oar bank. Quick now! If we hit them right, their oars will snap like kindling."

Ambrose watched in satisfaction as Alfred dropped his arm. Their own left bank of oars was quickly pulled onto the deck, and the three strong men assigned to the steering oar threw their weight against the massive beam. The vessel heeled right into the Viking oar bank. The Vikings manning them were thrown about like dolls in the hands of a young child having a tantrum. From the higher deck of the **Leaping Stag** came a torrent of spears and arrows. The Vikings who fled the partial shelter of the rowing benches were cut down.

Alfred looked down on the chaos his men had created in the Viking long-ship. Having crippled one ship, he was eager that they press on.

"Phillip! Those devils are not going anywhere for a while. Pass the word for the steering crew to veer away, and for the rowing crew to get those oars back into action just as soon as we are free of this mess! One of our lesser vessels should be able to finish taming this wounded beast.'

Alfred turned to Polonius with a look of satisfaction on his face. 'Polonius, I told you that higher sides were an advantage! We were able to shoot down on the devils and overwhelm them!"

Polonius had earlier in his life been a citizen of far-off Byzantium, and then an escaped Viking slave. He had even served for a time as chief military advisor for the audacious Rus Vikings who conquered an entire river system stretching for hundreds of Roman miles, all in the space of just a few years. He now served as spy master and senior military advisor to the king of Wessex. He was also one of the few men who dared to tell the unadorned truth to the young king he had tutored for years.

"Aye, Sire. The extra weight is a disadvantage, but you have made up for that by adding the extra oars and crew. She will track well on the open ocean, but she will not be useful in shallow water. Now what we used on the rivers of the Slav land were . . ."

Alfred smiled at his friend and advisor. "I know, Scholar! Wide hull and shallow draft allowed you to carry large cargoes and still sail through shallows. But this is the ocean, and we will not skulk far up rivers!"

"I hear you, Sire, but look ahead. Is it my imagination, or are the enemy vessels angling toward the shore?"

Alfred moved forward to get a better view. His bastard brother Ambrose followed the king to the bow, and Phillip, having relayed the king's commands, rejoined the party. Soon enough they all saw what Polonius' sharp eyes had spotted. The enemy captains, realizing that they were both outnumbered and losing the race, were veering gradually into where the surf foamed over shallows. Alfred's Viking-built long-ships, for the most part seized from Northmen foolish enough to be caught on the shore, should be able to follow through the shallows, but Alfred's larger flagship would find this impossible.

"By the bones of all the Saints, you are right, Polonius! Commander, make for the nearest vessel before it slips into shallow water where we cannot follow. They will not so easily escape us!"

The royal party watched in frustration as the Vikings sailed into shallower and shallower water. The **Leaping Stag** touched the gravel bottom twice, and the rowers hurriedly threw their backs into reversing the direction of the massive ship.

The other ten ships, built of the same design as the ships they were pursuing, were able to follow. Several caught up to the last of the fleeing vessels, but the pagan Northerners fought heroically, and the Saxon vessels did not now have the advantage of the larger vessel, with its higher sides and overwhelming numbers of crewmen.

The fights were indecisive, with considerable injuries on both sides. The Saxon captains called off the chase when the Viking vessels took a dangerous passage between two looming rocks. Less experienced and less desperate, the Saxon commanders were unwilling to risk the rocks and the treacherous current.

Alfred was furious. He turned to his captain. "Take us out to deeper water! Parallel the course of the God-cursed Vikings. We will attack any who attempt to escape by heading out-to-sea!"

Polonius stood by his side. "Look, Sire! Your long-ships are returning."

"Returning! I didn't order them to break off the fight. Hoist the flag to attack!"

"Sire, you can't get close enough to command the battle, let alone intervene. I think your commanders quite properly judged the danger to be too great, and broke off the chase."

King Alfred, still red-faced, turned to the thin Byzantine who had dared question his decision. "I know! Too deep a hull!' He suddenly grabbed Polonius in a fierce bear hug. 'Damn it, Polonius, but it is good to have a man who dares to tell me the unadorned truth! I don't know what would happen if I didn't have you and Ambrose whispering the truth in my ear . . . even when I don't want to hear it. Promise me you will always be bluntly honest, Scholar. Didn't you once tell me that the ancient Caesars used to do something similar to prevent themselves from becoming foolishly arrogant?"

"Well, Sire, when they rode in a Triumph and the Roman mobs cheered in adulation, they had a slave stand behind them on the chariot. His sole job was to constantly whisper to the Caesar that he was only mortal."

"My friend, I am grateful that you and Ambrose provide me the same service. You don't know how much I count on you two to tell me the truth. Too many tell a king only what they think he wants to hear.

And look! The Vikings escape, but at least we have savaged them. Commander, turn back and renew the attack on the long-ship we crippled. Let's at least add another ship to our fleet today."

The Saxon flagship swept down a second time on the crippled long-ship. The Viking commander had not been idle. He had shifted half of the crew from the unscathed side to replace the wounded and maimed. As the **Leaping Stag** returned, the long-ship was slowly making for the open sea.

Alfred stood surrounded by his royal party and the ship commanders.

"Order an all-out attack! If the heathen devils offer to surrender, we will find a stout rope and *offer them to Odin*! Either way, they will see their gods this day."

The officers ran to obey their king. The ship easily overtook the crippled vessel, and the archers and spearmen, resupplied, took up their harvesting again. The Vikings were brave men, and they fought as best they could, but the larger numbers and superior protection provided by the Saxon vessel's high sides made the battle cruelly uneven.

Outnumbered, and with a half-dozen more ships closing on his position, the Viking captain knew he could not escape. Suddenly, the long-ship turned toward its tormenters and steered directly for the **Leaping Stag**. Two naked Vikings stood in the bow waving their weapons and shouting curses at the Saxon foe.

Ambrose, standing amidships, saw the rapidly approaching danger. He had watched the havoc wrought by Viking berserkers in several battles. Well aware of the superstitious awe and fear the Saxon warriors felt toward these men, he rushed for the nearest rank of archers.

"Commander, tell your men to concentrate all their fire on those two in the bow. They must not be allowed to set foot on this deck!"

"You heard Prince Ambrose! On the count of three, I want every last one of you mothers' sons to shoot at the two crazy men. One. Two. Three. Release!"

Ambrose smiled in relief as first one berserker, and then the second one, collapsed under the concentrated fire.

As the ships veered together, Polonius ordered the corvus, his secret weapon, deployed. Once the two ships were near enough, the long gangplank pivoted and dropped. Its long metal spike struck the deck of the enemy vessel solidly, and the two vessels instantly became one.

The Viking crew, suddenly realizing the purpose of the massive plank, charged for the corvus, but the Saxons were on it first, and were soon pouring down onto the deck of the long-ship. Alfred ordered the entire crew to attack, except for a row of archers who continued to shoot down from their higher deck. The Vikings seemed to have known their fate if they were captured, for none even attempted to surrender. One by one they fell, fighting bravely to the very end.

BOOK ONE: KING GUTHRUM ATTACKS

CHAPTER 2

"AD 876: This year the army stole into Wareham, a fort of the West-Saxons."

"Polonius! Stand up, man. Here, in private, we are just friends. What is the word from the north?"

"Not good, Your Majesty. Guthrum and his Danes have crossed our northern frontier."

"May God strike down the devils! Do we have any idea how many warriors he has brought and where he is headed?"

"Our scouts are killing horses to get the latest information to us, Sire, but the short answer is no, we do not know as yet. The last reports were that he was definitely heading south and probably westward."

"I see!' Alfred called to the young *dreng* who stood stiffly at attention by the door. 'Godwin! Find Ambrose and Phillip. Have them report here immediately. Polonius, get out the maps. Let's try and figure out what these devils might be up to."

Within a thousand heartbeats, Ambrose and Phillip ran breathlessly into Alfred's Great Hall. Ambrose gasped. "Brother, what is it?"

"Grave news! Messengers from the north have just reported that Guthrum and his Danes have crossed the border into Wiltshire."

"That is serious indeed. Do we know their destination and numbers?"

Alfred looked grim. "Polonius?"

Polonius turned from the map he was spreading on the trestle table. He gave his best friend and companion a wan smile. "No, Prince Ambrose. The preliminary report indicates that several unprotected *tuns* were overrun, while more defensible *burhs* were bypassed. Guthrum seems to be in a hurry to go somewhere. A rough estimate of numbers might be over a thousand, all mounted, but that is just an unsubstantiated guess."

Ambrose looked at his brother the king. "Well, Alfred. We have faced worse than that before. The crops are in the ground. You have a standing force of almost three hundred drengs of your Personal Guard with you here, leavened with another hundred odd well-experienced *duguos*, all ready to ride at a day's notice, and the fyrds of the empire only await the call-to-arms. Let us show the pagans good Saxon steel!"

Polonius spoke without looking around. "First, my Prince, we have to have a better idea where they are headed. Brave as our fighting *thanes* of the Personal Guard may be, they would find themselves heavily outnumbered by the Viking army. It will take the combined fyrds of several shires to assure victory over Guthrum's Danes. And is this the only thrust we are facing?"

Alfred looked over Polonius's shoulder at the map of southern Angleland. "If Guthrum runs true to form, he will head for a strong defensive point, which he will further fortify. From there, he will raid in all directions. The real devastation will start once he is securely ensconced somewhere."

Ambrose looked over Polonius's other shoulder. "Unless, my brother, we are there with the fyrd to bottle him up."

Alfred stabbed at the map with his finger. "Here is Portchester, near where we met those ships last week. They were coursing westward when we met them. Our experience has been that the Vikings always try and choose a defensive site near water. More than once they have slipped away by sea when we finally manage to bring together enough resources that we could crush them. Could the fleet we met have been a prong of Guthrum's attack?"

Polonius stroked his chin. "Aye. If Guthrum wanted a southern port as his main base of operation, he would have been smart to send a ship-born expedition to take it. Coming from the north as he is, he has to fight his way across Wessex. Meantime, the local ealdormen, given warning of his approach, will do their best to deny the Danes any fortified positions. But a force that comes by ship - there would be no warning of an impending attack, and no time to adequately provision or garrison their target."

Ambrose smiled. "Unless a king's brand new fleet just happened to be cruising the southern coast and made an unexpected attack on the Viking fleet."

Alfred gestured at the large-scale map. "Well, my friends, we may have finally figured out what that fleet was up to. Exactly which southern ports would meet Guthrum's needs?"

Polonius pointed at several. "Too many to predict, Sire. Based on where we met the Viking fleet, I would guess Southampton or further west."

Alfred bent down to look closer at the map. "That leaves Southampton itself, Wareham, Exeter, Bredy, or a dozen small vills or monasteries that could be fortified. Polonius, which would you pick?"

"I would stay away from Southampton, at least once I found out that you have a fleet at the mouth of the river. It's also too central. Unless I was going direct for your throat in a lightning attack, I would stay away from the Wessex homeland entirely. Here, the people will rise to a man to defend you. To the east or west, in the conquered shires . . . it would be easier to sow discontent. You might not have the same level of support, and Guthrum might even manage to find a local *ealdorman* with pretensions to his ancestor's throne. It would not be the first time the Danes have installed an Angle or Saxon puppet."

Alfred straightened and started to pace. Man of action that he was, it was clear that he had come to some conclusions. "Diplomatically put, Scholar. What you are telling me is that Guthrum is probably moving his army toward our western shires. He is mounted, so he intends to move fast. He may be heading for the southern coast, and probably will attempt to seize a port, or at least some fortification convenient to the coast. We suspect that he has allies. Fortunately for us, we ran into and drove back what was probably one prong of his force. He may have more surprises for us. Guthrum may have turned some of our own leaders, or, at least, might be trying to.

Until more messengers arrive from the north with new information, let's work with this hypothesis. We can order the ealdormen to garrison the southern ports, particularly the ones that are fortified. We can send word to the eastern provinces and Cornwall to send mounted contingents, and we can call up the full fyrds of Wessex, Wiltshire, Hampshire, Dorset, and Devon.' The king sighed. 'My friends, Wessex is once again at war!'"

⚑

Ambrose, Phillip and Polonius watched from horseback as Alfred rode westward at the head of a long column of some six hundred mounted drengs and duguos. The king, impatient at the slow gathering of his fyrd, had impulsively decided to chase after the Vikings, even before his full forces had gathered.

Somewhere to the east, some ten columns and a total of eight hundred more churls and thanes, along with hundreds more retainers and dozens of cart loads of supplies, were wending their way toward their present position. As soon as Polonius had drawn up the marching orders for the late-arriving forces, the three companions intended to ride after their king with the new men.

As the late arrivals plodded past into camp, Ambrose noted that relatively few riders wore the chain-mail shirts that were almost standard in the Danish army. Each warrior, however, carried a spear, and all wore a battle-axe or sword strapped to their belt. They were *Jutes*, Angles, Saxons, Britons and Celts, but all owed military service to their king or ealdorman, and they were united in fierce hatred of the savage pagan Northmen who had invaded their lands. They were the fyrdmen; the militias of Alfred's empire that stretched from Cornwall to the Anglish Channel. With a last glance backward, Ambrose, Polonius and Phillip started out in pursuit of their king.

It had taken almost two weeks for the mounted thanes and the infantry to gather in one place, and in the interim, Guthrum and his raiders had ridden swiftly southward and westward, bypassing Alfred's position. The newly-arriving columns of infantry and late-arriving horsemen would continue to gather for another few days and then would march in Alfred's wake. Along the way, other columns were supposed to join up, until an army almost two thousand strong would arrive to support their king and his hard-riding vanguard.

As Ambrose and his two friends led the mounted fyrdmen in the wake of Alfred, they passed through devastated lands that had been plundered by Guthrum and his army as it had made its way south and west. The prince turned to Polonius and Phillip.

"It is all too easy to follow Guthrum's trail, my friends."

The three men stared at the still smoldering vill that had been, until recently, a prosperous settlement.

Polonius replied. "We saw the same in Mercia, Master."

"Aye, and along the Dnieper River, around Constantinople, and even in the Frankish coastal lands. This time, however, it is our own people who are dying, Scholar."

Suddenly, the normally taciturn Phillip spoke. "The heathen devils have been raiding our lands since the time of my grandfather, but never like this. This is not a raid - it is an invasion."

Ambrose replied. "I hope that Alfred is careful. He has good men with him, eager to show their king what they can do and win both land and glory, but if Guthrum decides to turn on them before all the *fyrdmen* have found their way to Alfred's side, he could easily find himself going into battle badly outnumbered."

Phillip spoke again. "Once we catch up with this force, Prince, King Alfred should have the men necessary to crush Guthrum."

Ambrose sighed. "I hope so, Weapons-master. There were few enough families who have not lost a son or uncle to the Vikings. North of the Wessex border, not a single Angle or Saxon kingdom has been able to hold out against them. We are the last unconquered *Angelisc* country on the island."

꘡

It took the mounted troop two days of hard riding, but eventually they caught up to Alfred's force of mounted infantry. Alfred smiled in greeting as his bastard brother and his two faithful companions rode up to his position, followed by a column a half-mile long.

"Welcome, gentlemen! Did I at least give you a merry chase?"

Ambrose grinned at his royal brother. "We had to ride hard, brother, but your trail was easy to follow."

Alfred suddenly looked very serious. "Yes, brother. As easy as it was for us to follow the Viking devils. We just followed the smoke from the burned vills."

꘡

The scouts rode hard for the Saxon column. When they spotted the royal banner, they swerved to report directly to their king. The commander of the little squad gasped.

"Yer Majesty! There be Viking raiders just ahead . . . just the other side of that there hill!"

Alfred turned a calm eye to the man. "Well? How many, and are there any other Viking forces around?"

"I know not, King! I rode directly to report to you!"

"Next time, I expect that you will bring me a complete report. Did you send out men to flank the Viking force and see what is behind them?"

The scout now looked thoroughly miserable. "No, King."

"And just what are the Vikings doing?"

"There is a little burh, Sire, just the other side of the hill, and they are looting it. I would guess that there are no more than a hundred of 'em."

"All right. Catch your breath, man, and wait. I may have some more work for you."

"Yes, King."

Alfred turned in his saddle to his two faithful companions. His childhood weapons tutor, Phillip, had ridden back to check on the slow-moving supply and infantry column. "Ambrose and Polonius, what do you think?"

Ambrose replied. "There are almost seven hundred of us in the vanguard, brother, all mounted.

I would propose that we send 300 to try and loop around them. The rest of us should wait a thousand counts, and then ride to the attack! Put Polonius' riders with the *pig-stickers* in front, and we will make an imposing array."

Polonius had been listening. "Could I add that we send out a screen of scouts so that we are not, in turn, ambushed ourselves? Remember that, not too far away, there is the main Viking force that, at least until Phillip's column catches up, still outnumbers us. They, too, are mounted. While we don't know their exact location, we are closing on them. Given an adequate warning system, however, I would concur with Ambrose. Let's attack!"

Alfred grew more excited. "So be it! Ambrose, please split up the force and get the first column moving. Tell them I want a big enough loop that the Vikings are not forewarned.

Polonius, be so good as to arrange for that screen of scouts ahead of and around the first column. Send them far. I want no surprises. Make sure that everyone knows we are to retreat toward the main body if faced with a superior force. I have no wish to have my gallant thanes crushed before the rank and file are here to support us."

Alfred signaled the main force to dismount. With no further words, he had the men walk their mounts to near the crest of the hill. The king strode back and forth dressing the line. When they crested the rise, he wanted a disciplined and organized force sweeping down on the hapless raiders.

Each man stood by his horse and waited silently for the word to mount. Firm discipline was kept. Not a word was spoken in the long line. Satisfied at last, Alfred led his horse to the middle of the line and then paused dramatically. Having carefully counted to one thousand, he raised his arm. The men swung into their saddles. When Alfred let his arm fall, the signal horns blared.

If the sounds of the Saxon war horns did not warn the Vikings, then the sudden thunder of hundreds of galloping horses certainly did. The raiders looked eastward to see a long line of armored men topping the rise and riding hard at them. The line was so long that it threatened to flank the Vikings on both ends.

The Northmen abandoned their loot and captives, and ran for their horses. It was a close thing. The Vikings had no time to form up into any kind of formation, but those few who managed to reach a horse rode hard for the west. Those who were a little slower were run through with the long lances Polonius had been training the Saxons with.

In the case of pockets of resistance, the Saxons preferred to leap from their horses and attack on foot. The fifty or so Vikings who had not made it to their horses in time were quickly cut down by the overwhelming numbers of attackers.

The other Danes, the ones who had been lucky enough to be on the other side of the settlement, managed to reach their horses. They rode desperately for their lives. The sounds of battle horns suddenly blared ahead of them, however, and a fresh line of horsemen suddenly stretched in front of them.

The Vikings were no cowards. Behind them was certain death, and ahead lay their only hope of escape. Some bunched up for support, but, to a man, they rode at the oncoming horsemen.

The two lines clashed, and most of the charging Vikings were killed in the savage melee. Some, however, lucky enough to find a chink in the on-rushing line of riders, made it safely through. The collision was so sudden that each rider got a quick jab or swing with spear, axe or sword, and then the surviving Vikings were away.

Alfred's men swung their horses around and pursued, but the king had instructed his thanes not to pursue blindly. Somewhere, not too far ahead, were between one and two thousand hostile Viking warriors. All were battle-hardened veterans, and all were mounted.

True to Alfred's prediction, Guthrum continued to lead his Danes south and west, until it became clear he was heading for Wareham. Messengers from Alfred's own nephew, Ethelwold, the Ealdorman of Dorset, reported that a lightning attack by Guthrum's best horsemen took the easily-defended nunnery just hours before Ethelwold had been able to garrison it with a strong force. Cursing Ethelwold as either a fool or a coward, Alfred pushed his mounted column hard along the trail of destruction, until the sturdy stone buildings of Wareham came into sight.

The king stared at the stone walls and palisades that blocked the end of the peninsula. "May God curse the wily heathen! It's Nottingham all over again."

Ambrose stared, too. "What do you mean, brother?"

"Guthrum uses our own defenses against us. We don't have enough men to storm those damn walls!"

Polonius spoke. "Let me be even more blunt, Sire. I fear that the fly has caught up with the spider."

Suddenly, Alfred grinned. "Well put, Scholar. Yes, I know we are no match for Guthrum, at least not until Phillip arrives with the rest of our men and our supplies. Fear not - I will do nothing rash.

Ambrose, spread the word. We will retreat to that natural strong point you noted earlier as we rode past it. We will camp there and wait for the rest of our army to catch up.

Polonius, I want you to organize a strong screen of scouts. I intend to use these eyes and ears not only to warn me of a serious threat, but also to allow us to locate any Viking foraging parties.

Once our position has been adequately fortified along the model of the old Roman marching camps, I want strong columns sent out on systematic sweeps of the area. I want any isolated raiding parties overwhelmed and killed.

Somewhere to the east, and the north, and the west, converging on this site and hopefully not more than a day or two away, should be the peddlers and the prostitutes, the ox-carts, the blacksmiths, the fletchers and bowyers, and the rest of my damn fyrdmen!"

Alfred sat on his horse on a high spot overlooking the peninsula made by the joining of the From and the Tarrant Rivers. Secure on the end was the nunnery of Wareham. His commanders and advisors were gathered around, and not far away sat his Personal Guard of three hundred young but battle-tested drengs.

The king turned to his brother and Polonius, once chief military advisor to the *Varangian* state of Kiev, and subsequently ambassador to imperial Byzantium. Polonius had followed his friend Ambrose to the frozen north, and then south, by way of the Asian rivers, to his own eastern homeland. Then, he followed again, all the way to Angleland. Now, Polonius served as chief advisor to Alfred, king of all the West Saxons.

Alfred looked at his two best friends. "Well, gentlemen, what do you think? Can we take the convent?"

Polonius spoke first. Military strategy was his specialty.

"Remember the teachings of *Master Sun*, Sire. 'If you outnumber the opponent ten to one, then surround them; five to one, attack; two to one, divide.'"

Alfred smiled. "Well, I hope that we will soon outnumber the heathens by at least two to one, but I am damned if I know how to divide them. What does the master strategist Polonius say?"

"Sire, when all of your forces finally gather, you could probably take it. It would be costly, however. You can only attack on one front, unless you bring in fleets of boats. The Danes fight well, and they have done a lot of work. It will be a tough nut to crack, even with a several-times advantage in numbers. I fear that you would only achieve a Pyrrhic victory."

Alfred looked puzzled. "Pyrrhic victory?"

"Prince Ambrose, do you remember your Latin history?"

"Probably not to your satisfaction, Scholar, but I do remember the story about Pyrrhus of Epirus."

"And so what is a Pyrrhic victory?"

"Did not Pyrrhus defeat a Roman army at the cost of most of his own?"

"Exactly, so, Prince."

Alfred interrupted. "I think, Polonius, that you are trying to tell me that if I attack, I might win, but it would be at a terrible cost."

"Or that you might not win at all."

Alfred nodded. "And if we lay siege?"

"It must eventually fall. We arrived too soon after them to have allowed them much time to build up supplies. Your aggressive sweeps have crippled their foraging expeditions. They cannot have much food. There is just one catch."

"Yes, Polonius. And just what is that?"

"Is there another prong to Guthrum's attack? We turned back one small fleet, but we have reports of another dozen scattered throughout Wales, northern Angleland, and Ireland. What if he has more reinforcements coming by water? There is a reason he moved his army close to the sea."

"Then the choice is between losing many of our finest young men on a frontal assault, or hoping that Guthrum will starve because he has no fleet to bring in either food or reinforcements?"

"In a nutshell, Majesty."

"If we attack and fail?"

"Then his army is loose in Wessex, and may God help us all. We run, and try to raise another army."

"And if we lay siege and he gets reinforcements?"

"Then we might be forced to retreat, but with an intact army. He can't go far, as long as we are sitting nearby with a couple of thousand men under arms."

"Except that these men will eventually want to go home to harvest their crops. Still, that's months away. Polonius, my friend, you make it all so simple.

I want the two of you to get to work organizing a siege. Don't neglect our own fortifications. We don't want an unhappy surprise early one morning. And if their reinforcements do arrive, the ramparts we build in the next few days may save all of our lives. It looks like we are going to sit in the mud here for a while. And Polonius, I want the entire southern coast put on ship alert. Send word that the signal fires are to be prepared and manned twenty-four hours a day. I want no surprises from the sea!"

CHAPTER 3

**"AD 876: The king afterwards made peace with
them; and they gave him as hostages those who were
worthiest in the army.....and that by night they broke
(out)."**

On the twentieth-sixth day of the siege, a lone warrior strode out of the
main gates of Wareham. He was dressed for war, wearing expensive
chain-mail, and with a sword at his waist, but he carried a white-covered
shield high over his head. Sentries ran to inform Alfred, and both the
king and his court retinue hurried to the ramparts opposite the main gate.
The throbbing note of a single war horn put the rest of the camp on alert,
but Alfred had ordered that one quarter of his men man the ramparts at
any given time, so there was no great panic.

The king and Ambrose watched the lone warrior climb down into
the dry ditch Alfred's men had dug so laboriously. The ditch stretched
from one side of the little peninsula to the other, effectively isolating the
solidly built nunnery from the mainland. It was not so deep that the
Danes could not clamber through it, but its depth, and the many
randomly placed stakes, ensured that no large formation of infantry or
horsemen could pass quickly through it. Thus, the defenses prevented
Guthrum's Danes from escaping the siege on horseback, and made it
difficult even for mass movements of infantry. The single man, however,
had no problem negotiating the obstacles. He stopped an easy spear cast
from where Alfred was idly watching him approach.

The man spoke in rough Saxon. "Great king, I am Jarl Ura, and my
master Guthrum has sent me to deliver a message to you."

"Then speak, Ura. What message has your master sent me?"

"Guthrum's army is strong, and in spite of the numbers of your
warriors, he feels he could cut his way through you at any time."

"But, Ura, he does not. Is this because he wishes to show Christian
mercy to me and my people?"

"You make a joke, I think. My king respects you, Anglishman, and
he admits that it will be expensive for us to cut our way out through your
army.' He smiled. 'You dig ditches well. Your peasants will be pushed
aside like tall blades of grass before a scythe, but your fyrdmen give a
good accounting of themselves. Instead of death for many of both our

nations, my master Guthrum has a proposal for you."

"I am listening, Ura."

"He wishes to call a truce. If you pull your army back, provide us with five hundred pounds of gold, a thousand pounds of silver, and enough cattle and pigs to supply all our needs, we will pack up and march north."

"I think Guthrum must have forgotten who is trapped on a peninsula. And by now you know your fleet isn't coming. Here are my terms. If you surrender half of your horses and all your slaves, we will let you keep the rest and march home unmolested. We would even provide the necessary food, as you request."

"King, we have not been defeated. We may yet be strong enough to destroy your entire army. If you refuse our offer, then we will soon find out. The choice is yours. My king instructed me to tell you that you have two days in which to ponder his proposal. In those two days we will make no hostile move."

"Take as long as you wish, Ura. Who knows, you might still have a few horses left that you can eat if you get hungry. I will agree, however, to make no hostile move until we receive your answer. Is that satisfactory?"

"Aye, king. I will convey your words to my master."

It was very late, but Alfred had asked all of his senior commanders and advisors to join him in his Command tent. Alfred paced the large single-roomed structure from end to end impatiently. He seemed in a foul temper, occasionally *holding his stomach.* He stared in turn at the various ealdormen, bishops, *athelings* and others who made up his advisory body.

"Well, Councilmen, what do we do?!"

Polonius looked up from the map he was studying. "Sire, that he offers any terms at all, means that he is worried, and probably hungry. But Ura is right. They are not defeated, and a sudden breakout might be very hard for us to stop."

"Then you are saying we should pay the bastard *Danegeld* and just let him ride home?"

Phillip spoke up, to everyone's surprise. "I would like nothing better than to crush this army, Majesty. It is the only language that Vikings understand. Say the word. Let us be a tide that rolls irresistibly, until no Vikings are left alive."

Alfred smiled fondly at the blond giant. "I, too, would like nothing better, Phillip. And yet, what will it cost us? How many widows will be grieving this winter? What if our men do break? Only our veteran thanes can be counted on to hold, and we have a high percent of raw levies. Dare I risk the fate of the entire kingdom on a mad attack? There is also the reason that they chose the nunnery. Guthrum is in a position to be easily re-supplied, and we know that the Danes have several fleets somewhere to the north of us, or in Ireland."

"Polonius, what does the Master Sun Tzu have to say on this matter?"

"I can remember nothing pertinent, Sire, but his student Cao Cao said 'When the enemy has called in its resources and is defending a city, to attack them in this condition is the lowest form of military operation.'"

Alfred sighed. "We don't know if they are adequately provisioned, but an attack would certainly be costly."

As the fire started to die down, Alfred rubbed a hand across his tired eyes and spoke to the men gathered before him. "Members of the *Witan*, the hour is late. I think that all that can be said has been said. I thank you for your thoughts. It has helped me come to a decision.'

Tired as the advisors were, they all roused themselves to listen. The king's next few words would determine if Wessex would have uneasy peace, or suffer further bloodshed.

'I have decided that we will agree to let Guthrum and his men through our lines, and I might consent to pay a small amount of Danegeld. I will, in turn, however, demand more than promises. I will only agree to a treaty if they give us some of their senior officers as hostages. We will work out the details in the morning.

Good night, my friends. Go to your beds, and sleep well."

Alfred stood, and the noblemen, warriors, and churchmen who made up the king's Council hastily rose and excused themselves.

Ambrose slipped naked under the deerskin covers of his bed and heaved a giant sigh. He had heard his brother's decision, but he was still not sure in his heart that it was the right one.

His body was exhausted, but his mind would not stop racing. He knew the army's ranks were full of ill-armed churls and retainers who had been called up especially to provide labor and support the mounted fyrdmen. These same men were beginning to melt away in the night.

Having faithfully served their time, and with the crops ripening at home, there was no keeping them for the onerous siege duty. Alfred had ordered some deserters hung, but his commanders only hung the slow and foolish ones. The rest just disappeared when no one was looking. Ambrose was not sure how long his brother could keep together a large enough force to contain Guthrum. Thus, he assumed that was why Alfred so suddenly agreed to come to terms with the powerful Danish king who had so brazenly invaded his kingdom.

For the thousandth time he cursed the fact that Wessex didn't have a professional standing force capable of dealing with an invading army. Polonius had warned him of the need many years before. With these thoughts roiling through his mind, it was dawn before he was able to fall into an uneasy slumber.

ß

It was near high noon of the second day when it was reported to Alfred that Ura was once again nimbly clambering down into the ditch and calling loudly for Alfred. Although Ambrose knew that Alfred was eager to talk to the man, the king intentionally delayed climbing into view for several minutes. At last, unable to contain himself, he climbed up onto the earth ramparts and casually looked through the gap in the palisade, down into the ditch. He stared at the Danish Jarl for some moments before he spoke. "Well, Ura. Have you come to surrender?"

"The fate of my people who surrender to your tender Christian mercies is well known, King-of-the West-Saxons."

"I would have hoped that such an object lesson would have kept you and your kind far from my lands, Ura."

"Once we were, like your own people, simple pirates raiding a foreign land. Now, King, we are conquerors of kingdoms!"

"Except Wessex, Dane. Except Wessex. We are the burial ground for some thousands of your countrymen. Any Dane who comes here is only entitled to the land it takes to bury him in."

"Alfred-of-the-West-Saxons, today you agree to pay Danegeld and my king rides north in peace, or your land will run red with blood, and we shall see who it will belong to."

"Do not push me, Ura! Rub your empty belly and ponder my words carefully. In order to prevent the needless death of some of my faithful men, I have decided that we would be willing to pay fifty pounds of gold and three hundred pounds of silver. Your king, however, must give me ten senior officers from amongst his High Council. These men will instantly pay with their lives for any treachery on your part."

"Guthrum is not accustomed to giving hostages to an enemy who has not managed to defeat him, King."

"Then tell Guthrum to either swim home or sharpen his sword, Ura.

I will pay the Danegeld to save Saxon lives, but I will have ironclad guarantees in return. I expect both a personal oath from Guthrum, and the ten hostages. I also expect half of your horse herd."

"King, you ask too much! Our horses are our means of transportation. It is many days hard ride to reach your northern borders. The loss of so many mounts would cripple us."

"An army half on foot will have no choice but to head north. That is the entire point, Jarl."

"King-of-the-West-Saxons, what you ask for puts us at your mercy. We cannot agree to such terms!"

"Ura, tell your king that Alfred will give him a second fifty pounds of silver after you turn over the horses. That will buy you a dozen horse herds in Mercia. Go now. Our discussion is at an end."

At dusk of that day, ten haughty Danish jarls clambered through the deep ditch, climbed to the narrow gap in the palisade, and surrendered to the astonished Saxon Officer-of-the-Watch. The ten men were disarmed and sent directly to King Alfred.

The king sat regally in his ornately carved chair. The outer walls of the large tent were lined with bishops and ealdormen, athelings and ambassadors. Directly before him stood the ten Viking jarls that he had demanded from Guthrum.

Polonius stood beside Alfred in his capacity of translator. Alfred addressed them all, knowing that Polonius would provide any necessary translating.

"Welcome to my court. You are all honored guests here, and will be treated as such, excepting only that you may not leave the encampment without permission, nor may you leave behind the men I assign to guard and protect you. I am a man of my word, and I tell you now that three months after your king and his army crosses our northern frontier, you will in turn be escorted north, with suitable gifts from me. If, on the other hand, your king breaks the oath he is to swear tomorrow morning, then you will pay for his treachery with your lives."

Alfred waited until Polonius translated his words. "Polonius, is what I said clear to each of them?"

"Perfectly, King Alfred. I translated exactly what you said."

Alfred spoke quietly to Ambrose. The king had agreed that the first fifty pounds of gold would be paid once the hostages had arrived, and Alfred wanted the Danegeld to be weighed and delivered to Guthrum.

"Brother, after you measure the gold and send it to Guthrum, please arrange with Ethelwold for a work detail. Starting at dawn tomorrow, I want them to widen the gap in the palisades and fill in a narrow stretch of the ditch. Tell Ethelwold that I want the work started just after sunrise, and it is to be complete by the noon hour oath-giving ceremony. It would not do for two kings to have to clamber up and down the steep banks of the ditch.

After the oath-giving, the Danes have promised to deliver several hundred of their horses. I told Guthrum I want a full half of the herd. We will need horse herders ready. Would you please take care of the details?"

Ambrose smiled. "Of course, Alfred."

Ambrose left his king's side and signaled for Ethelwold, atheling and nephew to Alfred, to join him. Ethelwold, as Ealdorman of Dorset, was overlord of most of the peasant workmen, and he commanded a force of thanes almost equal to Alfred's. As well, he was the night's Officer-of-the-Watch for the central portion of the Saxon siege-line.

"Ethelwold! The king has asked if you would arrange to have a ten-foot span of the ditch completely filled in. He would like the job started right after dawn, and it must be completed before noon. Once that's done, you may have your men start removing the equivalent length of palisade along the ramparts. Until then, Alfred expects that you will keep your Dorsetmen in full military readiness."

"Of course, cousin. If that's all, I hope that you will excuse me. I have a great deal to do before I sleep tonight."

⚑

A single Saxon war horn suddenly sounded in the distance. Its throbbing note was soon picked up and echoed throughout the camp. Only a full emergency merited such a series of calls. Alfred's advisors and commanders looked at each other and then grabbed their weapons. Something was very wrong!

A rider galloped through the camp toward Alfred's Command Center. In the wan torchlight, he looked scared. The sound of battle and many galloping horses managed to almost drown the blaring war-horns. Alfred and his comrades looked wildly about, but the sounds grew no closer.

Alfred focused again on the approaching man, and the messenger, in turn, recognized his king. He yelled out. "Sire! There has been a breakout! The Danes have escaped!"

Alfred stood straight. "What are you talking about? How could the Danes escape? Did they swim?"

"No, Sire! They rode across the ditch you ordered filled in, and through the hole in the palisade."

"The ditch was to be filled in and the palisades were to be pulled down after our entire army was drawn up in battle formation; after dawn!"

"Be that as it may, King, hundreds of Viking horsemen tore through the gap in the palisades. We had no chance to stop them! They rode west!"

Ambrose called out. "What sector are you from?"

"Ethelwold is our Ealdorman, Atheling! We are Dorsetmen."

Alfred turned to his commanders. "All right, commanders! I want all men in battle gear and on full alert. We designed the marching forts so that each separate section is defensible. We have no idea where that lying bastard is going to strike, or if he is at all, but he's loose, mounted, and very dangerous! Button up each of your defense perimeters tight until dawn. Come sunrise, report back to me here, and then we will see what can be done.

Phillip! Take a strong guard and put our hostages in chains! Assign a double guard on them, and then stay with them until morning. If any Danes are so much as seen in their vicinity - you are to cut their throats immediately. Commanders, on your way! Hold your positions at all costs, and may God be with us all!"

Dawn found the men exhausted. Only half had been allowed to sleep, and that only while in battle gear and in position, behind their various barricades and ramparts.

Soon after first dawn, Polonius' best scouts reported back directly to Alfred. The squad was led by Thane Burgtun, who stood stiffly at attention in front of his king.

"Your Majesty! Guthrum's Danes rode right through the Dorset sector. There were relatively few casualties. Most of Ethelwold's men just dove for cover, and the Danes were in a great hurry."

"And blocking the escape was supposed to be hundreds of men, a deep dry ditch, many sharpened wooden stakes, a log palisade, and numerous small strong-points designed to prevent just this kind of sudden escape! Just how the devil did the Danes fly over all that!?"

Thane Burgtun looked straight ahead. Alfred rubbed his stomach, trying to sooth the burning pain within. He was in a furious mood, and stress often turned on a raging furnace in his belly. Burgtun had no wish to be the one Alfred vented his rage on.

"Sire, my men report that the dry ditch was filled with dirt for over fifteen paces. The palisade on the ramparts was cut down. After that, the only obstacle was the men, and the Dorsetmen ran and hid against such a force as descended upon them."

"The ditch was full! How in God's name did the Danes fill the ditch without being spotted by the God-cursed sentries on the rampart above!? Ambrose! Bring me Ealdorman Ethelwold, and bring him to me now! You other commanders! Return to your sections, and prepare to break camp. I want at least the mounted fyrdmen to be on the road and after Guthrum within an hour at most. Well, move it!"

༆

Ethelwold, Ealdorman of Dorset, nephew of Alfred and son of a former king, stood before his king. "You sent for me, King Alfred?"

Alfred had changed to a dangerous calm. "Ethelwold, over a thousand mounted warriors managed to sneak up on your many alert sentries, filled in a huge ditch, dug through a rampart, removed several dozen sturdy logs, and rode out through a camp full of your men, who had been ordered to be extra alert. Would you care to explain to me just how any of that is possible?"

Ambrose noted that Ethelwold's face dripped perspiration. His voice, however, betrayed no nervousness when he spoke.

"Of course, Your Majesty. I asked myself the same question, and, by God, I got some answers!"

"Then please be so kind as to share your revelation with your king!"

"Thane Delwyn was commander on duty last night. He told the men to start filling in the ditch and remove the logs."

"He what!?"

"Told the men to fill in the ditch and remove the logs. After that, he told the men to stand down, Sire."

"Ealdorman, do you remember my specific instructions passed on to you last night by your uncle?"

"Of course, Sire! And I faithfully reported them verbatim to my assembled commanders, as they will no doubt be happy to attest. I am aware of the enormity of what happened last night because of Delwyn's misunderstanding of your clear instructions. You may rest assured, Sire, that Delwyn has already paid fully for his stupidity!"

Alfred was twitching in anger, but his voice became calm again. "And just how did Delwyn pay for his stupidity, Ethelwold?"

"When I realized what he had done, I ordered him hung at once. He is still hanging from a tree, Sire, in my camp. I wanted it to be an object lesson to my other officers. What he did was inexcusable. I have already declared his land and property forfeited, Sire."

"Ethelwold, you were in charge of your men last night."

"No, Sire. After being excused from your presence, I met a delegation of my people several Roman miles to the north. Bishop Asser rode with me. I left Delwyn in charge, Sire."

"Ethelwold, you are from the loins of my own brother. In spite of that, we may yet put you to God's justice. At this moment, your land and your very life is hanging by a thin thread! For now, I want you to go to your camp and prepare your forces to ride. This issue is, however, far from settled!"

Runnels of sweat poured down Ethelwold's face, but he just bowed to his king, and backed out of his presence.

CHAPTER 4

"AD 877: This year came the Danish army into Exeter from Wareham; whilst the navy sailed west about, until they met with a great mist at sea, and there perished one hundred and twenty ships at Swanwich. Meanwhile King Alfred with his army rode after the cavalry as far as Exeter; but he could not overtake them before their arrival in the fortress, where they could not be come at."

Alfred faced his chief advisors, though none looked into his eyes. The king was in pain, holding his belly again, and he was angry.

"I want only the men with horses, and I want them ready to ride by dawn. We will catch up to Guthrum and destroy him! Yes, what is it, Polonius?"

"Sire, with all due respect, at the moment you have fewer thanes than Guthrum has warriors. Running off after him will again be a case of the fly chasing the spider." Sun Tzu once said, "If you are fewer, then keep away if you are able."

"And is there anything wrong with a fly chasing a spider?"

"No, Sire, unless the spider turns to fight. We would be chopped to pieces and Wessex would lose its last hope against the Danes. Make no mistake, Sire. If you are killed, Wessex is defeated. If Wessex falls, there is no hope for all Britain."

"Then just what do you propose we do, Wizard? Let the devil's spawn destroy my entire country one vill at a time? As we talk, they are killing innocent men and raping their women. These are my people, and I must do something!"

"Then let us follow, Sire, but carefully. We must not be caught in the open until a lot more thanes join your banner."

"Look about you, Scholar. We have almost three thousand men in camp. How is Guthrum going to cut his way through so many?"

"Sire, what is the approximate number of Guthrum's warriors?"

"Probably thirteen hundred in total, though some will be walking wounded."

"And we have less than a thousand mounted thanes."

"We have almost three thousand under arms, Scholar. Even a

Saxon king can count!"

"You are correct, Sire, and over two thousand are churls who came to support their thanes. Most owe us no direct loyalty, Sire."

"My thanes and churls are brave men, Polonius, and they will stand and fight if I tell them to. You once told me that you went with the Rus tribesmen and conquered a river kingdom with fewer men than I have in camp today!"

"The Rus warriors became the core of a Slav force that numbered in the tens of thousands, Sire, and they also, not incidentally, recruited thousands more Vikings before they became a dominant force in the Dnieper River Valley."

"Then my thanes will be the core of my force, and they will support the churls. Any slaves who fight for me will be manumitted. You see, we have the men. Let us not waste more time arguing. I want to ride!"

"Sire, no one is saying that the churls are not brave men, and, they worked heroically building the defenses and manning the walls. Without adequate armor or a horse, however, they can not match the Vikings in the open, nor can they even keep up with your mounted thanes."

The king looked at Ambrose. "Well, brother?"

"Polonius is right, Alfred. We both know it."

"Well then, advisors, advise me! What the hell are we going to do? . . . Polonius?"

"By all means, Sire, let us follow the Danes, but carefully. We keep out a screen of scouts between Guthrum and our column. He must never be allowed to know our true numbers. We, in turn, must avoid being caught in the open at all costs."

"And just how, Scholar, do you propose that we do that?"

"By leapfrogging from defensive position to defensive position."

"And if there is no available position when the day ends?"

"Then we build a Roman marching-fort, Sire."

"Such a task takes immense effort, Polonius."

"The ancient Romans did it, nightly, in hostile territory."

"Yes. Yes, but it is time-consuming. It will slow us down!"

"But it also makes us unassailable, Sire. It means eight hundred behind walls can likely hold against thirteen hundred or even more."

"Hmm. I hate to admit it, but I suppose your plan makes sense . . . Ambrose?"

"Alfred, we have spare mounts. How many more men can we mount up? Let's ask for volunteers amongst the strongest and best equipped of the churls."

"Good thinking, brother. Phillip, how many men do you estimate you could mount if you took all the spare horses?"

"Perhaps four hundred, King."

"Now we are closer to Guthrum in number. But what do we do with the eighteen hundred men we can't take?"

Polonius spoke. "Send home those whose time is almost up, Sire. We can gather more as we need them. The rest march in our wake, along with the wagon-loads of supplies.

As well, we call up every thane on our path, along with their retainers. Meantime, your messengers guide in the mounted fyrds from the far eastern and western shires. Eventually, we will again be more than a match for King Guthrum, even if we are forced to meet him in the open."

Alfred looked at his advisors, and everyone waited with bated breath. At last, he spoke.

"You have convinced a stubborn king. I will give you twenty-four hours to bring in the horse herds and mount the extra men. Tell them there will be generous rewards for men who fight bravely under my banner. And Polonius, I expect you to study the maps and come up with easily-defensible positions for when we get close. I wish to avoid building marching-forts as much as possible."

Polonius smiled. "It will be done, Sire!"

Within twenty-four hours, Alfred led a force west of over twelve hundred men. As his mounted warriors rode after Guthrum, Alfred had his ealdormen send out messengers in all directions.

They stripped the vills and burhs bare of any remaining fighting men who could ride a horse. Many would serve for a few weeks, and then they had the right to return home, but Alfred planned to keep enough with the army at any given time that he would always have a force that would give Guthrum pause.

As it neared noon on the third day, Polonius rode up to his king. Ambrose smiled at the thin dark man, and used another of his titles.

"Well, Spy-master, what news have our spies and scouts brought us?"

"Not good, Sire. Guthrum's vanguard took the old Roman fort at Exeter, and his men are now busily strengthening its already formidable defenses."

"Damnation! Again he goes to ground. Exeter is in Odda's territory. Just what does the old rascal have to say about this?"

"He is upset, Sire. As you ordered, he garrisoned Exeter with a strong force of thanes, but he then sent you most of the garrison troops to support your siege at Wareham. It seemed a safe bet, with Guthrum trapped."

"You are right, Polonius. Odda is a loyal friend, and he is stripping Devon bare to support us. I don't think that we can blame him when it was us who let Guthrum escape."

Less than two days after Guthrum's main army arrived at Exeter, the vanguard of Alfred's fast-moving force caught up. As soon as Alfred came within sight of the old walls, he split the force into two.

"Ambrose, take the left wing and loop around Exeter. Try and stay out of sight of the town, but kill every Dane you can find! Kill the men of the foraging parties. Kill their scouts. I want Guthrum to be hungry and totally blind. Back away only if you are facing a large force. In that case, return here as fast as you can."

Ambrose grinned wolfishly. "And what will you be doing, brother?"

"Polonius is going to help me build a fine marching fort. We will have secure walls for you by the time you return."

The second column followed their king to a site recommended by Odda's local thanes. Following Polonius' advice, Alfred quickly put the men to work setting up another fortified marching camp based on the ancient Roman model.

Alfred knew that Polonius was right. Once Guthrum realized how numerically inferior the Saxon forces were, he would be tempted to attack. At all costs, Alfred's fyrdmen needed a strong defensive position, a secure base from which to harass the Danes.

Guthrum had no idea how many Saxons had arrived. His immediate priority had to be to have his men complete the repairs on the dilapidated defenses of the ancient city of Exeter.

Once the marching fort was completed, Alfred breathed a sigh of relief. Now he waited impatiently for his probing columns to return and for his infantry to catch up. Behind secure walls, he felt much less vulnerable.

⚐

The Weapons-master bowed to his king. "Sire, you sent for me?"

Alfred looked unsmilingly at his old tutor. "Yes, old warrior. We have the problem of our ten 'guests'. They are brave men and I feel no personal enmity toward them, but their lives were offered as a guarantee of Guthrum's word. He has broken his word, and they must pay the price. Let it be painless but public. Hang them from the trees near our main gate. Then I want you to ride back and see what is keeping the infantry and supply column. I wanted them here and safe last night!"

Phillip bowed low. "As you command, Sire."

Like industrious ants, the Saxons once again started construction of ditches, ramparts and palisades. Once again the local thanes and ealdormen called in every able-bodied man within several days' march. It would be days and even weeks before the masses of churls from far-away shires would be able to gather and march to join their ealdormen and thanes, but they would come; mounted thanes leading their own personal bands, and ealdormen with the armed might of their entire shires at their back. Both Alfred and Guthrum knew that Alfred's position, presently tenuous, would get stronger with time.

A grizzled thane called out to his king. "Sire, the Danes come!" The war horns were calling the men to the ramparts even as the breathless warrior reached his king.

Alfred looked impatient. "What exactly is happening?"

"Sire! It looks like the entire force of Danes is coming right at us!"

"Then thank the Merciful Lord for the protection of this fort. Get your weapons, man! Let's kill some Danes!"

The Danes rode right through the screen of Saxon scouts. In spite of the best efforts of Alfred's patrols, Guthrum obviously knew exactly where Alfred's marching fort was, and he was not put off by the irritating cloud of Saxon lancers and archers mounted on speedy horses. Instead, he led his men directly to the Saxon camp.

More than twelve hundred mounted and armored Danes rode right to the edge of the dry ditch. Leaping off their mounts and running past the swinging corpses of their own noblemen, waves of warriors charged headlong into the ditch. Alfred ordered his archers to the palisades, backed by a double row of spearmen.

Just behind the second row of spearmen, Alfred turned to his chief advisors and noblemen. "Well, gentlemen, I think we got Guthrum's attention. We have even made him cranky. This time, we are the ones behind the defenses, and we almost equal the devil's spawn in number. Let's give these Danes a bloody nose! . . . Polonius!"

"Yes, Sire."

"How far back is the supply column?"

"Not more than a day or so, Sire."

"Numbers?"

"Phillip's last report stated that he was leading some six hundred infantry and three hundred mounted, Sire, plus what they have been able to sweep up along the way. That might be another five hundred; lightly armed. The fyrds from Kent and Essex are on their way, but their arrival time is unknown."

"May God help the poor devils if Guthrum learns of the supply convoy's location and gets past us. If we can keep his attention here for a few hours, then Guthrum will have lost his biggest opportunity, and we will be strengthened immeasurably!"

The palisade had been built so that the archers could shoot through the spaces between the logs. Alfred's men emptied their quivers at the men leaping into the ditch and struggling through the maze of sharpened stakes. The defenses were not designed to stop any attackers; just slow them down. The Danes made easy targets as they struggled across the ditch and then started to climb the steep embankment. All too soon, however, they reached the ramparts. Some tried to climb the logs, while others set to with their axes.

The archers pulled back and headed for the supply depot and more arrows. The first rank of spearmen stepped forward and tried to stab through the spaces. Behind them, the re-supplied archers formed up again, and took aim at the rampart top.

Guthrum had thrown his entire force at one side of the marching fort, in the hope that a concerted push would break the defenders. Most of Alfred's men, however, were his drengs, young men with no property, whose only hope to hold land was to impress their king with their ferocity. The reckless young warriors were leavened with his old battle-toughened duguos, warriors who held land on the understanding that they would ride against Wessex's many foes whenever called upon. The tough Saxon thanes had conquered as far north as Mercia and Northern Wales, and had, between then, fought some dozen battles with various Viking war bands. They had won more than they lost. They feared the Danes, but they would fight until they could not stand. None among them were cowards.

The ditch filled with dead and wounded Danes, and more died as they struggled to get over or through the palisade wall. Those that reached the top were perfect targets for the archers.

Guthrum grudgingly accepted that he was wasting the lives of his men. With the sturdy walls protecting them, the Wessex fyrdmen were not about to break. His men were more than a match for poorly armed Saxon churls, but these veteran fyrdmen were the equal of his best Viking warriors, and the Saxons were using their defenses very intelligently.

Furious at the losses, the Viking king grudgingly ordered the retreat. The throbbing notes of the war horn brought his men stumbling back. Many of them, however, lay where they had fallen. Cursing *Loki*, Guthrum retreated to his strong fortification of Exeter.

The next day found the main body of Alfred's infantry arriving, along with some more late-arriving mounted fyrdmen from the far-flung shires. Straggling columns marched or rode in all day long. As each arrived, the men were quickly set to work unloading the ox carts and expanding Alfred's marching-fort.

Polonius and Ambrose stood beside Alfred, and Ambrose spoke.

"I am relieved, brother, that Phillip's screen of scouts kept Guthrum from catching the infantry in the open. Our Saxons are brave, but many are just raw levies. They would never have been able to stand against the Vikings."

Alfred turned to his brother. "Let us thank the Good Lord, Ambrose! God blinded Guthrum from the obvious. Guthrum threw his men at the wrong force, and do you know what?"

"What, brother?"

"It is going to cost him the war."

"So, Alfred, what do we do now?"

"Now I systematically crush Guthrum! Polonius, I want you to take charge again of designing and building inter-connecting defensive positions and ditches."

"Of course, Sire."

"Good. First of all, I want you to build a series of defensive fortifications, until they stretch all the way around Exeter. Put the new arrivals to work on that.

After that, we start systematically digging ditches and building ramparts from fort to fort, until they finally interconnect. Build the ditches first."

Polonius spoke. "Forts or ditches, Sire? Which do you want first?"

"I want it to be impossible for horsemen to ride out of Exeter. If Guthrum decides to break out again, I want him to have to walk."

"Sire, if we start with the ditches first, and he manages to get out, we will have no prepared defensive positions and he will go through our churls like a hot sax through butter."

"Of course, you are right. Polonius, I will leave the details to you. I have no wish to have any of our men massacred because of my impatience. Build some basic fortifications at the same time as the ditches. Once the ditches are complete, we can finish strengthening the forts. Then we build some serious ramparts along the ditches. I want them so high that not even a flea can jump out of there.

Oh, and Ambrose, once the construction is complete, I want roving patrols, night and day, so the Danes can't fill in a section of ditch without being heard or observed. Sentries found asleep on duty are to be flogged."

"Alfred, what about Ethelwold and his Dorsetmen?"

"I still do not know if Ethelwold is a fool or a traitor, but I don't intend to give the man an opportunity for treachery again. Keep the men of Dorset in reserve."

"And Ethelwold himself?"

"Send him on some important mission . . . how about - to raise more Dorset laborers?"

⚑

Alfred was looking eastward, toward the coast, when he noticed the plume of smoke climbing into the leaden sky. "Ambrose! What is that over there?"

"It's the coastal signal fire, brother!' Suddenly a second fire, much closer, struggled into being. 'The signal is coming from the east. There is an enemy fleet somewhere along our coast."

The rain which had fallen hard all day, and then slowed just the hour before, picked up again. The cold wind blew from the sea, causing the men to shiver from cold and wet, though by the calendar it was still summer.

Alfred turned to his friends and advisors. "There is little sense in standing here in the rain any longer. Our presence here will not speed up the news. We will know little more until the relays of messengers manage to ride here with a report. I do not envy them. It is a foul day to be riding muddy trails."

Polonius, visibly shivering, smiled as they headed for shelter. "Let us hope, good King, that the Vikings on the water are faring as poorly!"

⚑

The first messenger arrived late the next day. Though exhausted and covered in mud, he reported directly to the king's command tent, where Alfred greeted him.

"Stand up, lad. What is the news?"

"Sire! A massive fleet of over a hundred ships has been spotted just off the coast, near the Isle of Wight. They were last reported heading west and hugging the coast."

Alfred looked at Ambrose and Polonius with a frown. "By all the saints! A hundred ship-crews would make Guthrum unbeatable!"

Ambrose responded. "Plus give him the ability to leapfrog our armies. We saw Lodbrok's sons do that, all too well, *at Nottingham*."

"I understand that the summer storms have been fierce."

"The storms have been bad, Sire, and they continue."

"Most captains would head for the safety of the shore when the storms start to blow."

"They did, Sire. We almost lost Twineham."

"Oh? What happened?"

"The Viking fleet was clearly looking for shelter, King. They sailed boldly right into the harbor."

"And you say that the villagers there were able to beat off the combined crews of a hundred ships?"

"Yes, Sire. Not exactly."

"Did they or didn't they?"

"Ealdorman Halsig followed your instructions, Sire. He had placed a strong garrison at the port, but he later sent most of the men to Wareham when you sent out the call for more warriors."

"Then how in heaven's name did he hold the port?"

"When the fleet was sighted, he ordered all the women and men in the vill and the surrounding countryside into the fort. He had them don the surplus helmets and shields left behind by the rest of the garrison when it marched to Wareham."

"And that saved the port?"

"Yes, Sire. The sight of an apparently strong garrison of troops manning the defenses sent the ships back out into the stormy waters."

"This is good news, indeed. What else do you know of the progress of the fleet?"

"Thane Halsig ordered the few garrison troops he did have to mount up and try and follow, along the coastal trails. As each coastal burh or vill was passed, the thanes rounded up all the available able-bodied men and ordered them to head for the coast.' The messenger spoke proudly. 'I was one of the men who followed, King!"

"So what happened?"

"The ships themselves seemed to be in serious trouble, for they had furled their sails and even unstepped their masts.

Only backbreaking work with the oars kept the Viking ships from being blown unto the rocky shore. We waited impatiently, with our swords drawn. Farmers with sickles and mattocks ran through the driving rain to join us.

Thane Halsig was worried what would happen if large numbers of Vikings reached shore safely. We could have done little if they all tried to land at once.

Just before absolute darkness descended, however, we watched the Vikings turning back. Thane Halsig was sure that they were trying to reach the shelter of the Isle of Wight."

"But you don't really know what happened after that?"

"No, King. I was sent to bring you news of the sighting of the fleet."

⚑

The second messenger arrived two days later. The man was exhausted, but jubilant. The well-trained sentries wasted no time, but took him through the camp directly to Alfred's command tent. In the king's absence, Ambrose and Polonius, who happened to be working in the command tent, received the report.

The prince and the spy-master listened briefly to the man's story. Ambrose smiled at Polonius, then spoke to the messenger.

"What you have brought is truly wonderful news, man! Now, I want you to follow me, but you are not to say anything until I say so. Is that clear?"

"Yes, Prince Ambrose."

Ambrose led the man directly to Alfred's private tent, and, after the sentries snapped to attention, called out to his brother.

"May a prince disturb his brother? I have a report for you."

"Enter, Brother."

Alfred looked up from his table, and seemed surprised when he saw both Polonius and Ambrose. "There appear to be two of you! And just what have I done that merits a visit from both of you together?'

As he spoke, he saw the mud-encrusted messenger follow the two advisors into the room. 'And yet another. You have brought me a visitor.'

His eyes fell on the bulky burlap bag the messenger carried. 'It appears the visitor bears gifts. Could they be for me?"

Ambrose smiled. "Yes, brother-of mine. We felt sure that you would prefer this gift to even gold or choice jewels."

"Really? What could be so valuable? Ambergris? A piece of the holy cross? I concede defeat. What is in the bag?"

Polonius turned to the messenger. "Show the king his gift; kindly presented by Thane Halsig of Twineham."

The man seemed extremely nervous. "Aye, Master Polonius. 'Ere it is, Yer Majesty!"

The man reached into the bag and drew forth several pieces of weather-beaten oak planks.

Alfred held one, and looked into the eyes of the man who had handed to him. "It is no doubt fine oak, but I do not see great value in my hands."

Polonius smiled. He loved riddles. "Then, Sire, you are not looking closely enough."

"Polonius, once again your Byzantine convolutions of thought have lost a simple Saxon king. Perhaps you could help a befuddled king understand just why these pieces of wood are so valuable to me?"

"They are Danish planks, Your Majesty."

"Polonius, I suspect that you are trying to tell me something. Saxon or Danish, they seem rather short to be of much use, and they seemed to have been in the water for some time. Are these here not barnacles?"

Ambrose smiled. "Yes, my brother, and therein lies their value."

"You two had better give me a better hint than that, before I have the two of you stripped naked and treated to the exquisite joys of the Thousand Touches of a Feather!"

Ambrose broke into a grin. "They came from the sea."

"That is often where one finds barnacles. And this fact makes these somewhat short boards valuable to me?"

Polonius now grinned. "Oh yes, Sire. They used to be part of a much larger structure."

"A glimmer of light begins to reach the deep recesses of my poor brain. Did this larger structure once float on the sea?"

Ambrose took his turn. "Yes, brother-of-mine. Exactly right! And each board is from a different structure."

"Are you two trying to tell me that this is all that is left of the Viking fleet!?"

Ambrose laughed. "Brother, I told you that they are more priceless than gold or jewels."

"The pair of you are rascals!"

The messenger watched in awe as the king of all the West Saxons chased the thin dark man and the legendary prince around the room. Finally, the three collapsed together, laughing until they cried.

At last, Alfred was able to control his hysterical laughter. He slapped Polonius on the back, almost knocking the thin dark man over, and threw a last pretend punch at his more agile brother.

"You are right, my friends. This is a gift greater than gold or jewels. I feel the urge to share it. Messenger of Thane Halsig, what is your name?"

"Thawian, Yer Majesty."

"Well, Thawian, you have done well to bring these to me. And were there any Danes who did not drown?"

"Some ships escaped east, Sire. There were hundreds of dead bodies on the beaches and in the surf. We did find perhaps two dozen still alive, Majesty. Me master, Thane Halsig, felt sure that ye would want to question 'em, so 'e had 'em securely shackled and loaded onto an ox cart. They be following behind me. Some of the men were serious hurt, and a few may not make it 'ere alive."

"No matter. This is excellent news. Polonius, write my thanks to Halsig. Phillip, when they arrive, I want each of the Danes to be put to the question, until we know where they came from, and if there is more on their way. Once you have the information we need, choose the five healthiest, and chop their right hand off. Sear the stumps with fire and then turn the five loose. I want them to be allowed to report to Guthrum. Hang the rest, alongside the dead hostages."

Ambrose looked up at his brother. This was a much colder and more confidant man than he had seen before. "And what message do you want them to carry to Guthrum, Alfred?"

"I think the captives will know what to say when they get there."

On the third morning after the five maimed Danes had staggered into the Danish-held fort of Exeter, the main gates opened with a flourish of war horns. Jarl Ura, dressed in burnished but dented chain-mail, strode boldly forth, waving a white-covered shield. He was forced to scramble in and out of two separate ditches before he could get within hailing distance of the body of advisors and noblemen who surrounded King Alfred. Alfred strode to the edge of the last ditch from where Ura stood looking up.

"Hail, king-of-the-West-Saxons! I bring you greetings from my master, King of Denmark and East Anglia."

Alfred stared down at the burly warrior. "But not Wessex, Jarl. I am still king here, and you are still trespassing."

"King, you dig deeper ditches, and more!"

"Viking, you ride over the little ones."

"We may again, King-of-the-West-Saxons."

"But, Ura. There is a 'but' again."

"Yes, King. We grow hungry, and we both know that our fleet is not coming."

"We know both those things."

"Yet my king is the greatest warrior in all Denmark. We cannot ride away. You have made sure of that. But we can come out and fight. And we will kill three or four of your warriors for every one of us who dies. Who knows, your peasants may yet run, if we meet in a real battle."

"It is a risk that I have considered, Ura. I have gathered enough men that if you were to kill ten of my men for every one of yours that falls, yet we must still win."

"My master says that he is willing to retreat and never return to your country. We will kill no more, if we are allowed to march, unmolested, north to Mercia."

"Jarl Ura, we have had this conversation before. We were still discussing it when you slunk away in the night like a fox before a wolf. Your king had given us his word, yet he broke it within two days!"

"My king promised to make no hostile move for two days. He did not. He did not attack you. He rode away."

"With my gold, and through my men. Many were killed, Ura."

"King, we did not make a hostile move until your men stood in our way! Our purpose was not to attack Saxons; just to ride free."

"We waste time in arguing, Ura. How can I believe a man with no honor?"

"Guthrum has much honor, King. He gave you the hostages, but he had not yet sworn an oath to you. He told me to say to you that if we come to an agreement, you can choose as many hostages as you want, including anyone in his camp. As well, he has promised to swear an oath on his sacred armband."

"We had ten hostages before, Ura. We had to waste a great deal of hemp rope on them."

"It was hard to see our friends hanging from trees, King."

"What is the value of giving hostages if you don't care what we do to them?"

"We care greatly, King-of-the-West-Saxons, but it was your right to hang them."

Alfred stared down at the proud Jarl who stood before him. "Go back to your king, Ura. You will have your answer tomorrow."

Alfred paced the confines of his command tent. Benches along the outer wall were lined with the chief noblemen and advisors from all the constituent shires that made up his empire. Sprinkled amongst them were some senior clergy and several scholars. Alfred was a man with many different interests.

"Ambrose, what is the meaning of this oath he proposes?"

"Brother, it is one of the most sacred oaths a Viking can make. To break it is to have no honor before your fellow warriors."

Alfred raised his voice so all could hear. "Well, members of the

Witan. Guthrum has again offered us peace. What are we to do?"

Phillip spoke up. "Sire, I am a simple man. We can have true peace when we stand over the bodies of these pagans. I have lived amongst the Vikings, and I say that Guthrum will only respect strength. Let us pay him with steel, not gold! Only thus can we teach these Danes to stay out of Wessex."

Alfred looked with fondness at the blond giant who had faithfully protected his brother all the way from Denmark to Novgorod, Kiev, and Byzantium. There were few men in the world Alfred respected more than this taciturn man. The weapons-master was a man of action, however, and he rarely looked beyond the immediate.

"Thank you, Phillip. I concur that a dead Guthrum may be the only one we can trust to keep his word. Unfortunately, if the man makes an all-out attack on us, we will take serious casualties. Ura is not bluffing. Man for man, his army is amongst the best in the world.

We have some of my Personal Guard who are their match, but many of our thanes and churls are not veterans, and they might well break. I must balance the satisfaction of Guthrum's death against the possible loss of a thousand or more of my fyrdmen. The harvest season is here, and our people want to go home."

"The men will not abandon you, King!"

"The landed thanes will stay to the bitter end, my friend. The duguos are my chosen men, and any who do not will forfeit their hard-earned property! And I know I can count on the drengs to hold at all cost. They must prove themselves if they ever want to hold land in my name. Most of the conscripted churls, however, will soon fade away. Some are from far away, and their time is up. We can't just keep replacing them indefinitely, and it is no pleasure to hang men who just want to go home.

I am sure Guthrum's terms have not changed. If we let Guthrum go, he will ask for Danegeld and a food supply."

The Archbishop of Canterbury spoke next. "Your Majesty, he has pillaged and enslaved, and desecrated Holy Mother Church. Will we reward him for this with gold and food?"

Alfred looked sad. "I understand, Archbishop, and I will think about what you have said. Ambrose, what do you say?"

"Brother, I did not believe him for a moment the last time. I thought he might go north . . . if we kept the army just behind him. This time? He didn't offer a binding Viking oath before. It is a powerful oath to a Dane. Having lived among them for some years, I respect them greatly, and, in their own way, they have a very strong sense of honor.

The death of all invaders is the clearest message we can give the Danes. Yet I do not want to be responsible for the making of hundreds of widows. I would be tempted to sign a treaty, take the most important hostages we can, and dog him all the way to the border with the army, as long as we can cripple them a little first."

Alfred turned to Polonius. "Well, my Byzantine scholar, what do you say?"

"I am reminded of the saying of a student of the great Sun Tzu, who lived almost a thousand years ago, in far off China."

"And what did the student of the master say, Polonius?"

"The student, Cao Cao, said, 'When a people are desperate, they will fight to the death.'

Make no mistake, Sire. The Danes will attack before they starve to death. We are making them desperate.

Unlike the Saxons and the Danes, Sire, my people do not glorify war, though we are very good at it. Byzantium regularly faces invasion armies of fanatics that are more numerous than all the warriors of your entire island. We do not see war as glory. Rather, we see it as a necessary part of diplomacy, after the words and bribery have failed.

If we could kill Guthrum and his Danes at little cost to the people of Wessex, then I would recommend that without hesitation. A dead enemy cannot betray a promise, and the message to others is unmistakable. We are really, then, talking of the cost to destroy Guthrum . . . and the risk. You can have an easy victory for the price of a bag of gold and some cattle, or an expensive one where there is a chance your army will be crippled or even defeated."

King Alfred looked around the room, and listened one by one to his advisors and noblemen. In the end he sent them all to bed. "Good night, members of my Council, I think I will sleep on this. Please report here just after dawn. And gentlemen, I want fully half of our force to be on duty tonight. Commanders, see to it."

CHAPTER 5

A Truce is Signed

Jarl Ura stood again in the deep ditch, looking up at the Saxon king. "My master awaits your word, King-of-the-West-Saxons,"

Alfred stood tall in his magnificent shining armor. The warm sun reflected off the metal, and fleecy clouds scudded across the blue sky which color so closely matched his eyes.

"Then hear me, Jarl Ura. Under our laws, you all deserve death for what you have done to this peaceful land. Yet my heavenly Lord teaches me that we must try and forgive.

Ura the Dane, hear my words. Within two days you and all your people will ride directly to Mercia. Tomorrow, your king must come here and swear by his sacred armbands and all else that is holy to him, never to step foot in this land again.

I expect that he will bring with him twenty of his most senior officers and jarls. They will live with me as honored guests for one year, after which they will be free to return home. And I will not give Guthrum one more ounce of gold for Danegeld. Yet in honor of our agreement, I will present your king with some suitable gifts. In return, I expect Guthrum to present to me every Saxon and Jute, Celt and Angle, in your camp.

My Christian brethren will not go north to servitude while I draw breath. And I want those horses. We will never have a deal unless you turn over to us at least one quarter of your horses."

"King, it may surprise you to know that some of our finest warriors are Saxons and Angles from north of your borders. I can tell you now that Guthrum will not turn these men over to you."

"If they ride voluntarily with your host, then they are lost in the eyes of Almighty God, and I will consider them to be Danish. But I am firm on this. The others must be freed. Further, the men of Guthrum will not pillage on the way north. In turn, my reeves will supply you with cattle and pigs, so that no one starves. My army will march north behind you, and if there is any betrayal of our truce, then we will kill you to a man. Is all that understood?"

"I understand, and will take this to my royal master. I will have an answer for you by midday."

ᚱ

It took the Danes several hours to fill in the deep ditches that had so effectively kept them from riding out. Long columns of Vikings, as well as the Anglish captives, carried armloads of dirt and stones and threw them into the trenches. Alfred's force pulled back, and started further construction of its own.

At last the Danes completed their work. A wide portion of the ditches were filled in, and the ramparts painstakingly removed. In turn, Alfred's men had constructed, on their side, parallel ramparts steep enough to be impassable to horses, and then studded them with sharpened stakes. The twin ramparts stretched for hundreds of Roman feet. Any mounted column who wished to leave Exeter would be forced to ride the length of the ramparts. Lines of archers and spearmen stationed on the ramparts above would be able to easily launch a devastating hail of missiles on any force riding below.

Alfred waited. His main force of unmounted retainers, churls and peasants manned the new ramparts, while his mounted fyrdmen formed up and prepared for any surprises. As promised the day before, the main gates were thrown open and hundreds of horses galloped forth. They were funneled down the road and between the newly constructed ramparts. Skilled horse-herders waited for them in the open area beyond.

The gates opened a second time, and a mob of running figures erupted through them. Alfred's men watched carefully from the ramparts, bows or spears in hand. All of the running people were captives, which, as promised, Guthrum had released. They too, were forced to run the gauntlet, and eagle-eyed commanders checked the runners as they ran past to insure they were not Danes in disguise.

Polonius had warned Alfred that this would be a very dangerous time. Alfred thus had several dozen thanes ready to quickly herd the former captives directly into one of the lesser fortifications. There they were free to hug their countrymen and cry. Behind this screen of milling people, Alfred moved his best thanes into a shield-wall formation, backed by more lines of spearmen and archers.

Once the horses and captives were taken care of, Alfred signaled the men standing by with war horns. At the series of short staccato blasts, the Angles and Saxons formed up into marching formation and started a withdrawal, as Alfred had previously agreed.

Alfred had ordered his force to retreat to a low knoll nearby. His men rode and marched into cunningly designed defensive positions Polonius had laid out and had constructed earlier.

Guthrum waited until the Saxon force was well clear, and then led his long column forth. Once free of the restrictions of the Saxon earthworks, they rode in a thick column, obviously ready for battle.

Alfred, watching them ride out, wondered what would have happened if his men had jumped down from the ramparts to greet the running former captives. Loose, the full force of thirteen hundred Danes, with almost a thousand, mounted, fanatical and ready for battle, could have been an unmitigated disaster. He had ordered that the twenty Danish hostages be taken far to the rear, and temporarily shackled, but he was sure that Guthrum would have again sacrificed any number of hostages if it had meant the final defeat of the Wessex thorn.

The Danes headed north peacefully enough. Ambrose was pleased to see that many Vikings were forced to walk, and the horses they still had were weak from hunger. The famine had been severe enough that they had resorted to eating some of their mounts.

Alfred was relieved. It meant that Guthrum's Danes were not the mobile force they had been, just short weeks before. That, in turn, meant that his infantry could keep up. He had feared that Guthrum would have been able to outdistance the Wessex host. His mounted force, thanks to the arrival of more shire fyrds, was almost double that of Guthrum, but fully half of his force was churl infantry. Guthrum's army, however, even freed of the captives, was no longer in shape for another sudden escape.

Battle-hardened fyrdmen from Kent, from Cornwall, from Essex and Surrey, and from Wessex itself, rode proudly past their king and his assembled ealdormen. These men were the mainstay of the Wessex army. In return for the land granted them by their king or ealdorman, they provided military service when called upon. Each provided their own horse and equipment.

These heavily armored men were, in turn, supported by large numbers of churls. Some of these also rode horses, but many marched. Those of them brave enough, or lucky enough, to please their master, could hope to be provided enough land so that they would become thanes themselves.

Lastly, the large, shapeless mass of locally conscripted peasants and retainers marched by on foot. Few were in armor. All carried spears. Only some carried axes or swords, but their numbers provided necessary labor and support, and many had fought bravely.

To the north, Guthrum fled ignominiously north across the Thames River into Mercia. His army had been undefeated by the Wessex fyrds, but he had twice backed down from open battle.

Alfred turned his head toward his bastard brother. "Watch the Cornish contingent go by, brother-of-mine!"

"What do you want me to look for?"

"Oh, just describe the quality and quantity of what you see."

Just then, Alfred acknowledged the salute of the warriors from his most western province.

"Well, Alfred, I see a lot of men who, if they are fyrdmen, must have lost their horses somewhere."

"And I specifically commanded that only sworn fyrdmen be sent."

"I do see a small force of mounted fyrdmen, brother."

"Aye. I had Polonius check. Each of them are rivals or enemies of Ealdorman Anwell. That good man called up and sent only men who he hoped would die in battle. Their commander-in-chief is a thane called Aardwolf the Simple."

"Brother, I think that you are trying to tell me something."

"Aye. I guess I am. We have driven the foe from our land without as much as a battle. Yet as long as I have allies like Ealdorman Anwell, and nephew Ethelwold, I wonder how safe our empire really is."

"Brother, Anwell did not defy you. He sent the forces you told him to."

"Just barely, Ambrose. Just barely. What would happen if we really needed his support?"

Ambrose readjusted his harness and then replied. "Cornwall has long been our most rebellious province. I well remember Phillip telling us that, in *King Egbert's* time, the Cornishmen allied themselves with the Vikings in a major effort to break free of us. I hardly think, however, that there is a danger of them rising now. You have just driven a Danish army from our midst, and you have just had one of the most powerful armies under arms that you have ever had."

Alfred shifted his weight and tried to relax. "No, I don't think Anwell would dare anything now. His attitude tells me that he bears some watching, however."

"And Ethelwold?"

An expression of anger crossed Alfred's handsome face. "Ethelwold is either a fool or a traitor. He is of our blood, but I do not trust the man. The only way the Danes could have broken through his lines at Wareham was if Ethelwold intentionally withdrew the sentries assigned to guard that stretch of the ditch! We watched the Danes fill in the ditch at Exeter. How long did it take them?"

Ambrose pondered for a moment. "By using over two thousand soldiers and captives, they did it in about an hour."

Alfred pounced. "And the Danes did the same thing at Wareham, in the dark, and Ethelwold's men heard nothing? It is hard to believe, brother."

"Polonius checked with both Bishop Asser and several of Ethelwold's officers, as you asked him to do. What Ethelwold told us about his visit was true."

"Ambrose, Bishop Asser, a man we both love and respect, provides the perfect alibi. So Delwyn did call off the sentries. Maybe he even had a narrow strip filled in. Guthrum's men rode over a wide causeway! And who told Delwyn to do either?"

Ambrose replied. "He died conveniently quickly, brother."

Alfred looked grim. "Ethelwold bears some close watching, brother."

BOOK TWO: KING GUTHRUM RETURNS

CHAPTER 6

"AD 878: This year about mid-winter, after twelfth-night, the Danish army stole out to Chippenham, and rode over the land of the West-Saxons; where they settled, and drove many of the people over sea; and of the rest the greatest part they rode down, and subdued to their will; all but Alfred the King."

Alfred turned from his wife to stare at the gasping messenger. "You say there is a full army of riders galloping at this moment toward Chippenham! God's oath, man! Were you able to identify who the enemy is?"

"Aye, Yer Majesty. Guthrum's banners flew at the head of the column. Me brother recognized it. 'E served with you at Exeter last summer."

Ealhswith, Alfred's wife, gasped and threw her arms around her husband. "My husband, what does it mean?"

Their children were young, but they sensed the fear in their mother's voice. Edward, the eldest boy, broke into tears as he squeezed his mother's leg tight. His younger sister wailed and had to be picked up.

"God in Heaven! Am I never to be done with this man!?' Alfred sighed. 'It means that we are in serious trouble! We have a great deal of planning to do, and no time to do it in. My love, go to our bower. Pack yours and my clothes, and throw in some warm clothes for the children. Hurry now!"

"Where am I to go?"

"Head for the main jetty, and take the first boat across that you can. Once you get to the other side, wait for Polonius. He will put together a small escort and take the Court's women and children directly to Winchester. Push the horses until they drop, if need be!"

Ealhswith was a stubborn woman, married to a warrior king, but she knew that this was not the time to argue. She just looked at her husband for a moment. She then hugged him tightly, and shepherded the youngsters away to their private quarters.

Gretchen came and stood by her husband. Ambrose gently put his hand on her slightly enlarged belly. They embraced, and Ambrose whispered in her ear for her to prepare to follow the queen. "Ealhswith and her children will have a hard time of it in the dark and the cold. There will be too few men to escort you, at least until you get well away and can stop at one of the royal estates to gather some warriors. Please, my love, take Kuralla, Matilda and the rest of Phillip's brood, and help them get away . . . and make sure you take good care of yourself and our new baby!"

Gretchen, too, was the intelligent wife of a warrior. She did not bother to argue, but instead headed over to collect Kuralla and Matilda. The three women rapidly followed in Ealhswith's wake. Today men would die to buy time for the womens' and childrens' escape. Gretchen had no intention of wasting that preciously bought time.

Thane Pyt snapped to attention in front of his king. "Sire, what do you want me to do with the hostages?"

"Have them all escorted here immediately, under heavy guard. Send for the blacksmith and put them in chains. Then take them to the ramparts. If it is confirmed that Guthrum is the enemy, then I want you to hang them from the guard tower. I want Guthrum to know that Alfred keeps his word!"

The twenty captives stared at the king of Wessex. Only a few months previously their lives had been given as a pledge by King Guthrum, commander-in-chief of the Danish host who had shattered East Anglia and then set up a base in Mercia. Guthrum had promised to withdraw from Exeter, and all Wessex, after Alfred had doggedly followed him with his Saxon fyrdmen, and laid siege to the Viking base at Exeter.

Guthrum had retreated northwards, as he had promised. But it now appeared that soon after Alfred sent his army home for the winter, Guthrum dared to ride deep again into Wessex. His mounted army was even now reported to be sweeping down on the royal burh of Chippenham. Except for the chance sighting by several Saxon hunters, Guthrum might have totally surprised Alfred and his court, and soon have been comfortably ensconced in the Great Hall of Chippenham, with Alfred and his family in chains before him.

The hunters, alarmed by the size of the force they saw riding southwards, took off-road short cuts, drove their horses mercilessly, and managed to reach the king's winter burh before the northern invaders. At their shouted warnings as they galloped in, horses had been hitched to the massive beams that spanned the dry ditch, and the beams themselves were pulled into the settlement. They would serve to strengthen the main gate. The gate itself was quickly closed and barred, and the alarm horn blared. The thanes of Alfred's Personal Guard, well-trained, were no strangers to violence.

With the Avon river on three sides, and the fourth side protected by both a ditch and a palisade, the royal estate of Chippenham was eminently defensible, but only if Alfred had adequate troops. His army, one Guthrum had retreated from twice before, had been disbanded for the winter season! The only force Alfred had was the members of his court and the remnants of his Personal Guard. That added up to perhaps two hundred young thanes, drengs, who were still landless and thus stayed with their king for the winter. There were a few old veterans who had chosen to spend the Christmas season with Alfred, but pitifully few.

The problem of the hostages taken care of, Alfred became a whirlwind. He sent men running in all directions.

"Thane Byram! Collect all the boats tied up along the shore and have them moved to the main jetty, as far away out of sight of the Vikings as possible. The less the Vikings see the better. Man the ferries and get as many of the horses across as possible. Without them, there will be no escape for anyone.

Calldwr! Take some men and two of the boats. Send one upriver and one down. Destroy any other boats you can't bring here, especially on this side of the river.

Polonius! Our women are packing. Gather as many women and children as you can, and get them across the Avon as soon as possible! You are to escort the court's women and children directly to Winchester. Take only a small detail with you. We will need the rest of the men here, and you can pick up escort warriors at the next royal estate. Use some of the young lads as messengers. Send messages to all the nearer communities on the other side. I want all the horses they can spare, and I want them now.

Ambrose! Get the treasury out of here and unto that ferry. The devils will be here soon enough. I don't want that heathen Guthrum getting his greedy hands on any more of our gold and silver.

Well! What are the rest of you waiting for?! If you have nothing to do, get your weapons and man the palisade. It is the only thing between the enemy and your loved ones! And spread the word. Any slave who fights today at my side will be a free man by sunrise tomorrow. Issue weapons to any who want them."

Answering the strident summons of the horns, Alfred's Personal Guard raced to the ramparts. There, reinforced by the inhabitants of the little town, who had no illusions about would happen if the Vikings broke through the defenses, the Saxons prepared to battle the invaders.

Guthrum's banners flapped in the breeze as the hard-riding force neared. Soon the Danish king's emblem could be clearly seen. The twenty hostages, lined up on the ramparts, recognized the symbols on the flapping pennants, and knew they must pay the price of their king's treachery. They shuffled along stoically, their newly acquired chains clanking forlornly.

The large column of Viking horsemen quickly transformed into long lines of Viking infantry. Without pausing, they charged the ditch and fortified walls that was all that kept them from the Saxon king and victory.

Thane Pyt and his squad marched the luckless Viking hostages along the ramparts until they reached the guard tower by the main gate. They tied a rope around each hostage's neck, and one by one, they pushed the men over the edge, leaving them to flap obscenely and slowly strangle in front of their attacking brethren.

Any movement on the guard tower was met with torrents of arrows from the massed Vikings. Howls of outrage went up each time the Vikings realized that they had shot one more of their own. Soon all twenty hostages hung limply from the battlements of the main guard tower.

The Saxons manning the ramparts fought bravely. They emptied their quivers at the flood of Danes clambering down into the ditch and then struggling up to the base of the palisade. Spears greeted any Vikings foolish enough to make it to the top of the palisade, but while the ditch filled with dead and dying, yet the Danes just kept coming. Two replaced every one who fell, and the big Northmen systematically chopped or pulled at individual logs until the palisade became porous. The irresistible tide of Danes flowed over and then through, and the Saxon shield-wall began the fighting retreat that could only end in death or the river.

Behind the slowly retreating wall of men, however, the town emptied of women and children. Boatload by boatload, the refugees were hurriedly ferried across the river.

At last the Saxons only held the small area that blocked entry to the burh's main jetty. As their defensive lines shrank in length, they thickened, but the bought time was expensive. Hundreds of Saxons, many ill-armed retainers or townspeople, had already fallen to the horde of Viking attackers.

Phillip, Ambrose and Alfred were retreating slowly, easily fending off the Vikings foolish enough to try and challenge them personally. Ambrose finally turned to Alfred.

"Brother, it is time for you to take a boat. Polonius is holding it ready for you!"

"I cannot leave my people here to die like dogs. I am their king!"

"That is the reason why you must, Alfred! Only you can lead us to victory over these treacherous bastards. You must live to raise the army that will expunge this evil from our lands! Get out of here now! Good as you are as a swordsman, we need you more as a king!' He smiled grimly. 'And, most important, I told Polonius not to leave for Winchester until he saw you safe on the other side of the river."

"Ambrose, you are a devil! I'm just glad that you are on my side."

"Get out of here, brother!"

Alfred sighed. "May God be with us all this day! I will go, but I want you to follow. Is that understood?"

"Yes, Alfred! I will keep evacuating men as long as you send boats back and we are not overrun. But I will come."

At last there were only a few dozen Saxons left alive and unevacuated. The jetty was narrow, and thus the Vikings could not use their overwhelming numbers effectively. Their sheer weight, however, pushed the Saxons inexorably to the end of the pier. Ambrose had held the men who could swim to the last. The boats would not return again, but they would hover just out of reach of the Viking archers on the shore.

Ambrose did not even look at his giant companion at his side. "Phillip, my friend! I fear it is almost time for our bath! Are you ready?"

Even as he spoke, three heavily armored Vikings pressed forward. One swung a huge battle axe that was even heavier than the weapons-master's own mighty blade. The man was adorned with much gold, and was clearly a wealthy jarl. The giant Viking grinned. As his two companions protected him on either side, he started a mighty overhead swing that would be capable of penetrating the strongest armor, and a shield as well, if it was thrust in the way. He did not know Phillip, however.

The weapons-master's huge claymore, as long as Ambrose was tall, swung up in a counterstrike that cut deep into the axe handle. Both men's arms were numbed by the jarring collision. The brief pause allowed Ambrose to thrust his blade straight out. Suddenly the Viking on the left found a hole in his chest cut right through his chain-mail.

The construction of Ambrose's blade had been a mystery even to the experts in Byzantium, but the expert craftsmen Ambrose and Polonius had spoken to had guessed that it had probably been made in the Far East or by some unknown Arab metalworker. Its exact alloy composition could not be deduced, but it could be sharpened to an edge that allowed Ambrose to shave with it.

The Viking stared at Ambrose in silent wonder, and then toppled. Phillip's great blade was pulled back for another swing, but the wall of Vikings pressed forward again. There was no space for the claymore to be used effectively. A quick look behind him made Ambrose realize that they had little more room to back up.

"Are you ready for that bath, old friend?"

"On your command, Prince."

The weapons-master was a taciturn man, but he had helped raise Ambrose, and both his loyalty and his strength were prodigious. Ambrose knew that he would not go until he saw his charge hit the water.

The prince sighed and clipped a line to the handle of **Victory-Maker**. He had no intention of losing his precious sword if he could help it. It had been given to him by a gruff Dane when he had been the man's slave, and he had used it to protect himself from Sweden to Byzantium, and back again.

Realizing that one more push would force them all to topple backwards into the water, where none of them would have the chance to leap out of range of the battle-roused Danes, he knew they were out of time. The few remaining thanes were waiting for his signal. He pulled off his helmet and threw it at the head of the nearest Dane.

"Then let's go! Saxons, now!"

The remaining wall of battered warriors emulated their prince and hurled their weapons and armor at the nearest Vikings. Having cast off as much armor as they could, they turned and leapt into the chill river waters.

Alfred's Saxons had been lucky. Although a little ice had formed along the river's edges, the river itself was clear. Any Vikings who wished to cross would have to swim. Alfred's foresight had removed any boats for some distance both up and down-river. That was the only hope for the refugees on the far bank.

The warriors who leapt in the water, however, were not yet completely out of reach of the furious Danes. The Vikings were angry that their hostages had been slaughtered in front of their eyes, and their blood-lust was up from the savage fighting. An avalanche of arrow and spears followed the Saxons into the water, the numbers limited only by the number of Vikings who could crowd onto the end of the jetty.

Phillip and Ambrose swam deep for the waiting boats. They had not had time to shed all of their armor, and thus felt very weighted down. It was a close contest between the heavy weight, the various projectiles and the intense cold, as to which would kill them first. In the end, less than half of the men who had stood on the jetty managed to make it to the waiting boats.

CHAPTER 7

Ealhswith & Polonius Ride to Winchester

Queen Ealhswith, with Polonius at her side, and followed by the rest of the royal party, rode hard through the savage winter cold.

In spite of the poor trail, the queen moved her horse alongside Polonius. "May God protect all the men we have left behind, Polonius. I am afraid for them."

"Me too, your Highness."

"What do you think is happening back there?"

"I have no idea, my Queen, but the numbers are obvious and the conclusion foregone. It is not a question of if Guthrum takes Chippenham, but when."

Thus Polonius urged them on, in spite of the cold and the dark. The trace of snow that had recently fallen at least brightened the land, so that the road was easily visible, and the party could make good time.

The queen continued. "But what happens when Chippenham falls?"

"If Guthrum has any brains, and he isn't known for his stupidity, he is trying to pour his mounted warriors across the Avon just as fast as he can. Only your husband's quick thinking, seizing and destroying the boats, prevents Guthrum from immediately transporting his entire army across the river."

"But if Guthrum has no boats, perhaps Alfred can hold the river bank?"

"I know that he intends to try. He still has the remnants of his Personal Guard, plus whatever local people can be called up to fight."

"Thank the Good Lord!"

"The men will buy Wessex time, Majesty, but they will not be able to hold Guthrum for long."

"But if the Vikings cannot cross the river?"

"Guthrum will ride along the shores until he finds some boats, or he will build rafts, or he will find one of the fords. He has been delayed; not stopped.

And once he has crossed, it will be a thousand veteran Danes against, at most, a couple of hundred fyrdmen. Eventually, Alfred will have to tell his men to flee for their own lives."

"Surely Alfred can raise more than a few hundred men, Polonius?"

"It took a full month last summer to raise a force of thanes equal to Guthrum, Lady, and another month to double his numbers. Only the veteran duguos can stand shield to shield and match the Vikings. The other men can fight from behind walls, but they are no match in the open. To put them up in open battle against the Danes is to slaughter them. The Danes would carve through them as if they were butter.

Highness, the time necessary for the evacuation and escape of this royal court is being bought with gallons of Saxon blood. It is essential that we not waste the precious gift."

Polonius led the women, children and assorted servants toward the next royal estate along the time-honored royal circuit to the east. Normally these journeys were made in state, with the huge oxen-driven Saxon wagons ponderously moving from one estate to the next. The royal family would be comfortably ensconced inside, swaddled in precious furs, and surrounded by a large escort of the King's Personal Guard, as well as hundreds of royal servants and court hangers-on.

Tonight, most of that Guard were fighting, and dying, on the shores of the Avon River. Only an even dozen of them rode as escort to the Queen and the royal athelings.

They escorted over a hundred women and children, along with a handful of aged male advisors who were too old or sick for combat. Some of the children were so young that their mothers had strapped them to their own bodies. Others, a little older, were swaddled in fur or wool and loaded into wicker baskets on the packhorses.

The procession rode to the accompaniment of wails of the aggrieved youngsters, and the tears of some of the women. Queen Ealhswith and Polonius urged them on relentlessly, however. The present was being risked on the banks of the frigid river, but the future of Saxon Wessex was with Polonius, in the persons of the royal prince and his close cousins.

At last, numb from cold, the members of the refugee column saw the lone light that heralded their arrival at the royal estate that had been their target. Polonius spoke to Queen Ealhswith.

"My Queen, what are your wishes?"

"Polonius, let us stop just long enough to thoroughly warm up and switch horses. I would feel better if we put still more Roman miles between us and those savages. We can stop to sleep at the next royal estate. It is not more than a few hours ride further."

"Yes, my Lady."

Even as they spoke, an alert sentry called out to them from the guard tower.

"Who goes there?"

Polonius responded for the little column. "Open the gates for your queen! Rouse the servants and the guards!"

A sleepy steward, dressed only in his night clothes and visibly shivering, met the queen and her party as they rode through the gate.

"Yer Majesty, is it, in truth, yourself!"

"Of course it is, Claeg!"

"I uhh, don't understand. What kin I do for ye, Yer Majesty?"

"Many things, old friend. I have over a hundred women and children with me who need to be fed and warmed. After that, we need to exchange as many horses as possible. I wish to be on the road again within an hour. As well, I want you to send out messengers to call in as many of your local fyrdmen as possible. Can you remember all that?"

"Of course, Yer Majesty, but what is wrong? It is winter, and the men are not normally called out at such a time."

"I know that. Just do it! Not far behind me, your king and several hundred servants and the Personal Guard are fighting for their lives so that we can escape."

"Fighting against who, me lady? Wessex is at peace!"

"Not any more. Guthrum and his heathen devils are loose again in the land."

The steward blanched. He mumbled to himself. "Deliver us, oh Lord, from the fury of the Northmen!' He then responded to his queen. Her seemingly irrational demands suddenly made a lot more sense.

'I will send for the men immediately, Yer Majesty!"

The man was suddenly very awake. He burst into motion, clapping his hands. "Set roaring fires in the Great Hall! Bring blankets and furs for these people! Help them dismount, they must be frozen. Rouse the cooks! I want hot food prepared immediately!

Godwin, send runners to each of the nearest tuns and burhs. I want to see their lawful quota of men standing here, equipped and in fighting order, before the sun rises! If any fyrdmen quibble, tell them it is a direct order from their queen!

Grooms. Send me all the grooms! I want these horses rubbed down and stabled, and I want our entire horse herd saddled and ready to leave within an hour. Move now! Get to it!

My lady, if you would follow me, it would be my pleasure to escort you to your Great Hall."

Polonius continued to stare in the direction of the stables. It was very dark, but the people running around with flaring torches cast occasional illumination in the stables' direction. "A moment, Steward. Is that a royal wagon I see by the stables?"

"Aye, Lord. It were left when the royal party last traveled through here. The axle had broken a few miles out."

"Yes, I remember now. And is it repaired?"

"Of course, Lord Polonius."

"Excellent. Could you harness a half-dozen draft horses to it?"

"The harness was designed for oxen, but it should be a simple enough matter to readjust the harness, Lord."

Polonius smiled. "My queen, would you and the little ones like to again travel in comfort?"

"For myself, no. I will ride with the warriors. We Saxon women are not soft, Lord Polonius."

"So I have discovered, my lady. Would the wagon be satisfactory for the children and the infirm?"

"It would be eminently satisfactory, but do we dare? You yourself said that our best defense against the pagans is miles."

"It still is, my lady. But with the oxen swapped for horses, the wagon should not unduly slow us down. We intend to follow the road eastward from here, so it will move easily enough. And some of the children and old ones will suffer serious frostbite if they are forced to ride much further in the open."

"Polonius, what of the Danes?"

"It is better that some of us lose our fingers and toes than the Vikings catch them and kill us. There will be no mercy for the royal party. Guthrum wants our land, and the best means to that goal is to kill off as much of the royal family as possible."

"I agree, my queen. But we are now some miles from Chippenham, and Guthrum will have to pause after the fighting to establish a secure base. He cannot be certain that Alfred or some ealdorman will not raise enough of a force to at least threaten him in the open.

Since he did not manage to catch your husband, he will have to take some time to rebuild the fortifications of Chippenham.' Polonius shrugged. 'After that, then I suspect he will send out massive raiding parties in all directions, sniffing for the scent of the king.

It would be well that we are far away by then. But we would only be a secondary objective. His best hope of success is to kill or capture your husband. Next would probably be to terrorize the various shires so that they will not send their fighting men to Alfred come spring.

My queen, the capture of you and the royal children would be a very important long-term goal, but Guthrum should have more urgent tasks to deal with first. He will not know what direction you rode in, or, for that matter, where the king is. And each fortified burh we reach is another obstacle in his path, especially if they are forewarned and prepared to resist."

Claeg turned eagerly to his queen. "Aye, Yer Majesty! I will 'ave over a hundred more armed men come the morning, and I will send any mounted thanes to support King Alfred! I will have the churls bring in their families and livestock, and we will prepare for siege. If the heathen Vikings come this way, they will not get past us without a fight, me Lady!"

"I thank you, Claeg. I know I can count on you to hold them as long as possible."

Polonius spoke to the frightened but determined steward. "Try and get at least several hundred armed men within your walls. Once you reach a critical mass, the Danes will avoid you. They will look for easy nuts to crack, not ones that will bleed them dry. The stronger your defenses, the less likely it is that you will be attacked."

The queen then spoke. "Polonius, I know that you have tried to talk Alfred into establishing strong bases throughout the land."

"I did not need to convince him, my lady. He has told me repeatedly that no Saxon should be more than twenty Roman miles from a secure fortification. Only by providing such shelter to the women and children, will you get the men to march away to fight in another shire. They must feel that their own are protected and safe, or they will find excuses not to answer the call-to-arms."

Claeg stood by the open door of the Great Hall. "My Queen, please, enter, and warm yerself. I will go see personal-like to the 'orses and the wagon."

It was over two hours before the party had eaten, warmed themselves, and gotten themselves organized. Three of the refugees were so ill that it was decided the hazards of the trail in winter were greater than that of the Danes. Even the relative comfort of the wagon would be too much for them. Queen Ealhswith ordered them to stay. The rest, sore and exhausted as they were, mounted again, and started the arduous trek to the next royal burh.

The queen spoke quietly to Polonius. "Raven's Nest is not so far. I am convinced that we can reach it shortly after dawn. There we will stop and rest for twenty-four hours."

The Byzantine replied. "With your permission, Highness, I will put most of the escort at the rear."

"Are you afraid that the devil's hounds can catch up so fast?"

"No Highness. I am more concerned that there be a strong rearguard in order to help exhausted riders who might get disoriented or fall from their mounts."

"Agreed, Polonius. At least the younger children and the sick are safe in the wagon. But where will you be?"

"I will ride in the vanguard, along with two thanes who know the area."

"What about Gretchen and Kuralla?"

Polonius smiled. "They are as stubborn as you, Majesty. They will ride."

"Gretchen is pregnant. Surely she should be in the wagon."

"I agree, my Queen. She will still ride."

Ealhswith sighed. "So be it. Polonius, Alfred told you to take the armed men you need from the royal estates."

"My Queen, I intend to do just that, but I hope that you will agree that to strip the first royal estate on the road of its fighting men would be both cruel and short-sighted. Within days at most, the burh will, almost certainly, be forced to face a Viking onslaught. They will need every able-bodied man they have, and can find, in order to have any chance to survive."

ど

In the bitter pre-dawn cold, Queen Ealhswith pulled her roan mare up next to Polonius. Only the snow and the starlight had made it possible for Polonius and his two scouts to pick their way through the night.

The queen spoke. "Polonius, in spite of your cape and heavy coat, you seem to be shivering! Why on earth do you stay in this land, if you suffer so?"

"Well, my Lady, I *met your brother-in-law* many years ago when he was but a young tad. Frankly, when I first met him, he was spoiled and naive. The whips and chains of our masters soon taught him the true meaning of servility, however."

The queen smiled in the darkness. "Only him, Polonius?"

"I had already learned the lessons, my Queen. Several masters, in countries stretching from Byzantium to Frankland, had taught me the lesson well.

You know much of the story. We were lucky. We rescued Philip from death and escaped the Danes.

We fled by sea, and managed to make our way to Gunner of the Rus, master of a great trading house on the Viking Sea. With the Danes on our tail, he sent us to work as traders on the Asian rivers that flowed all the way to Imperial Byzantium."

"But that allowed you to return home again, to a climate that smiles on you in winter."

"It can be cold in Constantinople, too, in winter, when the winds come off the open steppes. The East is not a happy place for a man without money and influence, however. I had already been enslaved there once."

"But you and Ambrose became envoys of the rulers of Kiev! You were accredited ambassadors to the Imperial Court at Constantinople. And you know that Alfred feels he owes you much. He would give you enough gold to make you rich anywhere in the world."

"I am grateful that I have been able to serve your husband, the king, my Lady. But I will tell you the truth, my Queen, if you promise never to tell Ambrose."

"You have the solemn word of a queen, Polonius."

"If the truth be known, I find it hard to give up the role of tutor and confidant to Ambrose. He has saved my life more times than I can count, and he and Phillip have become closer to me than my own family.' He shrugged. 'I guess I continue to follow friendship . . . in spite of your abominable Anglish climate!"

A clattering of hooves on the hard-frozen ground warned them that a second rider had left the caravan and was catching up quickly. Polonius and the Queen reined in their horses.

Polonius searched for details of the face of the shapeless rider, trying to identify the person in the dark. To Polonius' surprise, he was eventually able to make out the caped and bundled figure of Kuralla, his beloved wife!

Polonius spoke. "Kuralla, is there trouble with the women?"

"No, my husband. Oh, Your Majesty! I didn't realize that it was you! Forgive me for interrupting."

"Don't be silly, Kuralla. I had some questions for Polonius, and I have asked them. Come, ride with your husband! I will go look and make sure that our faithful guardsmen in the rearguard are not falling off their horses from sheer fatigue."

As the queen rode off, Polonius spoke quietly to his wife. "My love, is there really a problem?"

"I just felt the need for a romantic night ride with my beloved husband. It seemed unfair that you were having all the fun."

"It is colder than the Greek Hades, my Sweet. Are you sure you would rather not ride in the great wagon of the queen?"

"I will do no less than the queen herself. I am the daughter of a

Slavic chieftain of the Volkhov River valley, sir! Unlike you soft southern Greeks, we have real winters. For a northern Slav, this is a mild spring evening."

Polonius laughed. "If that is true, my love, why are you wearing two coats?"

"All right, you Greek lout! It is cold even for a hardy Slav. Even yet, I intend to ride with my man. Don't get between me and my loved one, sir! Turn your mount and ride. Even as we stand here jawing, people are freezing."

"You are right, my tigress. You honor me by riding at my side."

"Then let's get going!"

The riders ploughed through the darkness, struggling to stay on the road. Fortunately, it was surrounded on both sides by trees and shrubs, and the snow thus showed a ribbon of white that hopefully stretched directly to the next royal burh.

At last, after hours of hard riding, a regular band of darkness that was too regular to be natural blocked the ribbon of white. Ambrose spoke to Kuralla.

"I sure hope that we are looking at the palisades of Raven's Nest. I don't think the women and children can go much further in this cold."

"Nor the Greek wizard."

Polonius smiled. "Nor him."

As they closed on it, the wall became more discernible. Pale dawn was approaching, and the sky was perceptively lightening.

Polonius spurred his exhausted animal forward, and he was followed by his three companions. Not far behind them were over a hundred innocent women and children. Without shelter sometime soon, some of those people were going to die. Salvation was close.

Polonius rode to the main gate and repeated the call he had used earlier that night. "Open the gates, in the name of your queen!"

For several minutes, nothing happened. Polonius yelled a second time. Suddenly the gate swung open just enough to allow a single man to squeeze through. More faces bobbed up on the palisade walkway above, and the torches they carried cast a flickering light on the heavily bundled riders.

"Who are you to be waking the dead with such noise?"

It was still dark enough that Polonius could barely make out the man's features. The torches only silhouetted him, as the torches were behind and above him.

"How dare you bar the gate to an emissary of the queen of Wessex!? This is a royal burh, and I am on royal business. Order the gates open immediately! Many lives may depend on it!"

"The gate remains shut. The burh is full. There is no room for the likes of you, sir! Go find yourself some other place in which to sleep."

Suddenly a voice called out from the upper walkway. "Master Polonius, is that you?"

"Is that you, Bayhard? Of course it's me. Open the gate at once! The queen approaches, and she is in desperate need of warmth and shelter. She has ridden through the night."

"I am sorry sir, but the gentleman you are talking to arrived before sunset, and forced his way in at sword point! He has almost a hundred armed retainers with him! My men have been disarmed."

Polonius turned back to the stout man standing in the shelter of the gate. "And who are you, sir, that you speak Anglish and yet you dare seize your sovereign's own property?"

The man spoke defiantly, but he stood close enough to the gate that he could quickly scuttle through if any of the riders tried to approach too closely. "You see before you Aiken, Thane of Hunter's Downs. I and my escort arrived cold and hungry, and we needed shelter. We need no other reason to demand hospitality from that simpleton on the wall!"

"Well, Aiken. I did not recognize you in the dark, but I do recognize your voice. You are far from your home territory. Alfred needs you at home, seeing to the defense of your land. Why are you so far from the land and the people who are your responsibility?"

"I know you, too, Wizard. The devil is loose in the land! Thousands of murderous Vikings are swarming across the land, killing all they meet! Just yesterday, more than a thousand fierce Vikings, flying Guthrum's own personal banners, galloped south, past my very burh! God knows how many more of the evil pagans are raping and pillaging!

"Aiken, where were they heading?"

"I know not. I only knew they were moving south."

"Toward Chippenham?"

"Aye, possibly, if they continued on that course . . . I am taking my family and going to Frankland, where we can make a holy pilgrimage and pray for our people's deliverance."

"Your place, sir, is with your people. Their only hope is your leadership. Alfred gave you land so you could defend it, not run for the continent!"

"Don't you lecture me, Greek! I know Alfred has been killed, and no man is safe in this land! Flee, and save your own life!"

"Alfred is alive and well! He was attacked at Chippenham, and he made a fighting retreat over the Avon River. Even as we speak, his queen and many innocent women and children of the court are on their way here. King Alfred is fighting a rearguard action.

In the name of your king, if you are unwilling to return to Hunter's Downs, then I command you to at least escort the Queen to Winchester. I need a stronger force, and dare not strip the estates of the men, thus leaving their women and children defenseless. You will win the king's forgiveness if you do this."

"Lord Polonius, the king is dead, and I am fleeing for my life. You may join me. We ride at dawn. I will take mounted warriors, but I will not be saddled with a large number of women and children. Our only hope of survival is to ride hard and make the eastern coast before the ravening hordes are upon us."

"Aiken, you are a thane of Wessex. Your duty is to your queen!"

"I have grown old fighting the enemies of Wessex. I have a dozen war wounds, and two of my sons have died fighting at my side! Don't lecture me about my duty! You're a Greek. You, of all people, should understand! I am told that your people have mercenaries do the dirty work of killing.

It's time my family and my life come before my duty. I am old and tired, and I just want to live out my remaining years in peace. I have had enough! Alfred, if he really lives, can have my *hides* of land."

"Aiken, Alfred will take back your land, and you will go to Frankland excommunicated and cast out of Holy Mother church. You will be stripped of your property, and will be declared an outlaw in all Christian lands! Think, man! You are betraying everything that you have both loved and fought for! You are a warrior of Alfred. Queen Ealhswith needs you!"

"She will have to find another. My ship awaits me in Kent. I ride an hour after dawn. I will agree to this and no more. If the queen wishes to ride with me as far as Winchester, I will escort her."

"The queen arrives even as we speak, but we have all ridden through the night, and need sleep, warmth and food before we hit the trail again. We cannot ride with you for some hours."

"I see a wagon approaching. I withdraw my offer. We do not have time to escort that damned thing over so many miles! I will take you, the queen, and your mounted warriors. All others must take their chances. Do you wish to ride with me or not?"

"Take your men, and be damned to you! You are a coward and a fool! I give you a hundred-count to move your party out of this burh or I will have the queen's escort hang you from the Watch Tower here!

Kuralla, please ride back and ask the queen to halt the column. Tell the commander that I want his troops drawn up and ready for battle; all of them."

Behind Polonius, a long column of riders slowly approached, led by the giant wagon. The riders were black against the snow.

As the column approached, Aiken would soon be able to estimate the raw numbers, but not see how many were women and how many were warriors.

Kuralla looked for a few moments at Polonius. Then she spoke. "As you command, husband." Having said that, she dug her heels into the sides of her horse, and the surprised mount galloped back toward the oncoming refugees.

Aiken chose not to call Polonius' bluff. He turned to the men above. "Order the men to mount up! It is almost dawn, anyway, and we have a long ride ahead of us."

⌖

When Aiken's party rode out of the royal burh, Queen Ealhswith's caravan had stopped well down the road. One by one, the heavily bundled riders were fanning out and moving into battle formation. Thane Aiken steered his mount over until he stood beside Polonius. He leaned close, and spoke quietly.

"I know you think that I am a coward, and perhaps I am, but Alfred's queen is worth her weight in silver to the Danes, and the children as well. I love my king enough that I will not sell his wife and family to Guthrum, even though it would buy safety for me, my family and my land. And Polonius, it is now bright enough that I can count how many warriors escort the queen."

"Then prove your love, Aiken. We need a strong escort to ensure the royal family makes Winchester safely. In one small gesture, you change from a traitor to a hero, and, you don't even go far out of your way."

"And if I do this thing Mother Church will not excommunicate me?"

"If you do this thing, then you may ride for the Kentish coast with the blessing of Alfred and his queen. There will be no excommunication. Beyond that, I make no promises."

The sky was still masked by clouds, but there was now enough light that Polonius could plainly see Aiken's pensive face. The man studied the snow at the feet of his horse for several long moments. At last he looked again at the dark-skinned Greek.

"Polonius, you have a smooth tongue. I have heard the ballads about you and Ambrose, and, having had the chance to talk with you, I begin to believe that the stories might even be true. It is understood that I only have to escort the queen as far as Winchester?"

"The queen and her entire retinue . . . as far as Winchester."

"What do we do if Guthrum's hounds find us?"

"We fight to defend innocent women and children until none of us are left standing."

Aiken snorted. "Some bargain, Greek, but you have bought yourself an escort."

"Then turn your men around. The queen and her people must be warmed and fed. I invite you and your men to join us for a repast. After some sleep, we will continue on our way."

CHAPTER 8

The Survivors Flee

Once the last boats were dragged onto the shore, Alfred ordered that they be chopped into kindling. Soon roaring bonfires helped warm and dry the bedraggled swimmers and other refugees. While women and children were mounted and sent on their way, nervous sentries paced the Avon shoreline. Desperate men, cold and tired, prepared to fight the savage Northerners if they managed to cross the river.

As the day dawned, the remaining thanes of the Personal Guard formed up. There were only a few horses left, and even fewer spears and arrows. Most of the other refugees had fled during the night. Alfred had been particularly relieved to see the royal women and children, led by Polonius, start on their way to Winchester.

Alfred faced his faithful men, and spoke. "No one could be prouder of what you did last night than me! You are all heroes. Today we will march in the wake of the Queen and the royal athelings. If Guthrum manages to cross and catches up to us, it will be our duty to hold them as long as we can. Once we reach my royal estate, I will release you from your pledge to protect me."

Looking very depressed, Alfred turned to Ambrose. "Brother . . . would you . . . ?"

Ambrose saw the despair written across his brother's face. He knew that without Alfred, Wessex would not survive. Alfred, however, had to regain his confidence, or he wouldn't survive. The prince raised his head and faced the column of thanes.

"Prepare to march! Left turn! Forward march!"

Ambrose got the little column moving. The ranks of the survivors were terribly thin.

"Alfred, we must keep moving! If you are captured, all of Wessex and all Angleland is finished! You are our only hope!”

"Ambrose, of what use am I now? My men lie dead at Chippenham! So many of my faithful men lie moldering and unburied. The cream of my Personal Guard died there. I should have died with them!”

"Alfred, you cannot blame yourself! You had a treaty with Guthrum. Our war band was dispersed for the winter when he so treacherously broke his solemn oath. We met the Vikings with villagers and churls, stiffened with too few of your Personal Guard. Our men were outnumbered by ten to one, and yet they held until most of the women and children could be evacuated. The walls were not strong enough to stop the horde Guthrum brought against us!

It's true many faithful warriors died or were captured, but others made it across the river, as did the young athelings, the women, and the treasury. Come spring, you can call up every warrior in the land and show Guthrum, again, how Saxons fight. Above all, however, we need a leader, and you are the only man who can successfully call upon the whole empire to march.”

"Yes, if there is an empire left by spring! The wolves are loose amongst us, and there is no shepherd to stop them.”

"Brother, it is not the first time the wolves have been loose in our lands. I suspect that it will not be the last. Each time, however, we have rallied and thrown them back into the sea.

Guthrum has gained a foothold by betraying his pledge and arriving in the winter season. We tried to defend Chippenham with too small a force, and we lost.

We can rectify the situation come spring, as long as you are there to lead us, brother. Ride now! We must stay ahead of the pagan devils. They would give anything to capture you!”

The distant and muffled sound of steel against steel indicated to the two riders that the rearguard had run into trouble. Ambrose turned on his horse.

"Phillip, would you please take the last of the King's Personal Guard with you and see what is going on back there? Let us pray that a merciful God will allow our king to escape Guthrum's long arm.”

"The Danes will not pass while I live, Prince!”

Alfred looked around the table at the tired faces of his closest advisors. They had all, like him, fought a desperate battle, and then had ridden hard for two days, only stopping briefly at various royal estates to obtain food and fresh horses. They had been pursued, but Guthrum's men couldn't possibly know which of the many groups of fleeing refugees the king had joined, and, thanks to Alfred's foresight in first taking, and then destroying the boats, Guthrum's force had been seriously delayed in crossing the Avon River in strength.

Now the royal party sat with Ethelnoth, Ealdorman of Somerset, and a loyal vassal of his king. When Alfred's messenger had arrived at Ethelnoth's Great Hall, he had immediately left his family and ridden directly to his king's side. They now sat around a trestle table in the burh of one of Ethelnoth's thanes.

At last Alfred spoke. "Well, my friends, I have sore need of your counsel. What shall we do about Guthrum and his Danes?"

Ambrose replied. "Brother, our forces are shattered. Most of your Personal Guard had returned home to their own families for the holidays. Those who remained and fought are badly mauled, and, throughout the empire, our levies have stood down for the winter. Now is not the time to try to call up all the warriors of the realm."

"Then, Ambrose, you are telling me I have no forces with which to fight. Obviously, I will have to hide in the forests of Selwood and endure being hunted like a royal stag."

Ethelnoth, Ealdorman of Somerset, spoke earnestly.

"Nay, Sire! I will call up as many of my loyal vassals as you wish, and we will form a new band to protect you. While I draw breath, you will not have to run and hide in your own land."

"I thank you for your loyalty, my old friend, but whatever force you can rally would not be sufficient to defeat the pagans, and yet would be a lode stone to attract them to my location. No . . . I fear that Ambrose is right and I am being a fool. I will hide in the fastness of Selwood Forest, and we will plan for spring.

The winter season will give us time to send out messengers and prepare the people for a summer campaign. This, I fear, will be the greatest challenge Wessex has ever faced."

Ambrose looked at his two old friends with relief. Alfred was animated as he spoke. It was the first sign that he had broken free from the bonds of deep depression that he had fallen into when he realized that the bulk of his vassals at Chippenham and many of his faithful Personal Guard were scattered or left dead in their desperate defense of Chippenham. He quickly turned back to Alfred, however, as their king and his brother spoke directly to him.

"Ambrose, I have a most important task for you. It is only a matter of time before Guthrum sends his minions to our royal seat at Winchester.

The few boys and old men who escorted our families back there after Chippenham fell will not be able to defend the column against any appreciable Viking force. I want you to go there and bring my beloved Ealhswith and my children here.

They will be safer in the forest here than within any fortification we presently possess. Bring Gretchen, Matilda and the children, and Kuralla too. And Polonius, I miss the man's sage advice and convoluted stories. Be careful, mind. You must not travel back as a royal party. Our protection this winter will not lie in the swords of our strongest men, but in the trees and in total secrecy. We must completely disappear from sight for a few months."

"My brother, my place is by your side!"

"Ambrose, the future of our family depends on you bringing my family to safety. And there is no one I would trust with their lives more than you! For now, I can hide better by not having a large retinue. I will ask Ethelnoth to show me the forest settlements so I will have a safe haven prepared when you return with our loved ones."

"Brother, what do we do with all the rest of the court?"

"I have been giving that much thought. I think they would be safest at Dover Castle. The walls are thick, and it is far from Guthrum's present field of operations. Failing that, there is the fleet and the Channel.

Strip Winchester bare for escort. Most can return as soon as they have escorted the court to the next tun. In that way, no one will be more than a day or two from their home base."

"Alfred, I hear and obey."

Alfred took two steps across the room toward his brother, and grabbed him in a fierce bear-hug. He smiled for the first time since the disastrous battle.

"Brother, I know you do! I count on it more than you know. I entrust to you everything that I hold dear to me. Take care, and go with God!"

The little cavalcade of three men and two packhorses moved quickly along the forest trails. Ahead loped two foresters of Ealdorman Ethelnoth, the loyal and powerful man who even now harbored and protected Alfred. The foresters knew the most secluded trails intimately, and they led the group without incident to the edge of Selwood Forest.

Once the party reached the old Roman road that ran eastwards from just south of Bath to Winchester, Ambrose sent the two men back, but with the strict injunction that they were to remain in the little village near where the group had exited Selwood Forest. Once the refugee party returned, it would need an escort to lead them to where Alfred was hiding, and the less who knew the real identity of the refugees, the better. The Saxons of Somerset were loyal subjects of their king, but large quantities of gold, or the torture implements the Danes knew how to wield so well, could loosen even the most recalcitrant tongue.

CHAPTER 9

Ambrose Reaches Winchester

Cold and stiff as he was, the bastard prince leapt from his horse. There, standing by the town gate of Winchester, mixed in with all the onlookers, was the object of all his desires and all his lust.

He had ridden for the better part of a week, and each and every weary mile he had dreamed of this moment. At last, as beautiful as in his dream, she stood within reach!

Gretchen put hand to mouth when she recognized Ambrose under his heavy winter cape. Almost before she had realized her husband had finally returned, he had run to her and swept her into his arms.

She gasped. "Oh, my beloved! I was so afraid that you would never come!"

"And I was so afraid that you might not have made it here safely!"

"You need have no fear of that, my husband. Polonius was able to scare us up a strong escort."

"I hope he didn't have to strip any burhs bare. They are weak enough with a full garrison. As we expected, Guthrum's devils are running amok. They are raping and pillaging even as we speak."

"You need not fear, my Lord and Master! We came across a thane fleeing to Frankland with a strong and well-mounted escort. Polonius threatened him with excommunication, until he agreed to escort us all the way to the gates of Winchester."

"Trust our smooth-talking Greek friend to find an effortless way to provide an escort. But I am grateful. I was terrified that you all were in mortal danger."

"My husband, all the danger was with you, defending our back trail. Did the heathen devils catch up to you?"

"Aye, we ambushed probing parties of Viking raiders several times, until they brought up so many men that it was all we could do to disengage. Alfred himself gave the order to disband and separate. We rode in a dozen different directions, and I think most were able to give the Danes the slip. But let's find Ealhswith. I have to report to her!"

As they spoke, the queen had approached. Unknown to the two lovers, she stood just behind them. "You do not have to look far,

Ambrose. Forgive me for interrupting you two, but I have to know!"

Ambrose turned around, and lifted his sister-in-law right off the ground. "The short answer is; yes, he was safe and well when I left him, and I have no doubt that he is still."

"Where is he? Was he injured in the fighting?"

Ambrose held his sister-in-law tight. "Relax, Ealhswith. He misses you greatly, too. In fact, he sent me to bring you to him."

"Oh, thank Merciful God! I will give the instructions for the court to prepare to travel . . ."

"No, Ealhswith. He asked me to bring you, your children, Polonius, Kuralla, Matilda and her children, and Gretchen. If you agree to come, we are to travel in secret. There will be no royal procession. No royal banners. No royal Personal Guard. The ride will be hard, and the journey will be cold and dangerous. He said the choice should be yours."

"If that is what my husband thinks is best, then that is what we will do. But what of the others? What are they to do?"

"Alfred's instructions were to send the rest of the court to Kent. Those who wish, may attempt to make it to their own homes, assuming that they are defensible. The court can travel by wagon, and with royal escort. Alfred felt they would be as safe in Dover as anywhere.

He instructed me to send a strong force with them, and to have Polonius draw up orders for the ealdorman there to protect them at all costs. His son is a member of the royal court. I think we need not fear on that account."

"Ambrose, why is the court not all staying together?"

"Sister, what I am about to tell you must not be repeated to anyone - even your most faithful servants. Alfred is deep in Selwood Forest. Most of his Personal Guard are dead, injured, or out of touch. We have no idea what the Danes are up to, but we know that we do not at present have the men to prevent them from doing whatever they want. There is probably not a fortress in the land that they could not overrun. There is therefore no safety for you behind stone walls. Thus he has chosen to just disappear.

He needs time; time to pull in allies and organize. The royal court with Alfred present would draw Danes like bears to honey. He therefore intends to send the court as far from the fighting as possible."

"Do you think Kent is safe?"

"I do not know, Ealhswith. Until we find out if there are other Vikings, or traitors, involved in this invasion, no one can be certain of anything. It is at least far from Guthrum's present theater of operations, and there are several long-ships of the fleet stored there for the winter, so, as a last resort, the ships can be used for an escape."

"What if Guthrum finds out about the court moving to Kent and chases after it."

"Then the only athelings left alive will be hiding in Selwood Forest."

"And if Guthrum finds us?"

"Then the Witan may choose from the royal cousins left alive in Kent."

Queen Ealhswith stared at Ambrose in silence for almost a minute. He reached out and put an arm on each woman's shoulders.

"Come, Ealhswith, Gretchen, let us seek some warmth, and after that, I would like to speak with Polonius and the fyrd commander."

The queen looked chagrined. "Oh, Ambrose, I was so excited to see you that I forgot that you must be both frozen and exhausted! Please, let me arrange for food and drink."

The three headed arm in arm for the Great Hall, where the riders would be warmed and feted. Ambrose smiled in turn at the two beautiful women who escorted him. "Both Alfred and I are blessed to have such intelligent and beautiful wives."

Gretchen poked him in the ribs. "Your reward for that, sir, will come when I get you to our quarters!"

⚑

Ambrose met Polonius in the privacy of the stout timbered home that Ealhswith had put at Polonius' disposal. The two men hugged each other hard.

"Ambrose, I had feared for you greatly! Thank God you are alive!"

"Polonius, my friend! I missed having you shivering at my side!"

"Long ago, when you told me about Angleland, you told me it was both beautiful and an exciting place to live."

"Well! And have we not had many exciting adventures here?"

"Aye, we have at that. And I fear that this one is not over yet. What news of Alfred?"

"We fought off a series of Viking probes, but their main force was finally able to cross the Avon, and we were forced to split up and ride for our lives."

"Is Alfred safe?"

"Aye. We sent word to Ethelnoth of Somerset that we were in his territory, and the man met us the next day with every man he could scrounge together. He is truly a faithful vassal, and a real friend. At present he is hiding Alfred deep in Selwood Forest. Alfred has asked me to secretly bring just his immediate family to him, along with you, and our wives."

"And the rest?"

"We are to send them to Dover, along with a strong escort."

Polonius looked thoughtful. "Alfred must be really afraid, if he is splitting up the young athelings."

"He cannot hide the full royal court in Selwood Forest, Polonius. There is also considerable danger for the royal procession, but at least they will eventually be far away, behind stout walls, and will have some ships of the Saxon fleet and the Channel at their back if need be."

"I understand, Ambrose. It is a wise man who does not put all of his eggs in one basket."

"Polonius, I know it will take some time for the court to prepare for its journey. In the meantime, Guthrum or one of his minions just might show up here. How secure is the tun of Winchester?"

Polonius thought for a moment. "The commander of the fyrd has called in all the churls and thanes, and their families, from the outlying areas. The men have labored daily on repairing the walls, but the truth is, I don't think Winchester could hold out long against a strong enemy force."

Ambrose nodded. "Well, my friend. It sounds like we had better help the court get organized. I would appreciate it if you would be so kind as to draw up the necessary writs and instructions. It is my intention that we slip out of the tun during all the excitement when the procession leaves."

CHAPTER 10

The Rule of Law

The exhausted band of riders finally broke out of the seemingly endless forest. Suddenly, they were among open fields, and children and pigs ran squealing. Even in the dusk, Alfred could see the palisades of the little tun and the welcoming plumes of smoke that rose into the darkening sky. Fire meant food, and, even more important, warmth.

Ethelnoth led the little cavalcade directly toward the main gate. He slowed a little, however, so Alfred would catch up to him.

"It appears, Sire, that word has yet to reach this settlement of the Viking invasion. The gates gape open, and a body of armed men are not challenged, let alone spotted, even this close to the tun! I am ashamed, Your Majesty!"

"Ethelnoth, be not too harsh on your thane. As you say, he may not know of our disaster. I would ask you, as well, not to refer to my title. I may be staying in the area for some time, and I do not for now want even your people to know my real identity. It bodes well that these people do not know what has happened. This is just the kind of isolation that I seek for my family and myself, until we are ready to react to Guthrum and his God-cursed Vikings."

"I understand, Sire. Yet what may I call you in front of my people?"

"Please identify me as a fellow nobleman who is staying with you. What title shall I use? How about just 'master'?"

"It will be as you wish . . . Master."

"Good man! And do I see a delegation finally assembling to greet their Ealdorman?"

"Aye, Master, and about time!"

The riders approached the gate, yet Alfred noticed that it stood invitingly open, and although a good two dozen armed men stood in front of it, yet they were not in any kind of military formation. Ethelnoth's angry voice rang out.

"Where is Aldwin, my thane?"

The men were bundled from the cold, but one man stepped forward when his master called his name.

"I am here! Is that Ealdorman Ethelnoth who calls my name?"

"Yes, you scoundrel! Where are your defenses, man!? Your tun is open to any who wish to take it!"

"After our last harvest, Lord, there are none around who would bother to take our humble tun!"

"Aldwin, I will not have you hung, for obviously you do not know the news."

"Know what, Ealdorman?"

"Guthrum and his Danes have crossed the northern border. They attacked King Alfred at Chippenham, and took the royal estate. Using it as their base, they even now rampage and loot unopposed through our land!"

"And our king! Is Alfred safe?"

"Aye. His Personal Guard made a heroic fighting retreat, and the king and his family was able to make it across the Avon River. God was with us; the river was not frozen, and the Danes were not able to immediately follow, since Alfred's men had taken all the boats. Many of the ealdormen and thanes who were at the royal court survived, but they are scattered and demoralized. Even now, the Danes hunt for the survivors."

"My Lord, we did not know! The last we had heard was that Guthrum had sworn a solemn and holy oath, and left hostages as a guarantee of good faith before he rode north to Mercia! I now understand your anger, and we will put the tun on a war footing immediately."

"Aye, do that, Aldwin. I want you to post watchers on all the trails around. Tomorrow, we will talk of a winter-long training program for the men. Make no mistake, we will be going to war in the spring. If the heathen come this way, we may be fighting long before then."

"Ealdorman, it will be done. Yet you and your men are doubtless cold and tired. I suspect that you have ridden far. Please, dismount and enjoy our hospitality. You and your followers are welcome here for as long as you need a place to stay.

Boys! Take our visitors' horses! Rub them down well and then feed them. They have served their masters well today . . . Honored guests, please follow me!"

Alfred followed the respective rulers of the tun and the shire through the gate. He looked at the rude thatched huts and the sturdy folk who came to stare at the strangers. He was master of uncounted small settlements like this, scattered from Surrey to the Devon coasts and beyond. He knew well that they were the source of his real strength.

As long as the Britons, Angles, Jutes, Saxons and Celts continued to answer his summons to war, he was invincible. The people of the forest and the downs, the plains and the coast, they were the backbone of his empire; the spear points that could cut the Danes down like the devil-spawn they were.

What he feared most was not the abandonment of the people, but the abandonment of his ealdormen. Alfred well knew the enticements Guthrum would blandish to Wessex's shire lords.

The Vikings had set up puppet rulers to the north, ruling the newly conquered lands through Saxon satraps. Their lives would be spared, and the ravaging of their land, if they would but submit and offer yearly tribute.

If enough of his leaders were swayed, then Saxon Wessex and its king were doomed. He suspected that the standard twin prongs of Danish policy were already in motion; the ravaging hordes devastating whole regions, while peace and protection were offered those who submitted.

His eastern and western shires were, in the lifetime of many living, independent kingdoms. Not all of his ealdormen were as brave as they boasted around the fires in the evenings. Not all loved their West Saxon king.

He sighed, and followed his hosts. For the next few weeks he could not even begin to deal with the politics of his realm. First he would have to find a safe haven, where he could bring his family. Then he would start to strike back at the heathen, and to organize the mighty host that would gather in early summer to crush the treacherous Guthrum!

The visitors were led to the Great Hall of Aldwin. It was solidly made of logs, and large enough to permanently support several dozen retainers. Ethelnoth was led to the High Seat, but he paused and looked askance of his master. Alfred smiled.

"Nay, Ealdorman Ethelnoth. You are master here. I am but a humble visitor to your lands. Please, sit in the Seat-of -Honor!"

The exhausted men were shown to the benches that largely circled the room. Trestle tables were brought and set up in front of the men, and soon ale and mead in drinking horns was distributed by smiling women.

Aldwin, seated next to his shire lord, spoke so all could hear.

"You all honor us with your presence. Please, drink and warm yourselves. The women even now are arranging a feast. I apologize that food is not ready, but we truly did not expect visitors today."

The churls of the settlement joined the thanes and noblemen who had just ridden in, and all settled down to serious drinking while the food was being prepared. The men and women of the isolated settlement were eager to hear of the latest news, and furious that the Danish king would break his most sacred oath, sworn on his own holy armband.

They applauded when they heard that Alfred had ordered the hostages to be hung directly in front of their attacking brethren. The news of the desperate battle, and of who was known to have perished, sobered many of the older men. They knew that they would train hard all winter, and then march at their master's bidding come spring. Every kingdom north of them had succumbed to the northern heathens, and only the grace of God and a massive empire-wide gathering of the fyrds could defeat Alfred's nemesis.

At last the talk of politics ceased, and men started the ritual boasting of their greatest deeds. The women distributed bowls of warm water and clean towels to the gathered menfolk and guests. They listened with a great deal of scepticism to the heroic stories. While they felt pride in the strength of their men, yet they, the wives and mothers, were the ones who buried the young lads and grizzled warriors foolish enough to think there was glory in battle.

The stories continued, and the women brought out heaping wooden platters of bread and steaming pork. At last Aldwin turned to Ethelnoth and the tall man who his master so clearly deferred to.

"Masters! May I have our *scop* sing you the ballad of Prince Ambrose, he who stole a Saxon princess from an Irish Norseman, and also marched in the Danish *Great Army* as a spy?"

Aldwin noticed that the tall stranger and Ethelnoth exchanged smiles. Ethelnoth replied. "Aye, I think that my guests and I would like very much to hear the story."

Aldwin clapped his hands twice. A slave scurried over immediately. "Find the scop. He is to earn his keep tonight. He is to sing for our guests."

⚑

Aldwin spoke earnestly to his master, Ealdorman Ethelnoth. "My Lord, while you are here, and in the absence of the king's shire Reeve, may I impose on you and call a *Moot*? I have a most grave accusation, and I fear that it will tear my community apart."

"Of, course, Aldwin. But what is the charge, that you are so concerned about it?"

"The daughter of one of my churls has accused her distant cousin of forcing himself upon her sexually. Whichever way I rule, the other side will take offense, and both are my relatives."

"Ah, you want me to take the heat. How does the man plead?"

"None will question your impartiality, Ealdorman. The man protests his innocence, and asks for us to allow him to clear himself by *compurgation*."

"Has she officially made her accusation?"

"Yes, Ealdorman. She did so at the last Hundred Court just a few days ago. I ruled he was to find his oath helpers and be prepared when I called the Moot."

"Are there witnesses?"

"No, Ealdorman, although her mother has already testified as to the state of her daughter when she returned home. The girl claims that she was gathering cooking wood in the forest when he came upon her and forced himself on her."

"Does the story collaborate?"

Aldwin shrugged his shoulders.

"It seems to, Lord. Both the girl and the young man were in the forest at that time. Our medicine woman tells me that the girl is no longer a virgin, and may have been forced. Yet in spite of mother Church's teaching, our young maidens are lusty, and there are several festivals where drink and tradition allow unbridled behavior."

"It is unusual for me to interfere at this stage, yet I understand the politics, and with Guthrum loose, I am not sure that the Shire Court will be in regular session for some time. By all means; call your Moot, my friend! I will preside."

⌐⌐

Ethelnoth sat in the High Seat, which had, for the special occasion, been placed outside on the commons. On one side his thane sat close beside him, and on the other side sat the parish priest. Aldwin stood and spoke to the assembled crowd. All churls and thanes who lived within a day's walk had been called to the Moot. Only those on sentry duty were exempted.

Aldwin stood before his master and called out to the assembled crowd. "Ealdorman Ethelnoth has kindly consented to sit in-authority for this special Moot. Are there any here who question his authority in this matter?"

Both Aldwin and Ethelnoth swept the crowd with their eyes. Seeing there were no replies, Ethelnoth then spoke deliberately and sonorously.

"Is the accused present today?'

A stir in one clump of people and a waving arm indicated that the defendant and his supporters were indeed present.

'The maiden Naomi is to stand before this Moot and repeat her accusation for all to hear. None shall interrupt her until she is through. Naomi, step forward!"

A beautiful maiden with flashing blue eyes and straw-blond hair walked slowly forward until she stood by the High Seat. She bowed to her thane and ealdorman, and then faced the crowd. She stood modestly and silently for several moments, but then she suddenly raised her head and pointed her finger at the accused who stood amongst his family.

"Honored sirs! That boy there! Cliftun. 'e come across me in the forest, and 'e forced 'imself upon me."

Ethelnoth spoke. "And did you agree to make love to him?"

She stood defiantly. "No, My Lord! I told 'im to leave me alone!"

"And did he?"

"No, My Lord! 'e hit me again and again, until I agreed to do what 'e said.' That said, Naomi threw her woollen cape down on the ground, unpinned the top of her dress, and allowed it to drop to her waist. Although Ambrose was distracted by the lovely rose-tipped conical breasts, he, and all present, could see large purple bruises on her arms and chest.

'See what 'e did to me!"

"Thank you, Naomi. You can put your dress back on. Did you then make love to him?"

The tears flowed down her cheek, and she flushed a bright red. "We didn't make love! 'e put his disgusting thing inside me and hurt me! Then 'e told me that no one would believe me if I accused 'im of rape. 'e said that no one would ever want to marry me if I told anyone what happened."

"Did you believe him?"

"No, Lord. Maybe. Well, even if it be true, it was wrong what 'e did to me, and me mother encouraged me to speak up, no matter what the cost."

"Thank you, Naomi. You are very brave to be here today. Pray step back now until I call you again."

"Thank you, Me Lord!"

Her mother, an older and more bosom copy of Naomi, led her crying daughter away.

"Cliftun! Stand before me."

The young man who Naomi had so recently pointed at took his place in front of the High Seat. He stood silently before his two masters.

"Cliftun, what do you say to the accusation that Naomi has made against you?"

"My Lords! It is not true! I ask you now to let me swear to my innocence."

"That is your right, Cliftun."

"Thank you, Master. Then before you and all of the Moot, I declare that by the Lord God, I am guiltless both of deed and instigation of the crime of which Naomi accuses me."

"And do you have oath-helpers to support your oath?"

"Aye, Me Lord!"

"Then have them come forward."

A group of three men stepped forward. Two others took a step forward and then stopped, carefully looking away from the accused. Aldwin turned to Ethelnoth, and spoke quietly. "These be Pearroc, Halebeorht, and Lindesig. All three are brothers of Cliftun."

Ethelnoth signaled each of the three to step forward one at a time. Each of the three looked at Cliftun, and then stated "By the Lord God, the oath is pure and not false that Cliftun swore."

Ethelnoth listened to the oaths, and then asked each oath-helper to step back. The ealdorman spoke quietly to the thane beside him. "Aldwin, what is the name of the two who decided not to come forward?"

"They be Rapere and Okedene the Younger, Ealdorman."

Ethelnoth stood up and spoke loudly. "I now command Rapere and Okedene the Younger to come before me."

The two men stood nervously before their shire lord. Ethelnoth spoke to both of them together. "Did you two promise to act as oath-helpers today?"

Both men looked carefully at the ground near their feet. Neither spoke. Ethelnoth's voice thundered. "This is a court! You will answer your ealdorman or be subject to heavy fines! Speak up! You!' With that he pointed to the shorter man. 'Rapere, did you promise to swear on behalf of Cliftun?"

"Aye, Me Lord."

"And why did you not?"

I . . . ah . . . had not seen the bruises on Naomi, Master"

"And so?"

The man looked as if he were hoping his busy right foot could dig a hole deep enough for him to hide in. He looked twice in the direction of Cliftun. At last he muttered. "I do not feel I can so swear."

Ethelnoth's voice thundered. "Speak up, Rapere!"

"I do not feel I can so swear."

"Thank you. Okedene?"

"Me, neither, Ealdorman."

Ethelnoth waved the men back into the crowd, and then had the accused step forward. "Cliftun, the only oath-helpers I have heard from are your own brothers. I do not find this to be satisfactory. Do you have others who would speak on your behalf?"

Cliftun glared at his two friends, who continued to carefully inspect the ground at their feet. "It appears that I do not, Me Lord."

"Do you have anything else to say for yourself?"

"Me Lord, before God and my own people, I am innocent!"

Ethelnoth spoke again. "I fear that the accusations are too serious for us to accept only the word of your immediate family. It is clear, then, that the truth of the matter has not yet been ascertained. I will therefore ask that the Holy Father beside me kindly lend us his good offices today. If man cannot ascertain the truth, then we must put our trust in God's divine revelations.

Cliftun, you may choose between the fire and the water. You have three days in which to fast and make confession. Which ordeal do you choose?"

"Me Lords! I swear to you that I am innocent! I will swear on whatever holy artefact you ask me to!"

"My judgement is that God will tell us of your guilt or innocence. Choose, Cliftun. Will it be fire or water?"

"Me Lords! I cannot swim, and I will need my sword hand to do battle against the king's enemies!"

"If you are pure in God's eyes, then your hand will heal swiftly and cleanly. If you are guilty in God's eyes, the very waters will reject your body. Have no fear. God will not let an innocent man drown before we can pull you out. Am I right, Holy Father?"

"Yes, my son. Cliftun, trust your soul to God! He will help you if you are innocent."

Aldwin spoke next. "Cliftun, you must choose, or you will be judged guilty right now."

"Oh, Master! Have mercy on a poor sinner! I meant no harm to Naomi. Ask the village boys how many of them have had her! I did not do what a dozen other boys have not also done!"

Pandemonium broke out in the crowd. Ethelnoth now stood. He slowly raised his right hand over his head, and the people slowly quieted.

"Silence! Cliftun, you have condemned yourself before your lord and before the people of this Moot!

Men of the Moot! You have heard Cliftun's statements. What is your judgement?"

The words thundered in Ethelnoth's ears. "Guilty! Guilty!"

Ethelnoth looked around the commons. Even some of Cliftun's original supporters slowly picked up the chant. They had watched him break, and then heard his confession. The cowardice he showed was as great a crime as the rape. In the end the vote was almost unanimous.

Ethelnoth stood regally in his cloak-of-office. His voice rang out sonorously. "Cliftun, you have been declared guilty by your own peers. I hereby sentence you to pay 100 shillings, in coin or kind, to Naomi's family. If you have not done this in three month's time, you will be sold into slavery to pay off your debt. I further decree that if, after you pay the fine, Naomi is unable to find a husband because of what you have done, you will marry and support her. The ultimate decision, however, is to be hers; not yours. I now declare this special Moot to be at an end."

CHAPTER 11

Ealhswith Is Reunited with Alfred

The massive gaily-painted wagons creaked across the ancient Roman bridge. Fore and aft, more than three hundred grim and well-armed fyrdmen rode escort. The serpentine column headed north, taking the old Roman road toward Silchester.

Babies cried, and the oxen-whips cracked. The royal court; ambassadors, bishops, young athelings, scholars and servants, all headed for the dubious protection of Dover. At least its Roman-built fortress, towering so high above the sea that the Continent could be seen from the upper battlements, was as strong as any in all of the West-Saxon Empire.

Almost all rode toward Dover. Not riding east were thirty veteran warriors, Queen Ealhswith, Polonius, Ambrose, Gretchen, Kuralla, Phillip's wife Matilda and her children, and Alfred's children. Most of the Queen's escort of thirty thanes had taken the other Roman road, leading north and west, before first light. Polonius had instructed them to be inconspicuous, so they rode in small groups, scouting ahead along the road the queen and her little group would follow.

The queen's road led to Cirencester, but passed through Selwood Forest. The last ten thanes would follow the disguised royal party, but at a distance.

The nondescript family of merchants; children, adults, and escort, rode past the slow-moving and gaudy royal caravan, and then forked left, toward the lands savaged by Guthrum's ruthless Viking brigands.

The arrogant soldier waved brusquely at the little mounted party. "Make way, there! In the ditch with you! Make way for your betters!"

Queen Ealhswith bridled. She turned her horse so she could confront the armored soldier. Ambrose grabbed the horse's reins and pulled the animal to the side of the road.

"Hold, Ealhswith! Just because you have the same name as a great and gracious queen doesn't mean that you can act like one! Off the road, woman, and be quick about it!"

The armored lout overheard, and laughed. "Good advice, sweetums! You better learn to make way for your betters, or you'll feel a taste of me whip! And if you have the sense God gave to you, you'd all turn around and get the hell away from here! There's wild Vikings somewhere behind me.' He leered at the queen. 'And they're just looking for tasty little vixens like you, sweetie!"

As the man spoke, Ambrose and Polonius managed to manoeuver the entire party into the drainage ditch beside the road. They were just in time. Within seconds, forty warriors rounded the bend in the road. Riding in a column of two, they thundered past, quickly followed by two wagons, and then another column of forty riders.

Ambrose looked grim. "And there go more rats deserting the sinking ship."

The queen was not to be distracted. "Ambrose! I have never been so humiliated in my life!"

"Ealhswith, be grateful that it is not summer. You would now be covered in mud. And if you think that his whip is just for show, then you're dreaming. If he chose to kill you because you did not obey a lawful command, he would, at worst, be forced to pay a fine. Your life today is worth less than 200 shillings. You are only the wife of a poor but hard-working merchant, woman, and you had better start behaving like one!"

Suddenly Ealhswith burst into laughter. "Thank you, oh great merchant, for reminding me of my place in life. I'm sorry, Ambrose. You are absolutely right. It's just hard being a peasant!"

"You have no idea, sister-in-law. But it can also be much worse. I have seen the slave marts of Constantinople and Rome. My body still carries the marks of the chains and the whips of my own captivity."

Ealhswith was suddenly sober again. "Aye. And if my husband is unable to raise enough warriors to beat this pagan devil Guthrum, then long lines of our people will be going to the slave markets of Europe. You are right, brother-in law. I will try and remember my place. And by the way, great-and-noble-merchant, where is this humble family sleeping tonight?"

"Not at a royal burh. Don't fool yourself. The Danes have their own spies scouring the length and breadth of this land, and don't think there are no Saxons on their payroll."

"You mean spies like your friend 'Harold the Frisian'."

"I hope that I don't find him spying again on Wessex, my Queen. Sitric Ivarsson has saved my life at least twice, and, without his help, I would never have been able to rescue my Gretchen."

"And if you see him?"

"I have told him that if he enters Wessex again as a spy, I will kill him."

"And what did he say to that?"

"He laughed and said that he understood. He has, as far as I know, tried to keep his father and the other Ragnarsson brothers out of Wessex."

"Can he actually do that?"

"I hope so, but he is only one of several commanders, and we are the last honey pot left intact. Eventually, they will have to come south to conquer . . . if Guthrum does not beat them to it."

"You have avoided the question, sir. Where does a merchant's wife sleep?"

Ambrose suddenly grinned. 'Fear not, my Lady. You are in luck. When Thane Galar last rode past us, he reported that he had been able to arrange for the loan of a hay loft in a small vill just a few miles ahead. We will sleep in comfort tonight. The cows below will even keep us warm!"

"A hay loft! Did you know that . . .' She looked contrite. 'A merchant's wife would be grateful for such a warm and comfortable place to sleep. I am grateful that Galar was able to find us such a palatial establishment for the night."

"That's the spirit, Ealhswith!"

Ealhswith looked serious again. "Ambrose, why have you sent our escort on? Wouldn't we be safer if they rode with us? There are so many desperate people on these roads."

"Everyone is fleeing the Viking threat, but a family of traveling merchants would hardly have thirty royal thanes as escort, my queen. They would simply draw attention to us."

"But how can they defend us if they are not at our side?"

"Easy, sister-in-law. They ride ahead, scout, listen to rumors, and receive official reports from the shire reeves. As you have already seen, small groups of them regularly ride past, on various pretexts."

"I bet they even sleep in comfort at the royal burhs!"

"Perhaps in the royal bed! Polonius gave them a writ commanding all and sundry to provide whatever they need, in your husband's name. And they keep a close eye on anyone ahead of us. If they see any signs of Vikings, or any hostile force, they will ride their horses to death to get the word to us here."

"And the ones behind us?"

"At least one of them is never far behind, and he carries a war horn. They will move in fast, if there is an unexpected threat. They just don't want to be seen riding with us. That could bring us the kind of attention we are trying to avoid."

"Thank you, brother-in-law. I really am grateful that you and Polonius are with us. I know that you are risking the lives of your own loved ones to deliver me to my husband. So lead on, oh mighty merchant!"

"'Humble' is the key word today, Ealhswith."

↦

As the little group rounded the curve, they saw that a heavy wagon had lost its wheel. It and its contents, stretched right across the road. The two draft horses were tied to saplings, patiently waiting until they were needed again. Three armed men were trying to manhandle the wagon to one side. Ambrose was alarmed, and he raised his arm to stop his own little troop.

"Polonius, take the women and children back until I can check this out. There are only two horses for a large wagon. It does not feel right!"

"Too late, Prince. Look behind us."

Ambrose twisted in the saddle, and there, across the road, was a band of ten armed men. A short heavy man, probably the leader by the quality of armor and clothes that he wore, advanced from the wagon. He was flanked by two men who wore simple leather armor and carried only spears and *saxes*.

The leader called out to them. "Advance, friends. You can't go back."

"What is that you want, sir?"

"My wagon has broken."

"That appears clear, sir, and although I am a merchant, I regret that I do not carry a spare wheel in my packs that I can sell you."

"I regret that, too, friend. For without that wheel, I am going to need horses."

"I regret that we have none to sell."

"Merchant, I wasn't asking you, nor do I have the spare silver to buy yours."

Ambrose smiled. "I am relieved. Then if you would be so good as to move out of the way, I think we can just about slip by."

"Friend, I fear that you don't understand. You are surrounded. You have women and children to protect. Take your weapons, and what supplies you wish, and start walking back the way you came. You and family only face death or slavery if you continue. I am really doing you a favor."

"What do you say that you and I settle this man to man? If you win,

I will freely give you the horses."

"And if I lose?"

"Then your men will get out of our way. Is that fair enough?"

"Nay. I fear not. You see, if we let you live, you will probably report us to the nearest king's reeve. It would be inconvenient if we were to have to tarry here awhile. The Danes are close behind!"

"And so you had no intention of letting us walk away. You would kill innocent women and children?"

"It's not my preference for the women, but I can't take the chance of one of the bitches talking. I'm truly sorry, friend. You should have taken our first offer. At least then, it would have been quick and painless.' The man raised his voice. 'Take them!"

Ambrose's blade snicked from its scabbard. Polonius threw back the folds of his cloak so his belt full of throwing daggers was within easy reach.

Ambrose's voice thundered. "Forward all! Polonius, kill these three! I will guard the rear."

Polonius performed his slight-of-hand, and suddenly both hands filled with throwing daggers. The man's eyes widened in shock, and he spoke. "Sweet-mother-of-God! A dark foreigner who makes knives appear magically. You're the dark man in the ballad! It's said that . . ."

Polonius' first dagger penetrated the man's throat, and his words turned to a gurgle. His comrades were a little quicker. They threw up their shields in unison, and both were struck by daggers. Without hesitating, however, Polonius threw the next ones low.

Twin screams told him that both blades struck truly. Neither wound would be fatal, but one man dropped his shield in pain and surprise. A blade smashed into his eye. The other staggered backward, large shield protecting most of his body. A flurry of daggers flew at him. He was able to catch most of them on his shield, but one more slipped below its protection, and he screamed again. He fell to the ground in agony, a dagger protruding from his leg. In the second when his shield slipped, he died.

The women were no fools, and even though the thieves in front of them were still standing, yet they grabbed the reins of the childrens' mounts and pressed forward. Kuralla, a daughter of a Slav chieftain of the Volkhov River Valley, had been trained from childhood to fight like a man.

While Polonius threw his daggers and Ambrose leapt from his horse to meet the approaching line of attackers, she unslung her light bow and notched the first arrow. While Gretchen and Ealhswith got the crying and screaming children over the dead bodies and past the wagon, Kuralla started calmly shooting at the Saxon attackers.

The line of attackers moved forward steadily. Ambrose had leapt to the ground to act as a rear guard, and his blade flicked out again and again, slowing their advance. The prince watched the approaching men carefully. He knew that if they moved on him as a group, or just used their spears as javelins, he was dead. At all costs, he knew that he had to distract them.

One of the attackers had heard his leader's words just before his death rattle. He spoke to his comrades. "Tom, what did the master say?"

Ambrose replied for him. "He said that the thin dark one is known as Polonius the Greek, who never misses with the throwing daggers. Polonius! If you are through playing with those men, come and give these gentlemen a demonstration of your skills!

And I have another puzzle for you, good gentlemen. Who carries a magic sword that penetrates all armor and cannot be stopped?"

"Me God! You must be Ambrose, bastard prince of Wessex!"

"Watch how the steel can slice right through chain-mail.' With that, Ambrose made a lunge at the nearest attacker. A whistling blow cut the spear point from the man's shaft, and suddenly the thin blade leapt forward in a manoeuver rare for Anglish swordsmen. It penetrated deep into the man's side.

Ambrose withdrew his blade before it lodged too deep and stuck. 'Which of you would like to be the next to try and match yourself against my magic sword?"

The men hesitated, even while one, and then another, were wounded by the arrows shot by Kuralla. Polonius, by now busy collecting his daggers, was almost ready to rejoin his companion.

The men withdrew a few paces, shields high. Ambrose was worried. There was no way he and Polonius could stop seven spears thrown in unison. He had managed to cause some fear and distraction, but the thieves were too committed to stop now, though they no longer seemed quite so eager.

The depressing thought had just entered Ambrose's mind when the echo of a Saxon war horn could be heard over the screams of the wounded. The very ground trembled as ten heavily armored horsemen arrived at a gallop.

With a wall of mounted thanes on one side, the arrows of Kuralla, the hurtling knives of Polonius, and the flashing blade of Ambrose on the other, the odds quickly changed. Within less than a single minute, most of the thieves were lying dead on the ground or were seriously wounded. The last three standing, realizing the futility of fighting the expert warriors they faced, threw down their weapons and raised their hand above their heads.

"We didn't know it were you, good Prince. Have mercy on God's poor sinners!"

Galar's thanes stepped forward and quickly trussed the three. Ambrose signaled for the three to be brought to him. Galar spoke to his prince. "Prince Ambrose, what are your instructions?"

"Find a stout tree, and hang them."

The first one panicked. "You can't do that, Prince. We 'ave not 'ad a trial!"

Ambrose looked sternly at the three of them. "You dared to attack honest citizens of Wessex. And the woman over there, on that horse, is your queen. The king's law is clear on both issues. The sentence for outlawry is death. The punishment for attempting to harm a member of the royal family is death. Do you deny these charges?"

The eldest, clearly the group's leader spoke. "Sir, there is no royal escort. There are no royal banners. How can you accuse us of attacking our queen if we did not even know who she is?"

Ambrose smiled grimly. "You have made a valid point, which I really cannot refute. I'll tell you what - I will drop the charge of attacking a member of the royal family."

The man smiled at his two companions. "You see, there is mercy and justice here."

Ambrose interrupted. "So you will only be hung for the single crime of outlawry. Are you prepared to meet your Maker?"

The silence and the downcast eyes signaled the answer.

"I now therefore sentence you to death by hanging. My Queen, do you wish to hear an appeal on this matter?"

Ealhswith looked hard at each prisoner, in turn. "These men intended to ruthlessly kill innocent travelers in order to save their miserable lives. If they live, they will have the power to betray their queen, and endanger my entire family. Galar, please take these men away and carry out the sentence."

"With pleasure, my Queen."

The Saxon woodsmen trotted ahead of the little party. Behind them came the cavalcade of women and children, escorted by a small blond man and a dark foreigner. The thirty thanes had been sent off with another runner to a small vill, where they would rest and be billeted.

Each of the small forest vills surrounding the tun chosen by Alfred for his winter stay was receiving similar small garrisons. Ethelnoth had called in several hundred men to provide a protective perimeter. As far as most knew, they were there for the defense of their ealdorman. Alfred's thanes knew the truth, but were sworn to secrecy.

Even reinforced as they were, however, everyone knew that their primitive defenses would do little to stop or dissuade Guthrum's Viking army if it happened to ride their way.

The woodsmen took the party along little-known paths. At intervals they were forced to stop and converse with sentries who materialized beside the trail.

Ambrose saw no sign of armed men who could have stopped them, but he was sure that the men were there. He assumed the fact that they didn't see them was evidence that they had passed inspection. His two faithful guides had assured him that the woods were alive with Ethelnoth's watchers.

ᚠ

The little party emerged from particularly dense woods. Suddenly they were surrounded by what would be, in summer, pastures and fields. Not far away, in the middle of the clearing, was a small tun. The tun was surrounded by a crude wooden palisade, and the number of columns of smoke that climbed into the air indicated that it was made up of no more than thirty or forty separate dwellings.

Even the horses picked up their pace. They sensed warmth and companionship.

Ambrose rode next to Polonius. "Well, old friend, are you ready for some food and drink?"

"First, Prince, I want to find a roaring fire! My body is numb from the Arctic cold of your lovely land!"

"Polonius! How can a veteran of a Novgorod winter complain of our mild winter?"

"It is easy, Ambrose. I was cold there, too!"

"Scholar, I see no welcome ahead. Do you think they know we are coming?"

"Look in the snow at your feet, Prince."

"All I see are footprints."

"And are they far apart or close together?"

"I would say very far apart, unless the man is a giant."

"Then they know we are coming, Prince. A woodsman has already reported our arrival."

Even as Polonius spoke, the gates swung open, and a column of armed and mounted men burst forth.

Ambrose turned to Polonius in sudden anxiety. "I hope that these are our friends. They come in a wild gallop!"

Three men quickly outpaced their heavily armored companions. All three wore warm capes that swirled around them, but one was a giant of a man. The first man brought his horse to a shuddering halt directly in the path of the little group, but the second vaulted from his horse and ran forward. He grabbed Ealhswith from her horse, and swung her around him in a great circle. At last he held her tight, still with her feet far off the ground. He held her and kissed her long and hard.

The eldest boy shrieked and yelled, "Daddy! Daddy!" His sisters joined in the din, until all were swept from their saddles and swung around in the air by their father, the king of Wessex.

The third man clambered down from his oversized mount, and went over to greet his sharp-tongued wife and his three children. Phillip hugged Matilda tight.

Ethelnoth slowly dismounted, as well, and waited quietly until Alfred finished greeting his family. At last, Ealhswith noticed the tall ealdorman, and went over to him.

"Greetings, Ethelnoth. It is good to see you again!"

"Welcome to Selwood Forest, my Queen! It is an honor and a privilege to have you here."

"For the first time in days, Ethelnoth, I feel safe again."

"My people will defend you with every breath of their bodies, Queen."

"I saw the watchers as we passed through the forest."

"I do not have the stone walls to protect you, Your Majesty, but I have the forest. Every trail is watched. Every stranger is turned away. Thousands of people watch for any sign of danger. I pray that it is enough."

"I thank you for all that you have already done to protect my husband, Ethelnoth."

"Come, Mistress. That is the name by which your husband wishes you to be known to my people. Let me get you and the children to a fire! You must be frozen."

CHAPTER 12

A Spy is Caught

Thane Aldwin approached his king as Alfred and Ethelnoth were exercising within the palisade. "A moment please, Sire?"

"Yes, what is it?"

"Sire . . ."

"Master. Here, I am but 'master.'"

Aldwin looked chagrined. "I am sorry, Master. We have caught a man skulking in the forest."

"Is he known to anyone?"

"No, Master."

"Does he have a good reason for being in the forest?"

"He says it is his right to travel where he pleases. He claims to be a scop."

"Was he warned that the forest is closed, on penalty of death?"

"I can send for Toft, the blacksmith's son over in Smithy's Tun. Just two days ago, he reported a foreigner asking how to find Ealdorman Ethelnoth. Toft swears that he told the stranger that the forest was closed, and the penalty for trespassing was death. Would you like me to send for Toft, Master?"

Ambrose replied. "Don't send for him yet. Let's meet this stranger first. Send in Prince Ambrose, and then have the man brought before me. He is not to know my real identity. Ethelnoth, would you please take the Seat-of-Honor?"

"Aye, Master," responded Alwin, heading for the door.

Ethelnoth echoed the answer. "Yes, Master."

Two burly churls dragged the stranger into the room on the heels of Ambrose. His arms were tied behind him. A third churl followed through the doorway, carrying an untidy pile of clothing and equipment. Ambrose and Alfred stood some distance away, saying nothing.

Alfred ignored the man, who was now held upright by the two Saxon guards. Instead, the king walked over to the pile of equipment that the third guard had tossed on to the trestle table. He poked through the packs, finally extracting a sword, along with a small harp.

Alfred turned to face first Ethelnoth, and then the captive.

"Ealdorman, this is an odd combination of tools for a scop. What have you to say, stranger?"

The man spoke for the first time, in an accent that Alfred could not quite place. "I am a man of peace, Lord, but the land is full of brigands, and even a peaceful man must be prepared to defend himself."

Alfred spoke again. "Untie his hands . . . Good. Stranger, hold out your hands toward me . . . now turn your hands over."

The man looked puzzled, but did as he was bid. Alfred carefully examined each finger of both hands, and both palms. The man, resigned, allowed the stranger to have his way. The churls who stood at each side were a hint that he actually had little choice. At last Alfred was done. He spoke to the man.

"I can see the calluses derived from the playing of the harp. I also see, however, the calluses of a fighting man. Why would a scop have the calluses of a swordsman? Think carefully before you answer. A lie could cost you your life."

"Lord, I sing for a living. I will defend myself if necessary, and, yes, I have joined fighting bands when times are hard and people parsimonious."

"I see. And were you not warned when you entered this shire that the Ealdorman Ethelnoth had closed the forest to travel?"

"Since when did a traveling singer listen to the prattling of minor officials? The entire world puts up obstacles to prevent people from doing what they want. Of course I was told that Ealdorman Ethelnoth had closed Selwood Forest to travelers. But I am not a traveler; I am a scop! If you doubt my word, bring me my harp or a holy bible so that I may swear a sacred oath in the presence of a consecrated priest!"

"Who in this land will step forth in your name for compurgation? Who will swear that you are an innocent minstrel?"

"I know not, Lord! I am a stranger to this land, having come just last year from Saxony. There are probably none here who can vouch for me."

"Stranger, why were you discovered far off the trail; in dense woods?"

"Honored sir, I was but performing a natural act that all, king and slave, must perform daily."

"And are you so modest that you must scramble so deep into the forest for a simple act of nature?"

"I confess, sir, that I did not know the location of the next village, and I was intending to have a nap."

"Why, pray tell, would you nap so far off the beaten track?"

The man started to sweat profusely, yet he argued valiantly. "That be simple, sir. Would you sleep openly on the road where any passing traveler could rob or harm you?"

Ealdorman Ethelnoth spoke. "A good answer, stranger. And I have a question for you."

"Ask, good sir, and I will answer honestly."

"Why is it that, although you were seen several days ago on the old Roman road, yet you were not seen by any of the people of the vills which you seemed to have magically bypassed? Would not a scop want to stop and entertain the very people who would feed him and provide him shelter?"

The man began to wilt. Perspiration poured down his brow. Ethelnoth turned to the tall stranger who stood near the prisoner.

"Well, Master! And what do you think we should do with a man who would wilfully flout my lawful instructions?"

"Ealdorman, it is never an easy task to order the death of a man. Yet in our code of laws promulgated by that great ruler of Wessex, King Ine, it states clearly that, "If anyone within the boundaries of our kingdom goes through the wood off the track, and does not shout or blow a horn, he is to be assumed to be a thief, to be either killed, or redeemed."

If I caught such a man in forbidden territory, who could not be vouched for, and who spoke with a Danish accent, I suspect that I would feel obliged to apply the full force of the law. If he is a Viking spy, then good riddance. If he is a devout Christian, well, he has had the opportunity to escape this mortal earth, and his next memories will be to awaken to join sweet Jesus walking on Earth. If but one successful spy returns to Guthrum's side, then Wessex could be lost!"

Ealdorman Ethelnoth looked down from his Seat-of-Honor. "I defer to Ine's commandment, young Master. The man was duly warned. Better a hundred innocent minstrels hang, than Alfred's location is ferreted out and reported to the Northmen.

Guards! Take this man away. Find a stout oak and hang him."

CHAPTER 13

"And in the winter of this same year the brother of Ivar and Halfdan landed in Wessex, in Devonshire, with three and twenty ships, and there was he slain, and eight hundred men with him."

The flames climbed high into the rapidly darkening sky. Far to the west, and also to the east, plumes of smoke rose in response. While lookouts stood at their pyres, other sentries whipped their horses madly as they galloped to the tuns or burhs where their people lived.

Twenty-three raven-sails had been spotted closing on the coast, and for the West Saxons of the North Devon coast, that was a sighting of great import. Within minutes, half a hundred beacon fires had been lit both up and down the coast, and a hundred men ran or rode to warn of impending danger or to man coastal observation points. Within hours, entire coastal villages were on the move, and, farther inland, militia contingents were marching to predetermined assembly points.

Somewhere to the east, King Guthrum and his Danes ruthlessly pillaged the Wiltshire countryside. King Alfred hid somewhere, like a hunted stag, and now another entire army was landing on the northern coast!

Even as the signal fires leapt to life, the crews of the twenty-three long-ships dropped their sails and manned the oars. The coast was dangerous, and the winds contrary.

The army of Ubbi rowed its way into the little harbor he had chosen for his landing site. The Vikings had timed their landing carefully. The sun set, but a brilliant full moon cast light on the beaches as more than twelve hundred Danes splashed ashore. There was no resistance. The villagers had fled inland, taking their herds of cows and flocks of sheep with them.

A few pigs which had escaped the roundup squealed in protest as the heavily armed warriors took possession of the village. A line of pickets spread out, prepared for a surprise attack from the forest, but none came. All the Saxon warriors within two day's walk were, at that moment, collecting their arms and preparing for a morning march, but there were, as yet, no forces capable of contesting the landing. The powerful army of the West Saxons had been sent home weeks before, after Guthrum the

Dane had solemnly pledged to take his raiders north into Mercia.

With the dawn, small bands of Viking foragers spread out in various directions, while the majority remained behind to fortify the little coastal village. High on the foragers' list were horses. Once the host had stolen adequate food supplies and was mounted, the men intended to ride swiftly eastward. Somewhere between them and King Guthrum was Alfred, with only the remnants of his Personal Guard and some local fyrdmen to protect him.

Ubbi smiled as he personally led a strong force due south. Once he and Guthrum crushed Alfred's pathetic forces between them, and performed the *Blood Eagle* on the man's body, the last major obstacle to the Viking conquest of all Britain would lie dead in the snow.

中

Ealdorman Odda stamped angrily through his Great Hall. His retinue of thanes cast their eyes down when he glared at them.

"You mean to tell me that no one met them on the beach!? Twenty-three shiploads of Vikings sail into one of my harbors, and not one of you morons sent men to at least harass them as they landed?"

Thane Axton, an old friend and confidant, was more willing than his comrades to face his master's wrath. He finally spoke up.

'Ealdorman, the men felt their job was to get the livestock and their families out of reach. As you commanded, they particularly made sure to remove the horses and as much food as they could. They only had an hour's notice, yet they managed to strip the village of most of the foodstuffs. The Vikings will have gone to bed hungry, if they were counting on eating Saxon food!"

"I am not unhappy about that! If the devils can steal enough horses to form a mounted band, they will be able to move much more quickly against our tuns, and, eventually, Alfred himself. That I want to avoid at all costs, but once the women, children and livestock were out of the way, I expected my thanes to mount up a strike force and ride back to ambush and harass! And I expect every surrounding village to send its full quota of men to help out. Only in this way can we stop the heathen devils!"

"Master, the men wanted to stay and protect their families, in case the Vikings moved their way."

"Do you mean that you were too afraid to obey my command, or that your men refused to obey you?" It was a dangerous question to answer, and the gathered thanes quietly admired the fresh rushes at their feet. Of them all, only Axton, a grizzled warrior of unquestionable loyalty and bravery, dared try again.

"Ealdorman, men gather even as we speak. The villages not threatened have sent us their finest young men. The Saxon host gathers, as you have commanded."

"All right! Tell the thanes of the threatened villages they can keep their men at home. But I want strong contingents from everyone else! These Viking devils will not march through my territory unopposed! Alfred has enough trouble in the east. He does not need these heathens breathing down his neck!"

"Ealdorman, by dawn, we should have more than sixty thanes and maybe eight hundred churls ready to march!"

"Send messengers to all of our burhs and tuns! I want triple that number!"

"Ealdorman, we are only entitled to one man per five hides of land. That is the condition by which the men hold the land."

"I am well aware of the law! Without a sufficient strike force to threaten the Vikings with, no holding is safe. Damn the terms! Tell the thanes that, for all our sakes, I need everyone who can hold a spear!

You say the Vikings were flying a banner with a single raven?"

"Yes, Ealdorman."

"Then it is probably the God-cursed Ubbi and his pirates. If so, we are going up against veteran warriors who have previously fought their way across our island, and have this very fall been pillaging southern Wales!

Twenty-three boats may have landed upwards of a thousand warriors. I want more than a thousand fyrdmen at my back before I march against the *spawn of Ragnar Lodbrok* and his ilk!"

༃

Ubbi questioned the messenger a second time, until he had extracted all the information the man carried.

"Yes, Jarl! We were just returning from the raid on the village when hundreds of mounted Saxons attacked us!"

"Exactly how many of them were there?"

"I do not know, Jarl! Our main body formed up around the supply train, and the rest moved back as a rearguard. I was in the vanguard. When Jarl Farulf saw the riders sweeping down on us, he ordered me to ride with all haste to let you know of the attack!"

"Next time, at least wait long enough to find out what we are facing! Korni! Take four hundred men south at double time. The raiding party is under attack! And Korni, before you leave, just in case it is all a feint, tell the rest of the men to prepare for a possible attack on the town. At last, the elusive Saxons appear. May Loki be visiting the Christians today!

Odda, from the hill overlooking the valley where his men had ambushed the Viking convoy, ordered his second rank, the infantry, to follow the mounted warriors down the hill. Shrieking war cries that were as wild as the Celtic tribesmen of Wales, the line of warriors hurtled toward the enemy.

The first wave of mounted men had leapt off their horses and charged at the surprised Vikings. While the Danes were reeling from this attack, hundreds of running men hit as one. The Viking line broke under the intense pressure, but the men did not panic. Some stood stubbornly and resisted to the end. Most of the men, however, ran for the line on the other side of the wagons. Slipping through, they proceeded to form a new outer wall of shields there.

The Vikings were expert warriors, and the difficult manoeuver was made smoothly. The Saxons followed eagerly, and intense hand-to-hand combat ensued. While a triple row of Saxons pressed the attack home, the rest looted the supply wagons, taking back the stores that the Vikings had gleaned from the empty villages.

Mounted scouts, riding exhausted horses, soon arrived panting to Odda's side. "Ealdorman Odda! A large body of Viking infantry is coming up the road at double time!"

"How many?"

"More than I had time to count, Ealdorman! Enough that we should worry."

Odda balled his fist in anger. "Damnation! With the loot and so many infantry, we could be caught with our pants down. Signaler! Sound the recall. God damn those parsimonious thanes who refused to send all their fighting men! We have to retreat when we should be overwhelming their main base!

Commanders! To me! Listen up! I want you to take the supplies we have captured and head east to the old fort at *Cynwith*. Our scouts report a large Viking force coming our way!"

Thane Axton spoke up. "Ealdorman, let us first finish off the heathen bastards here, first!"

"Look at them! They are veterans. We outnumber them four to one, but they coolly re-form their skjaldborg."

"Skjaldborg?"

"What they call their shield-wall formation. We are losing several warriors for every one of them we kill. We have their wagons and supplies. It is enough. Now start the men moving before we are caught in the open by the new force!"

Ealdorman Odda and his thousand men retreated to the ancient and ruined fortress that had sat on top of Cynwith for countless generations. The dry moat was not yet completely filled in, and the old stone and dirt walls, though dilapidated, were still capable of providing shelter to a besieged force.

Odda knew that the Vikings would have to pay dearly to overwhelm the Saxon force sheltered there. Even better, he knew that the Viking commander would be very reluctant to march on and leave such a strong enemy position to his rear, especially near to where his fleet was sheltered. Time was on the side of the Saxons. Every delay to the Viking force meant that the ealdorman had more time to raise more fyrdmen. The Saxon forces would only grow, but any Viking losses could not be replaced. The old man knew that Alfred was right. They must kill, even if it cost them two or three dead for every Viking dispatched. Eventually the Viking army would be bled dry.

꙰

Ubbi sat his horse and gazed upwards at the imposing ruins at the top of the hill. He turned to his commanders.

"The Saxons appear to be afraid to meet us in open battle. So be it! Send messengers to bring up the rest of our army. Korni, make sure that an adequate force remains that our fleet will be properly protected while we move east. If this is the best force that the Saxons can throw together to face us, then we have already won this land!"

The small band of mounted Vikings rode around and around the perimeter of the hill, looking for weaknesses in the old fortress. The infantry, by far the majority of the Viking army, chose various strong points and settled in.

A few Saxon arrows, and many jeers flew at them, but no overt hostile moves were made. There was no way the Saxons were going to abandon their fort in the face of Ubbi's Vikings.

꙰

Odda, famous for his hot temper, was furious once again.

"By Jesus' holy robe! What the hell do you mean that we have no water?! You told me that there was a spring within this fort!"

"Ealdorman, I did. There is. I did not know that it was dry!"

"You dolt! We are besieged, with more than a thousand thirsty men, and several hundred horses that the God-cursed Vikings are desperate for, and we have no water!

Your stupidity is going to cost us all our lives! Look over the walls. The Vikings are encircling us, and don't think for a moment that Ubbi has not sent for the rest of his men. Only we stand between him and our helpless King Alfred!'

Ealdorman Odda sighed. 'Tell the men to gather as much snow as they can. There is little enough on the ground, but it might buy us a few more days."

The contingents of armored men linked shields and slowly advanced up the hill. When the first arrows fell on them, they just raised their shields higher and plodded stoically forward. Strong columns of warriors marched separately, partially screened by the skjaldborg line.

Odda and his commanders watched the enemy approach with great interest, walking the length of the ruined walls to keep the columns in sight.

At last, the grizzled old ealdorman turned to his friend and chief thane. "Axton, what do you make of it?"

"I think, Ealdorman, that the devils are just probing our defenses. If they find a weakness, however, I have no doubt that Ubbi would ruthlessly throw a strong strike force at that weak point, perhaps while the rest run toward another wall to distract us."

"I think you are right, old friend. We must be ready. Once the Vikings breach the walls, we are done."

"Ealdorman, without water, we will soon enough be forced to surrender anyway. Already the men have drained the last of the supply, and we will have to order all of the horses killed before another day passes."

"Are they that far gone?"

"The weakest among them is suffering from thirst. More important, you know they must not fall into Viking hands. Ubbi's warriors mounted would be a catastrophe for King Alfred and the whole kingdom."

Odda turned. "You are right, my friend. If the Vikings make it over that wall, I want all of the horses killed! These devil's spawn can only harm Alfred if they obtain sufficient horses to mount most of their warriors. They will not be using ours!"

"Do you want me to send a squad of men to be ready to help the horse handlers, just in case?"

"Do it, and don't stint on the number of men you send. It is a high priority."

"Ealdorman, should I just tell the horse handlers to start now?"

"Not yet, but have the men ready . . . Hold it! The Vikings are up to something!"

As the ealdorman spoke, a phalanx of infantry burst through the skjaldborg, the Viking shield-wall screen. The solid column, several hundred strong, ran for the point where the ditch was mostly filled in and the walls had crumpled.

Axton spoke. "They are going for where the wall is lowest."

Odda smiled. "I told you that would be their first choice. Ubbi spotted it right away."

"So what are we going to do about it?"

"Did you send most of our archers, and all of our spare infantry there, as I instructed you, earlier?"

Axton smiled in return. "Of course, Ealdorman. Those were your orders."

"Excellent. Make sure the horse handlers have all the assistants they might need, and then let's join our men!"

The Vikings threw themselves into the ditch and scrambled up the crumbling stone walls. To their surprise, there was little opposition. Ten, and then a hundred of the bravest Vikings neared the top of the wall.

The Saxon infantry, out of sight behind the wall, stood in a neat line. On command, they threw their spears in unison.

Some of the attackers were able to get their shields up in time, but many of the Vikings were struck by the volley. The infantry line instantly threw itself flat onto the frozen ground, and the lines of archers behind them let fly.

The shields and bodies of the attackers absorbed hundreds of arrows. When the archers had shot their six allotted arrows, a horn sounded. The infantry stood, and, drawing their swords or axes, they charged.

The Vikings were brave men, but they had had enough. Without any commands, the men broke and fled.

Axton watched in relief, and spoke to the gruff ealdorman who was his master. "A victory for you, Ealdorman!"

"We won a skirmish, Axton, not the battle. If the God-cursed Vikings had been truly serious, they would just have accepted their losses and kept coming. We only have a finite number of spears and arrows, and, eventually, they could have cut their way through our line."

"Well, at least we taught the Vikings to respect the Saxons as fighters, Ealdorman. The irony is, however, that if the God-cursed Danes would just sit outside our walls for another day or two, they would win at no cost to themselves."

⚑

Ubbi watched in anger as his men fell back. He had thought for a few hundred heart-beats that the preliminary probe might actually take the fort, but the shrunken numbers that now returned angered him. He knew that the Saxons could eventually replace any fallen. His reinforcements were far away, however, in Ireland or northern Britain. If his numbers fell below a critical mass, he was in deep trouble.

⚑

Odda looked down on the sprawling Viking encampment. He tried to count the number of tents and multiply according to their size. He wasn't sure yet how many Vikings faced him, but he estimated that it was at least fifteen hundred. Against that, he had less than a thousand men left standing on their feet. The snow was long gone, and, within another two days, his men would be dying of thirst.

He was already steeling himself to order the slaughter of the faithful horses. His men would drink their blood, but it would be salty, and wouldn't much help. He noticed several sharp-eyed Viking scouts watching him from outside the walls, and he suddenly had an idea.

He shouted for his faithful lieutenant. "Axton!"

"Yes, Ealdorman?"

"Where is that last wagon-load of mead that we took from the Vikings?"

"Under guard, as you ordered. Tomorrow we will distribute its contents. After that, we will have nothing at all left to drink."

"Excellent! I want you to take a detail and move it to the area where the old stone wall has collapsed and the ditch is filled in. Make sure that the wagon is outside of the inner perimeter wall that we are using for defense. I want a strong detail of archers on the inner wall, but I want them well hidden."

Axton knew the exact place. At the point Odda had referred to, time and gravity had so battered the crumbling defenses that the Saxons had abandoned that portion of the outer wall in favor of having the men laboriously pile up a new, inner wall of rubble on the rise just above.

Although the indicated spot was within the outer perimeter of the ancient fortification, it was terribly exposed, and only a small screen of guards was kept there. In the event of an attack, they were expected to retreat to the much stronger wall they had so recently built with their own hands.

The faithful lieutenant was confused. "Ealdorman, if the Vikings see the wagon there, we may not be able to keep them away from it!"

"Then move the wagon in the daylight, so that they will be sure to see it."

"Master, without that liquid, we will soon die."

"There is enough mead there to slake our thirst for only another day or two. After that, we die anyway!"

"But what good will it do us to give it to the Vikings?"

"First, I expect that you will make it very costly for them to take it, and if we must sally out of here within a day or two, what condition would you prefer they be in when we attack?"

"Ah. Why, drunk enough that they can't raise their sword arms to defend themselves."

"So, move the damned wagon."

Axton grinned suddenly. "Yes, Ealdorman!"

The wagon was mostly hidden by the low and crumbled wall, but Odda watched carefully, and he saw alert scouts observing. He smiled when he saw them moving off toward the raven banner that undoubtedly marked the tent of Ubbi, commander of the Viking force.

⚑

The attack, when it came, was well executed. The sun was setting over the cold land when a strong body of unarmored men ran forward from hiding, carrying only large shields. Wearing no armor, they had not made any noise approaching, and the Saxons were caught off-guard, even though they had been expecting an attack all afternoon.

The token Saxon defenders took to their feet and ran for the inner wall, while the strong force of waiting archers ran to the higher rubble wall and started pouring a shower of arrows into the running Vikings. The northerners were protected by their shields, however, and a counter-line of Viking archers ran out and let fly their shafts from behind the ancient crumpled rampart.

The Saxons managed to kill or wound a good portion of the attackers, but they, too, started taking casualties. More and more Viking archers appeared, to cover the attack. One by one, the barrels were removed from the wagons and rolled away, in spite of everything that the Saxons threw at the enemy. Amidst Viking jeers, the last of the kegs finally disappeared over the ruins of the ancient wall, and down the hill.

There was great merriment in the Viking camp that night. Large fires roared, as, unlike the besieged Saxon force, the Vikings had unlimited firewood. The Danes happily spent the evening toasting the Saxons with the good Devon mead.

Odda, with his throat so dry that he was barely able to force down any food, yet listened with satisfaction. Then he went to meet with his commanders. They had a lot to do, and little time left.

Each cold and thirsty warrior woke up his neighbor with a silent shake. The first light of day was just beginning to streak the eastern sky, and the Saxons were finally ready to fight. The men, still numb from cold, wrapped all their metal accouterments in rags. Then, still without more than the occasional whispered word, the men formed up by the main gate.

Odda had ordered sixty archers and forty of his finest fighting thanes to form a wedge behind him. The men, proud that they had been so chosen, took their place silently. They had practiced forming up in the daylight, so each knew his exact place even in the dim pre-dawn light.

Odda climbed to the hilltop battlements one last time to look down on the enemy camp below. The roaring Viking fires of the evening before had sunk down into glowing embers, and the camp still slept. The cold, and the copious quantities of mead imbibed by the Vikings, helped them slumber soundly.

Directly below, not moving in the dawn stillness, hung the raven banner that was a source of dread from Ireland to Italy. The Vikings, secure in their superior numbers, had not even bothered to erect a barrier against the besieged Saxons.

Odda smiled suddenly in the pre-dawn light. He was about to show Ubbi that he had underestimated the men of Devon. Odda climbed down, out of sight of the Viking camp, and then waved the torch Axton held ready.

Over three separate low spots in the battlements, lines of warriors clambered down rope ladders. Once the three groups were clear of the dry moat, the main gates squealed open, and the entire horse herd was driven out with whips and fire. On the heels of the terrified animals came the main force of Saxons.

The Viking war horns started calling the men to arms, but the thunder of the hooves almost drowned them out. The terrified horses knocked over tents and trampled on sleeping warriors. Scant seconds after the horses, the screaming Saxons arrived.

The Vikings were veterans, however, and, drunk or sober, they kept their weapons close at hand. Isolated clusters formed together, and then sidled toward others, so that their formations grew, even while screaming Saxons hurled themselves at them.

Odda's compact column pushed itself ruthlessly through the disorganized mobs, heading unerringly toward the raven banner. When the knots of enemy warriors slowed them, Odda paused only long enough to have the archers fire volleys that broke up any incipient opposition.

Before the Vikings could recover from the fusillade of feathered shafts, the battle-hardened thanes cut through them. Thus, while most Saxons fought in individual combat, Odda's force penetrated all the way to Ubbi's tent.

Ubbi stood at his doorway, in his magnificent burnished armor. Large and intricately decorated gold armlets encircled both his wrists and his neck supported a massive *torque* of the same metal. The gold flashed in the early morning light, as if daring any Saxon foolish enough to come and try to take it.

Ubbi was surrounded by his faithful commanders, who had drank the night through with him, and then had lain in drunken stupor on the floor of his luxurious tent. They were awake now, however, and angry; looking around and trying to make sense of what was happening.

Odda cried "For God and for Devon!", and charged head on. The cry was picked up by his fighting thanes, and then the two groups collided. Even the archers threw away their bows and drew their swords or battleaxes. They had suffered much at the hands of the God-cursed Vikings, and for once they had the opportunity to strike back.

Odda tried to move diagonally toward the enemy commander, but both Saxons and Vikings were in the way. He did briefly see Ubbi cut down two thanes in as many strokes, and then he was forced to fight desperately to save his own life. A blond giant in chain-mail armor swung a huge battleaxe at his head. He ducked, and then cut at the Viking's unprotected legs.

Suddenly the Vikings cried out in rage and anger. It had been a long time since the Saxons and Danes had lived in close proximity on the continent, but Odda could easily enough understand the cry. He knew, then, that Ubbi, the scourge of both Europe and England, had at last fallen!

With the commander's death, much of the stubborn will went out of the Vikings. They had no intention of being slaughtered, however, so they continued to try and coalesce into a fighting unit. Once the majority of the survivors managed to gather, the enemy force started a fighting retreat toward the little town to the west where they had beached their ships.

Odda's force continued to cut down wounded and stragglers, but the ealdorman called his men back when they started to break formation to pursue the retreating foe. Axton, covered in blood and clutching a broken sword, yet reproached his master.

"Ealdorman, they escape! If we hurry, we may yet massacre the lot!"

"Nay, good Axton! Look about you! There must be over eight

hundred of the bastards all prepared for *Asgard*. I think we have given their *Valkyries* enough work for today. We too, have suffered greatly. We will camp here tonight, treat our wounded, and then follow in the morning, on horseback."

"But Ealdorman!"

"Fear not. As soon as you can catch an adequate number of our horses, you can send out a force of mounted warriors to harry if you wish. We have stopped them cold, even if we are not able to stop the remnants from reaching their ships. They are no longer a threat to either Devon or Alfred. And look, my friend!"

With that he pointed to the flag pole that stood beside Ubbi's tent. There, flapping gently in the cold early morning breeze, was the dreaded raven banner, left behind by the fleeing Vikings. Odda and Axton, followed by a retinue of lesser thanes, walked toward the beckoning banner. Theirs was a great victory, and a trove of gold or documents would make the victory even sweeter.

The messenger and his well-armed escort mounted up and kicked their horses into a gallop. They knew not where they rode, but they knew that their king was somewhere to the east, and Odda, Ealdorman of Devon, had given them strict instructions. They were not welcome back in the arms of their families until they found their king and reported directly to him.

In a leather pouch, the messenger carried both secret documents and news of Odda's great victory over Ubbi. The Viking leader's personal jewelry and a pass demanding all loyal subjects provide the men with both fresh horses and supplies, completed the contents.

The messenger did not know that what he carried might change the course of the war, but he well understood his master's imprecations to hurry. The riders rode for the fastness of Selwood Forest, where they hoped to find their sovereign.

CHAPTER 14

The Puzzle

"Polonius, we are missing something here. There must be another piece to the puzzle."

"How so, King Alfred?"

"Let's think this through logically. We corner Guthrum and he comes to terms with us. He then sneaks past us in the night.

Again we ride after him, and again we corner him with an overwhelming host, at Exeter. For the second time, he agrees to terms; this time offering us more hostages, but also giving us his most solemn oath. He marches north to Mercia, and we order the army to stand down for the winter."

Polonius spoke. "Pray continue, my King."

"Well, several months ago we had an army that was more than he could handle. He twice backed down from a final confrontation."

"So far your logic would satisfy even the most disputatious Greek philosopher, Sire."

"But now, a few months later, he returns. From the little we saw at Chippenham, his host is considerably smaller than when we last faced him. What is different? Why would he break his most solemn oath and sacrifice the lives of his hostages to attack us with only a portion of the force that he had before us just months ago?"

Polonius spoke again. "With all due respect, Sire, may I point out two things?"

"Speak, Wizard. I was rather hoping that you might."

"Thank you, Sire. One. You do not at present have an army. It went home for the winter. Thus you are not the danger you were just a few short weeks ago."

"True, Polonius, but he knows that in the spring the army will re-form again. And if he defeats that army, we could probably raise another one, and perhaps another after that. We are, after all, the only nation in all of Britain that has consistently defeated the Viking hosts."

"True again, Master. Which brings me to point number two."

"Speak, Polonius. I listen."

"Thank you, Sire. Point number two is you!"

"Me! I fear I cannot follow the Byzantine convolutions of your thought. You will help a simple Saxon king out by explaining further."

Polonius smiled. "As you command, Sire. Point two is actually quite simple. You are a national symbol, and at your command various forces of Angles, Saxons, Jutes, Britons, and even Celts of Cornwall abandon their families and farms and march to battle. They have little in common and often do not much like each other. They march because of you."

"They march because they have sworn a holy oath to obey their lawful king, and that is the condition by which they hold title to their land."

"It may be true, Sire, that the threat of losing their land may bring them to your side. But that does not explain why they hold when heavily pressed. It does not explain why they do not disappear in the night when facing a formidable enemy."

"Polonius, they stand because they are proud men, and they have an obligation to me, their rightful king."

"With respect, Sire, that is not completely true. Many still feel that their rightful kings are in exile or were killed. And if I had to choose between respecting an oath or abandoning my family in its time of need, well, I'm sure that it wouldn't be hard to find an excuse why I could not join this year's gathering of the fyrd.

Sire, they march because of you. You have proven to be a great commander, who generally brings victories. For this reason only will they abandon their home shires and march to battle, far away from their loved ones."

"I accept the compliment, Polonius. But I don't see what that has to do with Guthrum suddenly deciding that he can beat the very army he retreated from, just months before."

"Majesty, what would have happened if Guthrum had caught you at Chippenham?"

"I would be dead. The Witan would meet, and another atheling would be chosen as the new king."

"And who else would have the prestige and the experience to successfully call up and lead the powerful but disparate forces that make up the West Saxon army?"

"The most likely candidate on my list would be Ambrose. He is a legend in our land. I am king, but I am not blind to the fact that I owe much of my success to the two of you."

"You are very kind, Sire. And I agree that Ambrose might be one of the very few athelings who would be able to fill your boots, but he is almost always at your side. What if he, too, had been taken at Chippenham?"

"Then, Polonius, they would choose another. It has been the way of our people for countless generations."

"And if the ealdormen do not have the same degree of confidence in the new leader that they have in you two, will they risk all by sending their forces out of their home shires?"

King Alfred hesitated for a moment before he spoke. "And if they do not, then, like an individual twig, they will easily snap before the Danish host. The only hope of victory is to gather an overwhelming host; more than any single shire could field. That was a lesson you taught me many years ago, with a handful of straw.

I have subsequently seen it repeated many times more recently, in the short sightedness of the ealdormen of the northern kingdoms of Britain. None were solidly united, and all fell."

"I am gratified you remember, Sire. So the difference seems to be that Guthrum saw an opportunity and tried with a version of our own Long Ride, to capture possibly the only two people in the entire kingdom who would be capable of gathering enough loyal forces to defeat him."

"But it was sheer chance that he almost caught us at Chippenham. In a few days we could just as easily have been at any of a dozen different royal burhs."

"Make no mistake, King. Guthrum is no fool. I have no doubt that he has informants and spies amongst us all the time. We certainly know of Sitric's scouting of your lands in the past. It is the ones that I do not know about that worry me the most."

"I can accept your premise, Polonius, but I wonder that Guthrum would risk so much on a single throw of the *bones*. If he missed catching us, then he knows he will be soundly thrashed come spring."

"And if he did catch you, he has possibly won a war without fighting a single major battle. Further, if I was Guthrum, I would have loaded the bones in my favor."

"Ah, now we get to the meat of the matter. And how would you do that, my friend?"

"I would look for allies to join me, preferably before the Wessex fyrd could be reconstituted. Alternatively, or probably as well, I would attempt to sow discontent amongst your various shires.

If I could sway several of your ealdormen, or even just make them insecure enough that they refuse to leave their home shires, then your national army is crushed before it can even be called up."

"Polonius, you put into words thoughts that have troubled me greatly, and yet they must be said, or I am blind and foolish. Let us take those two thoughts one at a time. You suggested Guthrum might have allies. Who were you thinking of?"

"Sire, our own spy reports indicated that many of the Danes who rode north last fall really did plan to settle in Mercia. They have been at war for many years, and I think that some of the Danes just want to settle down. It is possible, of course, that some of these warriors will come south when they hear of Guthrum's success. Yet even with those late-arrivers, Guthrum would not be as strong as he was last summer.

Halfdan has a powerful army at his command, but the last reports indicate that he is presently parceling Northumbria out to his men. He is far away, and his forces are busy. I would be more anxious about his brother Ubbi. He was last reported wintering in southern Wales with a strong force and a fleet."

"If he sailed when Guthrum rode, then we could easily have been trapped between two enemy forces!"

"Sire, we may still be. If Guthrum sweeps westward, and Ubbi lands in the west and sweeps east, then we could be trapped now."

"With this hypothetical force coming from the west, Guthrum would have a real chance of capturing or killing both Ambrose and me!"

"Yes, Sire, even if he misses you at Chippenham. And make no mistake. With both you and Ambrose out of the way, Wessex would fall."

"And if he could influence several of my ealdormen to send him men, or even to just stay out of any fight . . ."

"The Danes are guaranteed victory!"

"Polonius, what you say makes sense. Obviously I must stay out of sight for some time to come; until we know what Guthrum is up to."

"That would be a wise precaution, Sire. We do not currently have sufficient men to protect you if the enemy finds you. Even if Ealdorman Ethelnoth raised the entire shire, we would be fighting with unprepared and semi-trained men; against professionals. The outcome would be unclear without a much larger core of experienced thanes. With the limited forces at our immediate disposal, you have no chance."

"Polonius, my friend, I hope that you enjoy living in the forest. I fear that we are here for some time yet."

Alfred spoke. "Ambrose, find Polonius and Phillip, and join me in my Command hut as soon as possible!"

Ambrose ran to find his friends. Alfred had looked grimly serious, and that worried his brother. A messenger from Ealdorman Odda had been brought blindfolded into the village late the night before. He wondered what news the man had brought.

He found his two friends resting in their hut, and the three rushed directly to the daub and wattle hut that masqueraded as the king's royal residence and command center. They found their king pacing restlessly, in front of the trestle table that was normally set up only at meal time.

On it were spread large parchment maps of all Southern Angleland. A leather pouch lay on top of the map, and around it were scattered several letters.

By the way the king glanced at the papers, Ambrose was sure that they were the cause of his disquiet. Whatever they reported, it was clearly both important and upsetting. No one else, not even the normal king's thanes who acted as messengers and guards, were present. Alfred had clearly ordered the hut cleared.

"Brother, you seem very troubled. What is the news from Devon?"

"I have news of a great victory, and also a hint of a possible catastrophe."

"What victory, brother-of-mine?"

"Ubbi sailed from southern Wales and landed on the north Devon coast . . ."

"That is hardly good news, Alfred."

". . . where Odda gathered all the local fyrd, and retreated to the ancient fortress at Cynwith. Ubbi besieged him, and Odda's men ran out of water."

"This is still not good news that you are sharing with us."

"Patience, brother. It gets better. Odda allowed the Vikings to steal a wagon-load of mead, and when they were through drinking it, the entire Saxon force sallied forth."

Polonius couldn't contain himself any longer. "I know it is rude of me to interrupt a king, Sire, but would you please tell us what happened?"

Alfred smiled. He was both elated and anxious, yet he enjoyed treating Polonius to a taste of his own medicine. The thin dark man was famous for his convoluted stories that only gradually meandered to the point. He smiled.

"Even the realm's senior strategist must learn some patience. But the answer to your question is here."

With that he reached into the leather pouch and drew forth two massive gold armbands, and an intricately carved silver ring.

"These, my friends, used to belong to Ubbi! God was with Odda. The Saxon force surprised the Vikings, and more than eight hundred pagans fell in the ensuing battle. Bloody but victorious, Odda and his men chased the remainder back to their fortified encampment, where the Vikings climbed aboard their ships and fled north."

The four men just stared at each other. Ambrose spoke first.

"But this is truly wonderful, brother! Our greatest fear, that of a second prong, has come true, but has subsequently been eradicated. The land is hungry for news of a victory. We should be shouting this news from the church steeples!"

Alfred's grin faded. "True enough, my friends, and tomorrow we will declare a day of rejoicing. If that was all the news, I would be as elated as you. Unfortunately, it isn't."

"Then speak, brother. What else did you learn?"

Alfred picked up a sheet of parchment from the trestle table. He had only learned to read as an adult, and he was very proud of the skills that Polonius had taught him. He held it out to his brother and his two advisors.

"You were right, Polonius! We now know why Guthrum had dared to move against us with his smaller army when he had been forced to retreat only months ago. It is obvious that he intended to trap us between two rocks before our army could be reconstituted.

As he swept south to the coast, Ubbi would have ridden from the west. With our fyrdmen sent home for the winter season, we were helpless. This letter states unequivocally, however, that there was a third prong in their plan."

Ambrose just stared at his brother in silence. Alfred finally spoke. "Ealdorman Anwell wrote this letter that was found in Ubbi's tent, along with the silver ring there with his crest on it. In exchange for nominal independence under King Guthrum, Anwell promises to bring the entire Cornwall fyrd against me!"

Phillip spoke at last. A taciturn man, he was clearly shocked by the treachery. "Sire, he would be a pariah among all Christian nations! He swore on the Holy Bible to be your vassal!"

"True, Weapons-master. But he would hardly be the first Christian to break his word. And the threat of excommunication has been lifted more than once in exchange for enough bars of gold. Perhaps he thought to use part of the Wessex treasury to purchase forgiveness from Holy Mother Church."

Polonius spoke seriously. "Sire, today you have told us of a great threat lifted from us, and another one imposed. Yet it seems to me that your people need to hear of victory if they are not to despair. It would not hurt if Odda were to be acclaimed across the land for his bravery and his loyalty."

CHAPTER 15

A Message Comes from Ethelwold

The thane was furious. He blinked his eyes, shook his head and, now able to see for the first time in hours, stiffly clambered from his horse. The two churls who had escorted the man tied up the three horses and stood stoically by, suffering the man's continuing verbal abuse in silence.

Prince Ambrose heard the commotion, and stepped out of the rude hut that he shared with Phillip and Polonius. The angry Dorset thane recognized the prince, and he turned angrily to him.

"This is an outrage, Atheling! I am a loyal thane of Ealdorman Ethelwold. My master sent me with an important document for King Alfred. Instead of treating me as a respected messenger of one of your own chief ealdormen, I have been treated as a common criminal!

These thugs here!' With that he gestured toward the two silent churls who stood patiently right behind the thane. 'These thugs disarmed me and stuck my head in a God-cursed bag! These bastards kept that bag on me for almost a full day, while they led my horse God-knows where! How dare they treat a loyal thane of Dorset in such a way! I want their balls for this!"

Ambrose recognized the thane as Seger, one of Ethelwold's most loyal and trusted minions. He strode over to the angry thane.

"Welcome to Alfred's camp, Thane Seger."

"What are you going to do about the way I was treated, Ambrose?"

"Prince Ambrose to you. Thane Seger, let me review the facts with you. You arrived in a tiny village with more than a hundred armed men at your back, in a land where only our Viking enemies ride openly. You loudly demanded that you and all your men were to be guided directly to Alfred's side, though there was no one in the village who could so much as identify you. Is it any wonder that they feared and distrusted you?

Under such circumstances, they did the only thing possible. They brought you here, as fast as they could, without giving away your king's location.

Thane Seger, I apologize for your treatment, but these two men were just following the strict instructions of their king. No one is allowed to ride here directly. I am sure you understand the peril Alfred is in, and see the logic behind his command."

"I understand that a loyal vassal has been abused by thugs, Atheling, and stripped of his weapons and his escort!"

"Thane Seger, you must understand that the villagers who met you did not know who you were. Even if they did, they are only allowed to bring you here blindfolded. And they could have hardly brought a hundred of you blindfolded. I know that what was done to you it is a great imposition, but the fate of your king is dependent upon none of his enemies finding his secret location. Anyone who can not be positively identified once they arrive here is summarily hung.'

Saying that, Ambrose waved the two churls away. Seger did not fail to note that both had their right hands on their saxes.

Ambrose continued. 'Surely, sir, you would not wish us to risk your king's life? The alternative is a few hours of discomfort. Is this too great a price for you to pay for your king's safety?"

The thane was still angry, but he at least started to calm down. "Well, I suppose if it protects King Alfred . . . But it's still a poor way to treat a loyal vassal."

"Come, Thane Seger. You are truly welcome here! Let me take you directly to your king. He will be eager to hear your news."

The thane followed Ambrose, gazing about curiously as he walked. He noted that the vill was very poor, and the defenses were, at best, rudimentary. The settlement looked to have been only recently carved out of the virgin forest, and only had thirty or forty crude buildings.

Ambrose led Seger directly to the largest building in the vill. A couple of thanes lounged idly by the entrance, but Seger noticed that they wore swords and their spears were close by.

Ealdorman Ethelnoth met Seger just inside the door, and greeted him warmly. "Welcome, Thane Seger. Welcome to my little domain. Here the man you are looking for is just called 'master'. He would be very unhappy if you were to use any other name. Do I make myself clear?"

"Perfectly, Ealdorman. Now may I be allowed to deliver my message without further interference?"

Even as he spoke, a tall blond man stepped briskly out of the deep shadow within. Seger had only seen his king up close one time, but he instantly recognized the man with golden hair and a warrior's physique. He started to kneel in obeisance.

Alfred spoke. "Nay, Thane! Don't kneel to me here. The less who know I am here, the better."

"Of course, your M . . . Master. I have the honor of bringing you a letter from Ealdorman Ethelwold." With a grand gesture, Seger reached into his courier's pouch, withdrew a carefully folded sheet of parchment, and held it out toward the king. In his excitement, he didn't even notice the dark thin man who, still in shadow, rested his hands on his belt of throwing daggers.

Alfred gravely took the document and slit the wax seal open with his sax. He stepped over to the open doorway so that he would have adequate light to read it. The king was very proud of his newfound skill. All present watched their king intently.

At last Alfred turned back to the little group now gathered around him. "Thane Seger, you must thank your master on my behalf. It says here that Ethelwold offers the royal family safe sanctuary in Dorset. He has even been kind enough to send a full hundred thanes to escort me back.

Please tell Ethelwold that I am very grateful for his generous offer. I fear, however, that my traveling to Dorset would only bring down the wrath of the God-cursed Vikings on an innocent people. I am particularly appreciative, however, Thane, of the great gift that you have brought me."

"Your . . . Master, I fear that I do not understand."

"Why the one hundred mounted warriors, of course! It was a great sacrifice for Ethelwold to send me so many stalwart men at a time when his own lands are threatened by the pagan menace."

"Sire . . . Master. I brought them as an escort. The lands between here and Dorset are crawling with Vikings."

"Of course. Of course, Seger. But look here." With that, Alfred held out the letter to Seger.

"Master, I was told that the letter is in Latin. I regret that I neither speak Latin, nor am I able to decipher the markings on that page."

"Oh. Let me translate part of it for you, Thane."

"I would be honored, Master."

"It says right here - see these squiggles? - that the hundred thanes are at my complete disposal."

"Master, the warriors were forced to wait far back, at the edge of the forest."

"Of course, Seger. This vill could not possibly support such a large force. My Personal Guard is scattered all through the forest; at more than a dozen vills and burhs. I think that I will attach your men to a large force belonging to Ethelnoth. His men have taken heavy casualties, and need reinforcements."

"Master, I am honored to take a reply back to Ealdorman Ethelwold, but I will need that escort if I am to make it back alive."

"Of course, Seger.' Alfred gestured magnanimously. 'I understand completely. Please, take any ten men you wish as an escort. You will travel faster and draw much less attention to yourself with a small and fast-moving force. I will even provide you with a royal writ demanding that all loyal to Wessex are to facilitate your journey."

Thane Seger had beads of perspiration breaking out on his forehead. His master had certainly said nothing about leaving ninety crack warriors for Alfred. He had a sinking feeling that his life was at serious risk if he dared to return and report that he had managed to leave ninety thanes behind to fight for Alfred's cause, yet he could hardly contradict his king.

He cursed himself angrily. He had hoped that Alfred's forces were so scattered and demoralized that his men could ride right into town and arrest the entire royal family. Should that fail, he was expected to bring the royal family to Dorset. At all costs, he had been instructed to capture or bring the royal family to Ethelwold. A crown for his master depended on it!

"Thank you . . . Master. May I then stay with you and your court, and command the men on your behalf?"

"Thank you for the generous offer, but it is incumbent that Ethelwold gets my reply as fast as humanly possible. There is no one I would trust more than you to get my letter through. Can I count on you, Seger?"

"Of course, Master, if that is what you wish."

Seger, already angry about his treatment at the hands of Ethelnoth's churls, was now going beet red. Not only had his mission failed, but it appeared that he was about to lose most of his men. To top it all off, he was being sent back home like an errant schoolboy. Still, he tried to force the corners of his mouth up. It was vital that Alfred consider Ethelwold to be a loyal vassal. Seger thought of the consternation come spring when two of Alfred's most powerful shire fyrds, that of Cornwall and Dorset, marched with Guthrum's Vikings!

CHAPTER 16

The Cakes Are Burned

Ethelnoth, Ealdorman of Somerset, followed his king deeper and deeper into the tangled forest of Selwood. Grasping his bow in one hand and his boar spear in the other, he ran breathlessly after his royal master. A trace of overnight snow had made the big buck's tracks prominent, and King Alfred, an avid hunter, refused to turn back. The sounds of the other mounted huntsmen and their hounds had long faded into oblivion.

"Come, Ethelnoth! Damn the horses and damn the men! We go on! I want venison for supper tonight. Tomorrow I may be hunted again by Guthrum and his God-cursed minions. Today, for a few hours, I am the hunter. Come on, Ethelnoth, let's get that stag!"

The two men trotted on, easily following the trail of footprints. The deer followed a game trail, and it was clearly spooked by the two pursuing men, for its stride lengthened.

At last, after over an hour of breathlessly pounding along the trail, Alfred swerved to miss a patch of ice, and, instead, slipped on some moss. He went down hard. Ethelnoth was right behind him, and the ealdorman stopped immediately.

"Are you all right, Master?"

"Yes, yes. Just help me up, if you please."

"Of course, Master."

Alfred stood on his own, but when he started to head over to where his boar spear had fallen, his right leg almost buckled.

"Master, what is wrong with your leg?"

"Nothing serious, old friend, but I will not be walking too far on it for a few days. Oh well, my body is sweaty, but my hands and feet are almost numb from the cold. I guess that your king will have to concede defeat. Tonight we will eat the bounty of whatever your villagers see fit to feed two famished noblemen. I am in your hands. Lead me back home, Ealdorman."

"My king, I but followed you. 'Whither thou goest, I will go.' But I hope you don't think that I know the way back."

"Ethelnoth, must I remind you? Somerset is your shire. We are in Somerset."

"Your logic is impeccable, Master, but Selwood is a royal forest. That means that it belongs to you!"

Alfred looked at Ethelnoth with consternation in his eyes, and then burst into loud laughter. He slapped Ethelnoth hard on the back, and then hugged him.

"Well, old friend. The two most important people in this entire shire are completely lost! What do you say to that?"

"I say that one of the two is the most important person in all Angleland."

"Now don't flatter me, Ealdorman. At the moment, my only subjects are you and your people, and a lot of deer, which, I might add, I can't even catch. What you say may even be true, Ethelnoth, but I have to tell you that this important personage you mention is still lost . . . and in your shire."

"Master, I smell smoke. There must be a habitation nearby. I regret that it is not likely to be one of your royal estates, or even one of my forest tuns, but if they have a fire, at least you can warm your royal toes."

"And perhaps get directions. Pass me my boar spear, and lead on, good Ealdorman!"

A plume of smoke rising straight into the sky located the dwelling for the two men. They openly approached the thatch and wattle hut, for they saw that it was a modest dwelling, likely the home of a churl.

Their presence was announced by a brindle cur, which set up a great din as soon as it spotted the two of them. A burly man stepped out through the doorway, an axe in his belt, and a spear in his hand.

"What does ye want, strangers? There be no treasures for the taking in this 'umble 'ome."

Alfred whispered to Ethelnoth. "Remember, I am but a visiting friend."

Ethelnoth smiled. "Aye, Master.' He threw back the hood of his heavy cape. 'Do you recognize, me, sir?"

"Be it truly Ealdorman Ethelnoth? Of course I recognize ye, Master! I served under ye when we joined King Alfred last summer and drove the heathen Danes north, out of Wessex! It made me proud to watch that rascal scuttle away like that. Sir, what may I do for ye and yer companion? Ye be a long way from yer home burh."

"We were hunting a choice stag, but he escaped us. We found ourselves near here, and smelled your wood smoke."

"Excuse my manners, sirs! Please, come in and warm yerselves by me fire. Ye must be frozen."

"Thank you, uhh."

"Eadric, Ealdorman. Me name be Eadric."

"Thank you, Eadric."

The two noblemen were led to the hut, where Eadric thrust the hide curtain aside and invited his two guests over to the hearth.

"Come in, sirs! Please, sit by the fire where ye may warm yerselves! Gyldan, this be Ealdorman Ethelnoth and his companion. They be cold, so bring them a bench so they can sit by the fire! Sirs, this be me Gyldan. Sometimes she has a shrill tongue, but she be the best wife a man could have."

The two men sat before the fire and stretched their extremities toward it. Alfred stretched his twisted ankle very carefully. Ethelnoth then spoke to his churl.

"Eadric, I need you to do something for me."

"Name it, Ealdorman, and consider it done."

"I need you to lead me by the quickest way to the tun of Deer's Yard. If separated from us, my men were to ride there and wait for us in the tun."

"Of course, Ealdorman, but what of your companion?"

Ethelnoth turned to Alfred. "Master?"

"I know what you're thinking, old friend, and you're right. My ankle is still sore. It would be best if you were to bring the horses back here. I can certainly ride with no problem."

Eadric turned to his wife. "Gyldan. Our guest will stay here with ye. Ye see that he be well taken care of, or ye'll get the back of me hand when I return!"

"Get out of 'ere, or I'll take me broom to ye now!" Holding the broom high off the ground, Gyldan advanced on her husband, who scuttled toward the door.

"Our holy father says the Good Book tells ye to love, honor and obey yer husband, woman!" said Eadric.

"Aye . . . Of course it does. It were written by men! Now get ye gone."

Beating a strategic retreat, Eadric went out the door. "I will wait for ye just outside, Ealdorman. Me love, I should be back before supper time."

Alfred dozed lightly as the warmth of the fire slowly permeated his extremities. Gyldan bustled around importantly, cleaning and preparing food.

"Excuse me, sir, but I must put these barley cakes by the fire so me man will have supper ready when he returns from his errand. We have but humble fare, but I suppose that if ye are still here, we could manage to find some food for the likes of ye, come supper time."

Alfred smiled. "I thank you, good dame, but I should be gone long before your supper time."

The woman looked relieved. "Well, if yer here, we will feed ye. Ye are a guest in our 'ouse. And now would ye please watch that the cakes do not burn while I go fetch water from the creek."

"Of course, good lady."

Alfred kept an eye on the barley cakes, but he was exhausted, and the heat of the fire made him very sleepy. He gradually slipped into a deep sleep.

He woke with a start as a broom struck him a good blow across the shoulders. "They burned! Ye let our supper all burn! Ye haven't even got enough of God's good grace to watch a fire, and that's a fact!"

As she was yelling at Alfred, her broom still raised menacingly, the hide door was thrust aside, and Ethelnoth and Eadric entered, followed by Phillip and Ambrose. Eadric just stood still in shock, but Phillip instantly drew his sax and stepped toward the suddenly frightened woman. Ethelnoth, too, stood in shock.

The ealdorman caught his breath, and spoke in a furious voice. "Master, I will arrange to have her whipped and then hung! Woman, you have no idea what you have just done. Gyldan, the life of you and all your family are hereby declared to be forfeited!"

The woman just stared in shock at the noblemen who had suddenly invaded her home. Her eyes were focused on the weapon that threatened her.

"But Me Lord! He let all our barley cakes burn in the fire! Me man will go to bed hungry this night!"

Alfred stretched to his full imposing height. His voice thundered in the confines of the small one room hut.

"Hold! Phillip, put away your weapon! This woman is right. I promised to watch the cakes, but I fell asleep. Their supper is ruined because of what I did, and her husband did us a service this day. Ambrose, give this man a gold coin. Eadric, you have earned the gratitude this day of Alfred, your king.

Woman, you were right to be angry, and I apologize for my neglect. You treat a guest poorly, however. Eadric, I will pray, for both our sakes, that your wife will learn proper Christian meekness."

At Alfred's name, Gyldan threw herself down on the rush floor and wailed. "Oh, Sire! Forgive me! Forgive me! Cut off me right hand that struck ye!"

"Woman, rise! You did not know who I was. Nothing more will be said of the matter. Ask forgiveness of your husband. It is he to whom you owe obedience and respect. Phillip, bring the horses. We ride!"

CHAPTER 17

The Saxons Finally Strike Back

The man staggered through the door, a cold and biting wind following him into the room.

"Me Lud, the heathen devils come!"

Ethelnoth, at first annoyed that his king's peace had been so rudely disturbed, quickly realized the importance of what he had just been told. He rose from his bench and strode rapidly toward the exhausted runner."

"Sit you down, man! Catch your breath and tell us the news!"

At last the man could speak again. "Me lud, I am from the tun of Owl's Head. As ye instructed, we sent out sentries on the roads leading from the east. Me brother was doing his shift, when he saw a body of mounted Vikings coming along the road. He took the forest trails back to our vill. We started an evacuation of women and children into the forest while the men armed and prepared to man the palisades. I was sent to report to you! The Vikings might be attacking even now as we speak."

"What's your name, man?"

"Brok, lud!"

"Well, Brok. And how many enemies were approaching?"

"I don't know, me lud! Me brother saw a mounted body of mayhaps a hundred men, but he had no idea how many might've been following. He slipped into the woods before he could be seen and caught!"

"You did well, Brok. Rest, and I will have food and drink brought to you."

"Me lud, I beg permission to run back and fight. Me people may be dying!"

"Catch your breath, Brok, and have some food so you can regain your strength. You are exhausted. Wait just a little, and we will decide what to do."

The tall man sitting in the far corner rose and walked into the light of the fire. Brok saw that the stranger was very well dressed, and he noted the deference the ealdorman paid to the stranger. Ethelnoth was lord of some two hundred thanes and more than three thousand churls. He deferred to very few men in the lands that his family had held for generations. The village rumor was that his master was hosting some very important noblemen, but no one had said who they were.

The man walked with a regal air, and his clothes were cut from expensive cloth. Brok wondered again just who this person was. Ethelnoth spoke to the man.

"Master, the heathen are no more than a day's march from here. What are your orders?"

The tall stranger replied. "What is your military situation?"

"I have ordered every able-bodied man to practice archery and spear casting daily. When the weather permits, the men are also ordered to practice formation maneuvers. They understand that come spring we will be going into battle. I have told all the thanes that I will have no mobs. We will lead men capable of maneuvering as units. I don't think they are ready yet for serious large-formation fighting, but they should be at least partially trained. Sprinkled amongst them, of course, are veterans who have served their king in other campaigns."

"Ethelnoth, do you think that the Danes know we are here and are coming for us?"

"Nay, Master, I am sure that they are simply on a foraging expedition. They will have stripped the Chippenham area bare by now."

"Aye,' the well-dressed stranger smiled ruefully, 'Even the treats lovingly collected for our king. And how many men would you send out on a foraging expedition?"

"A fairly small number, but all mounted and equipped to travel fast. Into such hostile territory as ours; perhaps one or two hundred, with as many more following to occupy villages, drive back livestock, and be prepared to reinforce if there was some unexpected resistance.

The vanguard would have to be large enough to overawe or overcome individual vills or local garrisons, but capable of quick movement in order to use the element of surprise. I would not expect them to hold, in the face of serious opposition."

"Hmm. Polonius, how many men can we call to arms?"

"Master, we have perhaps ninety of the king's thanes sequestered in various villages within a day's ride. The rest have been sent home to defend their vills and burhs, and to prepare for spring. He smiled suddenly. "Of course, there are almost ninety faithful Dorset thanes I know of who are just sitting around."

"Ethelnoth, what about you?"

"I can immediately call up more than a hundred thanes, and, given enough time, perhaps up to two thousand churls, if we are willing to take every able-bodied man to the age of fifty. Of prime men in fit shape; a little over a thousand. It would take some time to get such a force together, however.

I hesitate to call up the men of the villages near where the Vikings are raiding. It would leave their women and children helpless in the face of an unexpected attack.

If I wanted the force together in a day or so at the latest, however, I would have to call upon the local vills and burhs. I suspect that I might be able round up some six or eight hundred warriors within two days."

"So be it! I will call up my personal thanes, and you do the same, as well as five hundred of the best armed and most fit churls. I want only men who are mounted. Call up only local men so it will not take long to put the force together. It's time the Vikings felt our steel!"

Ambrose turned to his brother. "With all due respect, brother, if your banner, and any Personal Guard thanes, are recognized in battle, the entire Danish force will be on their way here at a full gallop. Much as it pains me to say it, you should not yet be visible. Our position here in the forest is too precarious."

"Ambrose, you know I am not a skulker. I hear what you say, but I do not like what I hear."

"Brother, forget your personal safety. Your appearance in battle will draw the Vikings to your hiding place like bears to honey. How then will we protect your wife and children?"

Polonius spoke quietly. "Master, what your brother says is true. Do not let your pride make you sacrifice your family. First they must be safe. Then we can strike!"

Alfred let his gaze sweep over his advisors. "Brother-of-mine, I do not mean to snap at you, but I am anxious to hit back at these devils. I want them to bleed for every elbow-span of land that they take! I must admit, however, that what you say has merit. What do you propose?"

"Brother, I also do not think that they should go unpunished. I just do not want Guthrum to locate you. First we must find a safer haven; one that we could defend, if necessary.

In the meantime, why do we not let Ethelnoth take a levy of his troops and hit the heathen? I would be pleased to go with him, and we can even use Ethelwold's Dorsetmen. I just do not want you to be identified with the attack. We will all ride under Ethelnoth's flag. No one will be surprised to see the Ealdorman of Somerset's flag in Somerset."

The king sighed. "Ethelnoth, you know that I would rather attack than breathe. Yet I suspect that Ambrose is right. If the full force of the Danes head here to catch me, then you and your isolated tuns and vills would have no hope. If the local lord alone faces them, they are most likely to just seek an easier area to pillage. Would you be willing to lead a force against the pagans, old friend?"

"Of course, Master. I would be derelict in my duty if I did not try to save my people."

"Good. Then it's settled. Ambrose, Polonius, and Phillip will ride with you, and they will bring a token force of my Personal Guard, but no one will fly royal emblems.

Ambrose! I need you and Polonius to break out our maps and start planning. Ethelnoth will add his knowledge to yours shortly, just as soon as he sends off his messengers."

Brok watched in awe as the young man ordered Ethelnoth around as if the grizzled veteran was a child. The messenger realized that only the king of all Wessex and its tributary domains could have so much authority.

The mention of Ambrose and Polonius were the final arguments. Even in his isolated village, wandering scops had sung of the legendary bastard prince, brother to Alfred, who had stolen a princess from an Irish Viking king by first capturing a Welsh town, and then attacking the Viking king's ship on the high seas. The ballad was almost as popular as the other, which told the story of Ambrose and his companions spying on the Great Army by joining it as recruits.

The man who stepped into the light was small in stature, though with the blond features of the royal house. A third man, thin to the point of emaciation, followed his companion. He was as dark-complexioned as his companion was light. This stranger could be none other than the master strategist who had come from far-off Byzantium, and now served King Alfred. Brok now knew with a certainty who the tall blond lord was. He also understood why his name was not uttered. This man, king of the only kingdom not yet prostrated before the Viking invaders, was also the most hunted person on the island. The Vikings had offered his weight in gold for his capture, dead or alive. This was possibly the only man left in all of Britain who was capable of driving the pagans from their shores, and both sides knew it.

Brok looked in awe at his king. He had only been in the presence of his ealdorman once before in his life, and this is the first time he had so much as glimpsed Alfred!

Alfred noted the various emotions flit transparently across the messenger's face, however, and he spoke directly to the man. "Yes, Brok, I am Alfred, king of Wessex. Here, however, I am only known as 'master', and now my very life is in your hands."

Brok slipped from the bench and knelt upon the rush-covered floor.

"Yer Majesty! Red hot tongs will not tear words from me mouth! We are your sworn men, and we will fight for ye until death! No man in these forests will betray ye! Without ye, Wessex has no hope."

"I thank you, Brok, for those kind words. With a few thousand more like you, we will yet drive the God-cursed heathens from our shores!"

↦

"The West Saxons are fools! Look! The gate swings open, and, even now, villagers gather wood outside. There are even cattle loose on the commons. Surely they know we are in the area. We enjoyed the hospitality of their neighboring village just last night! I would hang a jarl who was as lax as that."

"Do not underestimate our cousins the Saxons, my Jarl! They have proven a formidable foe, several times driving our armies from their shores. And I have sensed watchers."

"Bah! We crushed them at Chippenham. And if they knew we were here, they would be buttoned up tight and prepared for us."

"At Chippenham we caught them by surprise and overwhelmed a portion of the King's Guard with sheer numbers. We did not face an army. Even so, the king and most of his noblemen escaped, after giving us a bloody nose. Now, without Alfred in our grasp, the whole nation will answer a call-to-arms in the spring."

"And our cousins will have landed to the west by now, and, with their reinforcements and our new allies, we will easily crush the Saxon dogs!"

"Maybe, but for today, let's just concentrate on crushing that tun. Order the charge!"

The war horns blew their throbbing notes across the open ground surrounding the tun. The sounds were quickly followed by the rolling thunder of more than two hundred galloping horses.

The riders were, in turn, followed by a wave of running infantry carrying logs to be used as battering rams or, notched, as ladders. The attack was primitive in its simplicity, but it would be devastating if the riders could reach the open gate before its defenders could close it.

The wood gatherers dropped their loads and ran for their lives. They were all young and lithe, and easily made it to the gate before the first of the riders could cover the distance from the woods. The gates swung shut behind them, and they were securely barred before the riders could reach them.

The Vikings were not deterred, however. They knew they should outnumber the fighting men several fold, even if the villagers had called in all the fighting men from the area. Further, it was February, and they needed to take the village if they intended to sleep in comfort that night.

The Viking riders, frustrated in their attempt to ride through the gates before they were closed, leapt from their mounts and ran for the walls. The dismounted men with the ladders and battering rams would join them soon, and together they would climb the palisades. They would suffer a few casualties, but the nut looked no harder than a dozen others they had cracked in as many days.

The wave of running men caught up with the now dismounted riders. In short order, the logs were thrown against the wall, and, covered by a line of archers, a wave of climbers started swarming up.

Twenty men swung their legs over the top of the wall, and twenty men fell back or dangled dead from the heights. The second wave reached the top, only to suffer the same fate. The third wave was swept from their ladders by their dying companions. The rest refused to climb into the flying death that awaited any who dared to surmount the top.

The jarl looked at all of the dead bodies. Some looked like porcupines, with as many as a half dozen shafts in them. He cursed volubly.

"By Odin's beard! What magic is this; that they can kill all of our men! You! You climbed to the top! What is happening?"

The man saw the finger of his jarl point at him, and he ignored the arrow still embedded in his arm and ran to his master's side.

"My Jarl, there are some two hundred archers lined up and just waiting for us to show our faces. To reach the top of the wall is to die!"

"Then call back the men and order the battering rams to be put to work! I want that gate to be made into kindling. Order a second attack as a diversion over there, where the wall looks weakest."

"Jarl, do you want the archers to use fire arrows? It will keep them busy while we batter the gate and the wall."

"And where do you intend to sleep tonight, if we burn all the buildings? And what do you intend to eat, if we burn all their stores? Fool! Just do as you're told!"

The Vikings heeded the war horn's instructions, and soon the combined forces flowed into the requisite formations. These big men from the north were nothing if not master warriors. The heavy battering rams went into action. Lines of archers stood ready to fire if a Saxon enemy head dared to appear above the palisade. Since there was no walkway around most of the wall, the Vikings could move with near impunity. There were only occasional loopholes from which the defenders could fire in very restricted arcs. There were towers on either side of the main gate, however, and here the Saxons were able to fire down on the men handling the heavy battering ram. Dozens of Viking archers formed a line and attempted to retaliate.

A long eerie sound emanated from within the village stockade. The note was higher pitched than the Viking war horns, but it carried as well;

even over the screams of dying men.

Instantly, men thrust off the branches and hides that hid their dugouts under the bushes along the edge of the forest. They clambered out of their cramped hiding places, cold and stiff; grateful for action at last.

Other formations of Saxons ran from hiding places deep in the woods. They had practiced this, and they moved together like a well-oiled machine. Soon the thin line became a solid wall of spearmen and archers, six hundred strong, and it moved against the several hundred Danes. The Viking archers by the gate turned and started to form a shield-wall facing the attackers. Even as they re-formed in response to the new threat, however, the gates opened and Polonius led his mounted lancers into battle at a full gallop.

A solid wall of Vikings was impenetrable to even charging cavalry. The horsemen hit the men before they were reinforced with adequate swordsmen, however, and they broke. Suddenly hundreds of Viking archers and swordsmen were running for their lives. Once broken, they had no chance to form up again. The lancers spurred their way through the mob that had so recently been a disciplined fighting team. The attacking infantry, ill armed as they were, vastly outnumbered the broken Vikings. A flood of screaming Saxons from the open gate completed the rout.

Ambrose, watching from the edge of the woods, turned to Ethelnoth.

"My friend, your men have done well! Now turn your dogs and your foresters loose on them. Alfred would not want any survivors to reach Chippenham!"

Ethelnoth grinned at the brother of his king. "It shall be as you say, Prince."

CHAPTER 18

The Perfect Site is Found

"Ambrose! Ethelnoth! This is it!"

Ambrose and Ethelnoth looked at each other in puzzlement, then at their king. They had been poling his *punt* between seemingly endless thickets and reeds. Only the guides provided by Ethelnoth, close ahead, had prevented their being lost in the trackless wilderness, though Alfred had often hunted this area in his earlier visits.

Ambrose rose to the bait. "What is it, brother-of-mine?"

"Look around you! Is it not perfect?"

"I see a lot of alder bushes, and a lot of water. Perfect would be more ducks for my royal brother. What else am I looking for?"

Alfred smiled. "Ah, where is Polonius when I need him? He would understand."

He was clearly enjoying his little game with his older bastard brother. All too often, when he had been just a young man, Alfred had listened to Ambrose and Polonius discussing strategies they had learned in the Rus wilderness and from the sophisticated Byzantines. It was rare enough that Alfred had been able to stump his brother.

"Brother-of-mine, what happened when you made that attack against the Viking foraging party?"

"We cut the Danes to pieces, but without the use of either alder or water, as far as I can remember."

"Aye, true. But what happened after that?"

"Well, Selwood Forest filled with spies."

"And?"

"Alfred, you know as well as I. Ethelnoth here hung the lot of them. That was your edict!"

"And?"

"And we had to keep moving so that the Danes could not locate us."

"Good, Ambrose, and what was our problem there, my master strategist?"

"That we had no army, except for a few small groups of thanes, and Ethelnoth's loyal people. And we had no fortress large enough to hold off any kind of serious attack."

"And if we permanently called together a large force?"

Ambrose looked pensive. "A force large enough to protect us would have definitely attracted the attention of the Danes. Even the chance you were with Ethelnoth brought the spies. Calling together a large force would likely have been your death knell, unless you are able to call together and maintain a thousand or more warriors at one time and place."

Alfred smiled. "Excellent, brother, but I feel it is time that I strike back! Only by showing our people that we are alive and are successfully resisting, can we hope to eventually raise the kind of force that you tell me we will need to defeat these heathen devils! So I need to call together a force capable of at least successful defense of a place of our choice. And what is missing in this equation, learned brother-of-mine?"

"The men you can find. Ethelnoth has promised every man he has, for the asking, and you know that every fyrdman of Hampshire and Wiltshire will march on your command. I guess, therefore, that leaves a fortress strong enough to withstand a siege, or one that Guthrum can't find."

"Just so, brother! Look around you. I have hunted these marshes for years, yet I have no idea where I am. A dozen armies could disappear in here without a trace. Ethelnoth!"

"Yes, Your Majesty?"

"Is there an island in here where the land rises more than an elbow's length out of the water?"

"Yes, Sire. There is a fairly large island nearby. There is not much of a settlement on it, however."

"Is the island big enough to support the tents and shelters of several hundred men?"

"It probably has more than two acres of good dry land, even in the spring when the water is highest."

"Then take me there! I want to see if we have finally found a base from which we can strike back!"

※

Alfred was ecstatic. Two rivers made a barrier for horsemen, but, for men with punts and an intimate knowledge of the area, the rivers would provide either perfect highways or escape routes into vast marshes, whichever was needed. The island was deep in the alder swamps, and was very difficult to reach for those who did not know the secret paths. The area abounded in game, and the island was large enough that Alfred could have a fort built there that would be several hundred feet in diameter.

Alfred turned to his two companions after touring the perimeter of the little island. The four guides just rested quietly in their punts, waiting incuriously for their masters to decide what they wanted to do.

"My friends! I want to welcome you to Atheling's *Eig*. Our arrival here today is the start of a new dawn for Wessex. I swear by almighty God that I am going to make the Viking devils sorry they ever landed on our shores!"

Ambrose could not resist. "No, brother, it is almost sunset. Even my brother the king cannot change that."

Alfred grabbed his brother in a playful bear-hug.

"Now, brother, do not hit your sovereign!"

"Oomph! Do not crush your elder brother!"

The two men wrestled for a minute. Both had carried immense responsibilities on their shoulders for years, and all-too-rarely had the opportunity to roughhouse privately. At last, laughing uproariously, the two men let go of each other, and then hugged again.

"Ambrose! I have missed beating you up these last few years!"

"Beating me up! Alfred, your memory is short! Why, if you were not the king of me and all else you purvey, I would drown you in this swamp like a little puppy!"

"Come, brother. I admit it! You are right. It is almost sunset, and I want to return to our royal straw residence. We have much to plan!"

⚑

Alfred worked far into the night, ordering the extravagant use of the bulrush torches. He ordered his own family to temporarily move elsewhere, and he put his experts to work.

"Ethelnoth! Send word for all of the thanes of my Personal Guard to gather at this burh. We will have them punted to Atheling's Eig. I want a couple of tuns nearby designated to take care of horse-herds. Polonius, I want you to write to all my shire reeves within three day's journey. I want twenty of their finest horses from each of them, and no excuses!

Ethelnoth. I need enough lumber cut to make a palisade around the site we marked out today. The logs are to be green, so that they will not easily burn. I want the logs boated in, so that there is no obvious trail leading to the island. I want timber and wattle huts to be built. I want the necessary facilities so the island is able to permanently support perhaps three hundred men, and perhaps twice that in an emergency. Ethelnoth, I will need large levies of your churls for labor. I want this fort built in short order. Is any of this going to be a problem?"

Ethelnoth replied. "Not while I draw breath. If I can tell my people that it is for you, Sire, they will work themselves until they drop!"

"That will hardly be necessary, old friend, but yes, I am through with hiding from my own people. Tell your people that King Alfred has returned, and he needs the help of every able-bodied man in the shire!"

CHAPTER 19

"In the Easter of this year King Alfred with his little force raised a work at Athelney; from which he assailed the army, assisted by that part of Somersetshire which was nighest to it."

First the punts and coracles arrived by the dozen, and then the hundred. Ethelnoth had kept his word, and all the vills and burhs within a day's traveling time answered the summons by sending their adults; both men and women. Hundreds of sturdy peasants, dressed in warm clothes, set to with a will. Mixed in with all of the Somerset people were more than a hundred of Alfred's Personal Guard, and several dozen of Ethelnoth's own thanes.

Many of the local churls were sent out in their boats to locate and cut lumber. Alfred wanted a palisade several hundred Roman feet in diameter, and that would take an immense number of tree trunks. Several large oaks were also sought, to be used as Center posts for Alfred's Great Hall, and also for the timber and wattle huts that would shelter the remaining retainers and other fighting men Ethelnoth and Alfred intended to call in to join them.

Others industriously swung mattock and shovel, and started the backbreaking task of removing frozen soil and digging a ditch around the perimeter that Alfred had marked out. The excavated earth was used to build a high mound into which sharpened logs would eventually be driven. Gradually the shape of Alfred's fort began to take shape. The last hope of Wessex was literally rising from the ground.

In days, the army of workers accomplished the impossible. Hundreds of logs, hauled in from miles around, were cut, trimmed and floated to the island. By careful effort, no obvious trail was made to the king's swamp fort. No drag-marks would lead the Vikings to the island. Even Alfred took his turn at the heavy labor.

As the fortifications rose, so too did Alfred's spirits. Alfred finally had a secure place in which to leave his family while he struck back at the heathen foe. Messengers were sent out in all directions. Spring was nearing, and it was only a matter of weeks before it would be time for the shire fyrds to rally and march. Secret instructions were relayed to all of the major ealdormen and thanes of Wiltshire and Hampshire. Ethelnoth personally ordered the Somerset militias to join together into a single massive force that would itself outnumber that of the Viking invaders.

Each territorial unit was expected to provide its one man, armed and mounted. Ethelnoth made it clear, however, that he expected each fyrdman to bring as many retainers with him as he could. This was to be a gathering of not just the shire fyrd, but all the able-bodied men of Somerset.

While Ealdorman Odda had promised what support he could of the Devon fyrd, yet Alfred felt that he and his heroic followers had already done more than enough. Odda had sent messengers with news of victory, followed by news that his battered forces had marched against the seaside town where the Viking fleet had been tied up.

The Viking fleet, its rowing benches almost denuded of rowers, had slipped from the harbor with its tail between its legs. All together, they left behind more than eight hundred dead. While some escaped, the force itself was shattered as a fighting unit.

Not yet done, Odda had garrisoned the northern coastal towns against a second Viking landing, and sent the other half of his forces south, to sit on the northern border with Dorset and wait for further instructions from Alfred. He promised to follow up with a much larger force of conscripted infantry in the spring, when Alfred sent word he was ready.

CHAPTER 20

A Spy Goes To Guthrum's Camp

The little column ploughed steadily through the snow until the lead riders finally reached the main gate of the palisaded burh. A sentry, heavily wrapped in a cloak, appeared briefly on the walkway above the gate. He briefly held up a flaring torch, looked down at the snow-encrusted riders below, and then called out. "Strangers are not welcome here. Go away!"

With that, he ducked back into his shelter. Phillip shook some of the snow off his cape and looked at the prince beside him. "May I deal with this, Prince Ambrose?"

Ambrose peeked out from under his own voluminous cloak, and nodded. "With pleasure, my friend."

The giant man roared. "Open the gate for your lawful prince, you little turd! Open the gate or I will have the hide off your back before you can finish a 'Hail Mary'!"

The heavily cloaked visage appeared again almost instantly. "Who be you, daring to use a royal name?"

"You sniveling little pile of pig shit! You yammer while your betters freeze! Ambrose, Prince of Wessex, is waiting for you to open the damn gate. Run to the gate, fool, or lose your balls!"

Ambrose smiled as he heard the sentry frantically yelling to turn out the guard. The weapons-master was a frightening man when roused.

Within moments, the gates started to pivot open with a protesting groan. Phillip didn't wait for them to open fully, but forced his horse forward just as soon as the gap was large enough for his bulk to fit through. The giant thane was normally laconic, but Ambrose knew that his friend was just working off some of his anger and frustration. Ambrose could hear his booming voice as the horse and rider disappeared through the gate.

"Make way, you dolts! Put your pig-stickers down and greet an atheling of the royal house with proper respect!

You! Run to fetch Thane Hrycg.

You two! A royal prince is freezing his balls off right outside your gates! If you want to keep yours, you'll get that gate opened wide!"

The heavy gates slowly rumbled fully open, and Ambrose led the riders forward into the shelter of the walls. A semicircle of spear-carrying and shivering men awaited them, though Phillip's prancing mount was forcing a larger and larger area for the new arrivals.

The churls, intimidated by Phillip's size and demeanor, yet were unsure of the situation, and they were not yet ready to let strange armed men loose in their little settlement, whatever the threats. Thane Hrycg arrived at a run, with his cloak billowing behind him. As soon as he saw the weapons-master, he shouted out.

"By all that's holy! I know that voice which yells loud enough to wake the dead! Is that giant snowball on the horse really you, Phillip of Wessex?"

Ambrose answered for the giant warrior. "Of course that big oaf is Phillip, Hrycg."

The man stopped in his tracks. "Holy mother of God! I never thought to hear that voice again! It is Prince Ambrose himself!"

Ambrose threw back the folds of cloth that protected his head from the driving snow. "Not for much longer, old friend. Not if I don't get out of this damned snow pretty soon!"

"Forgive me, Prince Ambrose! You all must be frozen. Men! Put away your weapons and help our guests down. Then take the horses and rub them down thoroughly."

As Ambrose swung stiffly down to the ground, Thane Hrycg ran to his prince and hugged him in a great bear hug. "Prince, you are a sight for sore eyes! We became separated in the fighting when the Danes caught up with us after we made it across the Avon. I had been told that you and Alfred were killed!"

"No, my friend. That's just a rumor Guthrum's agents are busily spreading. Alfred is safe, and very much alive. We escaped with perhaps seventy of the Personal Guard, and Alfred is presently in hiding a long day's ride from here."

"God be praised! Prince, please bring your men to the Great Hall. There we will stoke the fire and provide you all with food and drink! When you are warm and comfortable, I want you to tell me of our king, and of our comrades who survived!"

Ambrose, his escort warriors, and Hrycg and all the churls who were not on guard duty, grabbed benches and clustered around the now roaring fire.

Ale and mead was brought by women still in their nightclothes, and gradually the riders thawed out. At last, Hrycg brought up the subject of Alfred again.

"Prince Ambrose, it brings joy to my heart to see you alive and well. The news you bring about your brother the king is wonderful. Yet I suspect you did not ride through such a bitter storm just to share a horn of mead with me.

You know I am Alfred's sworn man. He raised me from the ranks, and all the land that I hold, I owe to him. Command me, and I will obey. Does my king wish me to raise a force of my loyal Jutes?"

"Hrycg, Alfred knows of your loyalty, and is counting on it. The time to call up the fyrd is coming soon. Tell me; just what is the situation here in your home shire?"

"Prince, we will hold it, in Alfred's name."

"Hrycg, no platitudes please. What is your real military situation?"

"The blunt truth? Not good. I control eight different burhs and vills, and several dozen isolated farms. Each burh and vill has some defenses, yet they were primarily designed to keep cattle raiders at bay for a day or so, while the other settlements send support. The walls were never designed for defense against a real army.

None of the settlements have sufficient men to hold out against a determined foe, even after I called in all the churls working the isolated farms. I despair that we can stave off the Danish war machine when it reaches our lands. Already some of my more distant neighbors have been raided. That's the unvarnished truth, Prince. But that is not your problem. I have a sacred obligation to the king. Tell me what force you need, and I will raise it for you. I will ride within the hour, if you but wish it!"

Ambrose reached over and squeezed the man's arm tight. He knew his brother was terribly worried about how many of the ealdormen and thanes would remain true to their oath and their obligations. He felt a warm love for Thane Hrycg, a senior duguo who had chosen to leave the security of his estates to spend the Christmas season with his king. The move had almost cost him his life, yet he was clearly prepared to stand by his oath of obedience to the end.

After a long pause, Ambrose spoke. "Old friend, tell me how the thanes and ealdormen are dealing with Alfred's disappearance."

"They are sore afraid, Prince. Word had spread about your deaths, and there was despair. We all know that, without strong leadership, we can never stand against the Viking menace.'

He shrugged. 'Some have entered into negotiations with Guthrum. Without their king to lead them, they are just trying to protect their own people and property."

"Have you considered such a solution, Hrycg?"

"Prince, you ask me to speak treason to you.' He sighed. 'But the true answer is . . . yes. In the absence of instructions from a rightful king, I would take care of my own first. I have no wish to see my loved ones on the slave block at *Wyk Te Duurstede*.

You must remember that we all heard rumors that both you and Alfred were dead. We do not even know how many of the Witan are alive to meet and nominate another royal atheling for king. I know some of my colleagues have abandoned their lands and fled to the Continent. Some negotiate, and a few, only a few, build their defenses, in order to fight.

"Thane Hrycg, you are right. I came here for an important reason. Alfred has great need of a favor from you today."

"Prince, it is not a favor to obey your king."

Ambrose smiled. "I am glad that you feel that way. It is a big favor."

"Command me, Prince. How can I help King Alfred?"

"Hrycg, Alfred asks you to surrender your sovereignty to Guthrum, and offer him Danegeld."

Hrycg said nothing for several long moments. He sat immobile in his seat, and his dark blue eyes burned into Ambrose's. "Prince, if anyone other than you asked me to do what you have just asked, I would kill him! Better you just ask me to take my comrades here and attack Guthrum's citadel head on! That, I am willing to do."

It felt to Ambrose as if the temperature of the room had dropped by twenty degrees. He spoke earnestly. "Whoa, old friend! Let me explain my brother's needs."

Hrycg's words were ice cold. "I am listening, Prince."

"Hrycg, Alfred desperately needs to know who has betrayed him. How did Guthrum and his columns make it past the frontier watchers without us being alerted? Were throats cut at the border, or did gold change hands? How did Guthrum know that we were at Chippenham? Alfred understands that some Saxons will pretend to kneel to Guthrum only so they can protect their families and land. Others, however, will willingly align themselves with the Danes, even to the point of sending their fyrd to fight against Alfred himself, or, possibly, betraying their king to his enemies. Do you understand the need for what I am asking?"

"Aye. You want me to spy out Guthrum's camp in order to find the real traitors who have already betrayed Alfred, or who might do so, come summer."

"Exactly! Come spring, Alfred will send the call out to try and raise the greatest army Wessex has ever seen. But we must know who will ride with us, and if there are any who will bring warriors to fight on Guthrum's side. If we cannot identify our enemies by spring, and manage to counteract their threat, then the throne of Wessex could be lost. Soon after that, we will all be thrall to Guthrum, or dead."

"It is a hard thing that you ask, Prince. I am no spy. Yet I have to confide that I have considered paying Danegeld. Guthrum is no fool. He has treated the Saxons and Angles in Mercia and East Anglia who have submitted with great restraint. While they don't love him, yet a few now ride as Viking warriors, and they are treated with respect. Most of those who submitted kept their land."

"Old friend, the throne of Wessex is in grave danger. Alfred needs your help desperately. You do not have to spy on the Vikings. Alfred just needs you to ride into Chippenham, offer submission and pay the Danegeld. I have brought gold and silver from the treasury that you can use."

"Prince, if this is what my king commanded, I will do it. Yet I hardly see how this will help our cause."

"It is simple, Hrycg. A Swedish trader, whom you captured some time ago, would like to go with you."

"I have no captives here. If I capture a Viking, he dies!"

"Peace! The trader sits before you."

"Prince, you cannot do this! You have already used that ploy to fight with the Great Army, and again to travel amongst the Vikings of Ireland. You are already well known to many Vikings of different lands. They hear the songs the scops sing about you, and some grow angry.

If you are caught, you will suffer greatly for the embarrassment you have caused them. If one of us must become a spy, let it be me!"

"I thank you for your concern, old friend, and for your offer. Yet you do not speak the language, and you will not be given the run of the burh. Only a fellow Viking will be allowed to listen and see what we need to know."

"Aye. I suppose I see your logic. Yet it is a terrible risk, Prince Ambrose."

"If Alfred calls up traitors to his side, and is betrayed, then the royal house of Wessex is snuffed out, and the last free Angelisc kingdom on the island is irrevocably lost. Do I have a choice, old friend?"

⚑

The cavalcade made a brave showing. Thane Hrycg led his well-armed little force of twenty churls and lesser thanes forward. The Viking raiding party whooped and rode toward the Saxons at a full gallop. More than a hundred mounted Danes circled the slow-moving party, while waving their weapons and shouting bloodcurdling battle cries.

Hrycg did not even deign to look at the encircling horsemen, but his lieutenant hurriedly held higher the white shield that served the Vikings as a flag of truce. The white shield, and the reaction of the Jutish party when they had first spotted the larger Viking force, had made it clear that intended to parley, but the Vikings were just toying with the Jutes.

Finally tiring of the game, the commander of the Viking force rode up to face Thane Hrycg personally. He spoke in broken Anglish. "What you want, Saxon?"

"I wish to meet with King Guthrum."

"Saxon, why we not just . . . kill you now?"

"Because I am a Jute, and I have come to bend my knee before your king, Viking. He has sent word that any Anglish who are willing to pledge allegiance to him are welcome in his camp. What kind of greeting is this that you offer me, Viking? Why do you make your king into a liar?"

"Careful, Jute. I will . . . take you . . . to king. It be his command. But my choice is . . . kill all Jutes, and Saxons too."

"Then I am grateful that you are not king. Now call off your dogs before there is an unfortunate accident. We would not want to have to kill one of our 'allies.'"

"Ho! I think you - me would rather fight then be friend. But, if you wish to give we your gold and silver with no fight . . . ' The big man shrugged.' Then to follow me, Jute."

Hrycg's little party had penetrated to within an hour's ride of Chippenham before it had been spotted. The Jutish commander noted the lack of a secure security perimeter. He hoped that he, or Alfred, could eventually use that information against Guthrum. He rode next to the ragged man who wore leg irons fastened under his horse.

"Well, Hamar, have you noticed the lack of watchers? I am surprised that Guthrum does not have a stronger defensive perimeter."

Ambrose responded. "Aye, Hrycg. But remember that Guthrum doesn't have the force he had last summer. As well, Ethelnoth's thanes have been harvesting stray Danes whenever they were foolish enough to leave Chippenham in small groups."

"It means that we could sneak up on Chippenham, Prince!"

"Aye. If we had enough men to make it worthwhile. Come the spring, Hrycg, bring every man you can lay hands on to the gathering. It is our only hope!"

"I will be there, Prince, with every man of mine who can carry a spear."

ᕤ

The little party finally reached the burh of Chippenham, now Guthrum's stronghold. Ambrose noted that the ramparts had been raised and the ditch deepened. He knew that it would have been backbreaking work in the winter cold, when the ground had the consistency of rock. Now he knew what the Saxon captives had been doing under the Danish lash.

Haggard men looked up out of the dry ditch, staring at their countrymen still mounted on fine horses, until the crack of whips sent them staggering back to their task. Ambrose shuddered. He had once been a slave under the Viking lash, and he knew how hard the slaves' lot would be. From his own experience, he knew Vikings had little respect for men who chose to live as cowards rather than die in glorious battle. He prayed that the captives could be rescued before they were transported to Wyk Te Duurstede or some other continental slave market.

Ambrose rode across the same great oak beams they had so hurriedly pulled into the burh on the day of Guthrum's devastating attack. The gates swung open as they approached, and Hrycg's little group rode into what had once been one of Alfred's favorite royal burhs. Just before crossing the bridge, their Viking escort turned around and rode back the way they had come. Ambrose assumed that they were on their way back to resume their patrol.

The Vikings were either very well organized, or they had received word of the approaching Anglish party, for a waiting patrol of infantry stood fanned out across the road. The burly commander of the force, a giant of a man, spoke gruffly in rough Anglish. "Dismount! You will to follow me. I take you to my king!"

The Jutish squad looked to their commander. He echoed the instructions. "All right, men. Dismount. And Harold, unchain our guest. Form up and follow me!"

The shackles were removed from Ambrose, and the men obediently formed up behind their master. The Viking commander waited impatiently. He was not used to such good Anglish discipline within the Viking camp. It seemed that these were not cowed refugees, but undefeated fighting men.

King Guthrum sat in his Seat-of-Honor, set up at the edge of the burh's common area. The warmth of the winter sun allowed the Danes to escape the smoke and odors of the crowded Great Hall for a few hours. Crowds of hulking Viking warriors, in gaudy dress and warm cloaks, flanked him. Ambrose did spot the occasional Saxon costume amongst all the others.

Hrycg was led directly to Guthrum, but a line of fierce-looking and heavily armed warriors prevented the rest of the party from approaching too closely.

Guthrum spoke in his deep voice, and a Viking translator effortlessly translated what he said into Anglish. "Welcome, Thane. What brings you to my camp? Have you come to offer me your love and allegiance?"

"King, my name is Hrycg, and I am a thane of Wiltshire. I do not love you. I do not even like you."

Guthrum turned his head and conferred for a moment with a scholarly-looking man who stood just behind his chair. At last he turned back and resumed the conversation.

"Ho! I know of you, Thane Hrycg. You fought well when we attacked this burh. You cut down several of my best warriors. And you were a thorn in my side when we caught up to you on the other side of the Avon River. You are a dangerous man; a man to respect. You are no Anglish boot-licker. Why are you here, Hrycg of Wiltshire?"

"King, if I had my way, we would fight to the death. Yet we have heard disturbing rumors that Alfred and his brother Ambrose are dead. My people held a meeting . . . what you people call a 'thing', and we voted to pay you Danegeld if you will leave our lands alone. We know that we cannot hope to match your strength. I agreed only to spare widows on both sides."

"So you will just give me the gold and silver I would take anyway?"

"I would personally give you the point of my sword, but I swore to accept the decision of the majority."

"And so you will bend the knee to me?"

"And so I will bend my knee to you; not in love, but of necessity."

"You are an honest man, Hrycg. You dare to tell me your real thoughts. It is a welcome change from the sycophants who normally grovel before me. You see some standing in the crowds before you. They are cowards with no balls!

Yes, Thane Hrycg. I accept your offer, providing you do not insult me with a piddling amount of gold and silver. You and my . . . what do you call it . . . reeve . . . will settle the details later. In return, you promised to do something for me."

"Yes, King."

"From you, it will provide me little pleasure, Saxon, but it is necessary. Kneel!"

Slowly, grudgingly, Hrycg slid to one knee. "I and my people are Jutes, Guthrum, not Saxons. But I swear to you that, in the absence of my true king, I accept King Guthrum as my lord and master."

Guthrum smiled. "Grudging, and honest. Rise, Hrycg. I ask you to stay the night, and we will celebrate our new relationship. Perhaps over the mead we can even learn to like each other."

Guthrum snapped his finger. "Rolf! Go with this man, and get from him the boundaries of his land and the details of the tribute. I swear today that these lands will be sacrosanct from my raiding parties, as long, of course, as adequate tribute is paid me on a yearly basis. Go now."

Hrycg did not move. "King Guthrum."

The king looked back at Hrycg. A hush fell over the crowd. Others had died painfully for so interrupting their master.

"Yes, Thane Hrycg?"

"I brought you a present."

The king smiled. "Beside the tribute and your eloquent oath? This is an exciting day."

"King Guthrum, I brought you a one-eyed Swedish Viking.' Hrycg turned to his men. Let Hamar come forward!"

Ambrose moved in obedience. The Viking spearmen let him through their line. He stopped at Hrycg's side.

The thane spoke to Guthrum. "This man was shipwrecked on our coast when Divine Providence thrust your fleet onto our shores last year."

"Why he is little enough! Did you not feed him, Hrycg? If he came with a giant, carrying a mighty sword, and a thin dark man, I would be suspicious of such a gift."

Ambrose felt his heart pounding in his chest. *Guthrum's jibe* was frighteningly accurate. He felt a moment of sheer panic, but Guthrum continued.

"And yes, Thane, I remember. Somewhere in the crowd are five good men who lost their right hands at Alfred's command. How did this man survive the slaughter and mutilation of my brave warriors?"

"He convinced me he was more a trader than a warrior, which, as you can see by his size, was probably a wise thing. He entertained me, king. He both plays the harp, and juggles things. By amusing me, he saved his life. I thought that in honor of our new 'friendship', I should return him to his own. I now declare him to be yours to do with as you will."

"I thank you, Thane. Singer, come before me."

Ambrose made it through the men, and silently kneeled at Guthrum's feet. "What is your story, Singer?"

Ambrose replied in colloquial Danish. He had spent enough years in the Scandinavian countries and in the company of various Vikings on the Russian rivers that he spoke all the major dialects fluently.

"I was a trader who joined the fleet in Frankland. There is always lots of gold to be made when an army marches, especially when led by such a master warrior as yourself, Sire. *Aegir*, unfortunately, must have been angry that day, for he threw up a great storm, and many worthy ships went into Aegir's wide jaws. Most of the men had little chance. *Ran's nets* were full to over-flowing. I awoke on the beach to find myself chained and captive."

"And you lived with the Jutes for a year, Singer? You had the run of this man's house and did not escape?"

Ambrose unrolled the cloth that served as leggings. There was still dried blood where the leg irons had rubbed his ankles raw. "Great king, Thane Hrycg is a careful man. I was not provided the opportunity."

"Well, Swede, do you think you can earn a living in my camp?"

"I can entertain your men, and offer them some supplies from back home at only very modest mark-ups, Your Majesty. Hrycg has generously returned to me some of my trade goods. And I can fight, as long as the enemy come from the right direction!"

"Ho! I will expect you to sing for me some time, Singer. And you can juggle too?"

"Hrycg did not see fit to provide me with my customary daggers, but if I may, Your Majesty?" Ambrose gestured toward a basket of apples on the table, near the Danish monarch.

"Aye, help yourself."

Ambrose soon had six apples high in the air, one following the other through his hands in a movement that was faster than the eye could follow. Ambrose moved along the edge of the crowd.

The prince was not fooled by Guthrum's amicability. He was in as much danger as if he was leading a charge into the midst of the Viking king's finest warriors. If but one man recognized him, he was dead. Still, the eye-patch, the ragged clothes, the dirt, and the hair coloring that Polonius had painstakingly applied, had dramatically changed his appearance.

With a shock, he recognized Ealdorman Ethelwold of Dorset standing in the front rank of the crowd, and he moved toward him. He spoke in Danish to Guthrum.

"Sire, the Saxons in your crowd look to be a poor lot. I daresay they have already met a sharper trader than I!" With that, he adroitly slipped the ealdorman's dagger from its sheath, and it joined the procession of apples circling above his head.

"I do not understand Hrycg's reluctance to provide me with knives, Sire! But I would not want the Saxon to feel robbed. Let us trade, Saxon." He sent two apples hurtling at Ethelwold, who, visibly angry at being made the butt of a joke, yet dextrously caught them.

The crowd yelled its appreciation of the little man's skills with words and his hands.

Guthrum stood, signaling the end of the audience. "Singer, if you fight and sing as well as you juggle, then you are doubly welcome in my camp."

"No Odin-cursed Swede is welcome in this camp, little man."

"Friend, I am a trader and an entertainer; not a warrior. I have not done you any wrong."

"You breathe, Swede. My cousins in northern Ireland were massacred by you Swedes and your cousins, the Norse. *Your kind killed them and took their land.* Since then I have made it my goal in life to cleanse the world of Swedes."

"I think you mean Norse. I have already told you that I have no quarrel with you. My cousins are sailing the rivers of Russia, not poking around Ireland and stealing patches of dirt. I certainly have no wish to incur a blood debt or to break Guthrum's commandment. Yet if you would care to wager your sword against mine, we might practice swordplay until one of us draws blood. What do you say, Dane? Are you afraid of making a friendly bet with a puny one-eyed Swedish trader?"

The man's companions roared encouragement. Guthrum, aware of the dangers of keeping a force of some fifteen hundred violent warriors together, had ruled that, in the event of a dual that caused the death of one man in his army, he would perform the blood-eagle on the winner. A friendly dual, however, was not discouraged. Guthrum wished his fighting men to keep their skills honed to a razor's edge.

"Aye, pipsqueak! If you win, I will throw in all of my armor, for I will no longer be worthy of being called a warrior!"

"Dane, where I come from, we took weapons away from such louts as you, in case they harmed themselves!"

The crowd, once hostile to Ambrose, again roared with laughter. The little man was not intimidated, and he showed wit. The burly Dane, realizing that a lot of the laughter was aimed at him, drew his sword and charged Ambrose.

Ambrose saw an immediate opening, but if he used it, the man would impale himself on Ambrose's sword, and Ambrose had no wish to have his own lungs pulsating outside of his body. He swung his point aside, but twisted the blade enough that it struck the bigger man hard on his buttocks as he charged by. The crowd roared with laughter again, and the man turned red. He knew that the fickle crowd had turned against him and was now actively supporting the stranger. Roaring in anger and frustration, he flung himself again at Ambrose.

Again Ambrose slipped nimbly to the side, and the man's wild swing cut empty air. The Viking turned to face Ambrose a third time. "Stand still, you little pup, and feel Bjorn's steel!"

"As you command, you overgrown oaf!"

Ambrose then started stalking the Dane. Bjorn grinned at the change of tactics, and started to swing his sword in great whistling circles. Ambrose met the man blow for blow, and inexorably forced the man back toward the edge of the circle formed by the spectators. For a man to break the integrity of the circle in a friendly dual was to lose.

Bjorn fought back heroically, but the little man had blinding speed and surprising strength. Time and time again the Swede's blade slipped past his guard and touched his armor.

Rapidly nearing exhaustion, the big Viking gasped out words to his tormentor. "Who are you, stranger? No Swedish trader fights with such skill and strength."

"You are a fool, Bjorn! Before I lost my eye, I earned my living with a sword, just as you do. I can still defeat cripples and old women!" With that Ambrose swung low and caught Bjorn's left knee squarely. At the last moment, he twisted his blade, so the flat of his sword hit instead of the sharp edge. Bjorn's leg crumpled beneath him, and he fell hard. Even as he started to fall, Ambrose's blade leapt up and struck the Dane's sword away. By the time the big man recovered from landing hard on the ground, he was disarmed, and Ambrose's blade hovered by his throat.

Bjorn looked up at the dirty, brown-haired trader who stared at him with a single cold eye and a grim expression. For the first time, the Viking felt a stab of fear. This man, puny as he was, had a strength and power that almost visibly emanated from him. Bjorn prized martial skill and strength above all else, and he realized that he had met his match. The stranger made no further hostile move toward him, and the tip of his blade withdrew a little when Bjorn sat still on the ground, only grasping his injured knee. Ambrose's blade remained still in the air, and Bjorn's eyes showed a new respect for the man who could hold a heavy blade at that angle.

He rolled slowly over so he could get to his feet, and made no move toward his sword. He held his open hand out to the stranger. "Well done, Swede! I think I misjudged a man today. Help me to my feet, and I will fetch my armor for you. You have won it fairly."

The Danish warriors gathered around both Ambrose and the Dane, and heartily clapped both on the back. Ambrose put away his sword, and spoke to the big Viking.

"I think I, too, may have said some rash things today, Dane. I thank you for your armor and weapons. I wish to make a present of them to a brave man whom I would like to call friend. Will you accept them?"

The crowd roared with delight, and Bjorn shook Ambrose's hand in friendship. "Aye, stranger. I am very fortunate today. I have learned a valuable lesson. I have made a new friend, and I have been given armor that fits me to perfection!"

With that his friends roared anew. "Come, Swede. Let us find some of their abominable Saxon mead and celebrate our new friendship. And call me Bjorn."

"Bjorn, my name is Hamar. I accept your offer, but only if you and your friends let me pay for the drinks."

"None will say nay to that! Come, friends, we have some serious drinking to do!"

⚐

"Hamar, how did you come to Guthrum's camp?"

"It was not a simple trip, Bjorn. I sailed from Frankland with the Danish fleet, headed for Exeter and Guthrum's Army. A terrible storm overtook us off the town the Saxons call Swanage, and most of the fleet was dashed against the rocky shores.

The Odin-cursed Saxons waited for us on shore. They slit the throats of any of us who showed any fight, and chained the ones whom they found unconscious. They pumped my lungs dry of the salt water, but it was a small enough favor. We were taken to the local ealdorman, and some were then sent to Alfred himself.

The Saxon king ordered many of the Vikings to be put to the question. Alfred wanted to know the origin of the fleet, its destination, and how many ships had sailed from France. Brave men died slowly, and eventually Alfred's men got the knowledge that their master wanted."

"But you are here, in Guthrum's camp."

"Aye. I was lucky. I spoke their language and managed to convince them that someone as small and scrawny as myself was but a humble trader; not a warrior of Odin. It helped that, when they looted our wreck, they found my trading stock."

"So they let you go?"

"Hardly, old friend.' With that, Ambrose pulled up his pant leg so that the abrasions caused by the leg irons he had worn were clearly visible. 'They chained me like an animal, so I couldn't run. But I sang songs, and I juggled well, so the Ealdorman kept me for his amusement."

With that, Ambrose reached out for three apples, and quickly had them flying in the air. A fourth, fifth, and sixth then flew into the air to join the others.

"Some silly skills I had learned as a child kept me alive. I despaired, for although the Saxons did not abuse me, they had no intention of letting me go. I was sure that when they were no longer amused by me, I would be sent to a quarry or farm to work out the rest of my days."

"And you escaped?"

"No such luck, Bjorn. You and Guthrum intervened."

Ambrose could see that both Bjorn and his companions were leaning forward in curiosity. He knew that there was little Vikings liked more than a good tale.

"When you attacked Chippenham, the thane who held me captive rode home with his tail between his legs. He had been there at the attack, and he had barely escaped. He knew the might of Guthrum, and he was terrified that all of you were on his heels.

Once he reached his home, he called in all of his churls and started training them, but quickly realized that a force such as he commanded could not possibly hold off a serious Viking attack. Make no mistake. He is a brave warrior, but he knew that, after the slaughtering, Guthrum would just take the gold and silver, and sell his family into slavery, to boot. Thus he gathered his treasure, and rode to Guthrum to make peace. He thought it would be a grand gesture if he was to return me to Guthrum. Still, I won't complain. I am free of the bastard, and finally reached the army I had set out to join over a year ago."

"And what do you plan to do now, Hamar?"

"I have only a little of my trading goods left. The Ealdorman plundered them when I was in his captivity, yet I would like to try to trade with the remainder. If that doesn't work, I will hire out my sword. It is harder to fight with but one eye, but I am sure there is at least one man in this camp who would vouch for my fighting ability."

Bjorn grinned. "Have no fear about that, Swede. I have no intention of facing your magic blade again!"

The mead had flowed freely for several hours, and two of Ambrose's drinking companions had slid under the table. Ambrose had nursed his drink carefully, yet he was feeling the effect of the alcohol on his system. If he waited much longer, then he would himself pass out.

"Bjorn, ol' frien'! There was a Saxon ealdorman from Kent that cheated me several years ago, when I traded in the south. Wha' Saxon dogs have come to Guthrum's camp? I wan' to pay that bastard back!"

"From Kent? Nay, I don't think I have seen any from there. Some other ealdormen have come in to grovel, but I don't think any were from Kent."

"Wha' coward would sell out their king like that?"

"Without their king and his puking brother at their side, the *jarls of this land* are suddenly not so courageous. They flock to grovel at

Guthrum's feet."

"Hey. Your horn is looking very empty. Le' me fill it for you . . . I canno' believe that Saxon ealdormen 're such cowards."

"Guthrum is no fool! It doesn' matter if the Saxon dogs do gather their bloody forces come spring. He is terrorizing the areas where the ealdormen have not made submission, and he has signed enough secret agreements that our summer army will have as many Saxons in it as Alfred's. Don' you see . . . We will defeat the Saxon army with other Anglish!"

"I can't believe it. It is one thing to pay Danegeld. Wha' Saxon would march against Alfred?"

"Ol' frien', how do you think we escaped from the trap at Wareham? Do you really think we could've filled in a ditch with Saxon sentries all aroun'? The Saxons may be stupid, but they're no' that stupid! Yet another jarl has promised us a thousand warriors for this summer. An' when we add those men to Ubbi's army from the West, Alfred and any warriors he can raise will be crushed between two stones. An' that's if we don't get him handed to us on a platter first.

Lis'en! We got one ol' frien' whose goin' to try to lure Alfred into his clutches. Guthrum's plan is brilliant. If this fool Ethelwold succeeds in catching Alfred, we give 'im the gold an' the crown he has demanded. He runs Wessex for us, an' we cart away the rest of the treasures. If he fails, Alfred's so pissed at him that he has to support us come summer. Alfred'll take 'is 'ead if'en he kin catch the bastard."

"Why, that's a wunnerful plan! But ri' now I think I better lie down ri' here. I seem to be talking to two of ya and neither will stay in focus."

CHAPTER 21

The First Foray from Athelney

Alfred smiled in triumph. He and his men had laboriously dragged a dozen large boats all the way to the Avon River without being discovered by any of Guthrum's scouts or raiding parties. His little band of Saxons was now less than three Roman miles upriver from the fortified burh of Chippenham, where Guthrum and his Danes were headquartered.

Alfred signaled the men to climb into the boats. He trembled with excitement. For the first time since that terrible night when he had been forced to ignominiously retreat from Guthrum's overwhelming attack on Chippenham, he was going to strike back directly at the hated Vikings. He felt he had skulked long enough in the woods and the swamps. With his family safe at his island fortress, he felt it was time to let all Angleland know that Alfred, king of the West Saxons, was alive, and fighting mad! Even better, his daring attack on Guthrum's own citadel would not only be a symbol to his people, but also be the catalyst for Ambrose's escape. He feared for his brother's life, and was eager to be reunited with him.

The water was open, though the shore on either side had a thin covering of snow. The snow had made it easy to drag the boats into position, but it also meant that it would be easier for a Viking to see the Saxons silhouetted against the snow and water. Still, Ambrose, Polonius, Phillip and he had planned with care. All but the first two boats were roofed over with stout oak planks, and Alfred had brought only his highly trained drengs from his Personal Guard with him. There were no better warriors in all of Britain; Saxon or Viking.

The first two boats pulled ahead of the rest. Their task was to quietly drift down river and reach the twin ferries before the rest were spotted and the main force was ready to start their attack.

The thanes pulled in their oars and lay on the bottom of the boats. The carefully attached branches broke the shape of the two boats, so that they might be mistaken, at least from a distance, for two massive logs. Teams of Foresters had been launching old logs and branches from further upriver for days, and it was hoped that the Vikings had tired of watching logs float by.

With just one last bend of the river left before the Saxons came into sight of Chippenham, Alfred ordered the rest of the men to angle in and tie up beside a solitary gnarled oak that stood sentinel on the shore. Once all the boats were secured, he waited for the men to light the oil and wood in the metal sand buckets placed in the bottom of each boat. It was a dangerous thing to do in a small open boat, but it was necessary so that they could give the Vikings a warm surprise.

Alfred grinned again in anticipation of the little treat they had for Guthrum. A dark shape drifted toward them from the shelter of the woods, but no one raised a weapon. Polonius's mounted force was scouting the shore, and had been waiting for the boats to appear.

The men watched as Polonius himself strode through the snow to their location. His voice was quiet, but it carried to the crewmen. "Sire! The two boats are nearing the ferries. I have to ride now to get my troop into position. If you are ready, Sire, it is time to go!"

"Aye, Polonius! . . . You heard Lord Polonius! Cast off! Archers, prepare to shoot as soon as you come into range!"

Polonius' mounted force emerged from the woods, and then gradually faded from sight again as they worked their way along the shore toward the little fort that was their special target.

The ten boats dipped and danced in the current, as they floated toward the outer wall of the fortified burh of Chippenham. The steersmen brought the vessels as close to the burh's palisade wall as possible. Without a further word, the various crews lowered the wooden shields that helped hide the fires from the Danish sentry's eyes. Each archer then briefly dipped the tip of his arrow into the fire within the metal bucket, lit the flammable material wrapped around the head, drew the shaft to his cheek, and released.

Within moments, the sky lit up with thin flames of light that arced high and then fell into the burh. Most of the shots would miss, but almost all of the buildings had thatched roofs. Each archer attempted to empty his first quiver as fast as he could. As the first arrows arced, the men in all the boats took up a thundering chant. "Alfred! Alfred!" Alfred himself raised his personal banner on a makeshift flagpole.

Yells and throbbing war horns indicated to the Saxons that Guthrum and the Danes had woken to the danger. The boats kept floating down-river, and the archers continued the rain of fire arrows until the first quivers were empty.

The Danes were professional warriors, and the burh reacted to the blare of the war horns as if it was a giant hive that had been disturbed by a hungry bear. Hundreds of armed and angry Danes leapt the palisades or ran through the water gates, until a solid line of Vikings formed along the shore.

Many shook their swords or spears at the Saxons floating serenely past and shouted imprecations. The better prepared, however, who had thought to bring their bows, strung them and started a concerted effort to empty the boats. Alfred stood in the bow of his vessel, and the flickering light of the fire pot fitfully lit his body. He waved to the screaming men on shore.

The Saxon archers switched targets and proceeded to aim at the crowd of Danes lining the shore. Gradually, however, enough Viking archers arrived that the boatloads of Saxon warriors were forced to pull back toward the further bank. The Saxons rowed with good will. The amount of light over the burh indicated that they had managed to start some serious fires. In the winter cold, the loss of each house or storeroom was another major victory for the Saxons.

꙳

Ambrose had crossed on the last ferry at sunset. The little rectangular palisade he headed toward was right across from the tip of the peninsula that held the burh of Chippenham. Although the fort's location protected the two large ferries and a horse corral, it was garrisoned by less than two dozen Vikings. As long as the access to the ferries could be controlled, the garrison had all the resources of Chippenham on the further shore at its disposal; only a short boat ride away.

Ambrose waved to the two guards at the open gate. He was a regular visitor, and doubly welcome when he brought his harp. After dark, the little fort was buttoned up tight, and the garrison enjoyed the visits of the Swede who came to buy and sell, but was pleased to entertain them with both songs and stories.

꙳

"Sing the one about that bastard Prince Ambrose and the Irish!" Drud, already fairly drunk, pressed for the song that he knew would annoy his commander, a distant relative of the Jarl of Wexford.

Ambrose replied. "All right, ol' friend . . ."

Suddenly the sentry, stationed on the high walkway overlooking the river, called out. "Commander! There are lights in the sky, and a war horn sounds!"

The warriors were suddenly still and silent. Drunk or sober, they were brave and capable men. Each listened attentively, and soon all heard what the sentry was referring to. A single war horn sounded faintly in the distance. The sound was quickly picked up by others, however, and suddenly dozens were sounding."

A gaunt warrior cried out. "By Odin's beard! It sounds like a general alarm!"

Oskar, the burly commander of the little garrison, responded instantly. "Grab your weapons, my little chickadees! Man the walls!"

Ambrose laid down his harp and grabbed his own sword. No one questioned his right to join the warriors. It was understood that all of the Vikings would fight if threatened. The story of the fight between Ambrose and Bjorn was well known throughout the camp. The prince had earned his place beside the northern warriors in the only manner which they understood.

The men quickly climbed up the ladders to the walkway along the top of the palisades. There was no moon, but the snow effectively reflected the feeble light from the stars. The men could see, over the fortified burh across the river, dozens of fire arrows arcing high and then dropping below the battlements of the burh.

The little band watched in fascination for a few minutes. There was a certain beauty to the tiny fireflies of light. Gradually, more and more warriors started to exit the burh opposite their position and line up on the far bank. Above the sound of the war horns, a hypnotic chant could now be heard coming from upriver. Clearly, something was coming their way.

Ambrose pointed down-river and yelled. "Look there! There is a boat tied to the ferry! The Saxons are after the ferry!"

Oskar was an intelligent leader. The main reason for the little fort was to protect the vital communications link across the river. Alfred had escaped Guthrum's clutches here earlier in the winter because he had controlled the river, and the Vikings had been unable to cross the river in order to chase the fleeing refugees. The ferry was a vital link that allowed a quick transfer of men and horses back and forth across the river.

Oskar roared out in anger and sent the men running for the ferry. Two dozen men burst through the gate and charged for the landing. One last man ran out of the gate, but instead of following in the wake of the angry warriors, he turned and ran toward the woods. In the dark and excitement, only the hidden Saxon foresters saw him.

Once Ambrose reached the line of trees, he made the call of a hunting owl. The woodsmen threw off their white capes and quickly notched their arrows. While the howling Vikings threw spears at the fleeing boatload of Saxons, more than fifty archers started to harvest the Danes strung out and silhouetted against the water.

The Saxon boat that had been tied to the ferry fled downriver. The Danes from the little garrison jeered and lined up on the bank, weapons in hand, and waited for the small fleet of boats containing the Saxon archers. Suddenly, the Vikings standing on the river bank started dropping. They turned in confusion. With their backs to the water, and without any shelter, they were terribly vulnerable. The sound of a Saxon war horn startled them further. A long line of Saxon archers had stepped out of the forest and were targeting them. The snow muffled the sound of the horses' hooves, but the Danes, could also clearly see the shape of a mass of riders coming hard at them. Polonius' specially trained thanes with the double length lances led the charge. To their credit, not one of the Vikings tried to flee. One by one, each was either spitted on the end of a lance, or shot by the advancing archers. Within moments, the last Vikings on their side of the river were dead.

Ambrose ordered the woodsmen to retrieve their own horses and prepare to ride. First however, he sent out three squads to their predetermined tasks. A full two dozen ran to destroy the ferry. The men set to with a will, first dragging the heavy barge out of the water, and then proceeding to chop it into kindling with axes and swords.

Ambrose felt a moment's pang at the loss of the ferry. It had been a marvel of engineering. The barge, with a straight deep keel that the water could press against, was cunningly designed to travel in either direction; propelled by only the current of the river. A simple adjustment of the ropes that attached the barge to the heavy cable was all it took to reverse the barge's direction. After it was destroyed, the men ran to cut the cables of both ferries where they were attached to pulleys anchored by massive trees.

The second squad headed for the now abandoned fort, where they took burning logs from the fire and threw them onto the roof tops. Others poured flammable fluid on the palisade logs and lit it. Soon the flames rivaled those from across the river.

A squad of Polonius' riders mounted up and rode for the corral. Alfred's Saxons could always use more good horses.

Out on the water, the remaining boatloads of Saxons were forced to press against the banks furthest from Chippenham. The entire Viking army, except those desperately fighting the various fires, now lined the opposite bank of the river and shouted in frustration and anger. The sky filled with Danish shafts, and the stout oak planks looked like the nose of a hound which had got too close to a porcupine. Alfred's men kept rowing, however. Having just passed the little burning fort, they had to try one last close pass to the burh. The first boat had been unsuccessful in its attempt to land on the Chippenham shoreline, having been driven off with considerable casualties. While both cables across the river had been cut, the second ferry was safe on the other bank, along with a good dozen smaller boats flipped upside-down on the shore. They couldn't ferry horses, but they could carry Viking warriors. Worse, they could be used to bring a new cable across for the remaining barge. With even one barge in operation, Guthrum could send hundreds of mounted warriors after Alfred within twenty-four hours.

Try as they could, the Saxon planners had not been able to figure out a way to destroy the boats stored on the Chippenham side. The men who had drifted downriver ahead of the main force had promised to try, but they hadn't even gotten near the ferry itself. The archers hid behind their stout oaken planks while they peppered the boats and ferry with more fire arrows, in spite of the fact that they were within range of the Viking archers. Alfred himself grabbed a bow and shot carefully at the targets. The damage they caused was slight, however, and the Saxons were quickly driven back across the river by the steady rain of retaliatory arrows.

A series of short blasts of the Saxon war horns and a blazing fire recalled the men to the far shore and pinpointed their destination. There, horses awaited the exhausted rowers. As the boats were pulled from the water, they were soaked in oil and set on fire.

Surveying the flames greedily licking at the little fort, the brightness in the sky across the river, and the burning boats a little downriver, Alfred grinned and hugged his bastard brother. "God is good! You're crazy, brother-of-mine, but I love you! Let's get the hell out of here!"

The Saxons quickly formed up. Several of the rowers were dead, and one was mortally wounded. Alfred himself held the man in his arms. A tear slid down his cheek. After kissing the man on both cheeks, he drew his sax and quickly slit the man's throat so that he wouldn't suffer unnecessarily. The frothy blood the man had been spitting up indicated that he was beyond anything the wise old women could do, even if they were to reach the safety of a friendly village.

Alfred spoke. "Tie the wounded and dead men onto horses. We leave no one behind, dead or alive! We will leave no one for the Danes to wreck their vengeance on! When you have done with that, get a horse and mount up!"

The scouts led the mounted column eastward at a steady clip. The Saxons could not ride at breakneck speed through the dark, but each and every rider knew that not far behind them the entire army of King Guthrum was struggling to repair the damage to the ferry and transfer a large mounted force to their side of the river. Come the dawn, there would be pursuit. Alfred's personal banner had flown in the attack, and the Vikings would follow like dogs on the trail of a bitch in heat.

ॾ

The king of all the West Saxons reined in his exhausted mount. Just ahead of him was a roaring fire, and, in its flickering light, Alfred could see the ferry, the river, and a forest of sharp-spear-points. Each and every one of them was aimed at him and the host who streamed out behind him.

The king called out to the men barring his way. "Ethelnoth, you old rascal! Where are you? Is this any way to greet your tired and freezing king?"

The spearheads lowered instantly at the sound of the sharp Saxon words. A deep and gruff voice answered the king's summons. "I am here, my king! We feared for a moment that a patrol of Guthrum's Danes had found our fire before you could get back!

Please, Sire! If you would be so kind as to dismount and climb onto the ferry, we'll have you safe across in a jiffy! The horses are harnessed and in place, and we are ready to start the operation right away. Our horses are already across, but we have to work fast if you want everyone to be across soon after dawn!"

Alfred led Phillip, Ambrose, and his small clique of raiding party commanders over to the shore. They crammed on the flat-bottomed barge, along with as many fyrdmen as would fit.

A vigorously waved torch instructed the men on the other side to start up the heavy draft horses. The waterlogged craft lurched into deeper water, and then started a speedy journey across the frigid river.

As the heavily burdened barge nudged into the old log dock, King Alfred nimbly leapt ashore. Ambrose and Phillip came next, and they were in turn followed swiftly by the entire boatload of officers and warriors. Without instructions, the men fanned out in order to provide a security screen for their king, but there seemed to be little real likelihood of danger. Ethelnoth's troops who had been left on this side of the river to protect the barge and ensure that the ferry was ready for instant use, happily greeted their comrades. The only known danger was now on the other side of the river; though none doubted that it was speedily riding in their direction, and in overwhelming numbers.

It was essential that Alfred's band of raiders, now fleeing for their lives, had to get the entire group, horses included, across the river before Guthrum and his avenging demons arrived. To that effect, Alfred had left Ethelnoth's men instructions to cut towpaths and harness horses to the massive cables that spanned the river.

Even Alfred had been impressed how quickly a dozen strong horses could cause the old barge to plough across the fast-running river. An equally powerful team on the other side stood ready to quickly draw the ungainly vessel back. First the men, then the horses; Alfred prayed that all would cross before the Danes arrived.

The king strode over to the rough hut that, in time of peace, provided shelter for the enterprising Saxons who ran the little toll ferry. He was cold, and exhausted from all the action, and then the hard riding through the frozen countryside. At the doorway he turned to his officers. In all his fighting and riding, he had not had more than a few moments in which to talk with his brother, and he was impatient. He stopped at the entrance to the hut, and turned to his retinue of officers.

"Phillip, please stay by the door and see that we are not disturbed for a few minutes. Commanders, see to the men. It is imperative we get everyone across without any delays. And as for you, brother-of-mine, come and stand before your king. Your little brother wishes to talk with you!"

As soon as Ambrose crossed the threshold into the rude hut, Alfred swept the smaller man right off his feet in a fierce bear hug. "Ambrose, I was so worried! Next time, please tell your king what you are up to! We agreed you would send Hrycg to spy, not go yourself! But in the name of gentle Jesus, tell me, was your little jaunt worth risking the body of my only remaining brother and the country's greatest living hero?"

"Oof! It's hard to be crushed by a king and breathe at the same time! . . . Aye, I think it was, Alfred. Some time ago, Polonius said that Guthrum would never come south again with a diminished army unless he had some serious tricks up his sleeve. Do you remember that?"

"Yes, and we subsequently received the documents from Ubbi's camp that proved that Anwell of Cornwall was planning to commit treason and come over to Guthrum's side at the last moment."

"Guthrum intends to have more Saxons on his side than you'll have on yours!"

"God's breath! Why do I think you are trying to tell me that there is another traitor in our midst?"

"Because it is true, brother."

Alfred's face expressed his hurt, and then that fleeting moment passed and the look was replaced with one of anger. His visage hardened, and Ambrose knew that it was thus when Alfred was at his most dangerous. He rarely went into a blind rage. Rather, he burned with a cold anger that allowed his mind to coolly focus on an issue without loss of self control. It was part of what made him such a great king and a dangerous adversary. His voice, when he spoke, was tightly controlled.

"And just who else dares to betray me, brother?"

"In the Danish camp, Alfred, I saw several Saxon thanes and ealdormen. I heard names of several more who had visited and offered

Danegeld to protect their lands from being ravaged. But only one was offered a crown if he would bring a minimum of a thousand Saxon warriors against you this spring! Worse, the man intends, like Anwell of Cornwall, to send promises of numbers to you, and then change sides at the last moment. Thus the balance of numbers would change literally as you march to battle, and your army would be thoroughly demoralized."

"Two thousand men changing sides just before battle would take the heart out of any five armies I could cobble together! And worse; I would not call up distant fyrds if I thought I had adequate warriors locally for an overwhelming superiority! Just who is this perfidious traitor?"

"The one man who just might be able to force a civil war on our unhappy land. I refer to the Ealdorman of Dorset and the son of our own brother - Ethelwold. It was no accident that Guthrum escaped at Wareham. And he offered you sanctuary in his lands just last month."

"I wondered if that was a trick to scout out our secret location."

"It was that and more, Alfred. If you had put yourself in his hands, he would have had you put into chains and turned you over to Guthrum, along with your entire family."

Alfred sighed. "I see. And you think that Ethelwold could bring civil war to Wessex?"

"I fear it greatly. He is dangerous as ealdorman of a fyrd that numbers at least one thousand warriors, and probably as many again if Ethelwold digs deep. But, as the son of a former king, he is twice as dangerous."

"I did not usurp his throne! The Witan chose me over him because he was young and inexperienced! That is their function and their right."

"I agree, brother. But Ethelwold would be a perfect puppet king for Guthrum to play with. Many thanes and ealdormen, forced to choose between two close members of the royal line, would be confused and uncertain of what to do. It would be a certain recipe for disaster!"

"Well, brother, this requires some serious pondering. Let us talk no more of this until we are in our councils with Polonius and Ethelnoth."

The first light of an anaemic dawn found that all of the men and most of the horses had joined the Saxon war band on Alfred's side of the river. The draft animals were unhitched, blindfolded and led aboard the sturdy barge. The waiting men on the other side whipped up the other team of draft horses one last time.

Alfred smiled as he saw the last load of men and animals crossing the fast-flowing river. With no one remaining on the further bank, he ordered the barge pulled from the water and destroyed. The men set to with a will, and more than a hundred axes and swords rose and fell rhythmically. In minutes there was only a pile of splinters and boards.

Ethelnoth left his men finishing the destruction, and strode over to his king. "Sire do you want us to burn what is left?"

"The smoke would attract the Danes . . . But so what? Did your men scour the riverbanks for any boats?"

"Aye, Majesty, both up and down-river. We destroyed any boats on their side of the river for half a day's ride in both directions. This was the only barge in the area. It was part of a ferry service to replace the old Roman bridge upstream that had collapsed."

"Then by all means tell the men to warm themselves with a big bonfire. If Guthrum arrives before we are through, we will wave to the heathen devils! In this weather, if he tries to swim the river, half of his men would be dead in an hour. By the time they can drag enough boats here to get a force across that is big enough to threaten us, we will be again comfortably ensconced at Athelney."

CHAPTER 22

The Warriors Return, and Polonius Has a Plan

It was after sunset when Alfred and his officers approached the little forest hamlet. For the last few hours, squads of men had regularly broken off to head for the various burhs and vills scattered throughout the alder swamps, that either provided billets or boats for transportation.

The Saxon column that Guthrum was no doubt trying to follow was now just a skeleton of its former self. Viking trackers had no hope of tracing which of the many confusing paths led to the king of the West Saxons. The snow had held off, but the temperature was dropping. It promised to be a bitter night.

The anxious villagers quickly opened the palisade gate when Ealdorman Ethelnoth rode up and called out to the alert sentries. Youths ran to collect the horses, and the riders stumbled into what passed as the Great Hall, to warm themselves around the massive open-pit fire.

By dawn, the horses would be scattered across half a dozen forest and island holdings. As soon as the next snow fell, there would be no hint that the most influential men in Wessex had passed through the little vill.

The flat-bottomed swamp boats were pulled up on the nearby shore, ready to ferry the royal party to the fortress island of Athelney. From a dozen other similar villages, the various components of the warrior band would make similar journeys, until the main garrison was reunited at Alfred's fortress island.

The male adults of the little vill gathered in the Great Hall, behind the king and his officers. They were not sure if their king and their Ealdorman needed their services that night, and so they waited patiently for instructions.

Ethelnoth turned to Alfred. "Well, Sire, do you wish to rest, or do you want to press on?"

"I am sorry, old friend. I know that you are both saddle sore and exhausted, but I do want to press on. I am eager to reach the safety of our island and the arms of my loved ones. Are you, Ealdorman, up to a cold boat ride?"

"Sire, you are my king. Your wish is my command.' He turned to the thane by his side. 'Ryscford, can you arrange for enough rowers to get our entire party to Athelney tonight?"

"Yes, Ealdorman. We were expecting you. The men are ready to leave as soon as you are."

Within an hour, the tired Saxon officers, wrapped in warm furs, clambered stiffly into the boats that were held steady against the river bank. The little fleet pushed off in the intermittent moonlight.

With the royal party and the horses gone, it was as if Alfred had never visited. His entire war band had vanished from the face of the earth.

A little more than two hours after leaving the little vill, the fleet of narrow swamp boats crept near the highest point of land in the entire vast alder swamp. A single sentry announced their arrival from the security of a hidden sentry post located on a tiny island. His quick blast of a war horn was answered by the sentries on Atheling's Eig.

In moments, the entire population of the island was armed and manning the palisades. Athelney was Wessex's last hope. Its guardians were fanatical, and, in truth, there was no place else for these people to flee to.

As the little fleet neared the wharf, Alfred called out in his powerful voice. The gates of the island fortress swung open in response. The wives and children of the men who made up the war band joined the garrison in rushing to the shoreline. Many carried torches. Men died when the war band went into battle, and all were anxious to see if their menfolk had come home safely.

Alfred had his son and daughter hurtle into his arms, followed by Ealhswith. "Alfred! Thank you, oh God, for bringing my husband home to me!"

Kuralla, Gretchen, and Matilda as quickly found their loved ones, and, lit by flickering torches, the men and their families hugged and cried. The night rang with shouts of joy, and also wails of grief, when families discovered that some loved one would never return.

Alfred, supported by his son and wife, and carrying a small and shivering daughter in his arms, turned to the villagers who had managed to bring his men safe through the dark and the labyrinth of small channels to his island fortress. "Ryscford! I want you and your men to go direct to my Great Hall.

Warm yourselves, ask for food and drink, and then get some sleep. There is no need for you to make the journey back again right away. The temperature continues to plummet. I am grateful for what you have done this night."

"Thank you, Sire. We will do as you bid."

Alfred woke just as the sickly sun reached the zenith in the sky. It was bitterly cold outside, but his faithful servants had stoked the fire in his private hut until the air temperature was comfortable. He rolled off his sleeping pallet and called out to his wife who was bustling around quietly.

"Good morning, my love! I feel ravenous today!"

The queen called out to her lady-in-waiting. "Myrtle! The king wants to break his fast!'

She turned to her husband. 'Fear not, favorite-husband-of-mine. Your faithful cooks have labored for hours in order to have food ready for you when you awake."

"Thank you, my love. And would you please be so kind as to spread the word to Ambrose, Phillip, Polonius and Ethelnoth. I wish to see them here in a quarter hour."

Ealhswith stamped her foot in mock anger. "Now Alfred! They have just returned to their wives after a long and dangerous adventure. You let them be!' She looked coyly at him. 'Besides, your own wife would like to snuggle up a little with you. My great king fell asleep on me last night, after perhaps five or ten heartbeats."

Alfred now stood, wrapped only in a bearskin. "My love, I promise that I am yours to vent your lust upon . . . just as soon as I have a chance to meet with certain of my senior advisors. I need to see Ambrose, Polonius, Phillip and Ethelnoth. No others are invited."

Ealhswith threw a heavy woollen cape over her dress, and smiled at her husband. "I will go get your advisors. But I will hold you to your promise, sir!"

Alfred had barely finished his meal when the door opened to let in an Arctic blast of air and his wife, along with the men he had asked to see. He looked up as they trooped into the hut that served as royal bower.

"Welcome, friends! I am stiff and tired . . . and I have not felt this good since Guthrum galloped across our frontier!"

Ambrose hugged his brother. "Did I tell you, brother, how funny you looked in that boat, shouting your name and shaking your fist at the Viking host?"

"I did not look at funny as you, with your dirty hair and blackened teeth! You made a convincing villain, brother-of-mine.

Ealhswith, would you please serve our guests some mead? Myrtle, would you please stand guard outside the door for a few minutes. I do not want to be interrupted for a while, nor overheard. Ambrose has brought distressing news that we must discuss at some length."

As the faithful servant departed, Alfred waved his chief advisors to the benches nearest his special high-backed chair. "Sit. Relax. There are no ceremonies between us today. We must talk. Ambrose has returned with a further very disturbing piece of the Guthrum puzzle.

Let me just review what we know of his plans so far. Guthrum descended on us in a brilliant manoeuver that he probably learned *from Ambrose here*. Polonius, you said that Guthrum wouldn't come with his reduced army unless he had some other tricks up his sleeve. We now know just how right you were, Scholar!

Odda met Guthrum's second surprise, head on, in Dorset. Thank our merciful God that he was able to defeat Ubbi. The documents Odda sent us from Ubbi's tent told us that there was a third surprise, in the person of Anwell, our own Ealdorman of Cornwall.

Ambrose's spy mission, however, brought to light yet another little surprise that Guthrum has arranged for us."

Polonius spoke in a somber voice. "Please, Sire, tell us!"

"Ambrose, you risked your life to get the information, you should have the privilege of explaining what you found out."

"As you command, brother. When I was in the Danish citadel of Chippenham, I memorized a list of thanes and ealdormen who have agreed to pay Danegeld in order to save their lands from being ravaged by Guthrum's army.

Far more disturbing, however, I heard a story of a Saxon ealdorman who had already betrayed his king, and who intended to try and capture the entire royal family and turn them over to Guthrum's tender mercy. In return, he expected to be made a vassal king over much of Wessex. If that plan failed, he promised to betray the Saxon army and have his fyrd switch sides at the last moment. Between him and Anwell of Cornwall, they would be able to add almost two thousand warriors to Guthrum's force."

Phillip stood up in his agitation. "Tell me the culprit's name, and I will take fifty men and bring you his head in a week!"

Alfred spoke sternly. "His name is Ethelwold, and I forbid anyone to even mention this discussion outside of this room."

Ethelnoth spoke quietly. "And may I humbly ask why we cannot move against our own, who has betrayed his sacred oath to you, Sire?"

"Yes, of course you may, old friend. First, Ethelwold is a son of a former king. Between them, he and Anwell just might be able to garner enough support that Wessex could be forced into a civil war, at the very time we are trying to rally support to take on Guthrum. I remember, all too well, that it was just such a civil war that weakened Northumbria enough that it fell to the Great Army.

Second, how do we find an army to send against either Ethelwold or Anwell? Odda of Dorset is loyal and stands in Anwell's path, but his men suffered grievous losses at Cynwith, and he is attempting to garrison the northern coastal towns in case the Vikings in South Wales try again."

Polonius' face broke into a crafty smile that relieved both Ambrose and Alfred. Brought up in the Eastern Roman world of intrigue and deceit, he often had subtle solutions to problems that the Saxons hit head on.

"Sire, would you prefer a civil war while you fight Guthrum, or would you prefer that the Cornish fight faithfully at your side?"

"Do you have to ask, Polonius? Speak, you scoundrel! Just what is it that you are thinking?"

"Sire, I need a hundred archers, all mounted. Only your best, mind. I will also have to borrow your brother, Phillip, Bishop Asser, your signet ring, and, oh yes, the **Leaping Stag**. Yes, that should do it."

"You intend to conquer all Cornwall with that little force?"

"Well, if you are willing to lend me five hundred of Odda's men for a time, I will take Dorset out of the equation, as well."

Alfred leapt to his feet and hugged the dark man. "Polonius, if you manage to pull this off, I might even forgive your impudence!"

CHAPTER 23

Ambrose Rides to Cornwall, And Meets with Anwell

The column rode hard for the Cornish peninsula. The various royal estates they visited exchanged as many fresh horses as possible. Most of the royal stewards were reluctant to trade their fresh mounts for the lathered and exhausted ones, but Ambrose's name, and the royal ring that he wore, ensured at least grudging obedience. The column thus made good time.

On the border of Cornwall, the men rested for two days, while Boc, a senior thane of Alfred's Personal Guard, with two companions as escort, took the swiftest horses and rode ahead. Their task was to find Ealdorman Anwell, and deliver to him a royal summons commanding him to appear at his own home burh by the end of the week.

As the third day dawned warm and sunny, the cavalcade mounted up again. The warming weather reminded Ambrose that the day of reckoning with Guthrum was fast approaching. In less than a week, it would be determined if the Cornishmen were going to fight with Alfred or against him. The full fyrd of Cornishmen was a formidable force, and its loyalty could sway the entire summer campaign. In balance was nothing less than the fate of Wessex.

Less than a day's ride from the Ealdorman's home burh, Ambrose found the perfect place that he had been scouting for. They found a single dwelling far from any village, and surrounded by dense forest. He ordered the foresters to hide their horses and secretly surround the house, while Ambrose and Phillip changed their clothing, and then, escorted by a half-dozen other men in Viking armor, they rode openly to the dwelling.

The sound of the horses, and the jingle of their harness, brought the alert forest dweller to his door. Visitors were rare in winter, and were seldom a portend of good things. A burly man, dressed in homespun wool and wearing a brightly dyed cap, stood in his doorway and hefted a massive axe.

"What kin I do for ye, strangers?"

Ambrose replied in broken Gaelic. I need you . . . take a horse . . . and ride to Jarl . . . Ealdorman Anwell. Is very important . . . There be a gold coin in it for you."

The big man looked at the armored squad behind the blond man clad in Viking armor. He was alone except for his four young children who cowered inside, and his wife who stood just inside the doorway. The strangers all wore battered armor, and looked to be veteran warriors. Even with his bow and a quiver of arrows, he would have no chance against so many. He had no recourse except obedience.

"And ye will pay me gold just to deliver a message to my master?"

Ambrose casually tossed a shiny gold coin at the man. The churl caught it with easy grace, and then bit on it. He now held more money than he had even seen in his entire life, and he realized that it was real.

"Just what is the message that ye want me to carry?"

"You take this ring to Anwell, an' tell him he to come here, alone . . . right away! We stay here, and you wife remain as hostage. You obey . . . no harm come to her. You understand?"

The big man was dismayed to leave his wife in the hands of these pagan barbarians, but he knew he had little choice. Any attempt to rescue his family would probably cost them all their lives, even if he could raise enough men to take on the little force. On the other hand, the gold would make him a rich man.

"Aye, I will do as ye ask, if ye swear that my family will be safe."

Ambrose looked down at the anxious man. He felt great sorrow for the trick he was playing, but too much depended on this for him to take the man into his confidence. He steeled himself and continued.

"I swear by Odin . . . you family safe if you obey. I am ally with Anwell. We not make war on you."

At that, the big man nodded acceptance. Ambrose ordered Phillip, in Danish, to dismount and give up his horse. The churl clambered into the saddle and whipped the horse into a gallop. He was only a few hours from his master's home burh. Just the day before, he had been told that Anwell had moved into residence there. The sooner he reached his master, the sooner he could return and ensure that his family was safe.

Anwell and his two strapping sons stared at the churl who had so precipitously galloped into the little settlement. The fool told an incredible story of Vikings riding openly through Cornish lands, yet the man rode an obviously valuable horse that had a Viking saddle, and he carried Anwell's own signet ring, which had been entrusted to Ubbi himself. At last Anwell thanked the churl.

"I thank you for your efforts in bringing me this ring. You say the leader told you that I had to go alone to meet them?"

"Aye, Me Lord! He said it were most urgent, and that it had to be only ye."

"Very well. Wait outside until I call you!"

The man backed hastily out of his master's presence. "Aye, Me Lord."

Once the man had left, Anwell turned to his two sons. "Owein! Get that man out of sight - man and horse. The last thing we want is for Boc to see that messenger, or the Danish saddle! After that's taken care of, come back and post two guards outside the door. Saer! Look closely. My arms seem to be shortening of late. Is this truly the ring that we sent Ubbi?"

"Yes, father. There is no doubt."

"But the rumors were that Odda had crushed Ubbi's army!"

"Father, here is proof that the Vikings have landed. Perhaps they fled Odda but landed elsewhere."

⊫

The older man stood up and strode around the room. "Ubbi is supposed to be half way to Chippenham by now, with Devon thoroughly terrorized and Alfred trapped between a hammer and anvil. Still, thank God Ubbi's army is safe! Better he shows up late than never. My sons! By the end of this summer, Cornwall will again be free from the tyranny of upstart Wessex!"

"But father, Prince Ambrose might arrive at any time. What are we to do? You cannot leave now. To directly disobey a royal command would tip Alfred off before we have raised the fyrd. It was planned that we at least march east as erstwhile allies, until we are ready to declare our true allegiance and join Guthrum! Otherwise we will be facing Odda of Devon. He is loyal to the crown of Wessex, and thickheaded enough to attempt to bar our passage."

Anwell stared thoughtfully at his two sons. They were in the prime of their manhood, and he was very proud of them. He knew that either would make a worthy successor to the throne of Cornwall.

"Owein. How do we solve this conundrum? I obviously cannot be in two places at one time."

"Father, Alfred has specifically ordered that you meet with Ambrose. Unless we wish to make an open break now, and possibly alert Wessex, you must obey that order. Saer and I will ride out, in your name, and deal with the Viking messenger. We can take a dozen men, so we should be quite safe."

"I don't like it, but I see little choice. You and Saer are to choose only the best of my Personal Guard, and I want you to take no foolish chances."

Owein smiled fondly at his father. "I hear and obey, oh my king!"

ᕽ

Owein and Saer planned for various contingencies. One man was ordered to follow at a distance, so that at least one would escape if there was an ambush. On the last fyrdman's horse was two wicker panniers, each of which carried several homing pigeons. Alfred, himself, had told the court the amazing story of how some Hakim of Alexandria had used pigeons to communicate, and the Cornishmen had found the wondrous tale to actually be true. The birds wore different-colored ribbons on their legs, so prearranged messages could be sent in seconds. The two noblemen rode side by side, followed by fourteen well armed and veteran warriors.

The churl, now relegated to a spavined mount of indeterminate age, led the little force back toward his home. Owein spoke to the man as they rode.

"Be sure to use the game trails, and remember that I want to approach from the other side."

"We have already swung around, and are on the opposite side now, Master. My home is less than half a Roman mile beyond the large oak grove ahead."

"Excellent. There will be a silver coin in this for you if you do your job properly."

"Thank ye, Master!"

Owein waved his huntsmen forward. "Quietly now. Off your horses and scout ahead. I want no ambushes.

ᕽ

The scouts silently filed back to their young lord, and their leader reported. "We saw nothing suspicious, Master."

"Did you get close enough to see the house?"

"Aye, Master."

"And?"

"Just one man - a sentry by the look of him, and seven horses, saddled and tied behind the house."

Owein looked at Saer and smiled. "So, brother, we ride."

"We ride, but slowly, brother."

The little column advanced, but slowed as the house came into view behind a thin screen of woods. The leaves were just beginning to bud, and the forest views were still open.

Both brothers counted the horses tethered by the hut, and searched for any suspicious movements. There were just the seven horses already reported, and the single sentry, who continued to stroll around the house. A plume of smoke rose slowly into the sky, and delicious odors of cooking bacon hinted where the rest of the men were.

At last Owein gave the signal. The commander of the Personal Guard rode forward, unfurling a white banner as he rode. At a second signal, the rest of the troop broke cover and followed. The sentry, seeing the arrival of armed men, called out in a guttural tongue, and immediately an avalanche of men poured from the hut. Five heavily armored men, each dressed in Viking chain-mail, stood in a line, swords or axes naked in their hands.

The Guard commander eased his mount closer, and spoke authoritatively to the Vikings. "Who here requested the presence of my master, Anwell?"

The middle man, bigger by a head even than the big men on either side of him, stepped forward one pace. His naked sword was the length of some men's spears. His voice matched his size; deep and powerful.

"I will speak for us . . . Where is the man who would be king? My message for Anwell only."

"As a mark of honor, Anwell has sent both his sons to confer with you."

"My master say Anwell only."

"The sons speak with the full authority of their father."

"I come through much danger to see Anwell. My master say only Anwell."

"Then you have come a long way for nothing. The sons are willing to meet you."

The big man sighed. "Very well. We will talk. Tell them come forth."

The Viking force sheathed their weapons at a guttural command, and Owein and Saer, in turn, led their little force forward. One man held back, and discretely reached into one of his panniers. With a quick flick, he sent a pigeon high into the air.

Owein rode closer with his brother, alert, but not alarmed, as his force outnumbered the other two to one. He realized that two or three men might be missing, but they would not be decisive in any confrontation. He was intrigued by the size of the giant's sword. Very few men could handle such a blade, and he had last seen such a weapon at the royal court of Wessex.

Suddenly the man's face jarred old memories. A blond giant . . . armed with a sword bigger than most men . . . a thin dark man, armed with throwing knives . . . and a prince who carried a light sword that could yet cut through any armor . . . it was the stuff of legends, and ballads were sung about them around the fire on winter evenings. Yet Owein knew that the stories were true. He had met the bastard prince and his two comrades, and he knew that they had actually performed the feats of heroism alluded to in the ballads.

His eyes darted left and right, searching for the dark man. He had a premonition that something was very wrong. He shouted for the men to wheel and ride. Even as he spoke, his peripheral vision caught a flash of something somber in color, but moving.

The men reacted, but a thunderous voice checked them.

From the door of the hut strode a bishop in full regalia. He shouted at them in perfect Welsh Gaelic.

"Hold, in the name of your Heavenly Father and in the name of your lawful sovereign! He who rides from here will feel the wrath of Mother Church and the everlasting fires of hell!"

The party had started to wheel their horses when the command came, and they hesitated for brief moments. The command had come from no Viking throat, and they were confused.

In the end, it didn't matter. As they wheeled, they discovered a solid line of dozens of unarmored archers between them and the forest. The bows were strung, and the arrows were notched. A single command and no Cornishman would leave the clearing alive.

The horsemen wheeled their mounts again, searching for an escape. More archers ran out of the shadow of the house, and a commanding figure in burnished armor stepped from the doorway, followed by a thin dark man. Owein's premonition had been accurate. The bastard prince's voice now thundered at them.

"Those of you who stand still and drop your weapons are friends and allies of Wessex! Those of you who try to run are hereby declared outlaws and traitors. Your punishment will be swift. The archers will not let you escape the clearing. Owein and Saer will be the first to die if you attack.

Put down your weapons, as loyal friends of the Wessex crown. Do it now!"

Owein had drawn his sword, but, looking at the dozens of archers, at the bastard prince and his men, at the Bishop staring sternly at him, and at his brother, he threw down his sword in disgust. The other Cornishmen, following his example, meekly surrendered their weapons, as well.

Ambrose spoke to the now disarmed and dismounted group. "You have as yet committed no treason against your lawful king. We welcome you to the ranks of the men who gather even now to face the Danish King Guthrum. Owein and Saer, King Alfred bid me invite you directly to his side. He has great need just now of loyal and obedient vassals."

The two brothers looked at each other. They were obviously to be given no chance to communicate with their father. The panniers with the pigeons had been confiscated.

The Wessex mens' horses were fetched, and each Cornishman received an escort of at least four archers. Two kept their arrows notched. Satisfied, Ambrose led the cavalcade southward.

The prince knew that when the sons did not return or report, the bees' nest would be thoroughly shaken. Swarms of angry and anxious men would comb the land.

They headed due south, and within an hour they could smell the salt air. There was a headland that jutted far into the ocean. There, Polonius had arranged a rendezvous.

Hobbling and then leaving the horses, the entire group slid and scrambled down the steep slope to the rocky shoreline. There, sheltered by the cliffs above, a group of thanes uncovered a massive pile of dry wood, and, after soaking it with flammable liquids, they lit it. A smear of greasy smoke rose gradually into the sky.

The captain of the **Leaping Stag**, flagship of Alfred's fleet, crept closer to the headland. By the captain's calculation, this was the day when Ambrose should meet him here. He wanted to go in as close as possible so he would be able to spot the signal, but, on the other hand, he did not want to alarm the local inhabitants. Ships off this coast were rarely considered friendly since the God-cursed Vikings had started to cruise the waters around the island.

As he wavered, his lookout called out. "Master, there be smoke rising just above the cliffs!"

"Well, then! Steersman, take us in! Gently does it!"

The coast was dangerous, and the ship slid in only until shallow water threatened. While most of the crew manned the oars and kept the boat motionless against the tricky currents, the rest launched the two small boats they had brought as a precaution.

The sailors were drawn from the coastal vills, and were expert boatmen. The sailors smoothly transferred the group from the shore to the ship, though not without some excitement as the long rollers lifted the small boats precariously high into the air. Ambrose sent half of his men out to the vessel before he allowed his 'guests' to board.

At last, satisfied that the ship was loaded and safely underway, he and his now much smaller group climbed the cliffs again and chose the best horses from among the many that had been left hobbled and grazing. As he rode northward, the prince wondered if the ten archers chosen as herdsmen and riding eastward would be able to drive the horses all the way to the nearest royal estate. He had thought to abandon the horses. The loss of a hundred horses was as nothing, if Cornwall could be induced to fight at Wessex's side.

Polonius had won the argument, however. The horse herd was a fine distraction. Hundreds of Cornish thanes would likely be following the obvious trail within a day or two at most. Meantime, the ealdorman's sons and their retainers would be enjoying an invigorating sea voyage.

᛭

"Ealdorman Anwell, I greet you in the name of Alfred, your king."

"Prince Ambrose, I have been summoned like an errant schoolboy to meet you at my own burh. I demand to know the meaning of this impudent command."

"Can a lawful command from your king be impudent, Anwell? But you will know the meaning of your summons soon enough, Ealdorman. May we climb down off our mounts, or would you prefer we discuss the king's business in public?"

"It's all the same to me, but if you insist, you and your advisors may enter my Great Hall."

With no further word or glance, the ealdorman strode off toward his Hall, where he entered and then threw himself into his chair. Only then did he deign again to turn and see what had become of his royal guest.

Ambrose and his escort climbed down stiffly from their mounts. Bishop Asser joined Phillip and Polonius, and the small group followed the rapidly departing ealdorman whom they had come so far to see. The rest of their escort, following their previous instructions, remained by the horses.

"Well, Prince Ambrose. You requested a private audience. You have it. Now, just what is it that is so important that you could not say it in front of my own loyal men?"

"I see that you want to get right to the point. Very well. Ealdorman Anwell, there have been unpleasant and pernicious rumors that you have been involved in treasonous activities.

King Alfred does not wish to believe such heinous lies about such a loyal vassal. In order to prevent further rumors, therefore, I have brought Bishop Asser so that he can witness a ceremonial oath reaffirming your loyalty and obedience to King Alfred and his royal house. He will attest to the giving of your oath, and send written affidavits both to Alfred and the Holy Father in Rome."

Anwell reacted angrily. "I have already sworn an oath. How dare you imply . . ."

Ambrose held up his hand for silence. "Before you say anything, I would like to present you with a gift from your king."

Anwell looked startled, and puzzled. On the one hand he worried about being accused of being a traitor, and, on the other, he was receiving a gift! He decided that, until he knew which way the wind was blowing, the less he said, the better. "I am honored. Please proceed, Prince."

"Thank you. Polonius, if you would be so kind."

The lean Byzantine took the proffered carved wooden box from Phillip, and gently pried open the top. There, gleaming against a rich velvet cloth, was a beautifully and intricately carved gold armlet. Even Anwell was taken by its massive size and powerful beauty. He leaned forward and lifted the armlet from its protective box. He gently slid it onto his right arm, and then paused to admire its golden beauty against his woollen shirt.

Ambrose spoke. "It is with great pleasure that Alfred, king of Wessex and all its tributary states, offers you this small token of his esteem. He asks only that you treat it with great respect, for it cost the lives of hundreds of good Saxons to obtain."

Anwell looked puzzled. "It is truly beautiful, but I do not understand. It is obviously very valuable, but how could such an ornament have cost lives?"

Ambrose smiled. "Ealdorman, it was removed from the arm of Ubbi, son of Ragnar Lodbrok. He had no wish to give it up, and so it took many brave Saxons to kill him and destroy his army of invasion."

In spite of himself, Anwell visibly reacted. "Ubbi . . . dead?"

"You are no doubt overcome with joy that such an implacable foe of your sovereign has been dispatched. Alfred graciously allows you to declare a day of celebration throughout your lands."

"Please . . . please thank your royal brother for his generosity. Yet surely such an important person as yourself did not come all this way just to witness an oath-giving or bring me news of a Viking's death?"

"You are perceptive, Ealdorman. I also bring important instructions. We would like to arrange with Bishop Asser for the reaffirmation of your oath of loyalty as soon as possible.

I am instructed to tell you that Alfred commands you to personally lead a contingent of two hundred mounted thanes to the burh of Lyng before the end of April. There, you will be given new marching orders. Failure to appear, on time and with your full complement, will be construed as high treason, and punished accordingly."

"The king will surely excuse such an injured person as myself. I will, of course, have my personal doctor confirm these injuries, and my priest will attest to the truth of my condition."

"And your thanes, Ealdorman?"

"I will be pleased to send two hundred brave fighting men, and I will even increase the numbers if Alfred needs good Cornishmen to rescue him. I would not want it felt for one moment that I would shirk my responsibilities."

"Then your two sons will lead the fyrd?"

"Unfortunately, both sons are far away on a holy pilgrimage, and will not be back in time. If you wish, I will pay the *240 shilling penalty right now.*"

Ambrose spoke sternly. "Your sons' not fulfilling their oath to serve in the fyrd is subject to a much greater penalty than a fine, Ealdorman. At the very least, they will have their lands confiscated."

"Alas, your brother never saw fit to assign them any of the royal domains of Cornwall. But rest assured that, as their lord, I will confiscate all of their land as punishment, and make them pay their fine to Alfred's treasury. And fear not, Prince Ambrose. I will assign overall command to my most qualified commander, Aardwolf the Simple."

"Ealdorman, does not his very name intimate to you in any possible way that the man might not be up to commanding your Cornish fyrd?"

"While it is true that he is lacking in some intellectual capacities, yet this is also a blessing. When the kingdom of Wessex is threatened, he bares his sword and charges to the heart of battle. I believe the direct approach is best, and Aardwolf understands direct."

"Ealdorman Anwell, I am surprised to hear that your sons are away on a holy pilgrimage and unable to serve in the king's fyrd. Just last night, when I last spoke to them, they both said that they would be pleased to ride directly to Alfred's side to support him in his hour of need. Even as we speak, they are shrinking the miles between themselves and their royal master."

"Ambrose, if any harm comes to my sons . . ."

Ambrose's voice thundered. "Anwell, your sons are about to do their sworn duty! But I am glad that we are done with the language of diplomacy. Let us now talk some real truths. If any harm comes to Wessex as a result of your treachery, you will be officially declared an outlaw and harried from this land.

At this moment, your own life hangs by a thin thread! If you choose to ignore your king's ruling and decide to hide here in your mists, then know that, by our law, your children can be tried for their father's treason.

They will be drawn and quartered. We will send their remains to the four corners of the empire. Since you are at the western end of the empire, you will even receive part of them back.

Think carefully, traitor! Alternatively, you can swear another oath of allegiance, and lead a contingent of properly mounted thanes east in the spring, as your king commands. Not, mind you, that squad of misfits and family enemies you chose to send last summer, and not an army intending to make common cause with the Danes! Your sons will remain as honored quests of Alfred until he is convinced of your sincerity."

"And just what is to stop me from having the lot of you tortured and killed right now?"

Bishop Asser, who had until now been standing behind Phillip, now spoke up for the first time in his deep and sonorous voice.

"My son, the answer is your holy oath, the fact that one of your pagan allies has been crushed, and my promise to you that you will be excommunicated from Mother Church and damned through all eternity. If that is not sufficient, the point that your sons are being held hostage does leap to mind."

Anwell's face still showed a mottled red. He barely had his temper under control.

"Then I suggest we perform your damned ceremony today. You have far to ride tonight before you will be able to find shelter worthy of your exalted status!"

CHAPTER 24

Ambrose Meets Ethelwold of Dorset

Ambrose led his little delegation out of Anwell's burh and headed for the nearest royal estate to the east. Polonius rode alongside his royal friend and companion.

"I cannot say much for Ealdorman's Anwell's hospitality, my Prince."

Ambrose smiled at the thin dark man. "I, for one, am relieved to be out of his grasp! I'm willing to ride to one of our own royal estates, even if we have to ride half the night . . . Polonius, do you think that Anwell will keep his pledge to Alfred?"

"I would keep a close eye on those two sons, Prince. As long as they are kept at Alfred's side, I am sure that Anwell will not dare the king's wrath. If they escape or are allowed home, I would worry. He does *not love you West Saxons overmuch, I fear!*"

"Well, Scholar, that is just the first of our two little errands. Next, we must track down my royal nephew. If the second half of your plan works as smoothly as the first, then I think that we have a chance come spring. With the Cornishmen and the Dorset fyrd in full strength joining with Guthrum's battle-hardened veterans, we would be in deep trouble!"

The pillar of smoke gave away the location. Phillip took a troop of scouts ahead to ensure that whoever was ahead was friendly.

The royal party was quickly challenged by Saxon pickets. Almost before Phillip could rein in his party, a series of blasts on several war horns brought a cloud of armed Saxon riders at a gallop. Phillip recognized amongst the mounted officers two of his oldest friends. He greeted them warmly in his deep voice.

"Pitanig! And Radnor! Is this the way you greet loyal Wessex men!?"

Pitanig replied. "This is how Devonshire fyrdmen greet all strangers in this unhappy land, you big lummox!"

Radnor grinned at the blond giant. "You are coming from the wrong direction again, big man! I thought that you had learned to navigate the Asian steppes."

A grin crept across Pitanig's face. "Only if he has the little Greek with him to point the way."

The three men dismounted, and Phillip managed to lift both off the ground simultaneously with his big bear hug.

The weapons-master grinned. "Beware. The Greek's daggers are even sharper than his words. But, by the Good God, it's good to see even such bedraggled warriors as yourselves!"

Pitanig grunted. "If you would put us down long enough to look behind us, you overgrown ox, you would note that we brought several hundred more bedraggled warriors such as ourselves, who, incidentally, and with no help from you, just finished mopping up an entire Viking army!"

"The truth, little men. You were so thirsty that you tried to surrender, and you scared the Danes with your bleating!"

Pitanig was suddenly serious. "Phillip, how is Alfred and Ambrose?"

"Alfred is well and in hiding. Ambrose you will see before you can count your toes and fingers ten times. He is now just over that hill, probably still trying to decide if it's worth dealing with such a ragged bunch as yourselves."

Pitanig spoke. "Come, my big friend. Mount up. We will go find Ambrose and escort him to Odda. Our ealdorman eagerly awaits your arrival."

ಶ

Phillip led the procession direct to the main gate of the impressive burh. Unlike most of the Saxon settlements, where wooden palisades were favored as defenses, Ethelwold's primary burh had been built on top of old Roman fortification, and it was constructed solidly of stone. It was a formidable defensive position.

The giant reined in his horse, well aware of the many eyes focused on him. "Open in the name of Prince Ambrose, royal atheling and brother to the king!"

Phillip was known to the officers who manned the wall, and they immediately ordered the gates to be opened.

The burh was large, and the eighty men who rode in did not crowd the inner courtyard. The rearguard was slow to enter, however.

Ethelwold, surrounded by his senior thanes, came running to greet the prince.

"Uncle! Welcome! To what do I owe this honor? Do my eyes deceive me, or do I see Phillip and Polonius at your side? And is that really Bishop Asser? Please, dismount! My men will take your horses. You must be frozen through and through!"

Ambrose responded. "I thank you, Ethelwold. But I am waiting for the rest of my troop to arrive."

"Dismount, sir. All whom you bring are welcome here."

"I am glad you feel that way. I think that I hear them approaching even now."

There was a thunder of hooves, and the sentries cried out to their master below in alarm. "Ealdorman, there be another two hundred riders approaching!"

Ethelwold's eyes flicked to the massive gate. Ambrose's men were still trooping through slowly, however, and a powerful force had paused near the inside of the gate. Without Ambrose's permission, he had no hope of closing the gate in time to prevent the new riders from entering.

Suddenly, his capital town was about to hold more of Alfred's warriors than his own. He wondered how Ambrose had conjured up such a force, until he saw Odda ride in at the head of the larger force. With a sinking feeling, he realized that his citadel had been seized without a single sword lifted. He remembered the often sung story of how Ambrose had taken the major fort of Carnarvon, and he groaned inwardly. Then he shrugged mentally. As far as Odda and Ambrose knew, he was a most loyal vassal of the Wessex king. He decided to brazen it out. Perhaps he could yet use this visit to his advantage.

"Uncle, Thane Seger returned not long ago with the news that you and Alfred were alive. I was so relieved! Have you decided to take advantage of my offer of sanctuary? Both you and your brother have nothing to fear from Guthrum while you are under my roof!"

"Your offer is generous, Ethelwold, but Alfred cannot avail himself of it at the moment."

"I trust the king is well?"

"He is fine, Ethelwold."

"Is he close behind you?"

"He is in a safe place."

"Say the word and I will ride to him! Is he far from here?"

"Actually, I left his side some time ago. We have ridden all the way from Cornwall."

"Cornwall. That's a bleak place to visit in the cold winter season. Please come inside where you can warm up, and you can tell me exactly what has befallen the royal court! We will broach a keg of our finest ale in your honor."

Smiling broadly, Ealdorman Ethelwold led his visitors to his Great Hall. There, servants were hurriedly setting up trestle tables and benches for the many unexpected guests. Ethelwold waved his guests to the seats.

"Sit! Warm your selves by the fire. Drink is being brought even now, and warm food is being prepared. Uncle, it is really a great pleasure to see you again. You and your comrades are always welcome before my fire!"

Ambrose and his party warmed themselves around the open pit fire, and then allowed themselves to be seated. Polonius, however, stayed close to Ethelwold, and his heavy cloak was thrust away from his right arm. He was subtle, but Ethelwold noticed the man's careful movements. That Polonius could kill a man at twenty strides with his throwing daggers was legend, and the man wore a belt full of them.

After warming himself and settling down at the head table near Ethelwold, Ambrose spoke. "I thank you again for your kind hospitality, Ethelwold. I wish that I could report that I have brought you only good news, but I am afraid that I can't say that."

"Uncle, I suspected that you did not ride this long way for a social call. I certainly know how yon Polonius suffers from our brisk winter airs. The news must be grim indeed to take you all the way to Cornwall and then bring you here in the dead of winter. What is it?"

"Perhaps it would be better if we were to speak alone."

"Of course. Steward! Clear the hall. My uncle and I have royal business to discuss!"

"Yes, Ealdorman!"

In short order, the many thanes, churls and slaves that made up the Dorset court were bustled out of the hall, along with most of Ambrose's escort. Of Ambrose's party, only Phillip, Polonius, Odda and Bishop Asser remained.

"Now we are just family and close advisors, Prince Ambrose. From your demeanor, I fear you have very serious news."

"The news is serious, Ethelwold. What do you know of King Guthrum?"

"I know that we had the pleasure last autumn of chasing him out of Wessex. I am relieved to report that he has not yet raided deeply into Dorset. I am, of course, aware of his perfidious attack on Chippenham on Twelfth Night. Except for my illness, I would have been there with the king for the holidays!

Beyond the fact that you were defeated and driven into hiding, I know relatively little. There were terrible rumors that you and Alfred were killed. That is why I sent Thane Seger and a hundred warriors to you; to confirm that you were alive and well, and to offer my support."

"Your thanes were much appreciated, and they help keep the king safe, even as we speak."

"I am glad that I could help."

"We escaped Guthrum by crossing the Avon River in the only boats available, but many thanes laid down their lives so that the court could escape."

"And our king has found a safe haven?"

"Fear not. All of the royal family are safe. Alfred is presently building a secret base from which he can safely harass the Vikings."

"But that's wonderful news! Tell me where the court is at present, and I will send fifty more of my best thanes to Alfred's side this very night! Or better yet, accept my offer of refuge. Bring the king and the royal family here. Guthrum has not dared show his face in Dorset. It would be my pleasure to have Alfred stay here."

"I am sure it would."

Ethelwold stared hard at Prince Ambrose. He did not how to take Ambrose's comment. Surely, if they knew what he had plotted with King Guthrum, they would already have parted his head from his body. They had snuck an overwhelming force into his citadel, yet they were treating him as a loyal atheling. He was puzzled.

Ambrose continued. "Alfred's instructions for you are very specific. You are to stay in Dorset. If Alfred hears that you have sent out a call to the Dorset fyrd, he has told me to tell you that he will consider it high treason."

"But Prince Ambrose, if Guthrum arrives in force, our only defense is in the spears of our fyrd! Come spring, Alfred will need my men for his summer campaign. Even now, I have men training! I stand ready to send them for his defense."

"Ethelwold, you have been warned. Let me repeat. The act of calling up your fyrd will be construed as an act of treason against your king."

"Ambrose! Alfred is my father's brother. Why would I not call up my fyrd in defense of the realm?"

"Ethelwold, you were seen in Guthrum's camp."

Ethelwold deliberately rose to his feet, a furious expression on his face. "Whoever says that is a liar! Bring the man forward that I may challenge him to combat. By Almighty God, I will cut his lying tongue out!"

"Ethelwold, I was there. You caught an apple from an entertainer who told you that you looked like a hungry man. You ate my apple."

Ethelwold had swollen like an inflated pig's bladder in righteous indignation. Ambrose's words deflated him as surely as one of Polonius' sharpest daggers.

Ethelwold stammered. "That greasy little man was you?! Ambrose . . . I do not know what to say! Yes, I do admit, after Wessex was left defenseless against Guthrum's invasion, I did go to Guthrum and pay Danegeld to keep Dorset free from his hordes. But I did no more than Alfred himself did last summer at Wareham and Exeter. At no time did I intend treason to my own uncle, or to Wessex!"

Ambrose signaled Phillip, and the giant pulled a heavy and ornate armlet out of an ornate wooden box, and threw it down on the table in front of Ethelwold.

"What's this?"

"What do you see?"

"Why, a somewhat gaudy, but very impressive armlet. By its workmanship, I would say that it is Viking in origin, and by its size, I would say that it belonged to a very wealthy man."

"Alfred, your king, sends it to you with his compliments. It cost the lives of hundreds of Saxons to obtain."

"I don't understand."

"It belonged to Ubbi, son of Ragnar Lodbrok. He has no further use for it."

"I still don't understand."

"He and his men are dead."

"Dead? I thought that he and his fleet were in Southern Wales."

"He landed in Devon, and he and his men were cut down by brave Odda here, and the Devon fyrd."

"But . . . that's wonderful!"

"Yes, it is. And Odda has just left that same army on your northern frontier a scant day ago. I have instructed him to bring the rest of his army south, looking for your head, if so much as one man is called to arms in Dorset. I have further suggested that his men might provide you protection for the next few months. There are far too many traitors running around."

"Ambrose, I admit I panicked when I heard that Guthrum had crossed the frontier and that Alfred had nothing with which to stop him. I did what I could to protect Dorset from rapine and pillaging, yet I am a loyal vassal of King Alfred, and I want to support him any way I can!"

"Excellent! I was hoping that you would say that. Alfred was very upset to hear of your visit to Guthrum, but he has no wish to separate the head from the body of his own favorite nephew. The last thing this empire needs is civil war between its royal athelings.

Your king proposes that you demonstrate your support of him with a very generous offering of gold. His coffers are empty, and he greatly needs money if he is to survive. Considering the situation, he expects considerable generosity on your part. He understands and deeply regrets why the Dorset fyrd will not be able to ride to support him this summer. Do we thoroughly understand each other?"

"Perfectly. And the Dorset treasury will be as generous as possible, considering that most of our gold went to Guthrum just weeks ago."

"That was not authorized by your king, and he would not like to be reminded of it. Alfred assumes that you will not take that into account when you make your very generous donation."

"Yes, of course. And that being settled, may I call back the servants and arrange appropriate entertainment for my royal uncle?"

"It is always a pleasure to partake of your hospitality, Ethelwold. Oh, and did I tell you that Odda's men on your northern frontier desperately need supplies? Good food and copious fuel should keep them where they are, on the other side of the border."

"It would be my pleasure to send his men all the supplies they need."

"I thank you on Alfred's behalf. *Your generosity and support will be remembered.*"

CHAPTER 25

Alfred Fights Again, and Guthrum Seeks the Secret Base

"My king! Riders report that a major raiding party was spotted approaching from the south!"

King Alfred stared at Ealdorman Ethelnoth. "What are the numbers, and where exactly are they?"

"Last night they took the vill of Will's Crossing."

"Polonius, would you please unroll the map? Ethelnoth, where, exactly, on this map is the vill located?"

"Here, Sire." With that, Ethelnoth pointed out the location on the parchment map Polonius had spread on the trestle table."

"Gentlemen, do you think that Guthrum has found out our little secret?"

Polonius spoke. "I would be surprised if he knew the exact location, but he certainly knew what direction you took after the attack on Chippenham."

Alfred laughed. "He certainly did! Ethelnoth tells me his foresters have caught and hung an even two dozen spies. We'll never know how many others slipped into quicksand or set off a mantrap."

Ambrose had been staring at the map. "Well, brother. They come at last. What are your orders?"

"Brother-of-mine, I really enjoyed our visit to Chippenham a few weeks ago. Thanks to our little island fortress, I think the fox can again become the hound!"

Polonius looked extremely concerned. "Sire, there may be five hundred of them!"

"Relax, Polonius. We are not going to hit them head on. We are going to bleed them to death with a thousand little cuts.

Gentlemen, send out the orders. Any Dane who so much as steps behind a bush to piss is to have his throat cut. Tell the people in their path to use the escape routes. The women, children, and as much of the livestock as possible are to be transferred by water to safer locations.

Under no circumstance are the Vikings to get their hands on any boats! Burn the villages if they look likely to fall. Let the heathens sleep in the ashes. Ambush, ambush, and ambush! Ethelnoth, your people have been planning for this for weeks. Are they ready?"

"I think so, Sire. Every vill and tun has an escape route by water, and the necessary boats are stored."

"Excellent. Polonius, I want all of our garrisons to take to their boats. I expect them to encircle the Danes. If they can amass a local advantage in numbers, then they may fight. Otherwise they are to retreat and harass. I expect the men to make it very expensive for Guthrum's raiding party to advance any further into the marshes.

Ethelnoth, would you please arrange for boats and guides while Phillip gets together two hundred men? Gentlemen, let's give them another taste of Saxon hospitality!"

Ambrose eased his horse over toward his royal brother. Not far in front of them, ragged churls and armored thanes were hammering at the retreating square of Viking warriors. The Danes, though outnumbered, yet stubbornly held their formation, and the Saxons were losing two for every Viking that fell. Nevertheless, the Saxons were driving the Danish foraging party back. The Danes had abandoned their horses in the fierce fighting, and local village youths were leading them away. The Saxons, sensing victory, continued to attack ruthlessly, heedless of the cost.

Ambrose finally reached Alfred's side. "Brother, we are approaching their main base. We have made them pay dearly for their raid and taken back most of the food and loot. May I humbly suggest we now get the hell out of here? Soon we will again be the hunted!"

"Aye. You're right, big brother. It just feels so good to see the devils retreating!'

He turned to his small core of commanders and messengers. 'Sound the recall! Let's get the local men back to the boats! Get the Personal Guard mounted up, and let's head home!"

Four hundred hard-riding Danes followed the trail northward. Snow had recently fallen, so the trail left by Alfred's smaller war band was plain. The Vikings pushed the horses to the limit.

Much of their food supplies, and silver and gold looted from several churches, had been stolen from their own raiders. It was close ahead.

Even more important, however, the last unconquered Anglish king left on the entire island was finally within reach. Several warriors now riding in the host had not only spotted the royal banner, but had even recognized the tall king in his glittering armor.

Alfred was worth his weight in gold, dead or alive, and with him killed, Wessex would fall like a ripe apple from the tree. The rich land they were riding through would soon be theirs. All they had to do was to catch one man, and kill him.

"By Thor's hammer! Loki is playing games with us today!"

Oskar, commander of the strike force sent after Alfred and his raiders, pulled his horse to a stop. Behind him the entire column followed suit. The trail was still clear. The snow ensured that they would not lose it even in the alder forest. The land was marshy, however, and the trail continued along a thin spine of land that barely extended above the swamp water.

Uigbiorn, his chief sub-commander, just grunted. "Or Alfred."

"So what is your recommendation, Lieutenant?"

"Do you want to face Guthrum without Alfred, my Jarl?"

"Hardly! Guthrum was kind enough to allow me to rise from my sickbed to redeem myself after the disastrous attack at Chippenham. Do you think I have a choice? Alfred's death is worth the lives of a thousand Danes. With him gone, and his bastard brother, this island is ours.' He sighed. 'Order the advance."

The column was strung out for over a Roman mile, since riders could not ride more than two abreast. Suddenly, the vanguard came under fire. Arching shafts descended from the right.

The men quickly swung up their shields and dismounted, seeking the shelter of the trees on the side away from where the arrows originated. The men drew their swords, ready to do battle, but there was no one visible to fight.

Oskar crouched beside a thin alder that gave little enough protection. "Where are the Saxon bastards?"

Uigbiorn crouched nearby. "Look, my Jarl! There be boats behind the alder thickets over there."

Sure enough, when the commander peered out from behind his tree, he could vaguely make out several boatloads of Saxons arcing their arrows high and emptying their quivers at the Vikings. Suddenly, the warrior beside Uigbiorn grunted and fell forward. A shaft protruded from his back. Oskar realized that the arrow had come from behind him. Even as he turned, the air around filled with a shower of arcing shafts.

The commander roared to his men. "Look out! The archers are on both sides of us. Move back to back, and protect your partners.

Officers! Order the men to unsling their own bows! I want those boats emptied! Uigbiorn! Look at the thickets between here and where the archers are. The water is shallow. Take fifty men and kill those archers!"

The commands rang out, and a squad of some fifty warriors remounted their horses and charged the Saxons. Several horses in the first wave screamed in pain, however, and the charge was brought to an abrupt halt.

Oskar was furious. "You there! What stopped the charge?"

"Jarl! The horses went lame. There seem to be sharpened stakes everywhere under the surface of the water!"

"Curse Alfred and his entire pox-ridden family! Get your men back into shelter. Tell them to put their bows to work! I want those damned boats emptied."

The polished machine that was the Danish army went to work. In short order, there were two continuous rows of archers. Firing on command, they retaliated with showers of shafts, and the Saxon archers, much fewer in number, were quickly being decimated.

The Saxons were forced to paddle for their lives, taking with them a good percent of their force dead or wounded. The Danish force had suffered higher casualties, however, and many of the horses had also been shot. The Vikings were no longer completely mounted.

The Saxons driven off for the moment, the Danes mounted up again, and the column rode recklessly forward. Several more of the vanguard fell to hidden archers and various hidden man traps, but the force pressed resolutely on. Oskar refused to be stopped by mere gnat bites. His goal was clear; Alfred, dead or alive.

The trail led to the edge of a swamp. Oskar signaled his lieutenant. "So, where did they go?"

"Jarl, I have seen it's like before. The water is shallow, and the trail is clearly marked by a row of branches. If you stay on the trail, it is safe."

"And if you don't?"

"Quicksand. Maybe deep water."

"So where is the trail? They took it!"

"Aye, Jarl! And then they took the marker branches."

"So send some dismounted men in. They can feel the way across and we will mark it again."

"It will cost us both time and men, sir. The water is frigid."

"Just do it, you fool!"

Uigbiorn looked long at his commander's enraged face. At last he just nodded. "Yes, my Jarl!"

Several men stepped on the sharpened stakes and were crippled. Two fell into quicksand, but their comrades quickly pulled them out again. Eventually, the trail was marked and the obstacles were all removed. The column lurched into motion again.

Oskar rode near the vanguard. "Alfred has not got away yet! Soon we will find the secret fort that the peasants we have been torturing brag about. After I remove Alfred's testicles, you may perform the Blood Eagle on him. We will see how high this king can soar!"

The strip of high ground widened, and Oskar led the force at an increased pace. He felt victory close and almost in his grasp, until he reached the river. "Loki has definitely played his tricks today."

The Saxon tracks stopped by the water, and Oskar could see the many marks left in the snow and frozen soil by boats being beached and pulled ashore. It was clear that Alfred and his men had all been ferried across the wide and deep river.

"Uigbiorn! Send out scouts to see if there are any more boats on this side of the river. Without boats, we will have to swim the horses."

"Jarl, it is winter, and the river is wide. Neither the men nor the horses could take it. And look there. There are some of Alfred's men!"

Even as he spoke, a long line of men carrying bundles of spears and quivers of arrows moved into view. Secure on the far bank, they would be capable of devastating any Viking force that dared to swim the icy river. The Saxons waved saucily, and proceeded to relax on the far bank.

Oskar looked glumly at Uigbiorn. "Guthrum is going to have my balls, but signal the retreat."

CHAPTER 26

"Then, in the seventh week after Easter, he rode to Brixton by the eastern side of Selwood; and there came out to meet him all the people of Somersetshire, and Wiltshire, and that part of Hampshire which is on this side of the sea; and they rejoiced to see him. Then within one night he went from this retreat to Hey; and within one night after he proceeded to Edington; and there fought with all the army, and put them to flight...."

"Polonius!"

"Yes, Sire?"

"What is the date today?"

"Tuesday, May 10, Sire."

"Then today is the day. Phillip, was the signal fire lit last night on Stourton Hill?"

"Yes, Sire. It burned all night, and the smoke still climbs into the sky as we speak."

"Excellent. And what has happened?"

"Signal fires burn on every hilltop in Wessex."

"But only mine must burn throughout the day."

"That is understood, Sire."

"And do the men come?"

"They come, King."

"Then please have my chair taken to the hilltop. I will watch my fyrd gather and greet each contingent personally."

After a bitter winter of hiding, and then fighting skirmishes, the Saxon king was finally calling together his fighting men. Soon after the dawn, the king's chair sat high on Stourton Hill. Worried household servants brought his food to him, and he ate, but he insisted on sitting outside and personally greeting the forces as they rode and marched in.

Already, on the slopes below, the thanes of his Personal Guard had pegged out locations so that there would be some order to the army that Alfred prayed would materialize before his eyes this day. His officers gathered around their king.

Alfred turned to his bastard brother. "Ambrose, I worry."

"About what, brother?"

"If, by dusk, this valley is not full of West Saxon fighting men, then the Empire of Wessex is no more."

"Brother, you have done all that you can. We have had thanes and messengers riding tirelessly all spring. They have extracted pledges and promises from hundreds of Somerset, Wiltshire, and Hampshire thanes. Besides, if you do not get enough men to face Guthrum today, you can always retreat to the eastern shires and raise another army."

"I fear not, Ambrose. Somerset, Hampshire and Wiltshire make up the core of the West Saxon Empire. From them, I expect every able-bodied man. If I cannot raise adequate men from my own heartland, then we are finished."

"The ealdormen of Berkshire, Sussex, Essex and Kent are all sworn to obey you, Alfred."

"And they will, just as long as I have the strength to make them. We are still conquerors to the Saxons and Angles of the east, brother. They might welcome a chance at renewed independence."

"You did not tell the ealdormen of the east to bring their full fyrds, brother."

"No, but I asked for contingents of their best thanes. We will watch carefully today to see who shows up."

"And if everyone you asked for shows up?"

"Then I think I will finally have the manpower necessary to finish Guthrum once and for all. Oh, Ambrose, I just remembered one more task. Please send for the commander of the Devon men we separated from Ethelwold last winter."

"At once, brother."

‡

The burley warrior kneeled before his sovereign. Alfred spoke.

"Rise, commander, and come closer. I wish to speak with you . . . Ambrose, would you remove the sentries for a short time, so I can have words in private with this thane?"

"Of course, Alfred."

The king stared at the thane for several long moments. At last he spoke. "What is your name, Commander?"

"Thormond, Sire."

"Thormond, I will get right to the point. I know why you and Seger came looking for me last winter."

The big thane went red. "I am Ethelwold's sworn man, Sire, and I have never disobeyed a single command of his in my life."

"And Ethelwold has sworn to obey me in all things, Thormond. You do understand that you almost condemned your soul to eternal damnation, and your head to the block?"

The thane stood straight. "I obeyed the orders of my lawful lord, King."

"I understand that you fought well in several skirmishes this spring."

"I am a warrior, Sire, and I enjoy killing Vikings."

"Excellent. Thormond, if I was to give you and your men an opportunity to swear obedience directly to me, would you do it?"

"If Ethelwold is sworn to you, that would not cause a conflict, King."

"Good, because the alternative is to be convicted of treason, and I would not like to draw and quarter brave men who only obeyed orders."

"We will swear, King."

"Good. Tell your men that, after the oath-giving, I am going to put them in the vanguard of the Wiltshire fyrd. They will be given the opportunity to wipe away the stain on their honor with their swords. Tell them, also, that there will be generous rewards for the men who fight bravely against the Danes."

"I will tell them, King, and thank you."

"You can thank me after we crush the Vikings. Go now, and tell them to prepare for battle . . . and remember, Thormond, I will be watching."

"Yes, Sire."

Soon after Alfred's conversation with the Dorset thane, the first of the mounted fyrdmen arrived, followed by a horde of peasants. Most of the peasants wore only leather armor, and few rode. Without exception, however, the men all carried spears or bows, and also axe, sax, or sword. They marched into Alfred's camp singing, and Alfred and his advisors waved happily. In turn, most contingents cheered when they recognized their king's personal dragon-banner on the hillside. Terrible rumors had spread the length and breadth of the empire during the cold and bitter winter.

Their king, who had never yet lost a single campaign, was supposed to have mysteriously disappeared. Stories were rife that he had been captured or killed by the Vikings, and many of his sturdy subjects had feared for their future without King Alfred at their head.

Alfred beamed as, one by one, the militias of the various local shires showed up. Even Odda of Devon sent a small force, although Alfred had demanded none, as so many of the Devon fyrd had fallen in the struggle against Ubbi and his pagan warriors. Further, by keeping a strong force sitting on the border of Devon, and babysitting Ethelwold in his home burh, Odda was insuring that there would be no treachery by Alfred's nephew.

The eastern reaches of Alfred's empire were represented by small numbers of mounted thanes and noblemen. Small contingents from Berkshire, Sussex, Essex and Kent rode into the rapidly growing camp. Not numerous, for the distance was far, yet the newcomers were the fighting elite of the eastern shires, and they represented loyalty to the crown.

Alfred's marshals led the various contingents to their assigned areas, and soon the many men were industriously putting up tents and greeting old friends and relatives. By organizing the forces by shires, Alfred hoped to form an army that was dependable and loyal to its neighbors. He knew that the fyrd was only as strong as its weakest link, and if even a portion of his force broke in battle, then it was possible, even likely, that all would be both routed and massacred.

Ambrose clapped his brother on his back. "They come, brother. The valley is now filled."

"May the Lord be praised! With this size force, we will finally be able to finish off Guthrum."

Polonius approached. "I do not wish to rain on a king's parade, but our fyrdmen do not decisively outnumber the Vikings."

"I know, Scholar. Experience has taught me that my landed churls and thanes are probably the equal of the Viking veterans, but the large mass of retainers and peasants that march on foot are not capable of standing against the Vikings. Victory therefore hinges on numbers and judicious use of my battle-hardened veteran thanes.

What I need, more than anything, is an overwhelming force. Guthrum is no fool, and he has twice come to terms when faced with a Saxon army that he was not sure he could defeat.

And Scholar?"

"Yes, Sire?"

"I want a list of any thanes who did not answer my summons this day."

"Sire, there are still men on the road here, and others had had their regions decimated by the savage raiding that had gone on throughout the winter."

"I know, and I will take that into consideration, but I also know that some have been bought off, or frightened off, by Guthrum. Some even fled to the continent."

"And what will we do with the list, Sire?"

"When a host such as this goes into battle, there have to be rewards for the valiant. I intend to redistribute the estates of those who did not show up. Let me remind you, Scholar, except for the *Bookland*, all land in the entire kingdom is held on the sole understanding that, for every five hides of land held, I get one warrior, mounted and armored, when I call for it."

~

Two young noblemen, Owein and Saer, waited close by and anxiously scanned the ranks of the fyrdmen riding into the king's camp. The arrival of Cornish fyrdmen would mean that their father had decided not to openly oppose Alfred. They well knew that their lives were forfeit if Cornish forces were found to have joined Guthrum, or even if their father failed to show up.

At last, shortly before dark, the Cornish banner was seen and identified. Anwell himself, at the head of his two hundred well-mounted thanes, rode past the king's chair. The camp cheered the late arrivals; none louder than the two young men who had only been days from being drawn and quartered as traitors.

Alfred smiled in quiet satisfaction as the contingent rode past. Two hundred Cornish fyrdmen would not, in themselves, make or break his army. What it meant, however, was that up to a thousand Cornish warriors were not marching to join Guthrum. Best of all, because of Polonius' careful planning, Anwell had not, until he reached the burh of Lyng, known where the army was gathering. Even if the treacherous ealdorman had tried to send word to Guthrum about Alfred's gathering place, he did not have the necessary information in time to give Guthrum any chance to hurt Alfred.

~

Before the morning light of May 11 hit the camp, Alfred was up and about. His officers rushed to keep up with the restless king.

"Phillip! I want the fyrd ready to ride north in an hour! Look at that sun. We should be on the road by now!"

Ambrose caught up to his brother. "You seem to be worried about something, Alfred."

Alfred stopped, then smiled. "You are perceptive, as ever, Big Brother. I am worried."

"About what, brother-of-mine?"

"Well, yesterday, I worried if the ealdormen would deliver the men as promised."

"And today?"

"Are there more traitors out there? Does Guthrum have another surprise for us?"

"With luck, Alfred, we have found all the traitors, and dealt with them."

The king stared back at the camp that was starting to bustle. At last, he spoke.

"We already outnumber Guthrum, Ambrose, and stragglers are still arriving. We can only grow stronger day by day. Meantime, Guthrum has not only lost considerable numbers of men over the winter, but he has lost three major allies."

Ambrose looked puzzled. "And that worries you, brother?"

"Yes. I know that, if the boot was on the other foot, I would be attacking ruthlessly, before the various West Saxon shire forces could complete the gathering and coalesce into a real army."

"He has to find us before he can attack us, Alfred."

"Ambrose, as sure as you know there is a God, you know that Guthrum had out spies. He is already likely to know not only when we were to meet, but where."

"I think we took care of the 'when' with signal fires on every hill in the empire, brother, but how would he know the 'where.'

"We sent hundreds of messengers riding throughout the land, carrying both the date and the name of the gathering place. Who knows what information Ethelwold or Anwell might have sent. No, I think we can assume that Guthrum knows."

"And we are still vulnerable?"

"Not all of our men have yet arrived, we have just begun to organize the army, and, unlike this winter, we have no convenient fort to retreat to."

"Brother, what you are saying is that Guthrum knows our approximate location, and his best hope is another pre-emptive strike, before we can properly organize or find a defensive position. The obvious conclusion there, is that you think he is on his way here, prepared for battle."

"I would be, if I was him. Do you doubt it, brother?"

"Not really. So what are we going to do about it?"

Alfred hesitated. "We already outnumber him, in quantity, if not quality. I remember, however, the success Odda had against Ubbi, with the crumbling fortifications at Cynwith. I want the army on the move, so we can go northward, to a place called Iley Oak."

"Why Iley Oak?"

Alfred turned. "Polonius, why did we pick Iley Woods?"

"Because the local thanes reported that it was ideal for what we want, Sire."

Ambrose bit. "And just what, exactly, do we want, Scholar?"

"There is a hill there, flanked on either side by dense woods."

"And this is important to us?"

"Your brother thought so, Prince."

"The question is 'why', Wizard."

"Ah, that is a good question, Master."

"And the answer is?"

"With an earthworks flanked on both sides by dense woods, we will have a strong defensive position."

"I understand the usefulness of a fortification, but we will hardly chase Guthrum out of Wessex by hiding on top of a hill, however well situated."

Alfred smiled. "You are correct, brother. We will have to go hunting for him. Nevertheless, I want a secure position we can fall back on, in case things go wrong."

Ambrose grinned. "Then let's go build us some earthworks!"

As soon as the mounted column reached Iley Oak, Alfred put his men to work. Within hours, a dry ditch was dug, and the resulting heap of dirt was interspersed with sharpened stakes and surmounted by a palisade.

Alfred smiled at his bastard brother, who reined in his skittish mount near the top of the hill.

"Look, brother! It is not Athelney, but it could protect our asses if Guthrum manages to break our line and we have to run.

"Alfred, if God is just, then surely He will come to our aid when we face the Danes."

The king started to smile, but then he grimaced suddenly, and almost fell from his own horse. Only by clinging to his saddle was he able to stay seated.

Ambrose slipped quickly from his own saddle, yelled "Polonius!" and ran to his brother's side to help him dismount.

Alfred, bent over his beautiful horse, yet whispered to Ambrose.

"Brother! Leave me in the saddle! I cannot be weak, today of all days. The men must see their king mounted.

"Alfred, do not be a fool! If you are ill, I will get the doctors!"

"No! I have had these attacks before, and they always pass. It must again! I have no time today for pain!"

Polonius ran quickly to Ambrose's side, warned by the prince's voice that something was seriously wrong. "Yes, Prince Ambrose? . . . King Alfred, let me help you down!"

It had not taken Polonius long to see the pain on Alfred's face. He grabbed Alfred before he could fall from the saddle, but Alfred managed to speak.

"No, Polonius. The king will watch serenely from his mount. There is no alternative!"

"Then, Master, may I at least get you some more of the essence of the eastern poppy?"

Ambrose looked at his old friend in surprise. "Polonius, you knew that the king has had these attacks before, yet you did not tell me?!"

Alfred spoke clearly, though both of his companions could see the sweat pouring down his face, and they realized that even talking was a great effort.

"Do not blame Polonius, brother! He helped me once before, when I had an attack, and I swore him to absolute silence. And yes, Polonius, I will take the essence of poppy. Quickly please, I cannot sit my mount much longer!"

Ambrose called to ever-faithful Phillip. "Weapons-master, can you have the king's chair brought here, immediately?"

"It is in the wagon at the bottom of the hill. I will get it right away!"

Ambrose then spoke to his brother. "Off your horse, brother. You can serenely sit on your throne while the men work. Will you do that?"

Alfred tried to smile, but only grimaced. "It seems I have little choice. Please help me dismount."

Once the king was ensconced in his chair, his face betrayed no further signs of pain, but he held his stomach and eagerly drained the drought that Polonius prepared for him. At last, he was recovered enough to call out to his waiting brother and the small group of his closest advisors.

"Well, my friends. My stomach still burns like the fires of hell, but I am not going to pass out today. I saw more men arrive. Ambrose, how are we doing?"

"Better than expected, Sire. Two more contingents from the eastern shires are here, with word that more riders are following a day or two behind."

"And Hampshire, Somerset and Wiltshire?"

"All here, Sire."

"Excellent. Then we already have the army that matches Guthrum.

This is what I want you to do. Polonius, I want you to stay by my side, with some more of your poppy juice, just in case.

Ambrose and Phillip, I want you two to spread the word. Tonight we will have a great celebration. Each commander is to come before me and, in the presence of Bishop Asser, swear loyalty to Wessex and to his own companions. Each churl is to renew his oath to his immediate commander. The Bishop will then ask a blessing for all of us.

I will fast, and pray. Tomorrow, pure in heart, we will seek out the plague that has fallen on our smiling lands, and we will eradicate it!"

Well before the dawn broke, the Saxon army stirred. Men hurriedly ate what was left over in their common pots from the night before. More than a few felt hangovers, and many sipped on mead or ale. The men admitted to no fear, yet in their hearts they knew that they were marching to face a powerful and ruthless foe.

At last, in the dark of predawn, the new army of Wessex abandoned its base and marched forth in a long ragged column. Hundreds of horsemen were interspersed with the infantry, but the thanes wealthy enough to ride were not cavalry. As soon as the enemy was spotted, the thanes would abandon their mounts and form up in the time-honored shield-wall formation that both the Saxons and the Vikings favored.

Alfred had tried to estimate the number of fyrdmen as they had marched into the camp at Iley Oak. There were too many to accurately tally, but the king had estimated that there were more than twenty-five hundred. Of these, some five hundred were heavily armed and mounted thanes, interspersed with perhaps another five hundred mounted churls.

Alfred knew his fyrd to be a formidable force, and one that could easily destroy Guthrum if all went well. The great winding serpent of men and supplies stretched out for over a Roman mile. The column pushed on over the Wylye, and along the old white track that led up the steep chalk edge onto Salisbury Plain.

As the first glimmers of dawn streaked the eastern horizon, the West Saxon host spilled out onto the plain. The scouts' last reports indicated that Guthrum was at Alfred's own royal estate of Edington, near the huge White Horse carved in the turf long before the memories of the oldest living men.

The estate of Edington was palisaded and surrounded by a dry ditch, and had a comfortable Great Hall. No new scouts had arrived to report that the Viking army had moved, so Alfred assumed that Guthrum and his Viking army were still ensconced there. At last, Alfred was ready to meet him.

↰

Alfred posted the weapons-master ahead of the army, and ordered the long column to break right and left at Phillip's position. Thanes sent their mounts to the rear, and then leavened the front ranks of churls with their presence.

Shire by shire, the varied forces formed up into a long line, but with considerable depth. At all costs, Alfred did not want the shield-wall to break. Behind the veteran warriors were a mass of farmers and peasants who could absorb limited numbers of enemies, but would break if sufficient Vikings managed to cut their way to them. Panic was contagious, and if the mass of peasants broke, the veterans might collapse as well.

The king hoped that the shire organization would make the contingents functional in large units, but he hated to trust the fate of his kingdom to this. Polonius had often told him of the complex military formations of the Eastern Romans. Their infantry could function as a mass, or just as easily break into smaller centuries or maniples that were just as invulnerable to attack. Alfred dreamed of a professional army with such skills, but he knew that before he started to dream of a professional army, he had to defeat a very stubborn and competent Viking king, who waited to destroy the army of the West Saxons.

The entire West Saxon force was advancing slowly toward Edington, when the blare of Viking war horns brought it to an uncertain halt. Alfred and his advisors rode forward to see what was happening.

Guthrum had chosen to abandon the fortified estate, and the Saxons watched as rank after rank of armored infantry marched out onto the plain. The Viking ranks matched the length of the Saxon shield-wall, but it was of necessity thinner, since Guthrum had brought a relatively small force south with him. It had not been reinforced by Ubbi and his men, nor with the Cornish and Devonshire men Guthrum had counted on. Worst of all for the Danish king, many of his stalwart force had died in the endless skirmishes fought over the winter and spring, particularly after Alfred had started staging hit and run attacks. Unwilling to be besieged in an ill-supplied fortification where all the advantages went to the Saxons, Guthrum had apparently decided to throw the bones on one final confrontation.

To the chants and cheers of the entire Danish army, a dozen young men broke ranks and proceeded to strip in front of both armies. Naked, they retrieved their swords, and started screaming "Odin! Odin!" at the top of their lungs.

Alfred had seen the berserkers before, and knew they were a very dangerous element. The Saxons, in superstitious fear, often broke when confronted with the naked and screaming demons.

Guthrum would be sure to have a strong strike force waiting, just in case the berserkers managed to break the Saxon wall. Hundreds of armored veterans would follow their berserker comrades through any sort of breach.

Alfred had planned for this possibility, however, and he smiled in anticipation. He had instructed each ealdorman to put a row of slingers and archers directly behind the front ranks of swordsmen. They had firm instructions not to let any berserker get within reach of the front rank. The Vikings were drugged and truly fanatical, yet he knew that they could die. It just took a lot of arrows and rocks.

The berserkers started a raging attack against Alfred's Center. The Saxon front rank of spearmen cowered in superstitious terror of the madmen who charged recklessly at them, but they obeyed orders and sank to their knees. The archers were eager that the pagan demons not reach their ranks.

Hundreds of feathered shafts were released, and the berserkers began to look like porcupines. They each took many hits before slowing, but eventually even their raw will could not force the bodies to go further when they bled out. One by one, the human sacrifices dropped. None made it to the shield-wall.

The Saxons hooted in derision, but Alfred knew that the front rank just felt great relief that they had not had to fight madmen sworn to their gods. As the sun reached its nadir, the war horns blared again, and the full body of the Danish fighting machine rolled forward.

The Danes were outnumbered, but these same warriors had already helped to crush kingdom after kingdom to the north. All were veterans, and they had no particular fear of the lowly peasant army that had massed to defy them. They were better armed, and better trained, and, in the end, knew that the only way to *Valhalla* was to die in battle. They would either crush the last independent Angelisc kingdom in Britain today, or they would reach Asgard. The dressed ranks marched forward with confidence.

The two fronts struck, recoiled, and crashed together again. Shoulder to shoulder with their comrades, hundreds of warriors engaged in single combat.

The din was incredible, with various forces shouting to give each other support, and the sound of hundreds of spears and axes striking either weapons or shields. When someone was successful with their thrust or swing, the victim added high-pitched screams to the cacophony of sound.

The injured were pulled backward, and the dead were trampled on by their fellows, but both shield-walls held firm. The fallen were replaced with fresh comrades from the rear. The Saxon line was thicker, and the rear ranks were able to shower the foe with spears and arrows. The Vikings, however, wore better armor and were more successful in single combat. Both armies bled, yet neither had a marked advantage.

By late afternoon, the front lines had become a charnel house. The Saxons had pressed the Danes back, but at great cost, and were no closer than before to breaking the stubborn Danes. Alfred stood just behind the army, with his band of advisors and part of his Personal Guard that he had held in reserve.

"Well, friends, what do we do? We are thinning their ranks, but at great cost to ourselves. It will just take one shire unit to panic, and we are undone."

Polonius spoke. "Sire, they tried to break our center with their berserkers. Both armies are exhausted, and it looks like Guthrum has already committed his reserves. Why don't we take a leaf from his book, and send your Personal Guard through their center? If the Danes are forced to break formation, then our superior numbers guarantee victory."

"So be it. With God's help, we will today win a great victory. Ambrose! Phillip! Polonius! Take my Personal Guard and form them into a phalanx. Tell them to use the big pig- stickers until they achieve a breakthrough. Then they can throw the damn things away and go back to their swords! Go, and may God be with you!"

The Somerset fyrd were struggling mightily to hold the Danes. Man by man, their numbers were shrinking, and there were not many uninjured left in the rear ranks to plug the gaps. Already, old men and beardless youths were being thrust forward.

The fyrd was not far from breaking, when the sound of their own war horns blared behind them. Their officers yelled at them to clear an opening. "Make way! Make way! Move to the side! Form up to the right!"

Grateful for the break in the stubborn battle, for whatever reason, the fighting men of Somerset struggled to clear an opening. The Danes, sensing a lessening of pressure, pressed eagerly after the retreating foe. The Somerset ranks thickened into perpendicular lines that funneled the Danes through the main Saxon line. Several dozen brave Danish warriors dashed forward in an effort to fully exploit the apparent break.

At the end of the short corridor, however, they found a mass of heavily armored thanes and noblemen, each carrying spears some fifteen

Roman feet in length. This wedge of veterans started chanting "Alfred! Alfred!", and then charged forward.

The long spears struck the Danes before they could close on the enemy, and the Vikings died to a man. The same irresistible force swept on, and as quickly broke the thin line of Danish reserve troops who had tried to fill in the gap when the front rank had charged forward.

Suddenly a large and fresh formation of Saxons was behind the Danish skjaldborg. The Saxons, led by the bastard prince, threw away the oversized spears and started eagerly harvesting with their swords.

The Danes had had enough. Brave men, outnumbered, then attacked from both side and front, they broke. They threw down their weapons and ran. The panic was contagious, and, section by section, the skjaldborg collapsed. King Guthrum's army was in rout.

Alfred's army pursued until nightfall, but were unable to stop the Danes from re-forming into smaller bands as they retreated toward Chippenham. The king tried to get the Saxon thanes back from the hunt, so he could mount a sizable force and beat the Danes to their retreat. The Saxon thanes, however, had themselves broken into small bands and ranged far out of earshot of the recall horns.

The rest of the Saxon army, made up mainly of farmers and retainers of the thanes, did not have the discipline to quickly re-form, or even respond to the recall horns. They did manage to continue to savage the Danes, however, pursuing them eagerly.

The Danes liked to wear gold armlets and broaches, and, after looting many of the churches and abbeys of the island, many carried a fortune in gold. It belonged to the man who cut down the foe who wore it. A fortune was found on the battlefield and on the plain between Edington and Chippenham.

The warriors of the Saxon fyrds wandered back into camp separately and in small groups throughout the night. All were exhausted, and many were wounded, but they were triumphant. Many carried more looted gold and silver than they had seen in their lifetimes, and they were hopeful that the Danish threat to Wessex was finally over.

At dawn the next morning, Alfred spoke to his assembled commanders. "Ambrose, I want you and Phillip to form up my Personal Guard, and as many other mounted warriors as you can scrounge together. Let me know when you are ready, then together we will ride toward Chippenham. Guthrum's army may have broken, but this war is not over until the Danes are dead or out of Wessex."

"You think there is still a threat from Guthrum, brother?"

Alfred replied. "Guthrum is a brave and resourceful man, and he still has a strong fortified base only a few Roman miles away from here. A good portion of his retreating army is probably already ensconced there. With more reinforcements, or Saxon traitors at his side, he could yet be a formidable threat."

Leaving the rest of his army to make their way as best they could, Alfred led the mounted force of several hundred warriors after the Danish king. One way or the other, he intended to end the Danish menace once and for all.

CHAPTER 27

"(Alfred's army)...riding after them as far as the fortress, (Chippenham) where he remained a fortnight."

Alfred led the Saxon mounted force forward at a leisurely pace. The men were exhausted, and those of Guthrum's army who were going to make it back to Chippenham had probably already done so. The column passed dozens of Danes who lay dead and had been stripped of armor, weapons, and treasures during the night.

As the column advanced, Saxon stragglers joined the line of march. During the night, some of the fyrdmen had actually chased the fugitives as far as the Avon River. Thus Alfred's army reformed and grew as it advanced. Behind the mounted column of armored thanes, some still straggling out of the night's encampment, advanced the vast rank and file; many mounted, but many more on foot. Seven hundred Saxons reached the riverbank across from the burh by late afternoon, and a thousand more would arrive within twenty-four hours. Guthrum's remaining forces were probably equal in number to Alfred's advance guard, but the Vikings were demoralized, and many were seriously wounded. When Alfred's advance guard came within sight of Chippenham, it paused, and the leaders moved forward to hear their king's instructions.

Ambrose spoke first. "Well, brother, do we order an attack?"

The king sighed and held his belly. "I know Polonius' Chinese military strategist friend says that it is a low form of endeavor, and I am not prepared to throw away hundreds of lives on a frontal attack. I do not wish to have a . . . what did you call it, Polonius? . . . A Pyrrhic victory. I guess that means a siege."

Polonius spoke next. "What did you have in mind, Sire?"

"First we scour the banks for the boats, but while we make a big show of doing that, I want most of the army to quietly go upriver to the nearest ford and cross. It is summer, and we can string rope across for those who are not comfortable in the water."

"And then, Sire?"

"I am going to let you take care of the details, my clever Byzantine friend, but I envision a fortified camp built right by the main gate, so

Guthrum cannot devastate us with a surprise attack. Once the defensive position is completed, put the entire force to work digging a dry ditch surmounted by high earth ramparts and a palisade wall. Make it strong. This king has flown over altogether too many defensive walls."

Within days, the barrier stretched completely across the little peninsula. The Danes were now trapped in the very settlement where they had come so close to trapping Alfred and his immediate family during the Christmas festivities. Meantime, Alfred sent royal messengers to call up more of his eastern levies. It would take up to several weeks for them all to arrive, but he intended to have several thousand more fyrdmen on hand, in case he was forced to assault the fortified burh or face any more surprises.

Alfred sent others riding along both banks of the Avon River, to round up as many boats as they could find. He had escaped Guthrum's clutches only because of the boats. Thanks to a stubborn rearguard action that had decimated his Personal Guard, he had been able to get most of his forces across the Avon, while Guthrum had been unable to follow. He had no intention of letting Guthrum do the same to him.

Alfred called his chief noblemen and advisors to his side. All stared silently at the strengthened walls that protected the Danish survivors.

"My friends. As you know, I have sent for another two thousand men. Odda is on his way with every fyrdman he has not already sent me, but it may be up to several weeks before the eastern fyrds can be called up and arrive here. We thus have a major problem."

Ethelnoth, Ealdorman of Somerset, and loyal supporter of Alfred, spoke up. "How so, Sire?"

Alfred pointed. "There lies the enemy. We could probably overwhelm them now, but it would cost us dearly. Or, we can wait until a truly overwhelming force has gathered. The real question is, will Guthrum receive reinforcements before us?"

Polonius spoke quietly. "Sire, the longer we wait, the stronger we will become and the weaker Guthrum will be. Larger numbers in the attack will translate into both fewer casualties and surer victory."

"But more time also allows the Danes to prepare for the eventual onslaught, and may give them time to call up reinforcements."

Polonius replied. "Sire, the Danes survived all winter by sending out constant raiding parties and stripping the countryside bare. With us camped on their doorstep, the best they can do is fish in the river for food. They had been stripping the countryside around Edington when we caught up with them. Whatever supplies they had left stockpiled here cannot last long.

"That's clearly one vote for waiting. But what of the other threat? Should we not cut off Guthrum's head before his countrymen can come to his rescue?"

Ambrose spoke next. "Brother, from where will he get the forces? Much of his army of last summer has settled in Mercia, and most of the other Viking armies are settling far to the north, in Northumbria. Ubbi's force is reported to be back in Southern Wales, but the battle at Cynwith crippled it. It is without its leader, and the Welsh are now pushing back.

There are many Vikings in Ireland, but they, too, are facing rebellion. Best of all, the Norse are fighting with the Danes. Most of Guthrum's possible reinforcements are either fighting to hold on to what they have already conquered, or are busy settling down in new territories. With Ivar dead, Halfdan Ragnarsson is the only unknown variable in the equation that I can think of."

Alfred looked at his brother. "Ambrose do you think that Halfdan would attack? Of all of Lodbrok's sons, he is the last one, and, being master of both Dublin and Northumbria, he is a dangerous man."

"I know not, brother. Sitric is close to him, and he has been a friend to Wessex, yet we have killed Sitric's uncle. I can only pray that Halfdan stays in the north with Sitric, or returns to Ireland. I have no wish to face my old friend on the battlefield."

Alfred looked thoughtful for a minute, and finally seemed to come to a decision. "So be it! My friends, you have once again helped me come to a decision.

Commanders! My word is that we continue the siege. We will not waste good Wessex men on frontal attacks. I want the sentries doubled, however. Do not forget how Odda, our old friend here, destroyed Ubbi's army. And I want a full quarter of the army to be armed and standing-to, along the ramparts, at all times. They may rotate in six hour shifts. Is that understood?"

On the morning of the fourteenth day after the siege of Chippenham started, the heavy wooden gates of the burh swung open the width of a person, and a lone envoy stepped out of the main gate. He held a white shield over his head, and was unarmed. Alfred was called from his tent, and Ambrose hurried to join him.

The man boldly walked up to the ramparts erected by the Saxons across from the Viking ramparts. He stood patiently waiting, well within spear casting range.

Alfred turned to his brother, who had spent a year as a slave in Denmark, and then several years more working with the Varangians on the great river that led to the Black Sea. Ambrose was the adopted son of a respected Danish warrior, and was fluent in most of the dialects of the Vikings.

At a nod from his brother, he called out to the man in flawless Danish. "Identify yourself, Viking."

The man smiled at the Danish. His grasp of Anglish was rough, but solid. "I am Dagmar, Jarl of Jutland, and personal envoy sent by his Majesty Guthrum of East Anglia and Denmark. And who be you, that you talk with a Danish tongue?"

"I am Canuteson, adopted son of Canute, trader for Gunnar of the Rus and ambassador to the Imperial court of Byzantium. As Canuteson, I was a foot soldier in the army of Ubbi and Halfdan. But in this land I am best known as Ambrose, bastard prince of Wessex."

"Ho! I have heard of you, Ambrose the Dane-slayer. I spent several days chasing you across Mercia, until Sitric Ivarsson decided as an act of mercy to let you live. You then stole a princess from a distant cousin of mine in Ireland. Yes, Prince of Wessex, I know of you!"

"Where is Jarl Ura, Dagmar?"

"Alas, he died of metal poisoning. A Saxon spear, if I am not mistaken."

"My brother the king recognizes your status as official spokesman for King Guthrum. What is your message, Jarl Dagmar?"

"Please tell your brother the king that King Guthrum is prepared to agree to withdraw from Wessex forever, if your brother will accept his terms."

Ambrose looked at Alfred, who spoke quietly. "I would be thrilled to accept his surrender, but how do we know that he means it this time?"

Ambrose turned again to the envoy who stood below him in the ditch. "King Guthrum offered us a truce at Wareham. He took our Danegeld and at the first opportunity, he broke his word and escaped to the old Roman fort at Exeter. There we surrounded you once again."

"And we again came to terms with your king."

"Yes, after your supply fleet was caught in the storm and sunk. And then Guthrum swore his most holy oath, on his armband, that he would leave Wessex and never return."

The envoy shrugged again. "Only fools pay gold to robbers. You have lived among us. You know that we do not respect a man who is soft enough to pay for protection when his right arm can achieve it. Such an oath as was offered was worthless. But King Guthrum swore a holy oath to leave, and he kept his word, Saxon."

"And a third time your king broke his word to Alfred. He and his minions fell on this very burh as we were innocently enjoying our Christmas celebrations."

"And your king Alfred quite rightly hanged the hostages before our very eyes. It was hard to watch good friends die like that. We paid dearly for the treachery."

"And yet you expect King Alfred to yet again sign a truce with Guthrum?"

"Anglishman, we see your reinforcements troop into camp day after day. Campfires in the distance tell us that yet more warriors are answering your king's summons. You are already numerous enough that you could probably overrun us, but we both know how dearly it would cost you. My king accepts that his gamble has failed. It is time for talking. You have lived as a Viking. You know that when we sign a treaty with a man worthy of respect, we keep our word. Your king was all but defeated, and hid in the forest like a hunted stag. Yet by some feat of Christian magic he conjured up an entire army, and even now is in the process of raising another one. Such a feat can only be done with the support of the people, and perhaps powerful gods. Guthrum bade me tell your king that a man who can perform such magic is worthy of his respect."

"Your words are fine, and we are flattered, yet how do we know that Guthrum will not betray us yet again?"

"Please tell your king that Guthrum will give any number of hostages you want, and whoever you want. He asks for none in return. He swears to leave Wessex forever, and he asks to be baptized as a Christian. He has seen the terrible power of the cross, and he wishes to know more of it."

Alfred spoke quietly in Ambrose's ear while the entire Saxon army stood silently behind them. At last Ambrose responded to the envoy.

"Go back to your king, Jarl Dagmar, but return as the sun nears the horizon. Alfred promises an answer by sundown."

The Witan met in King Alfred's campaign tent. Alfred spoke. "Well, counselors? We have a big decision to make. We now have the manpower to finally crush Guthrum and his men, but it will leave a lot more grieving widows across the land. Alternatively, we can take this man's hand in friendship, and end the warfare between us. I am open to suggestions."

Odda, Ealdorman of Devon, spoke first. "Sire, the man has broken his word to us three times. What is to stop him from betraying us yet again?"

"I know, Odda. I know. I am the one who swore that any Viking invaders would only receive the land it takes to bury them. But think of what an incredible opportunity for Mother Church is being offered. This is the first time a Viking king of Angleland has asked to be baptized! If the savage Northerners truly accept the word of God, then perhaps we really can learn to live in peace and harmony with them. They are here, on our island, to stay. We may be strong enough to keep them out of Wessex, but there are not enough Britons and Saxons and Angles and Jutes left to completely drive them from the island. We can continue to fight wave after wave of them, or we can try to bring them to a new way of life!"

Odda looked at his king. "Sire, I am but an old and grizzled war horse. Like my old friend Phillip, my preferred strategy lies with my sword and my right hand. Yet I think I see what you are saying. But if we let Guthrum escape, and he returns with yet more Vikings . . ."

Alfred interrupted. "Then we call up the fyrds yet again and crush him again. We develop and train a standing army so that we never again have to sit idly by while Vikings plunder our land at will. And if he returns, this time we hang members of his own family, who will be left as hostages."

Odda nodded. "And if we convert him and his people to the True Faith, then they will be Christian neighbors."

Alfred smiled in triumph, and clapped Odda on the back. "You have it, old friend! Like it or not, Guthrum still controls East Anglia to the north. Better Christian Danes to our north than pagans. If Guthrum can be made to be a buffer between us and the pagan kingdoms farther north, then he would be valuable indeed."

The young king turned to his advisors and chief noblemen. Most nodded assent.

"So be it! Ambrose, meet with the envoy at sunset and tell him that we will accept Guthrum's surrender; on certain conditions. Tell him we expect his king's answer by noon tomorrow. Stay with me a moment, and I will give you more particulars.

Phillip! I want the men manning the palisades to be extra vigilant tonight. I also want the Avon River patrols doubled. There is to be no shirking, tonight of all nights.

Polonius! Your task may be the most important of all. I want you to have the men bring in an even dozen cattle, and I want them roasted whole. If the wind does not change tonight, Guthrum is going to smell cooking meat until it drives him crazy!

ॾ

Guthrum himself, King of part of Denmark, and all of East Anglia, stepped through the gate and advanced half way to the Saxon palisade, where he stood alone. He was a tall and burly man, and he wore the badge of his trade. He was dressed in fine chain-link armor, which, though burnished in sand for this occasion, showed considerable wear. It was the armor of a man-of-action, one who had fought long and hard.

His trousers were baggy, and tied across his shoulders was a beautiful woollen cloak. On both his neck and on his arms the man wore a king's ransom in gold.

Alfred, tall and blond, but slighter than his adversary, slipped through the opening in the palisade made by the removal of two logs. He nimbly dropped down into the dry ditch, and then scrambled up the further side to meet the advancing Danish king. Each was followed by only one man, unarmed, to act as advisor and translator. Guthrum had Dagmar at his side, and Ambrose followed his brother. There, between two armies, and watched by most of the men of both, the two rival kings met.

Each man looked his adversary over thoroughly. King Alfred spoke first. "Ambrose. Tell him that those armlets belong to me. He made a sacred oath on them that he did not keep."

Ambrose translated into flawless Danish exactly what his royal brother said. Guthrum looked startled for a moment, and then burst into loud laughter. He slapped Alfred on the back as he roared, and Ambrose reacted, but only Guthrum and Alfred were armed. Guthrum meant it in good humor, however, for he slipped off the massive pair of gold ornaments, and handed them to Alfred with a grin.

"Ho! You are right, Anglish king! I swore an oath on them to a man I thought was little better than a merchant. Time has proven me wrong. You are truly a man worthy of respect. Take these, not as the spoils of war, but rather as a token of my esteem!"

Alfred took the proffered armlets, and passed them back to Ambrose to hold. "Ambrose, tell him I thank Guthrum for his words, and his armlets. If we are to have a lasting truce, and perhaps even one day be friends, then we must have between us respect. A Christian does not break his sacred word."

Guthrum spoke in his deep voice. "Tell your master that, to a man such as himself, who has earned my respect, my word is also my bond. There will be no more betrayals on my part."

"Alfred says that he understands. He would like you to know that he respects you greatly as a leader, and would like to have you as a friend on his northern border."

Guthrum laughed again. "But out of Wessex, no doubt! Tell Alfred that I need several weeks to prepare my men to move north. Many have been wounded, and are not yet ready to travel. If he would supply me with adequate food, I will swear to hang any of my men who pillage either here or on the route north. Perhaps he could spare several of those cows that were so slowly roasted last night!"

Ambrose conferred, and Alfred agreed. The Vikings had to eat, and they would steal it if it was not freely given.

"My king agrees. He insists, however, that all slaves who are from Wessex must be freed."

"Again you take my slaves! You drive a hard bargain. We took many beautiful women in the last several months, but, yes, I will agree to once again release all my captives."

"There is the matter of the loot that you have taken."

"I am marching a shrunken army northwards. I will have close to a thousand widows, whose futures depend on the shares they receive from this expedition."

"Alfred understands, but insists that your men only take that which they can carry on their person. The rest must be returned to its rightful owners."

"Please tell King Alfred that his terms are acceptable to me. I promise to start trekking north within a month, and ask that the Saxon army be withdrawn a decent distance, so that there are no unfortunate misunderstandings between our warriors. I understand that your forces will not be disbanded until after I cross the northern border."

"Then there is the matter of hostages."

"I have already given my word. Alfred may demand any number, and anyone."

"Then he chooses your son and five of your jarls. He will give you the list of names later."

"So. Your spies are good! I have no choice but to agree. And, in turn, I ask that King Alfred meet me in two weeks, when he can teach me the way of the cross. If he will send me a suitable escort, I will meet him anywhere in Wessex that he wishes."

Alfred spontaneously reached out his hand to Guthrum, and the Danish king took it and shook it firmly.

CHAPTER 28

"They told him also, that their king would receive baptism. And they acted accordingly; for in the course of three weeks after, King Guthrum, attended by some thirty of the worthiest men that were in the army, came to him at Aller, which is near Athelney, and there the king became his sponsor in baptism; and his crisom-leasing was at Wedmore. He was there twelve nights with the king, who honored him and his attendants with many presents."

Ealdorman Ethelnoth raised his hand in greeting as the Danish king and his party of some thirty important princelings and jarls rode into the meadow. Behind the ealdorman stretched an escort-of-honor of over one hundred thanes, carefully selected from all parts of the West Saxon Empire.

Many of Alfred's surviving members of his Personal Guard sat as part of the line. The rest of the once considerably larger body had fallen in the lightening attack on Chippenham, or in the subsequent bitter struggle for survival and supremacy.

This time, Dagmar acted as translator for the two sides. Ambrose had remained with the royal household. Guthrum had put his life in the hands of Ethelnoth, and he was curious where he was being led.

"Ealdorman Ethelnoth, where do we ride?"

"His Majesty awaits you at Aller, which is less than a day's ride from here. It is an island near Athelney, which was our Center of operations against you this spring."

"Ah, now you tell me! Just two months ago I would have given a barrel of gold for the location of King Alfred's secret fort!"

Ethelnoth just grunted. "Many of your spies tried to earn that gold. You may still find some of their remains, hanging from the trees as we pass by."

꩜

Ethelnoth led the cavalcade deep into the alder forest. The land was swampy, and the riders had to keep to narrow tracks where only a few could ride abreast. Where there was no forest, there was water. Only occasionally did they come to clearings, and in each case local scouts rode ahead to inform the people just who was coming through. The common folk at each settlement crossed themselves and glared as the Danes rode through. Guthrum urged his mount closer to Ethelnoth, until he could easily talk with the gruff ealdorman.

"It appears that your people do not love us."

"Love you? You and your kind have raped and pillaged the length and breadth of the island. These people live in terror of the 'Northmen'. But more than that, you have cut off trade routes that we have used since the times of the Romans. You have tried to extinguish good Christian worship on our island.

Our people were learning to read. You have burned our libraries, and killed innocent priests and nuns. You have no idea what damage you have done to the Christian lands in your blindness and your greed!"

"Ethelnoth, teach me! I want to be baptized and learn the way of the cross. Show me that your three-gods-in-one is greater than Thor and Odin, and I will join you. And my people will follow me."

ᚦ

Alfred and his party traveled the last portion of the journey to the island of Aller by punt. It had only been a few months before that Alfred had stopped at the church on the little island to pray. Then, he had asked for God's guidance and divine intervention; just before he rode to the gathering of the shire fyrds and his eventual victory at Edington. It was thus at Aller where he decided to meet the Danish king and his chief advisors and Jarls.

Alfred had prudently left his own wife and son at Athelney, along with a strong garrison and most of his hostages. Guthrum's son had come with Alfred, to see his father and report that all of the others were safe and well.

Alfred waited with his own counselors and a small contingent of thanes from his Personal Guard. The men, dressed in their best armor and drawn up in a long single rank, stood rigidly still as Guthrum and his Danes were ferried the short distance onto the island.

Both Alfred and Guthrum had chosen this day to dress as kings instead of warriors. Each wore his sword and dagger, but no armor. Alfred's light crown of gold almost matched his hair, and around his waist was the belt given him as a child by *Pope Leo IV himself*

Guthrum was bareheaded, and his shaggy locks flowed down to his shoulders. The two men met as respected equals, and each embraced the other.

Guthrum spoke to Alfred through Ambrose and Dagmar. He pointed in the direction of the small fleet of punts that were securely beached on the far side of the island.

"Alfred, this place where you hid from my spies and my men, this Athelney, is it close to here?"

Alfred laughed. "It lies deeper in the marshes, Guthrum, much deeper."

"Then it is no wonder we could never find you. Without a guide, I could never have reached even this far."

"Without permission to approach, you would have been killed long since. Each settlement you passed through stood guard. Each has escape boats prepared for the women and children, and spears and arrows amassed for the intruder."

"Then it is as well that I come as a friend! I mean it, Alfred. I am going to take my men north to settle down. East Anglia has recognized my sovereignty, yet it is scarcely conquered. I think it is time to parcel it out amongst my faithful followers, while some of them still live. I will even allow your Christ-priests to come north and teach us the ways of the cross and the book. There is great magic in your books. It is one of the reasons that my people go out of their way to destroy them. We fear them."

Bishop Asser stood respectfully back from the two monarchs, but he almost rubbed his hands in glee. He was already mentally making lists of priests in his head whom he could send north. He had great hopes of increasing his influence throughout East Anglia.

The present church structure had been decimated by the rampaging Vikings, who had systematically looted each church they had come across for its gold and silver. The braver priests who had tried to defend their sacred treasures had died to a man. Many martyrs had fallen, but the priests he sent would have the official support of King Guthrum. Guthrum's offer was a wonderful opportunity for Mother Church, and for Bishop Asser, too.

Senior thanes were posted as guards, and only Alfred's most senior advisors were invited to the isolated cottage that was the king's temporary command headquarters. On the other side of the tun, at the Great Hall, the rest of the Saxons and Vikings were freely drinking and carousing.

Ambrose looked up from the parchment map they were perusing, and spoke to his brother. "Alfred, do you really think that this time they will march north and not dare us again?"

"I don't know, Ambrose. I have always remembered what you taught me long ago. You told me that, above all, the Vikings respect strength. And that reminds me. Ethelnoth, have you been able to scrounge up the drafts of men that I requested?"

"Aye, Majesty. Each village will be fully garrisoned as we ride through. All men within two day's march have been called in. If necessary, my thanes have instructions to leapfrog us, and use the same mounted levies in two different tuns. There are still mounted contingents of thanes arriving from the eastern shires, and their commanders all have instructions to use the road you are following. The road will be crowded with warriors marching to their king's side."

"Perfect. And Polonius, have you been able to arrange adequate food supplies for our scheduled stops?"

"Yes, King. The royal estates will be stripped bare, but we will be able to provide enough food for some extravagant feasting."

"Excellent. Wherever we go, I want Guthrum to see a land of plenty. Plenty of food, and, especially, plenty of brave young men. I want him to think that if he brings another five armies south, we have the forces to destroy them all.

Ambrose, to answer your question, I would like to think that his oath as a Christian would keep him north of our frontiers, but I honestly think that the real reason he will not return resides in the spears and swords of our warriors. But think, brother! What if he is sincere about learning about our Sweet Lord? What an opportunity it would be! Our own people were lifted from the darkness just a few hundred years ago by the Christian missionaries.

The truth - I believe that we can reside alongside our pagan neighbors - just as long as our sword is bigger than theirs. I also have no doubt that the Danes would come south again just as soon as they perceive that we are weak. But if we can convert Guthrum to the ways of God, or even the Viking children of the next generation, then there really may be a chance that we can share this island and all live in one brotherhood of Jesus Christ.

Let's declare peace, and send our priests north. We have a unique opportunity here to turn the forces of darkness from our shores. How can we not try? We will fight the northern menace with both the cross and the sword. And most important, the peace will buy us time in order to develop a fleet and build a string of defensive positions so our people are not so defenseless against surprise attack.

Once the women and children are protected, then the men are

willing to fight away from home. Until they have such security for their loved ones, the fyrdmen will continue to melt away as soon as we march them out of their home territory.

Having already secretly organized the trip, Alfred next invited his royal guest to visit the nearby royal estate.

"Guthrum, let us go to my hunting estate of Wedmore. There is a particularly fine church there that we can use for your baptism, and the boar and deer hunting in the area is excellent. It might be interesting if we are both on the same side of the hunt for a change."

"Ah, Alfred, I fear that even your fleetest royal deer will not be as challenging as chasing you!"

"However, my friend, you will have better success in the hunt, and at the end of the day there will be no grieving widows in our two lands."

"Aye. There are already too many of those now, I'm thinking."

The royal hosts and their Viking guests made a stately procession to Wedmore. They rode for only a few hours per day, but the trip was impeccably timed so that there was always a royal estate or tun to stop at for meals, or for the night. At each stop, they were lavishly feted and fed. What Guthrum did not know was that Alfred and Ethelnoth had sent messengers ahead to the shire reeves with strict instructions that no expense be spared to impress the visitors. At the same time, all of the tuns and burhs were heavily garrisoned by local levies of churls, and the thanes who had not been called up to serve in Alfred's fyrd were called up specifically for the royal passage.

Guthrum saw a well organized and very numerous fyrd wherever he went. As the royal party and the Danes rode the highway, strong bands of mounted churls and thanes continually blocked the road. The Saxon, Jute and Angle fyrds made way for the royal party, but each commander made obeisance to his king before he and his men resumed the long ride to where Alfred's main force held Guthrum's army captive.

At last, two days after leaving the marshes of Aller, the royal party, some two hundred strong, rode into the tun of Wedmore. Alfred passed the reins of his horse over to a servant, and put his arm on Guthrum's shoulder.

"Come, king. The mead is wasting. Tonight, come sundown, I have sworn to fast. King or not, I have need of your help in emptying the mead cask before the sun sets! Tomorrow I am to become your godfather, and I wish to pray tonight that I may be worthy of the task."

"Alfred, I know little of the way of the cross, yet I have hunted you across the breadth of these lands, and I have faced you in battle. I can tell you right now that you are worthy of the task. I hope that I will be worthy, as the child who must learn from his spiritual father."

The sound of shouted voices was the first hint of Alfred's surprise. Most of the people in the tun turned out in curiosity at the unusual sounds. It was not an attack, however, as some had feared. An even dozen giant ox-driven wagons rumbled slowly into sight, surrounded by a cloud of riders. Above them all flew the royal dragon banners of Alfred and Wessex. The rest of the royal household, which Alfred had originally left at Athelney, had finally caught up by an alternate road with the king and his guests.

Alfred himself strode forward to greet the newcomers. Several small shapes hurtled into his arms, followed quickly by his wife. Guthrum, following Alfred and curious about the turmoil, found himself face to face again with his son and the rest of the Viking hostages. With a whoop of delight, Guthrum hugged each in turn. Ambrose and Polonius pushed through the crowd until they could find Gretchen and Kuralla. After a winter of despair and a spring of anxiety, the royal court was once again together in a nation both united and at peace. Many of the crowd cried with pure happiness.

Bishop Asser raised his arms to allow his young acolytes to slip his alb over his head. This was to be a great day in his life, and in the absence of his arch-bishop, who was presently far away at Canterbury, he was the chief actor. Today he was to baptize a king, and, eventually, if all went well, perhaps Christianize an entire tribe of the ferocious northern barbarians. It was an incredible opportunity.

Clywd, his youngest acolyte, was busily unpacking the green chasuble from the bishop's kit. Asser despaired for the youngster. He would long ago have sent the lad packing, but he was the eldest son of his sister's brood. To send him home in disgrace would precipitate a family scandal that he couldn't handle. He mentally marked the boy down for one of the first openings in East Anglia when Guthrum allowed the Christian priests into his domain. Asser spoke irritably to the youngster.

"No, no, Clywd! Think, lad. I am dressing for the baptism of a king! What color would be appropriate for such an important ceremony?"

"Ah, perhaps purple . . . or white, Bishop?"

"Perhaps red or white, Clywd!"

Asser stood glowering as the boy stood indecisively. An abrupt wave of his hand stifled the answer one of the more intelligent acolytes had been about to shout out. At last Asser came to the boy's rescue.

"The red one, boy! Unpack the red one! You, Boda. Bring the Dalmatic and Stole. Kings are waiting for us!"

Hurrying into the rest of his costume, Bishop Asser grabbed his miter and staff, and rushed for the door. He was in charge of a very important ceremony, and he wanted it to go smoothly. A bishop who succeeded in this task might both bring lambs to God's church, and also much good Bookland. Alfred was known to be a generous man to those who pleased him.

ᚠ

Bishop Asser slowly led the brilliant procession toward the church. Behind him, and his solemnly chanting phalanx of priests, came two kings and sixty noblemen; thirty Saxon, and thirty Danish. Each of the Danes was to be baptized this day, and the Saxon thanes and ealdormen had volunteered to act as spiritual godfathers. Behind this glittering procession came over a hundred more of the most powerful of the king's thanes, foreign ambassadors, wealthy merchants, and several churls who were wealthy enough to qualify for the rank of thane, but had yet to be so honored.

The rays of the sun blazed down in unusual intensity on the July day, and several of the party felt faint under the burden of their various robes. The local churls and slaves, who had gathered to watch in fascination, had stripped off their outer garments, but the actors that day could not.

Bishop Asser had gone out of his way to showcase the pomp and ceremony of Mother Church. He was sure that this was part of what fascinated the pagan Danes.

He led the procession toward the tall wooden church that had been built along the lines of a Great Hall. His passage was marked with a cloud of incense, and the phalanx of priests chanted sonorously as they marched.

Alfred's royal church of Wedmore had huge beams stretching up to a high pointed roof. The dark interior was lit by flaring torches stuck into fixtures mounted on the wall.

Bishop Asser led his new converts through the towering doorway, to a position just before the font of holy water. The two kings and sixty noblemen formed a semicircle around the Bishop and the font. Asser stepped behind King Guthrum and tied the chrism, a white piece of linen cloth, around the king's forehead. At his signal, his subordinate priests and acolytes stepped behind the thirty Viking noblemen and duplicated the task. Each of the newly baptized Danes would wear the symbol of their new faith for eight days.

The volunteer godfathers stood beside their new spiritual children, while Bishop Asser, starting with King Guthrum, repeatedly dipped a scallop shell into the holy water and sprinkled a few drops on each Viking in turn. As he proceeded down the line, Bishop Asser chanted the mysterious Latin words that gave Guthrum and his followers hope of eternal salvation. "I baptize thee in the name of the Father, and of the Son, and the Holy Ghost. Amen.'

Once the task was completed, Bishop Asser returned and stood in front of the two kings. A smile on his face, he now switched to Anglish. 'And now, King Alfred, have you a Christian name for this new lamb of God?"

"Aye, Bishop, but first let us introduce our guests to the mysteries of the church. Turning to Guthrum, he spoke to the man. 'Dip your hand into the holy water, and make a sign of the cross, like this . . . Excellent. Now please follow me."

Alfred led the new lamb of God down the length of the nave to the altar, where he repeated the sign of the cross. Guthrum followed and carefully imitated him.

"Guthrum of Denmark, today your soul has been saved. Kneel with me before the power and glory of God, and then rise, as Athelstan of the Danes."

Guthrum followed the lead of Alfred, and when he rose, Alfred embraced the Viking king in a great bear hug. "Welcome to God's Holy Church, Athelstan of the Danes!"

One by one, the thirty converts were taught how to make the sign of the cross, and then brought forward to kneel at God's holy altar. One by one, they rose, and were greeted by their new Christian name.

Alfred smiled as he faced the sixty Christians. He turned to Bishop Asser. "My Lord Bishop, I hope that you can come and offer God's blessing to our joyous feast this evening."

"With the utmost pleasure, Your Majesty."

Guthrum stood silently, but he was amazed that the king of Wessex, indisputably now the most powerful man on the island, would so humbly ask the Bishop to join him. He wondered again at the power of this God and his spokesmen, who even kings deferred to. The Christ-priests he had met had died easily, though it was true that many had fought to their last breath. Some, citing their religious beliefs, had refused to fight at all. He was puzzled that out of humility grew such strength. He again complimented himself for taking the trouble to study these teachings.

He wondered if the time of Odin and Thor was passing. He had stolen many of the sacred books on his various raids. He decided to ask Alfred for a Christ-priest who knew how to interpret the strange runes within them.

Alfred sat in his intricately carved Seat-of-Honor, and beside him, in the chair that was normally reserved for the shire ealdorman, sat the Viking king who had decided to become a Christian. The king was flanked on the other side by Ealhswith, his queen.

By special decree, Alfred had ordered that she, in honor of the very special occasion, could join the men at the table. Slaves and churls hustled to set up the trestle tables and benches in the king's hall, while the women prepared the food and poured the ale and mead for the waiting guests. More than two hundred guests were milling around just outside the hall, or were in the process of arriving.

At Polonius' curt nod, the signal horn brayed, and the many guests hurried to receive a warm cloth and wash their hands. Once their ablations were completed, they lined up good-naturedly to file past the door-wardens, who had them escorted to their predesignated seats.

The trestle tables stretched the length of the hall. On either side of them were the ealdormen of the empire, mixed in with bishops of the church, ambassadors of foreign lands, and the bedrock of Alfred's power, the fighting thanes.

Close by, at the head of the long table, Alfred had commanded that his young son would join the adults for this special feast. Near to him were the Danish princelings and noblemen.

Bishop Asser intoned the blessing, and Alfred then clapped his hands to begin the feast. From the far end, close to the outdoor summer kitchens, began a procession of heavily laden servers. The servers started with large roasted portions of venison and boars, roasted with their heads still intact. Heaping platters of beef and lamb followed.

A second wave of servers brought out entire flocks of roasted chickens, and hundreds of smaller birds that had been roasted on skewers. The centrepiece for Alfred's table was a swan which had been cunningly cooked with its feathers neatly in place.

Some three dozen noblewomen circulated with huge pitchers of mead, ale and wine, which they poured endlessly into the waiting drinking horns. Baskets full of fresh loaves of bread, cheese, and spring vegetables were heaped between the platters of meat, until the tables groaned with their burden of food.

While the men and women got down to serious eating, Alfred's favorite scop tuned his harp and sang the epic ballads. To Ambrose's great embarrassment, Alfred insisted that he sing the ballads about Ambrose that had become so popular across the island. At the end of the first ballad, Guthrum toasted Ambrose with his horn of mead.

After the food was cleared away, Alfred rose to his feet, and the crowd quickly hushed. The king addressed the court.

"My friends, members of the court, and honored guests! Today I have had the honor of becoming a godfather to a Danish king, a great warrior, and a child under God. It is a great honor, and a trust that I will work very hard to fulfil. I hope that, this night, as we welcome Athelstan into our midst as a Christian in the sight of God, will be a memorable one. I pray that it brings lasting peace to both our people. I know that we will not entirely drive the Danes from our island. Athelstan knows that Wessex will not be defeated; not by any coalition of Viking forces. Thus it seems clear we must learn to live as brothers, sharing the island between our two peoples. I am prepared to help Athelstan settle in peace in East Anglia, and Athelstan has today sworn a sacred oath to God that he will live in peace with us and respect our borders.

In honor of this momentous day, I would like to present Athelstan and his noblemen with some tokens of our trust and esteem. At the point of a sword, Wessex will yield nothing. In true friendship, I am pleased to be generous."

With that said, Alfred clapped his hands rapidly three times. The curtains at the far end parted again, but this time it was not platters of steaming food that arrived. Thirty comely maidens marched in slowly, each carrying a small wooden casket. Solemnly, the maidens advanced until they were next to the Danish visitors. Each bent low, and ceremoniously presented her casket to the grizzled Danish veterans she stood beside.

Guthrum received his first. He thanked the pretty girl who presented it to him, and then eagerly opened the box. He withdrew a jewel encrusted golden crown and massive gold cross with inset jewels that matched the ones in the crown. Both were of exquisite workmanship, and the men closest to the Danish king gasped as Guthrum drew his gifts from their hiding place.

Guthrum, overcome with the value and beauty of the gifts, stood and embraced Alfred. He spoke in his deep voice, and Polonius translated his words so the Saxons and Angles could understand.

"I am overcome with the generosity of King Alfred's gift. He has shown himself to be as generous in victory as he was indomitable in defeat. Alfred is my godfather and my friend. I have no great treasury from which to respond to his enormous generosity. I wish, however, to offer all of Wessex a gift from me and my people. In a few days, when I return to Chippenham, I will move my army out of Wessex forever. My people are going to settle north of the Thames and the Avon River, and they will respect those boundaries as long as I am their king. There we will study the religion of the three-gods-in-one, and we will live in peace with our southern neighbors. *This I pledge to you in the name of Jesus Christ.*"

Guthrum's speech was greeted with cheers by all the guests at the tables. Alfred called him brother, and hugged him in friendship. Finally, Alfred ordered the servants to bring back the mead. The warrior nobles of two nations drank together, and swapped stories of heroic deeds. Finally, one by one, and in a stupor, each nobleman lay down or fell down on the fresh rushes spread on the floor. Danes and Saxons slept intertwined.

ᚱ

The Danish army marched forth with as much majestic pomp and ceremony as it could muster, though most of the mounts were weak from a lack of fodder, and some had to be led. The commanders carried their banners high, and each warrior was fully armed and armored. They were allowed to take only their personal possessions, however, and Alfred's treasury would soon be the beneficiary of the tons of loot that the Danes had not been able to stuff into their bags and onto their overburdened horses.

The Saxon host, under the direct command of Ealdorman Odda, had pulled down a portion of their ramparts and palisades, and withdrawn half a Roman mile to the west. Though their kings had pledged eternal friendship, yet Odda kept the Saxon fyrds prepared and in battle order. While many men of the fyrds had melted away or been released to return home over the weary weeks while the two camps waited for their respective kings to make peace, as many more fyrdmen had arrived.

Even during the truce, Odda had all the men, both veteran and new conscript, drill daily. He insisted on keeping sufficient men that they outnumbered the Danes by a margin of at least three to one, even though this meant that he had to send out the local thanes to scour the lands and conscript most of the churls within several days' ride. He and Alfred had agreed that the swollen army would escort the Danes every step of the way to the northern border.

There, they would build another fortified camp and sit for a few weeks, just in case. After the Saxon army finally disbanded, the border-watchers would be massively reinforced. Alfred had given strict instructions. Wessex would not ever again be completely surprised, as it had the winter before. Not if Alfred had anything to do with it.

APPENDIX I

The History of Wessex, of Russia, and of Ambrose and his Son and Friends in the Ninth and Tenth Century AD.

Historical facts are in plain text.
Fictional stories in this series and comments are in italics.
Parts specific to this story are in bold.

793: First recorded attack by (Norwegian) Vikings on England.

832-865 AD.: Danish Vikings attack East Anglia, Wessex, and Kent.

838: Cornwall surrenders to Wessex.

845: The king's mistress gives birth to AMBROSE.

849: Alfred the Great is born.

850: Vikings winter in Kent for the first time.

853: Alfred is sent to Rome where he is made a Consul by the Pope.

855: Ethelwulf, king of Wessex, takes his son Alfred to Rome again.

856: Ivar the Boneless and Olaf the White take Dublin.

858: Ethelwulf dies. Ethelbald becomes king.

(Trader of Kiev)
860: *Ethelbert becomes king. Vikings sack Winchester before being driven out of Wessex.* Ambrose and Phillip are enslaved in a raid on the coast of Wessex.

861: *Pope Nicholas sends envoys to Constantinople to investigate Photius' ascension as patriarch.*

862: Rurik, a leader of Varangian Rus Vikings, is invited to rule at

Novgorod.

Ambrose, Polonius and Phillip arrive in Sweden after escaping from Denmark. Pursued by their former captors, they hurriedly agree to go south with Rurik and his Rus tribesmen.

863: Dir and Askold, Rus jarls, take over the Slavic town of Kiev. Nb. There seems to be considerable debate about both this date and whether Dir and Askold actually really existed.

After setting up a trading post in Novgorod, the friends join Dir and Askold's force going south to Kiev.

864: The Pechenegs, a savage steppes tribe, attacks Kiev. Only with Polonius' expert help, and the fanatical fighting bravery of the Vikings, do they survive. An attack on the Pechenegs at their most vulnerable point not only ends the siege, but forces the Pechenegs to pay to cross the Dnieper River.

(Emissary to Byzantium)

865: Kent is invaded by a Viking force and Danegeld is paid for the first time to stop the destruction. The Great Army (Danish Vikings) arrives in East Anglia from France.

Dir and Askold lead a combined Slav and Varangian force against Constantinople because of a perceived injustice. With both the Byzantine fleet and army away, they manage to do considerable damage, although they never seriously threaten the city. On the way home, a savage storm sinks many of the Viking and Slav ships. Meantime, Kuralla is kidnaped in Kiev. That there was an attack by Varangians, and a storm, within a few years of this date seems inconvertible. Since the Russian Primary Chronicles set the date somewhere between 863 to 867, I arbitrarily assigned it to 865.

866: Reign of Ethelred in Wessex. The Great Army seizes York. Ambrose and Polonius are sent by Dir and Askold as official envoys to Constantinople. They return north to find word from Kuralla waiting for them. The friends rush north, free Kuralla, turn around, and travel again to Constantinople.

After attempts by Basil to involve them in a plot against the emperor, Ambrose, Kuralla, Polonius and Phillip sail for Wessex. Basil, aware they know altogether too much, sends agents after them.

(Southern Journey)

Basil is told by the Byzantine emperor, Michael III, to divorce his wife so he may marry Michael's mistress.

Bardas plans a sea campaign to retake Crete. Michael has Basil kill Bardas.
Michael adopts Basil and makes him junior emperor.
Ambrose and his friends are captured and enslaved by Muslim pirates operating out of Crete. Polonius' skills allow them to break out of their prison, and they escape to the dubious safety of a Byzantine Fleet. When they realize one of Basil's agents recognizes them and intends to kill them, they flee to Egypt, where they join a caravan heading west.
The Byzantine admiral harries them across North Africa, but Ambrose and his friends do manage to strike back and damage the Byzantine ships. Ambrose then finds a Muslim slaver to transport them to Calabria. Attacked and hunted, the friends finally cross the border from Calabria to Benevento. Ambrose feels that they are finally safe.

(Journey Home)
The friends start north. Ambrose and his friends pay a visit to Admiral Demetrious in Naples. They escape and make it back across the frontier just ahead of vengeful Byzantine soldiers.

Ambrose makes it to Rome, where he meets Pope Nicholas. He and his friends then head north for the mountain pass to France. They arrive after the pass is closed for the winter, and must spend the winter in Aosta.

867: Aelle, king of Northumbria, is killed trying to retake York.

Basil 'the Macedonian' kills his own sponsor, Michael III, emperor of Byzantium. (September)
Ambrose and his friends survive an attack by assassins, and in the spring they head north into the mountains where they are captured and enslaved. After Kuralla rescues them, they reach France and relative safety. They reach Paris and meet the king. Then they head for Calais and a ship to England. The Vikings, however, are raiding along the coast. Finally, after many

adventures, they reach Calais and Phillip finds a captain willing to risk the dangerous crossing.

867: Finally, Ambrose and his friends arrive in England, where Ambrose is welcomed back to the court. Ambrose meets a beautiful girl and falls in love.

(Warrior of the King)
868: The Great Army occupies Mercia. King Ethelred and his brother, Alfred, ride north to support Burgred of Mercia. The Vikings are besieged at Nottingham, but Burgred decides to pay Danegeld. The West Saxons go home.

Alfred marries a Mercian noblewoman - Ealhswith.
Ambrose and his companions return north and join the Great Army as spies. After finding out the Vikings are going north, they flee. Ambrose is wounded and nursed by his loved one. The Great Army pursues, and catches up. Strangely, the attack is called off.
Ahmad ibn Tulun, a Turk, is appointed by the Caliph to rule Egypt.
Pope Nicholas the Great dies.

(Gretchen; Future Princess)
Gretchen and her father head south for Wessex and her marriage. She is kidnaped and taken to Wales.
In Wales, Vikings attack the group, and Gretchen is taken to the Viking stronghold of Wexford in Ireland. Ambrose visits Wexford, but is unable to free Gretchen.

869: The Great Army returns to York in the north for a year.
Ambrose attacks the Viking ship carrying his beloved north. They are finally re-united.

870: Danes kill King Edmund of East Anglia, then invade Wessex under the Danish leader Halfdan.

871: Alfred becomes king. After fighting nine battles, Alfred pays Danegeld to buy peace for five years.

873: Ivar the Boneless, 'king of Dublin and York', dies in Ireland. His brother, Halfdan Ragnarsson, becomes king in his place.

874: Edward, son of King Alfred and future king, is born.

(Alfred the Great; Viking Invasion)
875: Alfred takes out a small fleet and routs seven Viking ships. (Nb. For dramatic purposes, I arbitrarily moved this event to the following year, where I tied it in with Guthrum's invasion.)

876: Danes under Guthrum break their word, slip past Alfred and seize Wareham.

877: Guthrum agrees to a truce, but slips away to Exeter, which the Danes fortify.
After a Viking fleet is dashed on the rocks in a storm, the Danes agree to withdraw.
Halfdan Ragnarsson is killed in Ireland fighting Norwegian Vikings.

878: Guthrum, a Danish chief, rides south across the Wessex border in winter.
Alfred at first hides in the forest of Selwood.
A second Viking army, led by Ubbi Ragnarsson and invading from Wales, is defeated in Devon.
As spring approaches, Alfred builds a military camp on the island of Athelney.

Battle of Edington: Alfred's forces meet the Vikings here in May. The Danes break and run to Chippenham.
The Saxons blockade the Danes within their fortress of Chippenham for 14 days.
At last Guthrum surrenders and agrees to be baptized.

879: Guthrum takes his retreating army to East Anglia, where the men eventually settle down.

882: Alfred fights a battle against four Danish ships.

883: Halfdan dies. Guthred is recognized as king of Jorvik.

884: Ethelflaed, daughter of Alfred, marries Ethelred of Mercia.

(Alfred the Great: King's Revenge)
885: A Danish army crosses to England and besieges Rochester. Alfred

relieves the city before it falls.

885: Later that summer Alfred fights a naval battle at the mouth of the Stour River. He takes all 16 enemy warships.
Guthrum breaks his treaty. He gathers every Viking vessel and attacks Alfred's laden fleet. He wins.
Alfred calls up his entire force and marches on London. He takes it and garrisons the city.

886: Alfred signs another treaty with Guthrum, where he gets London and control over part of Mercia.

889: Edgar, son of Ambrose and Gretchen, is born.

891: Danes in France suffer two serious defeats.

(Alfred the Great; Young Edward)

892: Five thousand Danes land in Kent and seize an unfinished fort at Appledore. A second fleet follows, led by Haesten, and lands at Milton Royal. Alfred arrives with his army, drives Haesten away, and then moves against the Danes at Appledore.

893: Haesten's fleet sails away, to Benfleet, and is eventually joined by the second, larger fleet. The Danes then raid deep into Hampshire and Berkshire. Edward, son of Alfred, inflicts a major defeat, and then chases the Danes across the Thames. After being forced to surrender, the Danes give hostages and depart. The Danes of Northumbria and East Anglia send two fleets to Dorset as a diversion. Alfred rushes to the west, while Edward marches on Benfleet. Edward wins a great victory.

The Danes gather all their forces and march along the Thames again. They are besieged, break out, gather fresh forces, and try again. Besieged at Chester, the Danes break out yet again and flee to Wales.

Late summer, 893: Edward, Ethelred, volunteers from the London garrison, along with reinforcements from the West Country, gather and march on Benfleet. The Viking army is away raiding, and the Saxons take the town.

All Danes now gather at Shoebury in Essex. They march west

to the Severn River. They build a camp at Buttington, in Montgomeryshire. Though besieged, the Danes break out and make it back to Essex.

Early autumn 893: The Danes in Essex march without pausing along the old Roman Watling Road, into Cheshire, where they seize the tun of Chester. Besieged, the Vikings break out yet again, though they suffer heavy losses. They flee to Wales.

Spring 894: The Danes split up and flee back to Essex via different roads.

Winter 894: The Danes sail up the Lea River and build a fort. London men attack, but are repulsed. Alfred arrives and guards the peasants who harvest the local crops. Alfred then moves his army to the mouth of the river, where he builds twin forts to blockade the Viking fleet. The Danes abandon their ships and ride north and west, to Bridgnorth in Shropshire.
Athelstan, future king and son of King Edward, is born.

895: In the spring the Vikings sneak back to Essex or move to Northumbria or East Anglia.
Guthfrith, king of Northumbria, dies on August 24.

896: *Sitric Ivarsson dies.*

(Edward the King)
899: King Alfred dies. Ethelwold seizes two royal estates and kidnaps a nun. Faced with an army under Edward, he flees northward. The Danes of Jorvik (Northumbria) accept him as king.

902: Ethelwold arrives in Essex with a Northumbrian fleet, and the Danes there submit to him.
The Norse are expelled from Dublin. Ingimund attacks Wales. Driven out, he settles on the Wirral Peninsula with the permission of Ethelflaed, since Ethelred is sick. (While the exact date is in doubt, the most likely year of this event was in 902.)
Elfweard, second son of King Edward, is born.

(Introduction to 'Ethelflaed, 'Lady of the Mercians')
903: Ethelwold convinces Eohric of East Anglia to join him, and

together they raid Mercia and Wessex as far as Cricklade and Braydon before retreating. In retaliation, Edward gathers his fyrdmen and ravages the Viking lands as far north as the northern fens. He then orders a retreat, but the Kentish fyrdmen are slow to obey and the Danes catch up with them on December 13. Ethelwold and Eohric are killed on the Danish side, while Sigehelm, the Ealdorman of Kent, falls on the other side. Both sides suffer serious losses. This is known as the Battle of the Holme.

(Ethelflaed, 'Lady of the Mercians')   (902 to 919)

905: The Norse under Ingimund demand land and the old fortress of Chester. When their demand is rejected, they revolt and besiege Chester. Ethelflaed provides extra fyrdmen and the garrison is able to hold the Norse off.

Edgar is Kidnaped by Ingimund and Ambrose goes after his family in Hitchingford.

906: King Edward concludes a truce with East Anglia and Northumbria, and probably pays Danegeld.

907: Ethelflaed refortifies Chester.

909: Ethelflaed & Edward raid Danish East Anglia and bring back the body of St. Oswald.

910: The Saxons and Mercians defeat and kill joint Jorvik kings Eowils and Halfdan II at the Battle of Tetenhall. Ethelflaed builds the fortress at Bramsbury.

911: Ethelred dies.
Ethelflaed is chosen by the Witan as 'Lady of the Mercians'.
Edward annexes London and Oxfordshire.

912: Ethelflaed builds two more burhs along the Welsh border - along the Severn River.
1. Bridgnorth - main crossing point to Wales.
2. Scargeat- location is unknown. Probably upriver north and west from Bridgnorth.
Edward takes his army to Essex, builds a fortress at Witham, and receives submission from Essex.
Some of Edward's supporters moves to the burh of Hertford and

work on it.

913: Danish forces at Leicester look west and see two new burhs: Tamworth and Stafford.

Danes march south to the village of Banbury, joining forces with Danes from Northampton for a coordinated attack. The Angles meet them in battle and defeat the Vikings.

914: Ethelflaed fortifies the largest town south of Danish Northampton - Buckingham.

She builds a fort on either side of the River Ouse.

Danish armies of Northampton and Bedford submit to Ethelflaed's army at Buckingham. Jarl Thurcetel submits.

A Viking army arrives from Brittany, led by Ohter and Hroald. They land in the Severn estuary. They go inland, but the men of Hereford & Gloucester meet them and put them to flight.

The Vikings finally leave in the autumn.

A Danish Viking, Ragnald, seizes power in Northumbria after Tetenhall, and defeats the Scots in the First Battle of Corbridge in 914.

915: This allows Edward to establish a fort at Bedford, directly across the Ouse from the former Danish camp.

Ethelflaed now had a nearly straight line of forts from Chester to Hertford.

There are two gaps. Ethelflaed closes the Mersey gap with several more burhs.

914 - Eddesbury. Warwick.

915 - Runcorn.

916: Edward builds a fort at Maldon.

Ethelflaed sends her army into Wales. An abbot had been killed. The army destroys a town and captures a Welsh king's wife.

917: Ethelflaed signs a treaty with two Scottish kings, both called Constantine, insuring their alliance against Jorvik.

Ragnald is unwilling to face Ethelflaed. He fights the Scots and Picts again at the Second battle of Corbridge. He wins again but the numbers of his army is cut in half.

Edward fights the Danes in the east - Towcester, Bedford, Wigingamere, Tempsford. He kills King Guthrum II at Tempsford and all resistance in East Anglia collapses.

Ethelflaed's troops march into the Danish center at Derby and take it.

All Danish leaders now submit to Edward and accept him as their protector.

They are granted their estates and allowed to live according to their Danish customs.

918: Edward builds a burh at Stamford. The Danes there submit without a fight.

To the west, Ethelflaed marches into Leicester, where Danes surrender without bloodshed, probably led by Danes seeking support against the Norse threat from the west.

The last two Danish enclaves, Nottingham and Lincoln, fall to the West Saxons by the end of summer, but Ethelflaed dies on June 12, 918.

(Elfwynn, Traitor Queen)

The Mercian Witan gives the title of queen to the twenty year old daughter of Ethelflaed - Elfwynn. Ambrose and Polonius kidnap her during the winter. They return to rescue the boys of the Royal School in the spring of 919.

919: Edward calls Elfwynn to his court and officially annexes Mercia. Edward moves his army to Gloucester and Betlic flees. Ambrose and Polonius chase him northward. They fight on the way, and Elfwynn finally kills Betlic.

Norse adventurer Ragnald storms York and establishes a line of Norse kings.

During his reign he gives nominal allegiance to Edward, who recognizes his new kingdom.

921: Edmund, son of King Edward, is born.

(Athelstan, First King of England)

924: There is a Mercian revolt in Chester. King Edward is killed at Fardon-on-Dee. Mercia supports Athelstan as king. Wessex supports Elfweard, his half-brother. Elfweard suddenly dies a few months after his father.

925: Athelstan is finally crowned as king. He is crowned at Kingston-upon-Thames, by Ayhelm, Archbishop of Canterbury. This is the first time a Saxon king is crowned with a crown instead of a helmet.

926: Athelstan arranges for his sister Edith to marry Sihtric of York. They agree not to invade each other's territory and not to support the other's enemies.

927: Sihtric dies. Cousin Guthfrith leads a fleet from Dublin to try and take the throne. Athelstan captures York and receives the submission of the Danes. (It is not known if he fought Guthfrith). The Northumbrians are outraged at this usurpation.

July, 927: at Eamont, King Constantine of Scotland (Alba), King Hywel Ddn of Deheubarth, Ealdred of Bamburgh and King Owain of Strathclyde accept Athelstan's overlordship, which leads to seven years of peace. Athelstan is now the first king of all the Anglo-Saxon people.

933: Prince Edwin drowns, possibly after a rebellion where someone called Alfred attempts to blind Athelstan.

934: Athelstan invades Scotland, though the reasons are unclear. Sometime thereafter, Constantine of Scotland marries his daughter to the Norse king of Dublin.

937: The Norse king of Dublin, Olaf Guthfrithson, joins with the Scots and Strathclyde Britons under Owain to invade England in the fall. Ambrose meets with the Scottish king. The opposing armies meet at the Battle of Brunanburh. Athelstan wins an overwhelming victory, though he also takes heavy losses. Ambrose and Polonius die protecting the king.

939: (October) Athelstan dies.

(Edmund, King of England)
939: Edmund is proclaimed king. Crowned in November.

939-940: King Olaf III Guthfrithson conquers Northumbria and invades the Midlands. Conquers as far south as Watling Street. Olaf marches south from York to Northampton. When that siege fails, he goes on to Tamworth, which he takes by storm. King Edmund besieges King Olaf and Archbishop Wulfstan at Leicester, but they escape by night. Battle is averted when

Archbishops Oda and Wulfstan reconcile the two kings and a truce is concluded. Watling Street becomes the new boundary.

941: Olaf Guthfrithson raids Bernicia and dies shortly thereafter. Olaf Sihtricson succeeds him on the Northumbrian throne. He has his cousin Ragnall as co-ruler.

942: Edmund defeats Idwal of Gwynedd.
Edmund reconquers the Midlands.

943: Edmund becomes godfather of King Olaf Sihtricson of York.

944: Edmund reconquers Northumbria.
Edmund drives out of Northumbria both Olaf Sihtricson and Ragnall Guthfrithson.
Congalach Cnogba, High King of Ireland, sacks Dublin.

945: Edmund conquers Strathclyde, but cedes the territory to King Malcolm I of Scotland in exchange for a treaty of mutual support.
Blacaire of Dublin driven out by Olaf.

946: Edmund is killed in a brawl by an exiled thief named Leofa.
Eadred, Edmund's brother, succeeds to the throne.

APPENDIX II

ALFRED'S ENGLAND

APPENDIX III

Glossary

240 Shilling Penalty Right Now: A thane was fined 120 shillings if he did not join the fyrd when it was called up. Since he held the land on the condition he provide military service, he was also likely to lose his land.

Aegir: was the Norse god of the sea, an omnipotent lord of the oceans of the world.

Angelisc: The name the Angle, Saxon and Jute tribesmen of England started to call themselves.

Angleland: England.

Asgard: The place of the gods, where Viking warriors go if they fall bravely in battle.

At Nottingham: This refers to the time in **Ambrose, Prince of Wessex, Warrior of the King**, when the Great Army used its fleet to bypass the massed Mercian army. This allowed the Danes to seize Nottingham.

Athelings: were 'princes of the blood'. The Saxon kings were chosen from the group by a Council, or Witan. The usual tradition was for the Witan to choose the eldest son, but this was not always adhered to.

Blood Eagle: When a person's ribs are broken and the lungs are pulled out through the back. The lungs will pulsate outside of the body until the man dies.

Bones: Dice.

Bookland was land given to individuals or the church in perpetuity. Unlike most land grants, they did not revert back to the king at the death of its possessor. For the church, this was vital, for it could not reach real power with its property only 'on loan' from the current king.

Burh: A Saxon fortified Great Hall, which belonged to an Ealdorman or the king.

Compurgation: A man accused of a crime could try to clear himself by asking others to come forward and swear that he was innocent.

Cynwith: Now known as Countisbury Hill.

Danegeld: Tribute paid to the Vikings on the condition they leave.

Dreng: Young warriors without land who resided with their lord.

Dromon: was a three-decked war galley of the Eastern Roman Empire's navy.

Duguo: The proven warriors who have been allotted land by the king. They are expected to answer the king's summons at the head of their own household troops.

Ealdorman: A nobleman next in power to the **Athelings**. The kingdom was divided into shires, and the Ealdorman was in charge of the shire. It was he who would call out the **fyrd**, or militia.

Egbert ruled Wessex from 802 to 839 AD.

Eig is 'island'. The area is now known as Athelney.

Frisian: Were sea-faring traders who were located on the mainland coast just south of Viking territory. One of their main cities was Wyk Te Duurstede.

From Ambrose Here: When Ambrose thought that his fiancé,

Gretchen, was being held captive at Carnarvon Fortress in Northern Wales, he seized the fort with a wily manoeuver. Saxons disguised as merchants and traders took position along all the roads between the border and the fortress. The main force, each with two mounts, started a *Long Ride* that did not end until the warriors arrived at their target. The fast-moving column out-rode most of the Welsh scouts and sentries, and the disguised merchants took care of any who got past the flying column. An overturned wagon blocked the main gate, and an infiltrated band of warriors fought to prevent the gate's closing until the main force arrived. The massive fort thus fell to Ambrose with very few casualties.

Fyrd or Fyrdmen: Militias were made up thanes and churls. For every five hides of land, one fyrdman, mounted and armed, was obliged to answer the call-to-arms.

Great Army: The name given to the large Viking army that invaded England in 865. Its leaders included Ivar the Boneless, Ubbi, and Halfdan.

Guthrum's Jibe...: Guthrum is referring to the time when Ambrose, Phillip (the 'giant'), and Polonius (the 'thin dark man') joined the Danish Great Army in order to ascertain the army's next target. This story was the subject of a very popular ballad that even many of the Vikings had heard.

A Hide is a unit of measure. It generally denoted enough land to support a single family. In Alfred's day, every so many hides (generally 5) held meant that you had the obligation to send one armed and mounted warrior to join the fyrd when so instructed.

Holding His Stomach: Bishop Asser reported that Alfred 'suffered from a nervous affliction' that affected him throughout his life.

Jarls of this Land: Ealdormen.

Jutes: The Jutes were, with the Angles and the Saxons, the three major Germanic tribes to have conquered Roman Britain. The empire of Wessex was made up of people from all three of the original tribes.

Leaping Stag: Alfred the Great's flag ship, built higher and longer than the typical Viking long-ship.

Loki: Is the Norse god of mischief.

Long Gallop or Long Ride: A technique Ambrose and Polonius used to seize Carnarvon. With multiple mounts, the riders start a fast ride toward the target from far away. By changing horses and posting scouts in advance to ambush any couriers, they attempt to outride any news of their approach, thus achieving complete surprise.

Master Sun: From **The Art of War**, by Sun Tzu. This text was written some time between the fifth to the third century B.C.

Met Your Brother-In-Law: He refers to his first adventures with Ambrose, in **Ambrose, Prince of Wessex; Trader of Kiev**.

Moot: is a gathering of men who both acted as a court, and could impose fines.

Norse: Norwegian

Not Love You West Saxons Overmuch, I Fear: I am not aware that the Cornish actually tried at this time to betray Wessex, but in 838 A.D. they allied themselves with a Viking army for an invasion of Devon.

Offer Them To Odin: i.e. They would be taken ashore and hung. The Vikings generally hung those they wished to sacrifice to Odin, and Alfred was known to hang the Viking pirates he captured.

Pig-Stickers: Polonius had been trying to teach the mounted Saxons the lance skills of the heavy cavalry of the

Russian Steppes. He had helped the Varangians of Kiev and of the Dnieper River Valley fight off a massive invasion of these fierce warriors. Though victorious, Polonius had learned to respect the steppe-warriors' skills. He had seen at first hand the shock value of their ferocious charge.

Pope Leo IV Himself: Alfred was the only Saxon king ever to be given the belt of a Roman Consul by a Pope.

Punt: is a flat-bottomed boat with a square-cut bow.

Ran's Nets: the wife of Aegir, she was the sea goddess of storms. She was reputed to collect drowned people in her net.

Reeve: a royal official responsible for keeping the peace throughout a shire on behalf of the king.

Sax: A long knife.

Scop: An Anglo-Saxon poet or minstrel.

Spawn of Ragnar Lodbrok refers to Ubbi, Halfdan, and Ivar the Boneless, the men who earlier brought the Great Army to Britain. They were the children of the powerful Danish chieftain Ragnar Lodbrok, who earlier had himself invaded Britain and France. Legend had it that he was killed in Northumbria by being thrown into a pit of vipers.

Thane: A Saxon nobleman.

Thing: The Viking assembly of free men that acted as a council.

This I Pledge To You In The Name Of Jesus Christ: Guthrum actually kept his word this time, at least for some years. In 885 AD he finally broke his promise and invaded again.

Torque: A heavy necklace; generally solid

Tun: is a town.

Valkyries were the divine maidens who took fallen warriors to Asgard.

Valhalla: Odin's Great Hall in Asgard, where half of those slain in battle go, to feast until Ragnarök.

Varangian: The name given to the Vikings who settled the river valleys of Russia.

Victory-Maker: Is the name of Ambrose's sword, given him by his Danish master. It was originally taken as loot from Arabs on the North African coast.

Witan: is the council made up of Saxon noblemen and Church elders. They had the final choice over the selection of each king.

Wyk Te Duurstede: Was a major port city of Frisia, and a major European Center for the slave trade.

Your Kind Killed Them And Took Their Land: The Norwegian Vikings did land in Ireland and seize territory from their cousins the Danes.

Your generosity and support will be Remembered: The Devon fyrd was not mentioned by the Anglo-Saxon Chronicles as being present at the battle of Edington when Alfred defeated Guthrum. Considering its geographical proximity, this would have been unusual. The Vikings generally set up a puppet king when they took over a kingdom, and Ethelwold would have been a likely candidate. That being said, I have not found any research that indicates that Ethelwold was, in fact, disloyal to Alfred at this time. He did, however, ally himself with the Danes shortly after Alfred's death.

APPENDIX IV

About the Author

After counseling teenagers and adults for more than forty years, Bruce Corbett retired to concentrate on his writing and photography. To date, he has written a collection of Science Fiction short stories and two Science Fiction novels. The project closest to his heart, however, is his series of well-researched historical novels based on a family of fictional heroes, set in the time of Alfred the Great, his children and grandchildren. **Alfred the Great; Viking Invasion**, is the seventh in this series, and starts with the surprise attack by King Guthrum's Viking army.

These novels are arguably the most comprehensive series of novels ever written based on the time of the Anglo-Saxon Chronicles. A complete description of the various novels, including samples, links and supplementary information, may be found on Bruce Corbett's web site:

www.brucecorbett.com

Bruce Corbett lives in Pincourt, Quebec, Canada. He is an avid landscape and wildlife photographer, and is generally found reading anything historic.

APPENDIX V

Other Books Released by the Author

In chronological order

HISTORICAL
I. The Ambrose Sagas
1. Ambrose, Prince of Wessex; Trader of Kiev
2. Ambrose, Prince of Wessex; Emissary to Byzantium
3. Ambrose, Prince of Wessex; Southern Journey
4. Ambrose, Prince of Wessex; Journey Home
5. Ambrose, Prince of Wessex; Warrior of the King
6. Ambrose, Prince of Wessex; Gretchen, Future Princess

II. The King Alfred Sagas
1. *Alfred the Great; Viking Invasion*
2. Alfred the Great; King's Revenge
3. Alfred the Great; Young Edward

III. The King Edward Sagas
1. Alfred the Great; Edward the King
2. Queen Ethelflaed; 'Lady of the Mercians' **2023 release**
3. Elfwynn, Traitor Queen of Mercia   **2023 release**

IV. The Anglo-Saxon Kings of all England
1. Athelstan, First King of England   **2023 release**
2. Edmund, King of England   **2023 release**
3. King Eadred of England   **2024 release**

SCIENCE FICTION
Bruce Corbett's Speculative Short Stories
The Vuorran Pogrom   (coming soon)
The Goldmines of Alpha Centauri   (coming soon)

The complete Prince of Wessex Sagas are available worldwide as e-books or paperbacks from Amazon or your favorite on-line bookstores.

www.ingramcontent.com/pod-product-compliance
Lightning Source LLC
Chambersburg PA
CBHW070105030726
47506CB00002B/602